FANTASY:
THE VERY BEST OF 2005

Other books by Jonathan Strahan include:

Best Short Novels: 2004

Best Short Novels: 2005

Fantasy: Best of 2004 (with Karen Haber)

Science Fiction: Best of 2003 (with Karen Haber)

Science Fiction: Best of 2004 (with Karen Haber)

Science Fiction: The Very Best of 2005

The Locus Awards: Thirty Years of the Best in Fantasy and Science Fiction (with Charles N. Brown)

The Year's Best Australian Science Fiction and Fantasy Volume: 1 (with Jeremy G Byrne)

The Year's Best Australian Science Fiction and Fantasy Volume: 2 (with Jeremy G Byrne)

Forthcoming:

Best Short Novels: 2006

Eidolon (with Jeremy G Byrne)

The New Space Opera (with Gardner Dozois)

The Starry Rift: Tales of New Tomorrows

FANTASY:
THE VERY BEST OF 2005

Edited by Jonathan Strahan

LOCUS PRESS
OAKLAND CALIFORNIA

Locus Press
PO Box 13305
Oakland, CA 94661
www.locusmag.com

For Karen, my partner in crime and dear friend,

and

For the Locus Press team,
Charles, Liza, Tim, Kirsten, Amelia, Carolyn, and Karlyn,
who made this book a reality.

CONTENTS

Introduction 1

Two Hearts, Peter S. Beagle 5

Snowball's Chance, Charles Stross 37

Sunbird, Neil Gaiman...............................47

A Knot of Toads, Jane Yolen...............................65

Boatman's Holiday, Jeffrey Ford............................87

The Language of Moths, Christopher Barzak 101

Anyway, M Rickert 125

The Emperor of Gondwanaland,
     Paul Di Filippo 141

The Pirate's True Love, Seana Graham.................157

Intelligent Design, Ellen Klages 163

Pip and the Fairies, Theodora Goss 167

Leviathan, Simon Brown 175

The Denial, Bruce Sterling..............................191

The Farmer's Cat, Jeff VanderMeer.......................207

There's a Hole in the City, Richard Bowes 213

Monster, Kelly Link 229

INTRODUCTION

As a lover of great fantasy short fiction, I have spent the last several years working to assemble books that represent everything fantasy has to offer, books that attempt to give some idea of the incredible richness and diversity of the field today. To me, that means looking to both acknowledge the excellence to be found in genre fiction, as well in the cross-genre "slipstream" work that has gained so much attention of late. In brief, it's a daunting proposition.

The fantasy short fiction field has exploded and diversified. Because of that astonishing diversity, fantasy fiction is as likely to appear in the pages of genre magazines like *The Magazine of Fantasy & Science Fiction, Realms of Fantasy,* or *Black Gate,* as in the pages of *The New Yorker* or the latest edition of *McSweeney's.* I found myself reading magazines, 'zines, chapbooks, anthologies, short story collections, and websites, and what I found as I read was that 2005 was a truly extraordinary year for fantasy.

Without a doubt, the big publishing event of the year was the publication of *Harry Potter and the Half-Blood Prince,* the wildly popular — and extremely long — sixth novel from J.K. Rowling. The most eagerly-awaited book, however, was George R.R. Martin's fourth "Song of Ice and Fire" novel, *A Storm of Swords,* which managed to live up to extraordinary expectations and saw *Time* magazine, no less, attempt to crown him the "American Tolkien." Elsewhere, it was a good year for fantasy novels: Neil Gaiman delivered his funniest and most accomplished novel with the Thorne Smith-influenced *Anansi Boys,* while his former collaborator Terry Pratchett continued the civilization of his Discworld with the funny and particularly resonant *Thud!.*

The strangest and most interesting fantasy of the year came, unexpectedly, from science fiction writer Cory Doctorow, whose fine *Someone Comes to Town, Someone Leaves Town* told the extraordinary tale of a man whose mother was a washing machine and whose father was a mountain. The most startling debut of the year was Hal Duncan's rich and strange *Vellum,* though Tim Pratt's cross-fertilization of Stephen King's "Dark Tower" and Charles de Lint's "Newford", *The Strange Adventures of Rangergirl* definitely repaid attention. Patricia A. McKillip delivered the best traditional fantasy of the year in *Od Magic,* Graham Joyce's powerful rumination on family and memory, *The Limits of Enchantment,* was a worthy follow-up to *The*

1

Facts of Life, and Jeffrey Ford's *The Girl in the Glass* was easily his finest to date. And then there was Paul Park's *A Princess of Roumania*. Every now and then a book gets published that is both extraordinary and unexpected. Park's startlingly powerful YA fantasy deserves to become a classic. If you only read one fantasy novel this year, make it this one.

At shorter lengths, things were just as exciting. While, unlike 2005, there were fewer stand-out anthologies like Ellen Datlow & Terri Windling's *The Faery Reel* or Al Sarrantonio's *Flights* published, there were four original anthologies that are well worth seeking out. The best fantasy anthology of the year was Marvin Kaye's strong collection of novellas set in Faerie, *The Fair Folk*, which featured outstanding stories by Megan Lindholm, Kim Newman, Patricia McKillip, and Tanith Lee. The fifth installment in Deborah Layne and Jay Lake's *Polyphony* series offered the usual slipstream blend of science fiction and fantasy that I've come to expect, including outstanding stories by Jeff VanderMeer, Robert Freeman Wexler, Theodora Goss, and others. Neil Williamson and Andrew J. Wilson edited *Nova Scotia: New Scottish Speculative Fiction* to coincide with the World Science Fiction Convention in Glasgow, and it included some very fine fiction by Jane Yolen, Charles Stross, and Ken Macleod, among others. And then there was the strange case of McSweeney's third anthology, *Noisy Outlaws, Unfriendly Blobs etc.* Edited by Ted Thompson, it featured truly wonderful stories by Kelly Link and Neil Gaiman, good stories by Nick Hornby and George Saunders, and a welcome reprint of Clement Freud's *Grimble*. Beautifully illustrated and filled with strong fiction, it's worth seeking out, even if I was left wondering if the book was aimed at younger readers, or just wanted to look that way.

It was a particularly impressive year for fantasy stories in the magazines as well — many featured excellent work. Gordon Van Gelder's *The Magazine of Fantasy & Science Fiction* had an extraordinarily good year, with fine stories by Kelly Link, Peter S. Beagle, Geoff Ryman, Jeffrey Ford, Bruce Sterling, Matt Hughes, and others. The other main genre fantasy magazine, Shawna McCarthy's *Realms of Fantasy*, had an even better year, with excellent stories from Christopher Barzak and Richard Parks, and good stories from Liz Williams, Tim Pratt, and others, and continues to deserve more acclaim than it gets. *Asimov's Science Fiction Magazine*, in its first year under editor Sheila Williams, published some strong fantasy by Liz Williams, Michael Swanwick, and others. I was also impressed by work from *The Third Alternative*, *Postscripts*, *Lady Churchill's Rosebud Wristlet*, *Electric Velocipede*, and *Black Gate*, among many others.

And there were short story collections. Two extraordinary short story collections garnered a lot of attention this year: Joe Hill's *20ᵗʰ Century*

Ghosts was simply the most impressive collection of horror fiction (and it was much more varied than that description implies) since Clive Barker's *Books of Blood*, while Holly Phillips's *In the Palace of Repose* was a collection of mostly previously unpublished fantasies that took my breath away. While I was also very impressed by Tim Powers's *Strange Itineraries*, Patricia McKillip's long awaited debut collection *Harrowing the Dragon*, and the Library of America's dauntingly definitive *H.P. Lovecraft: Tales*, the best collection of the year was Kelly Link's extraordinary *Magic for Beginners*. Like the Paul Park novel I've mentioned, it's simply essential.

That leaves just one last book to mention. Small presses have always published the occasional novella as small books. The best such book published this year, and at 60,000 words really a novel, was Jeffrey Ford's *The Cosmology of the Wider World*. The tale of a minotaur in his coral tower in the other-dimensional refuge of the Wider World looking back on his days in the lesser world of men and laboring on his great philosophical work, *The Cosmology*, it is truly exceptional.

Just as I was completing work on this volume SciFi.com announced its decision to close its online fiction magazine, *SciFiction*. Edited by Ellen Datlow, *SciFiction* published over 220 science fiction and fantasy short stories between March 2000 and December 2005, a number of which went on to win Hugo, Nebula, World Fantasy, Locus, and Theodore Sturgeon Memorial Awards. It will take a some time to assess the full impact of the closure of the highest paying market, and highest profile online publication, on the field, but it's likely to be dramatic. While SciFi.com is to be applauded for supporting the effectively non-profit *SciFiction* for six years, it's loss is definitely a blow for readers and writers.

Speaking of transitions, the publication of this volume, marks another period of transition. Last year saw the end of the *Science Fiction: Best of* and *Fantasy: Best of* anthology series' that I co-edited with Karen Haber. This book is a stepping stone on the way to a new book with a new publisher next year. I'd like to thank everyone who made that possible, especially Charles Brown and Karen Haber.

And so, I bring you the best of short fantasy for 2005, an important year for the field. Within these covers you will find fables and fairy tales, monsters and magic, and the welcome return of some old friends after far too long away. All are "fantasy," but more importantly they sparkle with the inescapable evidence of magic. I hope you enjoy reading them as much as I did.

Jonathan Strahan
November 2005

TWO HEARTS
PETER S. BEAGLE

Peter S. Beagle was born in New York in April 1939. He studied at the University of Pittsburgh and graduated with a degree in creative writing in 1959. Beagle won a Seventeen Magazine *short story contest in his sophomore year, but really began his writing career with his first novel,* A Fine and Private Place, *in 1960. It was followed by non-fiction travelogue,* I See by My Outfit, *in 1961 and by his best-known work, modern fantasy classic* The Last Unicorn, *in 1968. Beagle's other books include novels* The Folk of the Air, The Innkeeper's Song, *and* Tamsin; *collections* The Fantasy Worlds of Peter S. Beagle, The Rhinoceros Who Quoted Nietzsche, *and* Giant Bones; *several non-fiction books, and a number of screenplays and teleplays. He has a new novel,* Summerlong, *and a new collection,* The Line Between, *coming in 2006.*

My brother Wilfrid keeps saying it's not fair that it should all have happened to me. Me being a girl, and a baby, and too stupid to lace up my own sandals properly. But *I* think it's fair. I think everything happened exactly the way it should have done. Except for the sad parts, and maybe those too.

I'm Sooz, and I am nine years old. Ten next month, on the anniversary of the day the griffin came. Wilfrid says it was because of me, that the griffin heard that the ugliest baby in the world had just been born, and it was going to eat me, but I was *too* ugly, even for a griffin. So it nested in the Midwood (we call it that, but its real name is the Midnight Wood, because of the darkness under the trees), and stayed to eat our sheep and our goats. Griffins do that if they like a place.

But it didn't ever eat children, not until this year.

I only saw it once — I mean, once *before* — rising up above the trees one night, like a second moon. Only there wasn't a moon, then. There was nothing in the whole world but the griffin, golden feathers all blazing on its lion's body and eagle's wings, with its great front claws like teeth, and that monstrous beak that looked so huge for its head....Wilfrid says I screamed for three days, but he's lying, and I *didn't* hide in the root cellar like he says either, I slept in the barn those two nights, with our dog Malka. Because I

5

knew Malka wouldn't let anything get me.

I mean my parents wouldn't have, either, not if they could have stopped it. It's just that Malka is the biggest, fiercest dog in the whole village, and she's not afraid of anything. And after the griffin took Jehane, the blacksmith's little girl, you couldn't help seeing how frightened my father was, running back and forth with the other men, trying to organize some sort of patrol, so people could always tell when the griffin was coming. I know he was frightened for me and my mother, and doing everything he could to protect us, but it didn't make me feel any safer, and Malka did.

But nobody knew what to do, anyway. Not my father, nobody. It was bad enough when the griffin was only taking the sheep, because almost everyone here sells wool or cheese or sheepskin things to make a living. But once it took Jehane, early last spring, that changed everything. We sent messengers to the king — three of them — and each time the king sent someone back to us with them. The first time, it was one knight, all by himself. His name was Douros, and he gave me an apple. He rode away into the Midwood, singing, to look for the griffin, and we never saw him again.

The second time — after the griffin took Louli, the boy who worked for the miller — the king sent five knights together. One of them did come back, but he died before he could tell anyone what happened.

The third time an entire squadron came. That's what my father said, anyway. I don't know how many soldiers there are in a squadron, but it was a lot, and they were all over the village for two days, pitching their tents everywhere, stabling their horses in every barn, and boasting in the tavern how they'd soon take care of that griffin for us poor peasants. They had musicians playing when they marched into the Midwood — I remember that, and I remember when the music stopped, and the sounds we heard afterward.

After that, the village didn't send to the king anymore. We didn't want more of his men to die, and besides they weren't any help. So from then on all the children were hurried indoors when the sun went down, and the griffin woke from its day's rest to hunt again. We couldn't play together, or run errands or watch the flocks for our parents, or even sleep near open windows, for fear of the griffin. There was nothing for me to do but read books I already knew by heart, and complain to my mother and father, who were too tired from watching after Wilfrid and me to bother with us. They were guarding the other children too, turn and turn about with the other families — *and* our sheep, *and* our goats — so they were always tired, as well as frightened, and we were all angry with each other most of the time. It was the same for everybody.

And then the griffin took Felicitas.

Felicitas couldn't talk, but she was my best friend, always, since we were little. I always understood what she wanted to say, and she understood me, better than anyone, and we played in a special way that I won't ever play with anyone else. Her family thought she was a waste of food, because no boy would marry a dumb girl, so they let her eat with us most of the time. Wilfrid used to make fun of the whispery quack that was the one sound she could make, but I hit him with a rock, and after that he didn't do it anymore.

I didn't see it happen, but I still see it in my head. She *knew* not to go out, but she was always just so happy coming to us in the evening. And nobody at her house would have noticed her being gone. None of them ever noticed Felicitas.

The day I learned Felicitas was gone, that was the day I set off to see the king myself.

Well, the same *night*, actually — because there wasn't any chance of getting away from my house or the village in daylight. I don't know what I'd have done, really, except that my Uncle Ambrose was carting a load of sheepskins to market in Hagsgate, and you have to start long before sunup to be there by the time the market opens. Uncle Ambrose is my best uncle, but I knew I couldn't ask him to take me to the king — he'd have gone straight to my mother instead, and told her to give me sulphur and molasses and put me to bed with a mustard plaster. He gives his *horse* sulfur and molasses, even.

So I went to bed early that night, and I waited until everyone was asleep. I wanted to leave a note on my pillow, but I kept writing things and then tearing the notes up and throwing them in the fireplace, and I was afraid of somebody waking, or Uncle Ambrose leaving without me. Finally I just wrote, *I will come home soon.* I didn't take any clothes with me, or anything else, except a bit of cheese, because I thought the king must live somewhere near Hagsgate, which is the only big town I've ever seen. My mother and father were snoring in their room, but Wilfrid had fallen asleep right in front of the hearth, and they always leave him there when he does. If you rouse him to go to his own bed, he comes up fighting and crying. I don't know why.

I stood and looked down at him for the longest time. Wilfrid doesn't look nearly so mean when he's sleeping. My mother had banked the coals to make sure there'd be a fire for tomorrow's bread, and my father's moleskin trews were hanging there to dry, because he'd had to wade into the stockpond that afternoon to rescue a lamb. I moved them a little bit, so they wouldn't burn. I wound the clock — Wilfrid's supposed to do that every night, but he always forgets — and I thought how they'd all be hearing it ticking in the morning while they were looking everywhere for me, too frightened to eat any breakfast, and I turned to go back to my room.

But then I turned around again, and I climbed out of the kitchen window, because our front door squeaks so. I was afraid that Malka might wake in the barn and right away know I was up to something, because I can't ever fool Malka, only she didn't, and then I held my breath almost the whole way as I ran to Uncle Ambrose's house and scrambled right into his cart with the sheepskins. It was a cold night, but under that pile of sheepskins it was hot and nasty smelling, and there wasn't anything to do but lie still and wait for Uncle Ambrose. So I mostly thought about Felicitas, to keep from feeling so bad about leaving home and everyone. That was bad enough — I never really *lost* anybody close before, not *forever* — but anyway it was different.

I don't know when Uncle Ambrose finally came, because I dozed off in the cart, and didn't wake until there was this jolt and a rattle and the sort of floppy grumble a horse makes when *he's* been waked up and doesn't like it — and we were off for Hagsgate. The half-moon was setting early, but I could see the village bumping by, not looking silvery in the light, but small and dull, no color to anything. And all the same I almost began to cry, because it already seemed so far away, though we hadn't even passed the stockpond yet, and I felt as though I'd never see it again. I would have climbed back out of the cart right then, if I hadn't known better.

Because the griffin was still up and hunting. I couldn't see it, of course, under the sheepskins (and I had my eyes shut, anyway), but its wings made a sound like a lot of knives being sharpened all together, and sometimes it gave a cry that was dreadful because it was so soft and gentle, and even a little sad and *scared*, as though it were imitating the sound Felicitas might have made when it took her. I burrowed deep down as I could and tried to sleep again, but I couldn't.

Which was just as well, because I didn't want to ride all the way into Hagsgate, where Uncle Ambrose was bound to find me when he unloaded his sheepskins in the marketplace. So when I didn't hear the griffin anymore (they won't hunt far from their nests, if they don't have to), I put my head out over the tailboard of the cart and watched the stars going out, one by one, as the sky grew lighter. The dawn breeze came up as the moon went down.

When the cart stopped jouncing and shaking so much, I knew we must have turned onto the King's Highway, and when I could hear cows munching and talking softly to each other, I dropped into the road. I stood there for a little, brushing off lint and wool bits, and watching Uncle Ambrose's cart rolling on away from me. I hadn't ever been this far from home by myself.

Or so lonely. The breeze brushed dry grass against my ankles, and I didn't have any idea which way to go.

I didn't even know the king's name — I'd never heard anyone call him anything but *the king*. I knew he didn't live in Hagsgate, but in a big castle somewhere nearby, only nearby's one thing when you're riding in a cart and different when you're walking. And I kept thinking about my family waking up and looking for me, and the cows' grazing sounds made me hungry, and I'd eaten all my cheese in the cart. I wished I had a penny with me — not to buy anything with, but only to toss up and let it tell me if I should turn left or right. I tried it with flat stones, but I never could find them after they came down. Finally I started off going left, not for any reason, but only because I have a little silver ring on my left hand that my mother gave me. There was a sort of path that way too, and I thought maybe I could walk around Hagsgate and then I'd think about what to do after that. I'm a good walker. I can walk anywhere, if you give me time.

Only it's easier on a real road. The path gave out after a while, and I had to push my way through trees growing too close together, and then through so many brambly vines that my hair was full of stickers and my arms were all stinging and bleeding. I was tired and sweating, and almost crying — *almost* — and whenever I sat down to rest, bugs and things kept crawling over me. Then I heard running water nearby, and that made me thirsty right away, so I tried to get down to the sound. I had to crawl most of the way, scratching my knees and elbows up something awful.

It wasn't much of a stream — in some places the water came up barely above my ankles — but I was so glad to see it I practically hugged and kissed it, flopping down with my face buried in it, the way I do with Malka's smelly old fur. And I drank until I couldn't hold any more, and then I sat on a stone and let the tiny fish tickle my nice cold feet, and felt the sun on my shoulders, and I didn't think about griffins or kings or my family or anything.

I only looked up when I heard the horses whickering a little way upstream. They were playing with the water, the way horses do, blowing bubbles like children. Plain old livery-stable horses, one brownish, one grayish. The gray's rider was out of the saddle, peering at the horse's left forefoot. I couldn't get a good look — they both had on plain cloaks, dark green, and trews so worn you couldn't make out the color — so I didn't know that one was a woman until I heard her voice. A nice voice, low, like Silky Joan, the lady my mother won't ever let me ask about, but with something rough in it too, as though she could scream like a hawk if she wanted to. She was saying, "There's no stone I can see. Maybe a thorn?"

The other rider, the one on the brown horse, answered her, "Or a bruise.

Let me see."

That voice was lighter and younger-sounding than the woman's voice, but I already knew he was a man, because he was so tall. He got down off the brown horse and the woman moved aside to let him pick up her horse's foot. Before he did that, he put his hands on the horse's head, one on each side, and he said something to it that I couldn't quite hear. *And the horse said something back.* Not like a neigh, or a whinny, or any of the sounds horses make, but like one person talking to another. I can't say it any better than that. The tall man bent down then, and he took hold of the foot and looked at it for a long time, and the horse didn't move or switch its tail or anything.

"A stone splinter," the man said after a while. "It's very small, but it's worked itself deep into the hoof, and there's an ulcer brewing. I can't think why I didn't notice it straightaway."

"Well," the woman said. She touched his shoulder. "You can't notice everything."

The tall man seemed angry with himself, the way my father gets when he's forgotten to close the pasture gate properly, and our neighbor's black ram gets in and fights with our poor old Brimstone. He said, "I can. I'm supposed to." Then he turned his back to the horse and bent over that forefoot, the way our blacksmith does, and he went to work on it.

I couldn't see what he was doing, not exactly. He didn't have any picks or pries, like the blacksmith, and all I'm sure of is that I *think* he was singing to the horse. But I'm not sure it was proper singing. It sounded more like the little made-up rhymes that really small children chant to themselves when they're playing in the dirt, all alone. No tune, just up and down, *dee-dah, dee-dah, dee*...boring even for a horse, I'd have thought. He kept doing it for a long time, still bending with that hoof in his hand. All at once he stopped singing and stood up, holding something that glinted in the sun the way the stream did, and he showed it to the horse, first thing. "There," he said, "There, that's what it was. It's all right now."

He tossed the thing away and picked up the hoof again, not singing, only touching it very lightly with one finger, brushing across it again and again. Then he set the foot down, and the horse stamped once, hard, and whinnied, and the tall man turned to the woman and said, "We ought to camp here for the night, all the same. They're both weary, and my back hurts."

The woman laughed. A deep, sweet, slow sound, it was. I'd never heard a laugh like that. She said, "The greatest wizard walking the world, and your back hurts? Heal it as you healed mine, the time the tree fell on me. That took you all of five minutes, I believe."

"Longer than that," the man answered her. "You were delirious, you wouldn't remember." He touched her hair, which was thick and pretty, even though it was mostly gray. "You know how I am about that," he said. "I still like being mortal too much to use magic on myself. It spoils it somehow — it dulls the feeling. I've told you before."

The woman said "*mmphh*," the way I've heard my mother say it a thousand times. "Well, *I've* been mortal all my life, and some days...."

She didn't finish what she was saying, and the tall man smiled, the way you could tell he was teasing her. "Some days, what?"

"Nothing," the woman said, "nothing, nothing." She sounded irritable for a moment, but she put her hands on the man's arms, and she said in a different voice, "Some days — some early mornings — when the wind smells of blossoms I'll never see, and there are fawns playing in the misty orchards, and you're yawning and mumbling and scratching your head, and growling that we'll see rain before nightfall, and probably hail as well... on such mornings I wish with all my heart that we could both live forever, and I think you were a great fool to give it up." She laughed again, but it sounded shaky now, a little. She said, "Then I remember things I'd rather not remember, so then my stomach acts up, and all sorts of other things start *twingeing* me — never mind what they are, or where they hurt, whether it's my body or my head, or my heart. And then I think, *no, I suppose not, maybe not.*" The tall man put his arms around her, and for a moment she rested her head on his chest. I couldn't hear what she said after that.

I didn't think I'd made any noise, but the man raised his voice a little, not looking at me, not lifting his head, and he said, "Child, there's food here." First I couldn't move, I was so frightened. He *couldn't* have seen me through the brush and all the alder trees. And then I started remembering how hungry I was, and I started toward them without knowing I was doing it. I actually looked down at my feet and watched them moving like somebody else's feet, as though they were the hungry ones, only they had to have me take them to the food. The man and the woman stood very still and waited for me.

Close to, the woman looked younger than her voice, and the tall man looked older. No, that isn't it, that's not what I mean. She wasn't young at all, but the gray hair made her face younger, and she held herself really straight, like the lady who comes when people in our village are having babies. She holds her face all stiff too, that one, and I don't like her much. This woman's face wasn't beautiful, I suppose, but it was a face you'd want to snuggle up to on a cold night. That's the best I know how to say it.

The man...one minute he looked younger than my father, and the next he'd be looking older than anybody I ever saw, older than people are supposed to *be*, maybe. He didn't have any gray hair himself, but he did have a lot of lines, but that's not what I'm talking about either. It was the eyes. His eyes were green, green, *green*, not like grass, not like emeralds — I saw an emerald once, a gypsy woman showed me — and not anything like apples or limes or such stuff. Maybe like the ocean, except I've never seen the ocean, so I don't know. If you go deep enough into the woods (not the Midwood, of course not, but any other sort of woods), sooner or later you'll always come to a place where even the *shadows* are green, and that's the way his eyes were. I was afraid of his eyes at first.

The woman gave me a peach and watched me bite into it, too hungry to thank her. She asked me, "Girl, what are you doing here? Are you lost?"

"No, I'm not," I mumbled with my mouth full. "I just don't know where I am, that's different." They both laughed, but it wasn't a mean, making-fun laugh. I told them, "My name's Sooz, and I have to see the king. He lives somewhere right nearby, doesn't he?"

They looked at each other. I couldn't tell what they were thinking, but the tall man raised his eyebrows, and the woman shook her head a bit, slowly. They looked at each other for a long time, until the woman said, "Well, not nearby, but not so very far, either. We were bound on our way to visit him ourselves."

"Good," I said. "Oh, *good*." I was trying to sound as grown-up as they were, but it was hard, because I was so happy to find out that they could take me to the king. I said, "I'll go along with you, then."

The woman was against it before I got the first words out. She said to the tall man, "No, we couldn't. We don't know how things are." She looked sad about it, but she looked firm, too. She said, "Girl, it's not you worries me. The king is a good man, and an old friend, but it has been a long time, and kings change. Even more than other people, kings change."

"I have to see him," I said. "You go on, then. I'm not going home until I see him." I finished the peach, and the man handed me a chunk of dried fish and smiled at the woman as I tore into it. He said quietly to her, "It seems to me that you and I both remember asking to be taken along on a quest. I can't speak for you, but I begged."

But the woman wouldn't let up. "We could be bringing her into great peril. You can't take the chance, it isn't right!"

He began to answer her, but I interrupted — my mother would have slapped me halfway across the kitchen. I shouted at them, "I'm *coming* from great peril. There's a griffin nested in the Midwood, and he's eaten Jehane and Louli and — and my Felicitas — " and then I *did* start weeping, and I didn't care. I just stood there and shook and wailed, and dropped the dried fish. I tried to pick it up, still crying so hard I couldn't see it, but the woman stopped me and gave me her scarf to dry my eyes and blow my nose. It smelled nice.

"Child," the tall man kept saying, "child, don't take on so, we didn't know about the griffin." The woman was holding me against her side, smoothing my hair and glaring at him as though it was his fault that I was howling like that. She said, "Of course we'll take you with us, girl dear — there, never mind, of course we will. That's a fearful matter, a griffin, but the king will know what to do about it. The king eats griffins for breakfast snacks — spreads them on toast with orange marmalade and gobbles them up, I promise you." And so on, being silly, but making me feel better, while the man went on pleading with me not to cry. I finally stopped when he pulled a big red handkerchief out of his pocket, twisted and knotted it into a bird-shape, and made it fly away. Uncle Ambrose does tricks with coins and shells, but he can't do anything like that.

His name was Schmendrick, which I still think is the funniest name I've heard in my life. The woman's name was Molly Grue. We didn't leave right away, because of the horses, but made camp where we were instead. I was waiting for the man, Schmendrick, to do it by magic, but he only built a fire, set out their blankets, and drew water from the stream like anyone else, while she hobbled the horses and put them to graze. I gathered firewood.

The woman, Molly, told me that the king's name was Lir, and that they had known him when he was a very young man, before he became king. "He is a true hero," she said, "a dragonslayer, a giantkiller, a rescuer of maidens, a solver of impossible riddles. He may be the greatest hero of all, because he's a good man as well. They aren't always."

"But you didn't want me to meet him," I said. "Why was that?"

Molly sighed. We were sitting under a tree, watching the sun go down, and she was brushing things out of my hair. She said, "He's old now. Schmendrick has trouble with time — I'll tell you why one day, it's a long story — and he doesn't understand that Lir may no longer be the man he was. It could be a sad reunion." She started braiding my hair around my head, so it wouldn't get in the way. "I've had an unhappy feeling about this journey from the beginning, Sooz. But *he* took a notion that Lir needed us, so here we are. You can't argue with him when he gets like that."

"A good wife isn't supposed to argue with her husband," I said. "My mother says you wait until he goes out, or he's asleep, and then you do what you want."

Molly laughed, that rich, funny sound of hers, like a kind of deep gurgle. "Sooz, I've only known you a few hours, but I'd bet every penny I've got right now — aye, and all of Schmendrick's too — that you'll be arguing on your wedding night with whomever you marry. Anyway, Schmendrick and I aren't married. We're together, that's all. We've been together quite a long while."

"Oh," I said. I didn't know any people who were together like that, not the way she said it. "Well, you *look* married. You sort of do."

Molly's face didn't change, but she put an arm around my shoulders and hugged me close for a moment. She whispered in my ear, "I wouldn't marry him if he were the last man in the world. He eats wild radishes in bed. *Crunch, crunch, crunch,* all night — *crunch, crunch, crunch.*" I giggled, and the tall man looked over at us from where he was washing a pan in the stream. The last of the sunlight was on him, and those green eyes were bright as new leaves. One of them winked at me, and I *felt* it, the way you feel a tiny breeze on your skin when it's hot. Then he went back to scrubbing the pan.

"Will it take us long to reach the king?" I asked her. "You said he didn't live too far, and I'm scared the griffin will eat somebody else while I'm gone. I need to be home."

Molly finished with my hair and gave it a gentle tug in back to bring my head up and make me look straight into her eyes. They were as gray as Schmendrick's were green, and I already knew that they turned darker or lighter gray depending on her mood. "What do you expect to happen when you meet King Lir, Sooz?" she asked me right back. "What did you have in mind when you set off to find him?"

I was surprised, "Well, I'm going to get him to come back to my village with me. All those knights he keeps sending aren't doing any good at all, so he'll just have to take care of that griffin himself. He's the king. It's his job."

"Yes," Molly said, but she said it so softly I could barely hear her. She patted my arm once, lightly, and then she got up and walked away to sit by herself near the fire. She made it look as though she was banking the fire, but she wasn't really.

We started out early the next morning. Molly had me in front of her on her horse for a time, but by and by Schmendrick took me up on his, to spare the other one's sore foot. He was more comfortable to lean against than I'd expected — bony in some places, nice and springy in others. He didn't talk much, but he sang a lot as we went along, sometimes in languages I couldn't make out a word of, sometimes making up silly songs to make me laugh, like this one:

> *Soozli, Soozli,*
> *speaking loozli,*
> *you disturb my oozli-goozli.*
> *Soozli, Soozli,*

would you choozli
to become my squoozli-squoozli?

He didn't do anything magic, except maybe once, when a crow kept diving at the horse — out of meanness; that's all, there wasn't a nest anywhere — making the poor thing dance and shy and skitter until I almost fell off. Schmendrick finally turned in the saddle and *looked* at it, and the next minute a hawk came swooping out of nowhere and chased that crow screaming into a thornbush where the hawk couldn't follow. I guess that was magic.

It was actually pretty country we were passing through, once we got onto the proper road. Trees, meadows, little soft valleys, hillsides covered with wildflowers I didn't know. You could see they got a lot more rain here than we do where I live. It's a good thing sheep don't need grazing, the way cows do. They'll go where the goats go, and goats will go anywhere. We're like that in my village, we have to be. But I liked this land better.

Schmendrick told me it hadn't always been like that. "Before Lir, this was all barren desert where nothing grew — *nothing*, Sooz. It was said that the country was under a curse, and in a way it was, but I'll tell you about that another time." People *always* say that when you're a child, and I hate it. "But Lir changed everything. The land was so glad to see him that it began blooming and blossoming the moment he became king, and it has done so ever since. Except poor Hagsgate, but that's another story too." His voice got slower and deeper when he talked about Hagsgate, as though he weren't talking to me.

I twisted my neck around to look up at him. "Do you think King Lir will come back with me and kill that griffin? I think Molly thinks he won't, because he's so old." I hadn't known I was worried about that until I actually said it.

"Why, of course he will, girl." Schmendrick winked at me again. "He never could resist the plea of a maiden in distress, the more difficult and dangerous the deed, the better. If he did not spur to your village's aid himself at the first call, it was surely because he was engaged on some other heroic venture. I'm as certain as I can be that as soon as you make your request — remember to curtsey properly — he'll snatch up his great sword and spear, whisk you up to his saddlebow, and be off after your griffin with the road smoking behind him. Young or old, that's always been his way." He rumpled my hair in the back. "Molly overworries. That's *her* way. We are who we are."

"What's a curtsey?" I asked him. I know now, because Molly showed me, but I didn't then. He didn't laugh, except with his eyes, then gestured for me to face forward again as he went back to singing.

> Soozli, Soozli,
> you amuse me,
> right down to my solesli-shoesli.
> Soozli, Soozli,
> I bring newsli —
> we could wed next stewsli-Tuesli.

I learned that the king had lived in a castle on a cliff by the sea when he was young, less than a day's journey from Hagsgate, but it fell down — Schmendrick wouldn't tell me how — so he built a new one somewhere else. I was sorry about that, because I've never seen the sea, and I've always wanted to, and I still haven't. But I'd never seen a castle, either, so there was that. I leaned back against his chest and fell asleep.

They'd been traveling slowly, taking time to let Molly's horse heal, but once its hoof was all right we galloped most of the rest of the way. Those horses of theirs didn't look magic or special, but they could run for hours without getting tired, and when I helped to rub them down and curry them, they were hardly sweating. They slept on their sides, like people, not standing up, the way our horses do.

Even so, it took us three full days to reach King Lir. Molly said he had bad memories of the castle that fell down, so that was why this one was as far from the sea as he could make it, and as different from the old one. It was on a hill, so the king could see anyone coming along the road, but there wasn't a moat, and there weren't any guards in armor, and there was only one banner on the walls. It was blue, with a picture of a white unicorn on it. Nothing else.

I was disappointed. I tried not to show it, but Molly saw. "You wanted a fortress," she said to me gently. "You were expecting dark stone towers, flags and cannons and knights, trumpeters blowing from the battlements. I'm sorry. It being your first castle, and all."

"No, it's a pretty castle," I said. And it was pretty, sitting peacefully on its hilltop in the sunlight, surrounded by all those wildflowers. There was a marketplace, I could see now, and there were huts like ours snugged up against the castle walls, so that the people could come inside for protection, if they needed to. I said, "Just looking at it, you can see that the king is a nice man."

Molly was looking at me with her head a little bit to one side. She said, "He is a hero, Sooz. Remember that, whatever else you see, whatever you think. Lir is a hero."

"Well, I know *that*," I said. "I'm sure he'll help me. I am."

But I wasn't. The moment I saw that nice, friendly castle, I wasn't a bit sure.

We didn't have any trouble getting in. The gate simply opened when Schmendrick knocked once, and he and Molly and I walked in through the market, where people were selling all kinds of fruits and vegetables, pots and pans and clothing and so on, the way they do in our village. They all called to us to come over to their barrows and buy things, but nobody tried to stop us going into the castle. There were two men at the two great doors, and they did ask us our names and why we wanted to see King Lir. The moment Schmendrick told them his name, they stepped back quickly and let us by, so I began to think that maybe he actually was a great magician, even if I never saw him do anything but little tricks and little songs. The men didn't offer to take him to the king, and he didn't ask.

Molly was right. I *was* expecting the castle to be all cold and shadowy, with queens looking sideways at us, and big men clanking by in armor. But the halls we followed Schmendrick through were full of sunlight from long, high windows, and the people we saw mostly nodded and smiled at us. We passed a stone stair curling up out of sight, and I was sure that the king must live at the top, but Schmendrick never looked at it. He led us straight through the great hall — they had a fireplace big enough to roast three cows! — and on past the kitchens and the scullery and the laundry, to a room under another stair. *That* was dark. You wouldn't have found it unless you knew where to look. Schmendrick didn't knock at that door, and he didn't say anything magic to make it open. He just stood outside and waited, and by and by it rattled open, and we went in.

The king was in there. All by himself, the king was in there.

He was sitting on an ordinary wooden chair, not a throne. It was a really small room, the same size as my mother's weaving room, so maybe that's why he looked so big. He was as tall as Schmendrick, but he seemed so much *wider*. I was ready for him to have a long beard, spreading out all across his chest, but he only had a short one, like my father, except white. He wore a red and gold mantle, and there was a real golden crown on his white head, not much bigger than the wreaths we put on our champion rams at the end of the year. He had a kind face, with a big old nose, and big blue eyes, like a little boy. But his eyes were so tired and heavy, I didn't know how he kept them open. Sometimes he didn't. There was nobody else in the little room, and he peered at the three of us as though he knew he knew us, but not *why*. He tried to smile.

Schmendrick said very gently, "Majesty, it is Schmendrick and Molly, Molly Grue." The king blinked at him.

"Molly with the cat," Molly whispered. "You remember the cat, Lir."

"Yes," the king said. It seemed to take him forever to speak that one word. "The cat, yes, of course." But he didn't say anything after that, and we stood there and stood there, and the king kept smiling at something I couldn't see.

Schmendrick said to Molly, "*She* used to forget herself like that." His voice had changed, the same way it changed when he was talking about the way the land used to be. He said, "And then you would always remind her that she was a unicorn."

And the king changed too then. All at once his eyes were clear and shining with feeling, like Molly's eyes, and he *saw* us for the first time. He said softly, "Oh, my friends!" and he stood up and came to us and put his arms around Schmendrick and Molly. And I saw that he had been a hero, and that he was still a hero, and I began to think it might be all right, after all. Maybe it was really going to be all right.

"And who may this princess be?" he asked, looking straight at me. He had the proper voice for a king, deep and strong, but not frightening, not mean. I tried to tell him my name, but I couldn't make a sound, so he actually knelt on one knee in front of me, and he took my hand. He said, "I have often been of some use to princesses in distress. Command me."

"I'm not a princess, I'm Sooz," I said, "and I'm from a village you wouldn't even know, and there's a griffin eating the children." It all tumbled out like that, in one breath, but he didn't laugh or look at me any differently. What he did was ask me the name of my village, and I told him, and he said, "But indeed I know it, madam. I have been there. And now I will have the pleasure of returning."

Over his shoulder I saw Schmendrick and Molly staring at each other. Schmendrick was about to say something, but then they both turned toward the door, because a small dark woman, about my mother's age, only dressed in tunic, trews, and boots like Molly, had just come in. She said in a small, worried voice, "I am so truly sorry that I was not here to greet His Majesty's old companions. No need to tell me your illustrious names — my own is Lisene, and I am the king's royal secretary, translator, and protector." She took King Lir's arm, very politely and carefully, and began moving him back to his chair.

Schmendrick seemed to take a minute getting his own breath back. He said, "I have never known my old friend Lir to need any of those services. Especially a protector."

Lisene was busy with the king and didn't look at Schmendrick as she answered him. "How long has it been since you saw him last?" Schmendrick didn't answer. Lisene's voice was quiet still, but not so nervous. "Time sets its claw in us all, my lord, sooner or later. We are none of us that which we were." King Lir sat down obediently on his chair and closed his eyes.

I could tell that Schmendrick was angry, and growing angrier as he stood there, but he didn't show it. My father gets angry like that, which is how I knew. He said, "His Majesty has agreed to return to this young person's village with her, in order to rid her people of a marauding griffin. We will start out tomorrow."

Lisene swung around on us so fast that I was sure she was going to start shouting and giving everybody orders. But she didn't do anything like that. You could never have told that she was the least bit annoyed or alarmed. All she said was, "I am afraid that will not be possible, my lord. The king is in no fit condition for such a journey, nor certainly for such a deed."

"The king thinks rather differently." Schmendrick was talking through clenched teeth now.

"Does he, then?" Lisene pointed at King Lir, and I saw that he had fallen asleep in his chair. His head was drooping — I was afraid his crown was going to fall off — and his mouth hung open. Lisene said, "You came seeking the peerless warrior you remember, and you have found a spent, senile old man. Believe me, I understand your distress, but you must see — "

Schmendrick cut her off. I never understood what people meant when they talked about someone's eyes actually flashing, but at least green eyes can do it. He looked even taller than he was, and when he pointed a finger at Lisene I honestly expected the little woman to catch fire or maybe melt away. Schmendrick's voice was especially frightening because it was so quiet. He said, "Hear me now. I am Schmendrick the Magician, and I see my old friend Lir, as I have always seen him, wise and powerful and good, beloved of a unicorn."

And with that word, for a second time, the king woke up. His blinked once, then gripped the arms of the chair and pushed himself to his feet. He didn't look at us, but at Lisene, and he said, "I will go with them. It is my task and my gift. You will see to it that I am made ready."

Lisene said, "Majesty, no! Majesty, I beg you!"

King Lir reached out and took Lisene's head between his big hands, and I saw that there was love between them. He said, "It is what I am for. You know that as well as *he* does. See to it, Lisene, and keep all well for me while I am gone."

Lisene looked so sad, so *lost*, that I didn't know what to think, about her or King Lir or anything. I didn't realize that I had moved back against Molly Grue until I felt her hand in my hair. She didn't say anything, but it was nice smelling her there. Lisene said, very quietly, "I will see to it."

She turned around then and started for the door with her head lowered. I think she wanted to pass us by without looking at us at all, but she couldn't do it. Right at the door, her head came up and she stared at Schmendrick so hard that I pushed into Molly's skirt so I couldn't see her eyes. I heard her say, as though she could barely make the words come out, "His death be on your head, magician." I think she was crying, only not the way grown people do.

And I heard Schmendrick's answer, and his voice was so cold I wouldn't have recognized it if I didn't know. "He has died before. Better that death — better this, better *any* death — than the one he was dying in that chair. If the griffin kills him, it will yet have saved his life." I heard the door close.

I asked Molly, speaking as low as I could, "What did he mean, about the king having died?" But she put me to one side, and she went to King Lir and knelt in front of him, reaching up to take one of his hands between hers. She said, "Lord...Majesty...friend...dear friend — remember. Oh, please, please *remember*."

The old man was swaying on his feet, but he put his other hand on Molly's head and he mumbled, "Child, Sooz — is that your pretty name, Sooz? — of course I will come to your village. The griffin was never hatched that dares harm King Lir's people." He sat down hard in the chair again, but he held onto her hand tightly. He looked at her, with his blue eyes wide and his mouth trembling a little. He said, "But you must remind me, little one. When I...when I lose myself — when I lose *her* — you must remind me that I am still searching, still waiting...that I have never forgotten her, never turned from all she taught me. I sit in this place...I *sit*...because a king has to sit, you see...but in my mind, in my poor mind, I am always away with *her*...."

I didn't have any idea what he was talking about. I do now.

He fell asleep again then, holding Molly's hand. She sat with him for a long time, resting her head on his knee. Schmendrick went off to make sure Lisene was doing what she was supposed to do, getting everything ready for the king's departure. There was a lot of clattering and shouting already, enough so you'd have thought a war was starting, but nobody came in to see King Lir or speak to him, wish him luck or anything. It was almost as though he wasn't really there.

Me, I tried to write a letter home, with pictures of the king and the castle, but I fell asleep like him, and I slept the rest of that day and all night too. I woke up in a bed I couldn't remember getting into, with Schmendrick looking down at me, saying, "Up, child, on your feet. You started all this uproar — it's time for you to see it through. The king is coming to slay your griffin."

I was out of bed before he'd finished speaking. I said, "Now? Are we going right now?"

Schmendrick shrugged his shoulders. "By noon, anyway, if I can finally get Lisene and the rest of them to understand that they are *not* coming. Lisene wants to bring fifty men-at-arms, a dozen wagonloads of supplies, a regiment of runners to send messages back and forth, and every wretched physician in the kingdom." He sighed and spread his hands. "I may have to turn the lot of them to stone if we are to be off today."

I thought he was probably joking, but I already knew that you couldn't be sure with Schmendrick. He said, "If Lir comes with a train of followers, there will be no Lir. Do you understand me, Sooz?" I shook my head. Schmendrick said, "It is my fault. If I had made sure to visit here more often, there were things I could have done to restore the Lir Molly and I once knew. My fault, my thoughtlessness."

I remembered Molly telling me, "Schmendrick has trouble with time." I still didn't know what she meant, nor this either. I said, "It's just the way old people get. We have old men in our village who talk like him. One woman, too, Mam Jennet. She always cries when it rains."

Schmendrick clenched his fist and pounded it against his leg. "King Lir is *not* mad, girl, nor is he senile, as Lisene called him. He is *Lir,* Lir still, I promise you that. It is only here, in this castle, surrounded by good, loyal people who love him — who will love him to death, if they are allowed — that he sinks into...into the condition you have seen." He didn't say anything more for a moment; then he stooped a little to peer closely at me. "Did you notice the change in him when I spoke of unicorns?"

"Unicorn," I answered. "One unicorn who loved him. I noticed."

Schmendrick kept looking at me in a new way, as though we'd never met before. He said, "Your pardon, Sooz. I keep taking you for a child. Yes. One unicorn. He has not seen her since he became king, but he is what he is because of her. And when I speak that word, when Molly or I say her name — which I have not done yet — then he is recalled to himself." He paused for a moment, and then added, very softly, "As we had so often to do for her, so long ago."

"I didn't know unicorns had names," I said. "I didn't know they ever loved people."

"They don't. Only this one." He turned and walked away swiftly, saying over his shoulder, "Her name was Amalthea. Go find Molly, she'll see you fed."

The room I'd slept in wasn't big, not for something in a castle. Catania, the headwoman of our village, has a bedroom nearly as large, which I know because I play with her daughter Sophia. But the sheets I'd been under were embroidered with a crown, and engraved on the headboard was a picture of the blue banner with the white unicorn. I had slept the night in King Lir's own bed while he dozed in an old wooden chair.

I didn't wait to have breakfast with Molly, but ran straight to the little room where I had last seen the king. He was there, but so changed that I froze in the doorway, trying to get my breath. Three men were bustling around him like tailors, dressing him in his armor: all the padding underneath, first, and then the different pieces for the arms and legs and shoulders. I don't know any of the names. The men hadn't put his helmet on him, so his head stuck out at the top, white-haired and big-nosed and blue-eyed, but he didn't look silly like that. He looked like a giant.

When he saw me, he smiled, and it was a warm, happy smile, but it was a little frightening too, almost a little terrible, like the time I saw the griffin burning in the black sky. It was a hero's smile. I'd never seen one before. He called to me, "Little one, come and buckle on my sword, if you would. It would be an honor for me."

The men had to show me how you do it. The swordbelt, all by itself, was so heavy it kept slipping through my fingers, and I did need help with the buckle. But I put the sword into its sheath alone, although I needed both hands to lift it. When it slid home it made a sound like a great door slamming shut. King Lir touched my face with one of his cold iron gloves and said, "Thank you, little one. The next time that blade is drawn, it will be to free your village. You have my word."

Schmendrick came in then, took one look, and just shook his head. He said, "This is the most ridiculous...It is four days' ride — perhaps five — with the weather turning hot enough to broil a lobster on an iceberg. There's no need for armor until he faces the griffin." You could see how stupid he felt they all were, but King Lir smiled at him the same way he'd smiled at me, and Schmendrick stopped talking.

King Lir said, "Old friend, I go forth as I mean to return. It is my way."

Schmendrick looked like a little boy himself for a moment. All he could say was, "Your business. Don't blame me, that's all. At *least* leave the helmet off."

He was about to turn away and stalk out of the room, but Molly came up behind him and said, "Oh, Majesty — Lir — how grand! How beautiful you are!" She sounded the way my Aunt Zerelda sounds when she's carrying on about my brother Wilfrid. He could mess his pants and jump in a hog pen, and Aunt Zerelda would still think he was the best, smartest boy in the whole world. But Molly was different. She brushed those tailors, or whatever they were, straight aside, and she stood on tiptoe to smooth King Lir's white hair, and I heard her whisper, "I wish *she* could see you."

King Lir looked at her for a long time without saying anything.

Schmendrick stood there, off to the side, and he didn't say anything either, but they were together, the three of them. I wish that Felicitas and I could have been together like that when we got old. Could have had time. Then King Lir looked at *me*, and he said, "The child is waiting." And that's how we set off for home. The king, Schmendrick, Molly, and me.

To the last minute, poor old Lisene kept trying to get King Lir to take some knights or soldiers with him. She actually followed us on foot when we left, calling, "Highness — Majesty — if you will have none else, take me! Take me!" At that the king stopped and turned and went back to her. He got down off his horse and embraced Lisene, and I don't know what they said to each other, but Lisene didn't follow anymore after that.

I rode with the king most of the time, sitting up in front of him on his skittery black mare. I wasn't sure I could trust her not to bite me, or to kick me when I wasn't looking, but King Lir told me, "It is only peaceful times that make her nervous, be assured of that. When dragons charge her, belching death — for the fumes are more dangerous than the flames, little one — when your griffin swoops down at her, you will see her at her best." I still didn't like her much, but I did like the king. He didn't sing to me, the way Schmendrick had, but he told me stories, and they weren't fables or fairytales. These were real, true stories, and he knew they were true because they had all happened to him! I never heard stories like those, and I never will again. I know that for certain.

He told me more things to keep in mind if you have to fight a dragon, and he told me how he learned that ogres aren't always as stupid as they look, and why you should never swim in a mountain pool when the snows are melting, and how you can *sometimes* make friends with a troll. He talked about his father's castle, where he grew up, and about how he met Schmendrick and Molly there, and even about Molly's cat, which he said was a little thing with a funny crooked ear. But when I asked him why the castle fell down, he wouldn't exactly say, no more than Schmendrick would. His voice became very quiet and faraway. "I forget things, you know, little one," he said. "I try to hold on, but I do forget."

Well, I knew *that*. He kept calling Molly Sooz, and he never called me anything but *little one*, and Schmendrick kept having to remind him where we were bound and why. That was always at night, though. He was usually fine during the daytime. And when he did turn confused again, and wander off (not just in his mind, either — I found him in the woods one night, talking to a tree as though it was his father), all you had to do was mention a white unicorn named Amalthea, and he'd come to himself almost right away. Generally it was Schmendrick who did that, but I brought him back that time, holding my hand and telling me how you can recognize a pooka, and why you need to. But I could never get him to say a word about the unicorn.

Autumn comes early where I live. The days were still hot, and the king never would take his armor off, except to sleep, not even his helmet with the big blue plume on top, but at night I burrowed in between Molly and Schmendrick for warmth, and you could hear the stags belling everywhere all the time, crazy with the season. One of them actually charged King Lir's horse while I was riding with him, and Schmendrick was about to do something magic to the stag, the same way he'd done with the crow. But the king laughed and rode straight at him, right *into* those horns. I screamed, but the black mare never hesitated, and the stag turned at the last moment and ambled out of sight in the brush. He was wagging his tail in circles, the way goats do, and looking as puzzled and dreamy as King Lir himself.

I was proud, once I got over being frightened. But both Schmendrick and Molly scolded him, and he kept apologizing to me for the rest of the day for having put me in danger, as Molly had once said he would. "I forgot you were with me, little one, and for that I will always ask your pardon." Then he smiled at me with that beautiful, terrible hero's smile I'd seen before, and he said, "But oh, little one, the remembering!" And that night he didn't wander away and get himself lost. Instead he sat happily by the fire with us and sang a whole long song about the adventures of an outlaw called Captain Cully. I'd never heard of him, but it's a really good song.

We reached my village late on the afternoon of the fourth day, and Schmendrick made us stop together before we rode in. He said, directly to me, "Sooz, if you tell them that this is the king himself, there will be nothing but noise and joy and celebration, and nobody will get any rest with all that carrying-on. It would be best for you to tell them that we have brought King Lir's greatest knight with us, and that he needs a night to purify himself in prayer and meditation before he deals with your griffin." He took hold of my chin and made me look into his green, green eyes, and he said, "Girl, you have to trust me. I always know what I'm doing — that's my trouble. Tell your people what I've said." And Molly touched me and looked at me without saying anything, so I knew it was all right.

I left them camped on the outskirts of the village, and walked home by myself. Malka met me first. She smelled me before I even reached Simon and Elsie's tavern, and she came running and crashed into my legs and knocked me over, and then pinned me down with her paws on my shoulders, and kept licking my face until I had to nip her nose to make her let me up and run to the house with me. My father was out with the flock, but my mother and Wilfrid were there, and they grabbed me and nearly strangled me, and they cried over me — rotten, stupid Wilfrid too! — because everyone had been so certain that I'd been taken and eaten by the griffin. After that, once she got done crying, my mother spanked me for running off in Uncle Ambrose's cart without telling anyone, and when my father came in, he spanked me all over again. But I didn't mind.

I told them I'd seen King Lir in person, and been in his castle, and I said what Schmendrick had told me to say, but nobody was much cheered by it. My father just sat down and grunted, "Oh, aye — another great warrior for our comfort and the griffin's dessert. Your bloody king won't ever come here his bloody self, you can be sure of that." My mother reproached him for talking like that in front of Wilfrid and me, but he went on, "Maybe he cared about places like this, people like us once, but he's old now, and old kings only care who's going to be king after them. You can't tell me anything different."

I wanted more than anything to tell him that King Lir *was* here, less than half a mile from our doorstep, but I didn't, and not only because Schmendrick had told me not to. I wasn't sure what the king might look like, white-haired and shaky and not here all the time, to people like my father. I wasn't sure what he looked like to me, for that matter. He was a lovely, dignified old man who told wonderful stories, but when I tried to imagine him riding alone into the Midwood to do battle with a griffin, a griffin that had already eaten his best knights... to be honest, I couldn't do it. Now that I'd actually brought him all the way home with me, as I'd set out to do, I was suddenly afraid that I'd drawn him to his death. And I knew I wouldn't ever forgive myself if that happened.

I wanted so much to see them that night, Schmendrick and Molly and the king. I wanted to sleep out there on the ground with them, and listen to their talk, and then maybe I'd not worry so much about the morning. But of course there wasn't a chance of that. My family would hardly let me out of their sight to wash my face. Wilfrid kept following me around, asking endless questions about the castle, and my father took me to Catania, who had me tell the whole story over again, and agreed with him that whomever the king had sent this time wasn't likely to be any more use than the others had been. And my mother kept feeding me and scolding me and hugging me, all more or less at the same time. And then, in the night, we heard the griffin, making that soft, lonely, horrible sound it makes when it's hunting. So I didn't get very much sleep, between one thing and another.

But at sunrise, after I'd helped Wilfrid milk the goats, they let me run out to the camp, as long as Malka came with me, which was practically like having my mother along. Molly was already helping King Lir into his armor, and Schmendrick was burying the remains of last night's dinner, as though they were starting one more ordinary day on their journey to somewhere. They greeted me, and Schmendrick thanked me for doing as he'd asked, so that the king could have a restful night before he —

I didn't let him finish. I didn't know I was going to do it, I swear, but I ran up to King Lir, and I threw my arms around him, and I said, "Don't go! I changed my mind, don't go!" Just like Lisene.

King Lir looked down at me. He seemed as tall as a tree right then, and he patted my head very gently with his iron glove. He said, "Little one, I have a griffin to slay. It is my job."

Which was what I'd said myself, though it seemed like years ago, and that made it so much worse. I said a second time, "I changed my mind! Somebody else can fight the griffin, you don't have to! You go home! You go home *now* and live your life, and be the king, and everything...." I was babbling and sniffling, and generally being a baby, I know that. I'm glad Wilfrid didn't see me.

King Lir kept petting me with one hand and trying to put me aside with the other, but I wouldn't let go. I think I was actually trying to pull his sword out of its sheath, to take it away from him. He said, "No, no, little one, you don't understand. There are some monsters that only a king can kill. I have always known that — I should never, never have sent those poor men to die in my place. No one else in all the land can do this for you and your village. Most truly now, it is my job." And he kissed my hand, the way he must have kissed the hands of so many queens. He kissed my hand too, just like theirs.

Molly came up then and took me away from him. She held me close, and she stroked my hair, and she told me, "Child, Sooz, there's no turning back for him now, or for you either. It was your fate to bring this last cause to him, and his fate to take it up, and neither of you could have done differently, being who you are. And now you must be as brave as he is, and see it all play out." She caught herself there, and changed it. "Rather, you must wait to learn how it has played out, because you are certainly not coming into that forest with us."

"I'm coming," I said. "You can't stop me. Nobody can." I wasn't sniffling or anything anymore. I said it like that, that's all.

Molly held me at arm's length, and she shook me a little bit. She said, "Sooz, if you can tell me that your parents have given their permission, then you may come. Have they done so?"

I didn't answer her. She shook me again, gentler this time, saying, "Oh, that was wicked of me, forgive me, my dear friend. I knew the day we met that you could never learn to lie." Then she took both of my hands between hers, and she said, "Lead us to the Midwood, if you will, Sooz, and we will say our farewells there. Will you do that for us? For me?"

I nodded, but I still didn't speak. I couldn't, my throat was hurting so much. Molly squeezed my hands and said, "Thank you." Schmendrick came up and made some kind of sign to her with his eyes, or his eyebrows, because she said, "Yes, I know," although he hadn't said a thing. So she went to King Lir with him, and I was alone, trying to stop shaking. I managed it, after a while.

The Midwood isn't far. They wouldn't really have needed my help to find it. You can see the beginning of it from the roof of Ellis the baker's house, which is the tallest one on that side of the village. It's always dark, even from a distance, even if you're not actually in it. I don't know if that's because they're oak trees (we have all sorts of tales and sayings about oaken woods, and the creatures that live there) or maybe because of some enchantment, or because of the griffin. Maybe it was different before the griffin came. Uncle Ambrose says it's been a bad place all his life, but my father says no, he and his friends used to hunt there, and he actually picnicked there once or twice with my mother, when they were young.

King Lir rode in front, looking grand and almost young, with his head up and the blue plume on his helmet floating above him, more like a banner than a feather. I was going to ride with Molly, but the king leaned from his saddle as I started past, and swooped me up before him, saying, "You shall guide and company me, little one, until we reach the forest." I was proud of that, but I was frightened too, because he was so happy, and I knew he was going to his death, trying to make up for all those knights he'd sent to fight the griffin. I didn't try to warn him. He wouldn't have heard me, and I knew that too. Me and poor old Lisene.

He told me all about griffins as we rode. He said, "If you should ever have dealings with a griffin, little one, you must remember that they are not like dragons. A dragon is simply a dragon — make yourself small when it dives down at you, but hold your ground and strike at the underbelly, and you've won the day. But a griffin, now...a griffin is two highly dissimilar creatures, eagle and lion, fused together by some god with a god's sense of humor. And so there is an eagle's heart beating in the beast, and a lion's heart as well, and you must pierce them both to have any hope of surviving the battle." He was as cheerful as he could be about it all, holding me safe on the saddle, and saying over and over, the way old people do, "Two hearts, never forget that — many people do. Eagle heart, lion heart — eagle heart, lion heart. *Never* forget, little one."

We passed a lot of people I knew, out with their sheep and goats, and they all waved to me, and called, and made jokes, and so on. They cheered for King Lir, but they didn't bow to him, or take off their caps, because nobody recognized him, nobody knew. He seemed delighted about that, which most kings probably wouldn't be. But he's the only king I've met, so I can't say.

The Midwood seemed to be reaching out for us before we were anywhere near it, long fingery shadows stretching across the empty fields, and the leaves flickering and blinking, though there wasn't any wind. A forest is usually really noisy, day and night, if you stand still and listen to the birds and the insects and the streams and such, but the Midwood is always silent, silent. That reaches out too, the silence.

We halted a stone's throw from the forest, and King Lir said to me, "We part here, little one," and set me down on the ground as carefully as though he was putting a bird back in its nest. He said to Schmendrick, "I know better than to try to keep you and Sooz from following —" he kept on calling Molly by my name, every time, I don't know why — "but I enjoin you, in the name of great Nikos himself, and in the name of our long and precious friendship...." He stopped there, and he didn't say anything more for such a while that I was afraid he was back to forgetting who he was and why he was there, the way he had been. But then he went on, clear and ringing as one of those mad stags, "I charge you in *her* name, in the name of the Lady Amalthea, not to assist me in any way from the moment we pass the very first tree, but to leave me altogether to what is mine to do. Is that understood between us, dear ones of my heart?"

Schmendrick hated it. You didn't have to be magic to see that. It was so plain, even to me, that he had been planning to take over the battle as soon as they were actually facing the griffin. But King Lir was looking right at him with those young blue eyes, and with a little bit of a smile on his face, and Schmendrick simply didn't know what to do. There wasn't anything he *could* do, so he finally nodded and mumbled, "If that is Your Majesty's wish." The king couldn't hear him at all the first time, so he made him say it again.

And then, of course, everybody had to say good-bye to me, since I wasn't allowed to go any farther with them. Molly said she knew we'd see each other again, and Schmendrick told me that I had the makings of a real warrior queen, only he was certain I was too smart to be one. And King Lir...King Lir said to me, very quietly, so nobody else could hear, "Little one, if I had married and had a daughter, I would have asked no more than that she should be as brave and kind and loyal as you. Remember that, as I will remember you to my last day."

Which was all nice, and I wished my mother and father could have heard what all these grown people were saying about me. But then they turned and rode on into the Midwood, the three of them, and only Molly looked back at me. And I think *that* was to make sure I wasn't following, because

I was supposed just to go home and wait to find out if my friends were alive or dead, and if the griffin was going to be eating any more children. It was all over.

And maybe I would have gone home and let it be all over, if it hadn't been for Malka.

She should have been with the sheep and not with me, of course — that's her job, the same way King Lir was doing his job, going to meet the griffin. But Malka thinks I'm a sheep too, the most stupid, aggravating sheep she ever had to guard, forever wandering away into some kind of danger. All the way to the Midwood she had trotted quietly alongside the king's horse, but now that we were alone again she came rushing up and bounced all over me, barking like thunder and knocking me down, hard, the way she does whenever I'm not where she wants me to be. I always brace myself when I see her coming, but it never helps.

What she does then, before I'm on my feet, is take the hem of my smock in her jaws and start tugging me in the direction she thinks I should go. But this time...this time she suddenly got up, as though she'd forgotten all about me, and she stared past me at the Midwood with all the white showing in her eyes and a low sound coming out of her that I don't think she knew she could make. The next moment, she was gone, racing into the forest with foam flying from her mouth and her big ragged ears flat back. I called, but she couldn't have heard me, baying and barking the way she was.

Well, I didn't have any choice. King Lir and Schmendrick and Molly all had a choice, going after the Midwood griffin, but Malka was my dog, and she didn't know what she was facing, and I *couldn't* let her face it by herself. So there wasn't anything else for me to do. I took an enormous long breath and looked around me, and then I walked into the forest after her.

Actually, I ran, as long as I could, and then I walked until I could run again, and then I ran some more. There aren't any paths into the Midwood, because nobody goes there, so it wasn't hard to see where three horses had pushed through the undergrowth, and then a dog's tracks on top of the hoofprints. It was very quiet with no wind, not one bird calling, no sound but my own panting. I couldn't even hear Malka anymore. I was hoping that maybe they'd come on the griffin while it was asleep, and King Lir had already killed it in its nest. I didn't think so, though. He'd probably have decided it wasn't honorable to attack a sleeping griffin, and wakened it up for a fair fight. I hadn't known him very long, but I knew what he'd do.

Then, a little way ahead of me, the whole forest exploded.

It was too much noise for me to sort it out in my head. There was Malka absolutely *howling*, and birds bursting up everywhere out of the brush, and Schmendrick or the king or someone was shouting, only I couldn't make out any of the words. And underneath it all was something that wasn't loud at all, a sound somewhere between a growl and that terrible soft call, like a frightened child. Then — just as I broke into the clearing — the rattle and scrape of knives, only much louder this time, as the griffin shot straight up with the sun on its wings. Its cold golden eyes *bit* into mine, and its beak was open so wide you could see down and down the blazing red gullet. It filled the sky.

And King Lir, astride his black mare, filled the clearing. He was as huge as the griffin, and his sword was the size of a boar spear, and he shook it at the griffin, daring it to light down and fight him on the ground. But the griffin was staying out of range, circling overhead to get a good look at these strange new people. Malka was utterly off her head, screaming and hurling herself into the air again and again, snapping at the griffin's lion feet and eagle claws, but coming down each time without so much as an iron feather between her teeth. I lunged and caught her in the air, trying to drag her away before the griffin turned on her, but she fought me, scratching my face with her own dull dog claws, until I had to let her go. The last time she leaped, the griffin suddenly stooped and caught her full on her side with one huge wing, so hard that she couldn't get a sound out, no more than I could. She flew all the way across the clearing, slammed into a tree, fell to the ground, and after that she didn't move.

Molly told me later that that was when King Lir struck for the griffin's lion heart. I didn't see it. I was flying across the clearing myself, throwing myself over Malka, in case the griffin came after her again, and I didn't see anything except her staring eyes and the blood on her side. But I did hear the griffin's roar when it happened, and when I could turn my head, I saw the blood splashing along *its* side, and the back legs squinching up against its belly, the way you do when you're really hurting. King Lir shouted like a boy. He threw that great sword as high as the griffin, and snatched it back again, and then he charged toward the griffin as it wobbled lower and lower, with its crippled lion half dragging it out of the air. It landed with a saggy thump, just like Malka, and there was a moment when I was absolutely sure it was dead. I remember I was thinking, very far away, *this is good, I'm glad, I'm sure I'm glad.*

But Schmendrick was screaming at the king, "Two hearts! *Two hearts!*" until his voice split with it, and Molly was on me, trying to drag me away from the griffin, and *I* was hanging onto Malka — she'd gotten so *heavy* — and I don't know what else was happening right then, because all I was seeing and thinking about was Malka. And all I was feeling was her heart not beating under mine.

She guarded my cradle when I was born. I cut my teeth on her poor ears, and she never made one sound. My mother says so.

King Lir wasn't seeing or hearing any of us. There was nothing in the world for him but the griffin, which was flopping and struggling lopsidedly in the middle of the clearing. I couldn't help feeling sorry for it, even then, even after it had killed Malka and my friends, and all the sheep and goats too, and I don't know how many else. And King Lir must have felt the same way, because he got down from his black mare and went straight up to the griffin, and he spoke to it, lowering his sword until the tip was on the ground. He said, "You were a noble and terrible adversary — surely the last such I will ever confront. We have accomplished what we were born to do, the two of us. I thank you for your death."

And on that last word, the griffin had him.

It was the eagle, lunging up at him, dragging the lion half along, the way I'd been dragging Malka's dead weight. King Lir stepped back, swinging the sword fast enough to take off the griffin's head, but it was faster than he was. That dreadful beak caught him at the waist, shearing through his armor the way an axe would smash through piecrust, and he doubled over without a sound that I heard, looking like wetwash on the line. There was blood, and worse, and I couldn't have said if he were dead or alive. I thought the griffin was going to bite him in two.

I shook loose from Molly. She was calling to Schmendrick to *do* something, but of course he couldn't, and she knew it, because he'd promised King Lir that he wouldn't interfere by magic, whatever happened. But I wasn't a magician, and I hadn't promised anything to anybody. I told Malka I'd be right back.

The griffin didn't see me coming. It was bending its head down over King Lir, hiding him with its wings. The lion part trailing along so limply in the dust made it more fearful to see, though I can't say why, and it was making a sort of cooing, purring sound all the time. I had a big rock in my left hand, and a dead branch in my right, and I was bawling something, but I don't remember what. You can scare wolves away from the flock sometimes if you run at them like that, determined.

I can throw things hard with either hand — Wilfrid found *that* out when I was still small — and the griffin looked up fast when the rock hit it on the side of its neck. It didn't like that, but it was too busy with King Lir to bother with me. I didn't think for a minute that my branch was going to be any use on even a half-dead griffin, but I threw it as far as I could, so that the griffin would look away for a moment, and as soon as it did I made a little run and a big sprawling dive for the hilt of the king's sword, which was sticking out under him where he'd fallen. I knew I could lift it because of having buckled it on him when we set out together.

But I couldn't get it free. He was too heavy, like Malka. But I wouldn't give up or let go. I kept pulling and pulling on that sword, and I didn't feel Molly pulling at *me* again, and I didn't notice the griffin starting to scrabble toward me over King Lir's body. I did hear Schmendrick, sounding a long way off, and I thought he was singing one of the nonsense songs he'd made up for me, only why would he be doing something like that just now? Then I did finally look up, to push my sweaty hair off my face, just before the griffin grabbed me up in one of its claws, yanking me away from Molly to throw me down on top of King Lir. His armor was so cold against my cheek, it was as though the armor had died with him.

The griffin looked into my eyes. That was the worst of all, worse than the pain where the claw had me, worse than not seeing my parents and stupid Wilfrid anymore, worse than knowing that I hadn't been able to save either the king or Malka. Griffins can't talk (dragons do, but only to heroes, King Lir told me), but those golden eyes were saying into my eyes, "Yes, I will die soon, but you are all dead now, all of you, and I will pick your bones before the ravens have mine. And your folk will remember what I was, and what I did to them, when there is no one left in your vile, pitiful anthill who remembers your name. So I have won." And I knew it was true.

Then there wasn't anything but that beak and that burning gullet opening over me.

Then there was.

I thought it was a cloud. I was so dazed and terrified that I really thought it was a white cloud, only traveling so low and so fast that it smashed the griffin off King Lir and away from me, and sent me tumbling into Molly's arms at the same time. She held me tightly, practically smothering me, and it wasn't until I wriggled my head free that I saw what had come to us. I can see it still, in my mind. I see it right now.

They don't look *anything* like horses. I don't know where people got that notion. Four legs and a tail, yes, but the hooves are split, like a deer's hooves, or a goat's, and the head is smaller and more — *pointy* — than a horse's head. And the whole body is different from a horse, it's like saying a snowflake looks like a cow. The horn looks too long and heavy for the body, you can't imagine how a neck that delicate can hold up a horn that size. But it can.

Schmendrick was on his knees, with his eyes closed and his lips moving, as though he was still singing. Molly kept whispering, "Amalthea... Amalthea...." not to me, not to anybody. The unicorn was facing the griffin across the king's body. Its front feet were skittering and dancing a little, but its back legs were setting themselves to charge, the way rams do. Only rams put their heads down, while the unicorn held its head high, so that the horn caught the sunlight and glowed like a seashell. It gave a cry that made me want to dive back into Molly's skirt and cover my ears, it was so raw and so...*hurt*. Then its head did go down.

Dying or not, the griffin put up a furious fight. It came hopping to meet the unicorn, but then it was out of the way at the last minute, with its bloody beak snapping at the unicorn's legs as it flashed by. But each time that happened, the unicorn would turn instantly, much quicker than a horse could have turned, and come charging back before the griffin could get itself braced again. It wasn't a bit fair, but I didn't feel sorry for the griffin anymore.

The last time, the unicorn slashed sideways with its horn, using it like a club, and knocked the griffin clean off its feet. But it was up before the unicorn could turn, and it actually leaped into the air, dead lion half and all, just high enough to come down on the unicorn's back, raking with its eagle claws and trying to bite through the unicorn's neck, the way it did with King Lir. I screamed then, I couldn't help it, but the unicorn reared up until I thought it was going to go over backward, and it flung the griffin to the ground, whirled and drove its horn straight through the iron feathers to the eagle heart. It trampled the body for a good while after, but it didn't need to.

Schmendrick and Molly ran to King Lir. They didn't look at the griffin, or even pay very much attention to the unicorn. I wanted to go to Malka, but I followed them to where he lay. I'd seen what the griffin had done to him, closer than they had, and I didn't see how he could still be alive. But he was, just barely. He opened his eyes when we knelt beside him, and he smiled so sweetly at us all, and he said, "Lisene? Lisene, I should have a bath, shouldn't I?"

I didn't cry. Molly didn't cry. Schmendrick did. He said, "No, Majesty. No, you do not need bathing, truly."

King Lir looked puzzled. "But I smell bad, Lisene. I think I must have wet myself." He reached for my hand and held it so hard. "Little one," he said. "Little one, I know you. Do not be ashamed of me because I am old."

I squeezed his hand back, as hard as I could. "Hello, Your Majesty," I said. "Hello." I didn't know what else to say.

Then his face was suddenly young and happy and wonderful, and he was gazing far past me, reaching toward something with his eyes. I felt a breath on my shoulder, and I turned my head and saw the unicorn. It was bleeding from a lot of deep scratches and bites, especially around its neck, but all you could see in its dark eyes was King Lir. I moved aside so it could get to him, but when I turned back, the king was gone. I'm nine, almost ten. I know when people are gone.

The unicorn stood over King Lir's body for a long time. I went off after a while to sit beside Malka, and Molly came and sat with me. But Schmendrick stayed kneeling by King Lir, and he was talking to the unicorn. I couldn't hear what he was saying, but I could tell from his face that he was asking for something, a favor. My mother says she can always tell before I open my mouth. The unicorn wasn't answering, of course — they can't talk either, I'm almost sure — but Schmendrick kept at it until the unicorn turned its head and looked at him. Then he stopped, and he stood up and walked away by himself. The unicorn stayed where she was.

Molly was saying how brave Malka had been, and telling me that she'd never known another dog who attacked a griffin. She asked if Malka had ever had pups, and I said, yes, but none of them was Malka. It was very strange. She was trying hard to make me feel better, and I was trying to comfort her because she couldn't. But all the while I felt so cold, almost as far away from everything as Malka had gone. I closed her eyes, the way you do with people, and I sat there and I stroked her side, over and over.

I didn't notice the unicorn. Molly must have, but she didn't say anything. I went on petting Malka, and I didn't look up until the horn came slanting over my shoulder. Close to, you could see blood drying in the shining spirals, but I wasn't afraid. I wasn't anything. Then the horn touched Malka, very lightly, right where I was stroking her, and Malka opened her eyes.

It took her a while to understand that she was alive. It took me longer. She ran her tongue out first, panting and panting, looking so *thirsty*. We could hear a stream trickling somewhere close, and Molly went and found it, and brought water back in her cupped hands. Malka lapped it all up, and then she tried to stand and fell down, like a puppy. But she kept trying, and at last she was properly on her feet, and she tried to lick my face, but she missed it the first few times. I only started crying when she finally managed it.

When she saw the unicorn, she did a funny thing. She stared at it for a moment, and then she bowed or curtseyed, in a dog way, stretching out her front legs and putting her head down on the ground between them. The unicorn nosed at her, very gently, so as not to knock her over again. It looked at me for the first time...or maybe I really looked at *it* for the first time, past the horn and the hooves and the magical whiteness, all the way into those endless eyes. And what they did, somehow, the unicorn's eyes, was to free me from the griffin's eyes. Because the awfulness of what I'd seen there didn't go away when the griffin died, not even when Malka came alive again. But the unicorn had all the world in her eyes, all the world I'm never going to see, but it doesn't matter, because now I *have* seen it, and it's beautiful, and I was in there too. And when I think of Jehane, and Louli, and my Felicitas who could only talk with her eyes, just like the unicorn,

I'll think of them, and not the griffin. That's how it was when the unicorn and I looked at each other.

I didn't see if the unicorn said good-bye to Molly and Schmendrick, and I didn't see when it went away. I didn't want to. I did hear Schmendrick saying, "A dog. I nearly kill myself singing her to Lir, calling her as no other has *ever* called a unicorn — and she brings back, not him, but the dog. And here I'd always thought she had no sense of humor."

But Molly said, "She loved him too. That's why she let him go. Keep your voice down." I was going to tell her it didn't matter, that I knew Schmendrick was saying that because he was so sad, but she came over and petted Malka with me, and I didn't have to. She said, "We will escort you and Malka home now, as befits two great ladies. Then we will take the king home too."

"And I'll never see you again," I said. "No more than I'll see him."

Molly asked me, "How old are you, Sooz?"

"Nine," I said. "Almost ten. You know that."

"You can whistle?" I nodded. Molly looked around quickly, as though she were going to steal something. She bent close to me, and she whispered, "I will give you a present, Sooz, but you are not to open it until the day when you turn seventeen. On that day you must walk out away from your village, walk out all alone into some quiet place that is special to you, and you must whistle like this." And she whistled a little ripple of music for me to whistle back to her, repeating and repeating it until she was satisfied that I had it exactly. "Don't whistle it anymore," she told me. "Don't whistle it aloud again, not once, until your seventeenth birthday, but keep whistling it inside you. Do you understand the difference, Sooz?"

"I'm not a baby," I said. "I understand. What will happen when I do whistle it?"

Molly smiled at me. She said, "Someone will come to you. Maybe the greatest magician in the world, maybe only an old lady with a soft spot for valiant, impudent children." She cupped my cheek in her hand. "And just maybe even a unicorn. Because beautiful things will always want to see you again, Sooz, and be listening for you. Take an old lady's word for it. Someone will come."

They put King Lir on his own horse, and I rode with Schmendrick, and they came all the way home with me, right to the door, to tell my mother and father that the griffin was dead, and that I had helped, and you should have seen Wilfrid's face when they said *that!* Then they both hugged me, and Molly said in my ear, "Remember — not till you're seventeen!" and they rode away, taking the king back to his castle to be buried among his own folk. And I had a cup of cold milk and went out with Malka and my father to pen the flock for the night.

So that's what happened to me. I practice the music Molly taught me in my head, all the time, I even dream it some nights, but I don't ever whistle it aloud. I talk to Malka about our adventure, because I have to talk to *someone*. And I promise her that when the time comes she'll be there with me, in the special place I've already picked out. She'll be an old dog lady then, of course, but it doesn't matter. Someone will come to us both.

I hope it's them, those two. A unicorn is very nice, but they're my friends. I want to feel Molly holding me again, and hear the stories she didn't have time to tell me, and I want to hear Schmendrick singing that silly song:

> *Soozli, Soozli,*
> *speaking loozli,*
> *you disturb my oozli-goozli.*
> *Soozli, Soozli*
> *would you choozli*
> *to become my squoozli-squoozli...?*

I can wait.

SNOWBALL'S CHANCE
CHARLES STROSS

Charles Stross's first stories appeared in the early '90s, but he first attracted wider attention with 2001 Theodore Sturgeon Memorial Award nominee "Antibodies" and novella "A Colder War". His major work to date is the "Accelerando" sequence of stories, published as the novel Accelerando *in 2005, which details the lives of three generations in a family making its way through a Vingean Singularity. Individually, the stories have been nominated for the Hugo, Nebula, British Science Fiction, and Theodore Sturgeon Memorial awards. Stross's first collection,* Toast and Other Rusted Futures, *was published in 2002, and his first novel, Hugo nominee* Singularity Sky, *appeared in 2003. His short story "The Concrete Jungle" won the Hugo Award in 2005. Almost overwhelmingly prolific, Stross has also published novels* The Atrocity Archives, Iron Sunrise *(a sequel to* Singularity Sky*),* The Family Trade, *and* The Hidden Family. *Upcoming are* The Clan Corporate, Glasshouse, *and* The Jennifer Morgue.

The louring sky, half past pregnant with a caul of snow, pressed down on Davy's head like a hangover. He glanced up once, shivered, then pushed through the doorway into the Deid Nurse and the smog of fag fumes within.

His sometime conspirator Tam the Tailer was already at the bar. "Awright, Davy?"

Davy drew a deep breath, his glasses steaming up the instant he stepped through the heavy blackout curtain, so that the disreputable pub was shrouded in a halo of icy iridescence that concealed its flaws. "Mine's a Deuchars." His nostrils flared as he took in the seedy mixture of aromas that festered in the Deid Nurse's atmosphere — so thick you could cut it with an axe, Morag had said once with a sniff of her snot-siphon, back in the day when she'd had aught to say to Davy. "Fuckin' Baltic oot there the night, an' nae kiddin'." He slid his glasses off and wiped them off, then looked around tiredly. "An' deid tae the world in here."

Tam glanced around as if to be sure the pub population hadn't magically doubled between mouthfuls of seventy bob. "Ah widnae say that." He gestured with his nose — pockmarked by frostbite — at the snug in the corner.

Once the storefront for the Old Town's more affluent ladies of the night, it was now unaccountably popular with students of the gaming fraternity, possibly because they had been driven out of all the trendier bars in the neighbourhood for yacking till all hours and not drinking enough (much like the whores before them). Right now a bunch of threadbare LARPers were in residence, arguing over some recondite point of lore. "They're havin' enough fun for a barrel o' monkeys by the sound o' it."

"An' who can blame them?" Davy hoisted his glass. "Ah just wish they'd keep their shite aff the box." The pub, in an effort to compensate for its lack of a food licence, had installed a huge and dodgy voxel engine that teetered precariously over the bar: it was full of muddy field, six LARPers leaping.

"Dinnae piss them aff, Davy — they've a' got swords."

"Ah wis jist kiddin'. Ah didnae catch ma lottery the night, that's a' Ah'm sayin'."

"If ye win, it'll be a first." Tam stared at his glass. "An' whit wid ye dae then, if yer numbers came up?"

"Whit, the big yin?" Davy put his glass down, then unzipped his parka's fast-access pouch and pulled out a fag packet and lighter. Condensation immediately beaded the plastic wrapper as he flipped it open. "Ah'd pay aff the hoose, for starters. An' the child support. An' then — " He paused, eyes wandering to the dog-eared NO SMOKING sign behind the bar. "Ah, shit." He flicked his Zippo, stroking the end of a cigarette with the flame from the burning coal oil. "If Ah wis young again, Ah'd move, ye ken? But Ah'm no, Ah've got roots here." The sign went on to warn of lung cancer (curable) and two-thousand-Euro fines (laughable, even if enforced). Davy inhaled, grateful for the warmth flooding his lungs. "An' there's Morag an' the bairns."

"Heh." Tam left it at a grunt, for which Davy was grateful. It wasn't that he thought Morag would ever come back to him, but he was sick to the back teeth of people who thought they were his friends telling him that she wouldn't, not unless he did this or did that.

"Ah could pay for the bairns tae go east. They're young enough." He glanced at the doorway. "It's no right, throwin' snowba's in May."

"That's global warmin'." Tam shrugged with elaborate irony, then changed the subject. "Where d'ye think they'd go? The Ukraine? New 'Beria?"

"Somewhaur there's grass and nae glaciers." Pause. "An' real beaches wi' sand an' a'." He frowned and hastily added: "Dinnae get me wrong, Ah ken how likely that is." The collapse of the West Antarctic ice shelf two decades ago had inundated every established coastline; it had also stuck the last nail in the coffin of the Gulf stream, plunging the British Isles into a sub-Arctic deep freeze. Then the Americans had made it worse — at least for Scotland — by putting a giant parasol into orbit to stop the rest of the planet roasting like a chicken on a spit. Davy had learned all about global warming in Geography classes at school — back when it hadn't happened — in the rare intervals when he wasn't dozing in the back row or staring at Yasmin MacConnell's hair. It wasn't until he was already paying a mortgage and the second kid was on his way that what it meant really sank in. Cold. Eternal cold, deep in your bones. "Ah'd like tae see a real beach again, some day before Ah die."

"Ye could save for a train ticket."

"Away wi' ye! Where'd Ah go tae?" Davy snorted, darkly amused. Flying was for the hyper-rich these days, and anyway, the nearest beaches with sand and sun were in the Caliphate, a long day's TGV ride south through the Channel Tunnel and across the Gibraltar Bridge, in what had once been the Northern Sahara Desert. As a tourist destination, the Caliphate had certain drawbacks, a lack of topless sunbathing beauties being only the first on the list. "It's a' just as bad whauriver ye go. At least here ye can still get pork scratchings."

"Aye, weel." Tam raised his glass, just as a stranger appeared in the doorway. "An' then there's some that dinnae feel the cauld." Davy glanced round to follow the direction of his gaze. The stranger was oddly attired in a lightweight suit and tie, as if he'd stepped out of the middle of the previous century, although his neat goatee beard and the two small brass horns implanted on his forehead were a more contemporary touch. He noticed Davy staring and nodded, politely enough, then broke eye contact and ambled over to the bar. Davy turned back to Tam, who responded to his wink. "Take care noo, Davy. Ye've got ma number." With that, he stood up, put his glass down, and shambled unsteadily towards the toilets.

This put Davy on his lonesome next to the stranger, who leaned on the bar and glanced at him sideways with an expression of amusement. Davy's forehead wrinkled as he stared in the direction of Katie the barwoman, who was just now coming back up the cellar steps with an empty coal powder cartridge in one hand. "My round?" asked the stranger, raising an eyebrow.

"Aye. Mine's a Deuchars if yer buyin'..." Davy, while not always quick on the uptake, was never slow on the barrel: if this underdressed southerner could afford a heated taxi, he could certainly afford to buy Davy some beer. Katie nodded and rinsed her hands under the sink — however well sealed they left the factory, coal cartridges always leaked like printer toner had once done — and picked up two glasses.

"New roond aboot here?" Davy asked after a moment.

The stranger smiled: "Just passing through — I visit Edinburgh every few years."

"Aye." Davy could relate to that.

"And yourself?"

"Ah'm frae Pilton." Which was true enough; that was where he'd bought the house with Morag all those years ago, back when folks actually wanted to buy houses in Edinburgh. Back before the pack ice closed the Firth fro six months in every year, back before the rising sea level drowned Leith and Ingliston, and turned Arthur's Seat into a frigid coastal headland looming grey and stark above the the permafrost. "Whereaboots d'ye come frae?"

The stranger's smile widened as Katie parked a half-litre on the bar top before him and bent down to pull the next, "I think you know where I'm from, my friend."

Davy snorted. "Aye, so ye're a man of wealth an' taste, is that right?"

"Just so." A moment later, Katie planted the second glass in front of Davy, gave him a brittle smile, and retreated to the opposite end of the bar without pausing to extract credit from the stranger, who nodded and raised his jar: "To your good fortune."

"Heh." Davy chugged back a third of his glass. It was unusually bitter, with a slight sulphurous edge to it: "That's a new barrel."

"Only the best for my friends."

Davy sneaked an irritated glance at the stranger. "Right. Ah ken ye want tae talk, ye dinnae need tae take the pish."

"I'm sorry." The stranger held his gaze, looking slightly perplexed. "It's just that I've spent too long in America recently. Most of them believe in me. A bit of good old-fashioned scepticism is refreshing once in a while."

Davy snorted. "Dae Ah look like a god-botherer tae ye? Yer amang civilized folk here, nae free-kirk numpties'd show their noses in a pub."

"So I see." The stranger relaxed slightly. "Seen Morag and the boys lately, have you?"

Now a strange thing happened, because as the cold fury took him, and a monstrous roaring filled his ears, and he reached for the stranger's throat, he seemed to hear Morag's voice shouting, *Davy, don't!* And to his surprise, a moment of timely sanity came crashing down on him, a sense that Devil or no, if he laid hands on this fucker he really would be damned, somehow. It might just have been the hypothalamic implant that the sheriff had added to the list of his parole requirements working its arcane magic on his brain chemistry, but it certainly felt like a drenching, cold-sweat sense of imma-nence, and not in a good way. So as the raging impulse to glass the cunt died away, Davy found himself contemplating his own raised fists in perplexity, the crude blue tattoos of LOVE and HATE standing out on his knuckles like doorposts framing the prison gateway of his life.

"Who telt ye aboot them," he demanded hoarsely.

"Cigarette?" The stranger, who had sat perfectly still while Davy wound up to punch his ticket, raised the chiselled eyebrow again.

"Ya bas." But Davy's hand went to his pocket automatically, and he found himself passing a filter-tip to the stranger rather than ramming a red-hot ember in his eye.

"Thank you." The stranger took the unlit cigarette, put it straight between his lips, and inhaled deeply. "Nobody needed to tell me about them," he continued, slowly dribbling smoke from both nostrils.

Davy slumped defensively on his bar stool. "When ye wis askin' aboot Morag and the bairns, Ah figured ye wis fuckin' wi' ma heid." But knowing that there was a perfectly reasonable supernatural explanation somehow made it all right. *Ye cannae blame Auld Nick for pushin' yer buttons.* Davy reached out for his glass again: "'Scuse me. Ah didnae think ye existed."

"Feel free to take your time." The stranger smiled faintly. "I find atheists refreshing, but it does take a little longer than usual to get down to business."

"Aye, weel, concedin' for the moment that ye *are* the deil, Ah dinnae ken whit ye want wi' the likes o' me." Davy cradled his beer protectively. "Ah'm naebody." He shivered in the sudden draught as one of the students — leaving — pushed through the curtain, admitting a flurry of late-May snowflakes.

"So? You may be nobody, but your lucky number just came up." The stranger smiled devilishly. "Did you never think you'd win the Lottery?"

"Aye, weel, if hauf the stories they tell about ye are true, Ah'd rather it wis the ticket, ye ken? Or are ye gonnae say ye've been stitched up by the kirk?"

"Something like that." The Devil nodded sagely. "Look, you're not stupid, so I'm not going to bullshit you. What it is, is I'm not the only one of me working this circuit. I've got a quota to meet, but there aren't enough politicians and captains of industry to go around, and anyway, they're boring. All they ever want is money, power, or good, hot, kinky sex without any comebacks from their constituents. Poor folks are so much more creative in their desperation, don't you think? And so much more likely to believe in the Rules, too."

"The Rules?" Davy found himself staring at his companion in perplexity. "Nae the Law, right?"

"Do as thou wilt shall be all of the Law," quoth the Devil, then he paused as if he'd tasted something unpleasant.

"Ye wis sayin'?"

"Love is the Law, Love under Will," the Devil added dyspeptically.

"That's a'?" Davy stared at him.

"My employer requires me to quote chapter and verse when challenged." As he said "employer," the expression on the Devil's face made Davy shudder.

"And she monitors these conversations for compliance."

"But whit aboot the rest o' it, aye? If ye're the deil, whit aboot the Ten Commandments?"

"Oh, those are just Rules," said the Devil, smiling. "I'm really proud of them."

"Ye made them a' up?" Davy said accusingly. "Just tae fuck wi' us?"

"Well, yes, of course I did! And all the other Rules. They work really well, don't you think?"

Davy made a fist and stared at the back of it. LOVE. "Ye cunt. Ah still dinnae believe in ye."

The Devil shrugged. "Nobody's asking you to believe in me. *You* don't, and I'm still here, aren't I? If it makes things easier, think of me as the garbage collection subroutine of the strong anthropic principle. And they" — he stabbed a finger in the direction of the overhead LEDs — "work by magic, for all you know."

Davy picked up his glass and drained it philosophically. The hell of it was, the Devil was right: now he thought about it, he had no idea how the lights worked, except that electricity had something to do with it. "Ah'll have anither. Ye're buyin'."

"No I'm not." The Devil snapped his fingers and two full glasses appeared on the bar, steaming slightly. Davy picked up the nearest one. It was hot to the touch, even though the beer inside it was at cellar temperature, and it smelled slightly sulphurous. "Anyway, I owe you."

"Whit for?" Davy sniffed the beer suspiciously: "This smells pish." He pushed it away. "Whit is it ye owe me for?"

"For taking that mortgage and the job on the street-cleaning team and for pissing it all down the drain and fucking off a thousand citizens in little ways. For giving me Jaimie and wee Davy, and for wrecking your life and cutting Morag off from her parents and raising a pair of neds instead of two fine upstanding citizens. You're not a scholar and you're not a gentleman, but you're a truly professional hater. And as for what you did to Morag — "

Davy made another fist: HATE. "Say wan mair word aboot Morag..." he warned.

The Devil chuckled quietly. "No, you managed to do all that by yourself." He shrugged. "I'd have offered help if you needed it, but you seemed to be doing okay without me. Like I said, you're a professional." He cleared his throat. "Which brings me to the little matter of why I'm talking to you tonight."

"Ah'm no for sale." Davy crossed his arms defensively. "Who d'ye think Ah am?"

The Devil shook his head, still smiling. "I'm not here to make you an offer for your soul, that's not how things work. Anyway, you gave it to me of your own free will years ago." Davy looked into his eyes. The smile didn't reach them. "Trouble is, there are consequences when that happens. My employer's an optimist: she's not an Augustinian entity, you'll be pleased to learn, she doesn't believe in original sin. So things between you and the Ultimate are... let's say they're out of balance. It's like a credit card bill. The longer you ignore it, the worse it gets. You cut me a karmic loan from the First Bank of Davy MacDonald, and the Law requires me to repay it with interest."

"Huh?" Davy stared at the Devil. "Ye whit?"

The Devil wasn't smiling now. "You're one of the Elect, Davy. One of the Unconditionally Elect. So's fucking everybody these days, but your name came up in the quality assurance lottery. I'm not allowed to mess with you. If you die and I'm in your debt, seven shades of shit hit the fan. So I owe you a fucking wish."

The Devil tapped his fingers impatiently on the bar top. He was no longer smiling. "You get one wish. I am required to read you the small print:

> "The party of the first part in cognizance of the gift benefice or loan bestowed by the party of the second part is hereby required to tender the fulfillment of 1 (one) verbally or somatically expressed indication of desire by the party of the second part in pursuance of the discharge of the said gift benefice or loan, said fulfillment hereinafter to be termed 'the wish.' The party of the first part undertakes to bring the totality of existence into accordance with the terms of the wish exclusive of paradox deicide temporal inversion or other wilful suspension contrary to the laws of nature. The party of the second part recognizes understands and accepts that this wish represents full and final discharge of debt incurred by the gift benefice or loan to the party of the first part. Notwithstanding additional grants of rights incurred under the terms of this contract the rights responsibilities duties of the party of the first part to the party of the second part are subject to the Consumer Credit Regulations of 2026..."

Davy shook his head. "Ah dinnae get it. Are ye tellin' me ye're givin' me a wish? In return for, for... bein' radge a' ma life?"

The Devil nodded. "Yes."

Davy winced. "Ah think Ah need another Deuchars – fuck! Haud on, that isnae ma wish!" He stared at the Devil anxiously. "Ye're serious, aren't ye?"

The Devil sniffed. "I can't discharge the obligation with a beer. My Employer isn't stupid, whatever Her other faults: she'd say I was short-changing you, and she'd be right. It's got to be a big wish, Davy."

Davy's expression brightened. The Devil waved a hand at Katie: "Another Deuchars for my friend here. And a drop of the Craitur." Things were looking up, Davy decided.

"Can ye make Morag nae have ... Ah mean, can ye make things ... awright again, nae went bad?" He dry-swallowed, mind skittering like a frightened spider away from what he was asking for. Not to have ... whatever. Whatever he'd done. Already.

The Devil contemplated Davy for a long handful of seconds. "No," he said patiently. "That would create a paradox, you see, because if things hadn't gone bad for you, I wouldn't be here giving you this wish, would I? Your life gone wrong is the fuel for this miracle."

"Oh." Davy waited in silence while Katie pulled the pint, then retreated back to the far end of the bar. *Whaur's Tam?* he wondered vaguely. *Fuckin' deil, wi' his smairt suit an' high heid yin manners....* He shivered, unaccountably cold. "Am Ah goin' tae hell?" he asked roughly. "Is that whaur Ah'm goin'?"

"Sorry, but no. We were brought in to run this universe, but we didn't design it. When you're dead, that's it. No hellfire, no damnation: the worst thing that can happen to you is you're reincarnated, given a second chance to get things right. It's normally my job to give people like you that chance."

"An' if Ah'm no reincarnated?" Davy asked hopefully.

"You get to wake up in the mind of God. Of course, you stop being you when you do that." The Devil frowned thoughtfully. "Come to think of it, you'll probably give Her a migraine."

"Right, right." Davy nodded. The Devil was giving *him* a headache. He had a dawning suspicion that this one wasn't a prod or a pape: he probably supported Livingstone. "Ah'm no that bad then, is that whit ye're sayin'?"

"Don't get above yourself."

The Devil's frown deepened, oblivious to the stroke of killing rage that flashed behind Davy's eyes at the words. *Dinnae get above yersel'? Who the fuck d'ye think ye are, the sheriff?* That was almost exactly what the sheriff had said, leaning over to pronounce sentence. *Ye ken Ah'm naebody, dinnae deny it!* Davy's fists tightened, itching to hit somebody. The story of his life: being ripped off then talked down to by self-satisfied cunts. *Ah'll make ye regret it!*

The Devil continued after a moment: "You've got to really fuck up in a theological manner before she won't take you, these days. Spreading hatred in the name of God, that kind of thing will do for you. Trademark abuse, she calls it. You're plenty bad, but you're not that bad. Don't kid yourself, you only warrant the special visit because you're a quality sample. The rest are ... unobserved."

"So Ah'm no evil, Ah'm just plain bad." Davy grinned virulently as a thought struck him. *Let's dae somethin' aboot that! Karmic imbalance? Ah'll show ye a karmic imbalance!* "Can ye dae somethin' aboot the weather? Ah hate the cauld." He tried to put a whine in his voice. The change in the weather had crippled house prices, shafted him and Morag. It would serve the Devil right if he fell for it.

"I can't change the weather." The Devil shook his head, looking slightly worried. "Like I said —"

"Can ye fuck wi' yon sun shield the fuckin' Yanks stuck in the sky?" Davy leaned forward, glaring at him: "'Cause if no, whit kindae deil are ye?"

"You want me to what?"

Davy took a deep breath. He remembered what it had looked like on TV, twenty years ago: the great silver reflectors unfolding in solar orbit, the jubilant politicians, the graphs showing a 20% fall in sunlight reaching the Earth ... the savage April blizzards that didn't stop for a month, the endless twilight and the sun dim enough to look at. And now the Devil wanted to give him a wish, in payment for fucking things up for a few thousand bastards who had it coming? Davy felt his lips drawing back from his teeth, a feral smile forcing itself to the surface. "Ah want ye to fuck up the sunshade, awright? Get ontae it. Ah want tae be wairm..."

The Devil shook his head. "That's a new one on me," he admitted. "But — " He frowned. "You're sure? No second thoughts? You want to waive your mandatory fourteen-day right of cancellation?"

"Aye. Dae it the noo." Davy nodded vigorously.

"It's done." The Devil smiled faintly.

"Whit?" Davy stared.

"There's not much to it. A rock about the size of this pub, traveling on a cometary orbit — it'll take an hour or so to fold, but I already took care of that." The Devil's smile widened. "You used your wish."

"Ah dinnae believe ye," said Davy, hopping down from his bar stool. Out of the corner of one eye, he saw Tam dodging through the blackout curtain and the doorway, tipping him the wink. This had gone on long enough. "Ye'll have tae prove it. Show me."

"What?" The Devil looked puzzled. "But I told you, it'll take about an hour."

"So ye say. An' whit then?"

"Well, the parasol collapses, so the amount of sunlight goes up. It gets brighter. The snow melts."

"Is that right?" Davy grinned. "So how many wishes dae Ah get this time?"

"How many — " The Devil froze. "What makes you think you get any more?" He snarled, his face contorting.

"Like ye said, Ah gave ye a loan, didn't Ah?" Davy's grin widened. He gestured toward the door. "After ye?"

"You — " The Devil paused. "You don't mean..." He swallowed, then continued, quietly. "That wasn't deliberate, was it?"

"Oh. Aye." Davy could see it in his mind's eye: the wilting crops and blazing forests, droughts and heatstroke and mass extinction, the despairing millions across America and Africa, exotic places he'd never seen, never been allowed to go — roasting like pieces of a turkey on a spit, roasting in revenge for twenty years frozen in outer darkness. Hell on Earth. "Four billion fuckers, isnae that enough for another?"

"Son of a bitch!" The Devil reached into his jacket pocket and pulled out an antique calculator, began punching buttons. "Forty-eight — no, forty-nine. Shit, this has never happened before! You bastard, don't you have a conscience?"

Davy thought for a second. "Naw."

"Fuck!"

It was now or never. "Ah'll take a note."

"A credit — shit, okay then. Here." The Devil handed over his mobile. It was small and very black and shiny, and it buzzed like a swarm of flies. "Listen, I've got to go right now, I need to escalate this to senior management. Call head office tomorrow, if I'm not there, one of my staff will talk you through the state of your claim."

"Haw! Ah'll be sure tae dae that."

The Devil stalked towards the curtain and stepped through into the darkness beyond, and was gone. Davy pulled out his moby and speed-dialed a number. "He's a' yours noo," he muttered into the handset, then hung up and turned back to his beer. A couple of minutes later, someone came in and sat down next to him. Davy raised a hand and waved vaguely at Katie: "A Deuchars for Tam here."

Katie nodded nonchalantly — she seemed to have cheered up since the Devil had stepped out — and picked up a glass.

Tam dropped a couple of small brass horns on the bar top next to Davy. Davy stared at them for a moment then glanced up admiringly. "Neat," he admitted. "Get anythin' else aff him?"

"Nah, the cunt wis crap. He didnae even have a moby. Just these." Tam looked disgusted for a moment. "Ah pulled ma chib an' waved it aroon' an' he totally legged it. Think anybody'll come lookin' for us?"

"Nae chance." Davy raised his glass, then tapped the pocket with the Devil's mobile phone in it smugly. "Nae a snowball's chance in hell..."

SUNBIRD
NEIL GAIMAN

Neil Gaiman was born in England in 1960 and worked as a freelance journalist before co-editing Ghastly Beyond Belief *(with Kim Newman) and writing* Don't Panic: The Official Hitchhiker's Guide to the Galaxy Companion. *He started writing graphic novels and comics with* Violent Cases *in 1987, and with the seventy-five installments of award-winning series* The Sandman *established himself as one of the most important comics writers of his generation. His first novel,* Good Omens *(with Terry Pratchett), appeared in 1991 and was followed by* Neverwhere, Stardust, American Gods, *and* Coraline. *Gaiman's work has won the Hugo, World Fantasy, Bram Stoker, Locus, Geffen, International Horror Guild, Mythopoeic, and Will Eisner Comic Industry awards. His most recent novel is* Anansi Boys. *Upcoming are two short story collections,* Fragile Things *and* M is for Magic. *Gaiman moved to the United States in 1992 with his wife and three children, and currently lives in Minneapolis.*

They were a rich and a rowdy bunch at the Epicurean Club in those days. They certainly knew how to party. There were five of them: There was Augustus TwoFeathers McCoy, big enough for three men, who ate enough for four men and who drank enough for five. His great-grandfather had founded the Epicurean Club with the proceeds of a tontine which he had taken great pains, in the traditional manner, to ensure that he had collected in full.

There was Professor Mandalay, small and twitchy and grey as a ghost (and perhaps he was a ghost; stranger things have happened) who drank nothing but water and who ate doll-portions from plates the size of saucers. Still, you do not need the gusto for the gastronomy, and Mandalay always got to the heart of every dish placed in front of him.

There was Virginia Boote, the food and restaurant critic, who had once been a great beauty but was now a grand and magnificent ruin, and who delighted in her ruination.

There was Jackie Newhouse, the descendant (on the left-handed route) of the great lover, gourmand, violinist and duelist Giacomo Casanova. Jackie Newhouse had, like his notorious ancestor, both broken his share of hearts and eaten his share of great dishes.

And there was Zebediah T. Crawcrustle, who was the only one of the Epicureans who was flat-out broke: he shambled in unshaven from the street when they had their meetings, with half a bottle of rotgut in a brown paper bag, hatless and coatless and, too often, partly shirtless, but he ate with more of an appetite than any of them.

Augustus TwoFeathers McCoy was talking —

"We have eaten everything that can be eaten," said Augustus TwoFeathers McCoy, and there was regret and glancing sorrow in his voice. "We have eaten vulture, mole, and fruitbat."

Mandalay consulted his notebook. "Vulture tasted like rotten pheasant. Mole tasted like carrion slug. Fruitbat tasted remarkably like sweet guinea pig."

"We have eaten kakopo, aye-aye, and giant panda —"

"Oh, that broiled panda steak," sighed Virginia Boote, her mouth watering at the memory.

"We have eaten several long-extinct species," said Augustus TwoFeathers McCoy. "We have eaten flash-frozen mammoth and Patagonian giant sloth."

"If we had but gotten the mammoth a little faster," sighed Jackie Newhouse. "I could tell why the hairy elephants went so fast, though, once people got a taste of them. I am a man of elegant pleasures, but after but one bite, I found myself thinking only of Kansas City barbecue sauce, and what the ribs on those things would be like, if they were fresh."

"Nothing wrong with being on ice for a millennium or two," said Zebediah T. Crawcrustle. He grinned. His teeth may have been crooked, but they were sharp and strong. "But for real taste you had to go for honest-to-goodness mastodon every time. Mammoth was always what people settled for, when they couldn't get mastodon."

"We've eaten squid, and giant squid, and humongous squid," said Augustus TwoFeathers McCoy. "We've eaten lemmings and Tasmanian tigers. We've eaten bower bird and ortolan and peacock. We've eaten the dolphin fish (which is not the mammal dolphin) and the giant sea turtle and the Sumatran Rhino. We've eaten everything there is to eat."

"Nonsense. There are many hundreds of things we have not yet tasted," said Professor Mandalay. "Thousands perhaps. Think of all the species of beetle there are, still untasted."

"Oh Mandy," sighed Virginia Boote. "When you've tasted one beetle, you've tasted them all. And we all tasted several hundred species. At least the dung-beetles had a real kick to them."

"No," said Jackie Newhouse, "that was the dung-beetle balls. The beetles themselves were singularly unexceptional. Still, I take your point. We have scaled the heights of gastronomy, we have plunged down into the depths of gustation. We have become cosmonauts exploring undreamed-of worlds of delectation and gourmanderie."

"True, true, true," said Augustus TwoFeathers McCoy. "There has been a meeting of the Epicureans every month for over a hundred and fifty years, in my father's time, and my grandfather's time, and my great-grandfather's time, and now I fear that I must hang it up for there is nothing left that we, or our predecessors in the club, have not eaten."

"I wish I had been here in the Twenties," said Virginia Boote, "when they legally had Man on the menu."

"Only after it had been electrocuted," said Zebediah T. Crawcrustle. "Half-fried already it was, all char and crackling. It left none of us with a taste for long pig, save for one who was already that way inclined, and he went out pretty soon after that anyway."

"Oh, Crusty, *why* must you pretend that you were there?" asked Virginia Boote, with a yawn. "Anyone can see you aren't that old. You can't be more than sixty, even allowing for the ravages of time and the gutter."

"Oh, they ravage pretty good," said Zebediah T. Crawcrustle. "But not as good as you'd imagine. Anyway there's a host of things we've not eaten yet."

"Name one,' said Mandalay, his pencil poised precisely above his note-book.

"Well, there's Suntown Sunbird," said Zebediah T. Crawcrustle. And he grinned his crookedy grin at them, with his teeth ragged but sharp.

"I've never heard of it," said Jackie Newhouse. "You're making it up."

"I've heard of it," said Professor Mandalay, "But in another context. And besides, it is imaginary."

"Unicorns are imaginary," said Virginia Boote, "But gosh, that unicorn flank tartare was tasty. A little bit horsy, a little bit goatish, and all the better for the capers and raw quail eggs."

"There's something about Sunbirds in one of the minutes of the Epicurean Club from bygone years," said Augustus TwoFeathers McCoy. "But what it was, I can no longer remember."

"Did they say how it tasted?" asked Virginia.

"I do not believe that they did," said Augustus, with a frown. "I would need to inspect the bound proceedings, of course."

"Nah," said Zebediah T. Crawcrustle. "That's only in the charred volumes. You'll never find out about it from there."

Augustus TwoFeathers McCoy scratched his head. He really did have two feathers, which went through the knot of black-hair-shot-with-silver at the back of his head, and the feathers had once been golden although by now they were looking kind of ordinary and yellow and ragged. He had been given them when he was a boy.

"Beetles," said Professor Mandalay. "I once calculated that, if a man such as myself were to eat six different species of beetle each day, it would take him more than twenty years to eat every beetle that has been identified. And over that twenty years enough new species of beetle might have been discovered to keep him eating for another five years. And in those five years enough beetles might have been discovered to keep him eating for another two and a half years, and so on, and so on. It is a paradox of inexhaustibility. I call it Mandalay's Beetle. You would have to enjoy eating beetles, though," he added, "or it would be a very bad thing indeed."

"Nothing wrong with eating beetles if they're the right kind of beetle," said Zebediah T. Crawcrustle. "Right now, I've got a hankering on me for lightning bugs. There's a kick from the glow of a lightning bug that might be just what I need."

"While the lightning bug or firefly (*Photinus pyralis*) is more of a beetle than it is a glow-worm," said Mandalay, "they are by no stretch of the imagination edible."

"They may not be edible," said Crawcrustle. "But they'll get you into shape for the stuff that is. I think I'll roast me some. Fireflies and habanero peppers. Yum."

Virginia Boote was an eminently practical woman. She said, "Suppose we did want to eat Suntown Sunbird. Where should we start looking for it?"

Zebediah T. Crawcrustle scratched the bristling seventh-day beard that was sprouting on his chin (it never grew any longer than that; seventh-day beards never do). "If it was me," he told them, "I'd head down to Suntown of a noon in midsummer, and I'd find somewhere comfortable to sit — Mustapha Stroheim's coffeehouse, for example, and I'd wait for the Sunbird to come by. Then I'd catch him in the traditional manner, and cook him in the traditional manner as well."

"And what would the traditional manner of catching him be?" asked Jackie Newhouse.

"Why, the same way your famous ancestor poached quails and woodgrouse," said Crawcrustle.

"There's nothing in Casanova's memoirs about poaching quail," said Jackie Newhouse.

"Your ancestor was a busy man," said Crawcrustle. "He couldn't be expected to write everything down. But he poached a good quail nonetheless."

"Dried corn and dried blueberries, soaked in whisky," said Augustus TwoFeathers McCoy. "That's how my folk always did it."

"And that was how Casanova did it," said Crawcrustle. "Although he used barley-grains mixed with raisins, and he soaked the raisins in brandy. He taught me himself."

Jackie Newhouse ignored this statement. It was easy to ignore much that Zebediah T. Crawcrustle said. Instead, Jackie Newhouse asked, "And where is Mustapha Stroheim's Coffee House in Suntown?"

"Why, where it always is, third lane after the old market in the Suntown district, just before you reach the old drainage ditch that was once an irrigation canal, and if you find yourself in One-eye Khayam's Carpet shop you have gone too far," began Crawcrustle. "But I see by the expressions of irritation upon your faces that you were expecting a less succinct, less accurate, description. Very well. It is in Suntown, and Suntown is in Cairo, in Egypt, where it always is, or almost always."

"And who will pay for an expedition to Suntown?" asked Augustus TwoFeathers McCoy. "And who will be on this expedition? I ask the question although I already know the answer, and I do not like it."

"Why, you will pay for it, Augustus, and we will all come," said Zebediah T. Crawcrustle. "You can deduct it from our Epicurean membership dues. And I shall bring my chef's apron and my cooking utensils."

Augustus knew that Crawcrustle had not paid his Epicurean Club membership in much too long a time, but the Epicurean Club would cover him; Crawcrustle had been a member of the Epicureans in Augustus's father's day. He simply said, "And when shall we leave?"

Crawcrustle fixed him with a mad old eye, and shook his head in disappointment. "Why, Augustus," he said. "We're going to Suntown, to catch the Sunbird. When else should we leave?"

"Sunday!" sang Virginia Boote. "Darlings, we'll leave on a Sunday!"

"There's hope for you yet, young lady," said Zebediah T. Crawcrustle. "We shall leave Sunday indeed. Three Sundays from now. And we shall travel to Egypt. We shall spend several days hunting and trapping the elusive Sunbird of Suntown, and, finally, we shall deal with it in the traditional way."

Professor Mandalay blinked a small grey blink. "But," he said. "I am teaching a class on Monday. On Mondays I teach mythology, on Tuesdays I teach tapdancing, and on Wednesdays, woodwork."

"Get a teaching assistant to take your course, Mandalay O Mandalay. On Monday you'll be hunting the Sunbird," said Zebediah T. Crawcrustle. "And how many other professors can say that?"

They went, one by one, to see Crawcrustle, in order to discuss the journey ahead of them, and to announce their misgivings.

Zebediah T. Crawcrustle was a man of no fixed abode. Still, there were places he could be found, if you were of a mind to find him. In the early mornings he slept in the bus terminal, where the benches were comfortable and the transport police were inclined to let him lie; in the heat of the afternoons he hung in the park by the statues of long-forgotten generals, with the dipsos and the winos and the hopheads, sharing their company and the contents of their bottles, and offering his opinion, which was, as that of an Epicurean, always considered and always respected, if not always welcomed.

Augustus TwoFeathers McCoy sought Crawcrustle out in the park; he had with him his daughter, Hollyberry NoFeathers McCoy. She was small, but she was sharp as a shark's tooth.

"You know," said Augustus, "there is something very familiar about this."

"About what?" asked Zebediah.

"All of this. The expedition to Egypt. The Sunbird. It seemed to me like I heard about it before."

Crawcrustle merely nodded. He was crunching something from a brown-paper bag.

Augustus said, "I went to the bound annals of the Epicurean Club, and I looked it up. And there was what I took to be a reference to the Sunbird in the index for forty years ago, but I was unable to learn anything more than that."

"And why was that?" asked Zebediah T. Crawcrustle, swallowing noisily.

Augustus TwoFeathers McCoy sighed. "I found the relevant page in the annals," he said, "but it was burned away, and afterwards there was some great confusion in the administration of the Epicurean Club."

"You're eating lightning bugs from a paper bag," said Hollyberry Nofeathers McCoy. "I seen you doing it."

"I am indeed, little lady," said Zebediah T. Crawcrustle.

"Do you remember the days of great confusion, Crawcrustle?" asked Augustus.

"I do indeed," said Crawcrustle. "And I remember you. You were only the age that young Hollyberry is now. But there is always confusion, Augustus, and then there is no confusion. It is like the rising and the setting of the sun."

Jackie Newhouse and Professor Mandalay found Crawcrustle that evening, behind the railroad tracks. He was roasting something in a tin can, over a small charcoal fire.

"What are you roasting, Crawcrustle?" asked Jackie Newhouse.

"More charcoal," said Crawcrustle. "Cleans the blood, purifies the spirit."

There was basswood and hickory, cut up into in little chunks at the bottom of the can, all black and smoking.

"And will you actually eat this charcoal, Crawcrustle?" asked Professor Mandalay.

In response, Crawcrustle licked his fingers and picked out a lump of charcoal from the can. It hissed and fizzed in his grip.

"A fine trick," said Professor Mandalay. "That's how fire-eaters do it, I believe."

Crawcrustle popped the charcoal into his mouth and crunched it between his ragged old teeth. "It is indeed," he said. "It is indeed."

Jackie Newhouse cleared his throat. "The truth of the matter is," he said, "Professor Mandalay and I have deep misgivings about the journey that lies ahead."

Zebediah merely crunched his charcoal. "Not hot enough," he said. He took a stick from the fire, and nibbled off the orange-hot tip of it. "That's good," he said.

"It's all an illusion," said Jackie Newhouse.

"Nothing of the sort," said Zebediah T. Crawcrustle primly. "It's prickly elm."

"I have extreme misgivings about all this," said Jackie Newhouse. "My ancestors and I have a finely-tuned sense of personal preservation, one that has often left us shivering on roofs and hiding in rivers — one step away from the law, or from gentlemen with guns and legitimate grievances — and that sense of self-preservation is telling me not to go to Suntown with you."

"I am an academic," said Professor Mandalay, "and thus have no finely developed senses that would be comprehensible to anyone who has not ever needed to grade papers without actually reading the blessed things. Still, I find the whole thing remarkably suspicious. If this Sunbird is so tasty, why have I not heard of it?"

"You have, Mandy old fruit. You have," said Zebediah T. Crawcrustle.

"And I am, in addition, an expert on geographical features from Tulsa, Oklahoma to Timbuktu," continued Professor Mandalay. "Yet I have never seen a mention in any books of a place called Suntown in Cairo."

"Seen it mentioned? Why, you've taught it," said Crawcrustle, and he doused a lump of smoking charcoal with hot pepper sauce before popping it in his mouth and chomping it down.

"I don't believe you're really eating that," said Jackie Newhouse. "But even being around the trick of it is making me uncomfortable. I think it is time that I was elsewhere."

And he left. Perhaps Professor Mandalay left with him: that man was so grey and so ghostie it was always a toss-up whether he was there or not.

Virginia Boote tripped over Zebediah T. Crawcrustle while he rested in her doorway, in the small hours of the morning. She was returning from a restaurant she had needed to review. She got out of a taxi, tripped over Crawcrustle and went sprawling. She landed nearby. "Whee!" she said. "That was some trip, wasn't it?"

"Indeed it was, Virginia," said Zebediah T. Crawcrustle. "You would not happen to have such a thing as a box of matches on you, would you?"

"I have a book of matches on me somewhere," she said, and she began to rummage in her purse, which was very large and very brown. "Here you are."

Zebediah T. Crawcrustle was carrying a bottle of purple methylated spirits, which he proceeded to pour into a plastic cup.

"Meths?" said Virginia Boote. "Somehow you never struck me as a meths drinker, Zebby."

"Nor am I," said Crawcrustle. "Foul stuff. It rots the guts and spoils the taste-buds. But I could not find any lighter fluid at this time of night."

He lit a match, then dipped it near the surface of the cup of spirits, which began to burn with a flickery light. He ate the match. Then he gargled with the flaming liquid, and blew a sheet of flame into the street, incinerating a sheet of newspaper as it blew by.

"Crusty," said Virginia Boote, "that's a good way to get yourself killed."

Zebediah T. Crawcrustle grinned through black teeth. "I don't actually drink it," he told her. "I just gargle and breathe it out."

"You're playing with fire," she warned him.

"That's how I know I'm alive," said Zebediah T. Crawcrustle.

Virginia said, "Oh Zeb. I *am* excited. I am so excited. What do you think the Sunbird tastes like?"

"Richer than quail and moister than turkey, fatter than ostrich and lusher than duck," said Zebediah T. Crawcrustle. "Once eaten it's never forgotten."

"We're going to Egypt," she said. "I've never been to Egypt." Then she said, "Do you have anywhere to stay the night?"

He coughed, a small cough that rattled around in his old chest. "I'm getting too old to sleep in doorways and gutters," he said. "Still, I have my pride."

"Well," she said, looking at the man, "you could sleep on my sofa."

"It is not that I am not grateful for the offer," he said, "But there is a bench in the bus station that has my name on it."

And he pushed himself away from the wall, and tottered majestically down the street.

There really *was* a bench in the bus station that had his name on it. He had donated the bench to the bus station back when he was flush, and his name was attached to the back of the bench, engraved upon a small brass plaque. Zebediah T. Crawcrustle was not always poor. Sometimes he was rich, but he difficulty in holding onto his wealth, and whenever he had become wealthy he discovered that the world frowned on rich men eating in hobo jungles at the back of the railroad, or consorting with the winos in the park, so he would fritter his wealth away as best he could. There were always little bits of it here and there that he had forgotten about, and sometimes he would forget that he did not like being rich, and then he would set out again and seek his fortune, and find it.

He had needed a shave for a week, and the hairs of his seven-day beard were starting to come through snow white.

They left for Egypt on a Sunday, the Epicureans. There were five of them there, and Hollyberry Nofeathers McCoy waved goodbye to them at the airport. It was a very small airport, which still permitted waves goodbye.

"Goodbye, father!" called Hollyberry Nofeathers McCoy.

Augustus TwoFeathers McCoy waved back at her as they walked along the asphalt to the little prop plane, which would begin the first leg of their journey.

"It seems to me," said Augustus TwoFeathers McCoy, "that I remember, albeit dimly, a day like this long, long ago. I was a small boy, in that memory, waving goodbye. I believe it was the last time I saw my father, and I am struck once more with a sudden presentiment of doom." He waved one last time at the small child at the other end of the field, and she waved back at him.

"You waved just as enthusiastically back then," agreed Zebediah T. Crawcrustle, "but I think she waves with slightly more aplomb."

It was true. She did.

They took a small plane and then a larger plane, then a smaller plane, a blimp, a gondola, a train, a hot-air balloon, and a rented Jeep.

They rattled through Cairo in the Jeep. They passed the old market, and they turned off on the third lane they came to (if they had continued on they would have come to a drainage ditch that was once an irrigation canal). Mustapha Stroheim himself was sitting outside in the street, sitting on an elderly wicker chair. All of the tables and chairs were on the side of the street, and it was not a particularly wide street.

"Welcome, my friends, to my *Kahwa*," said Mustapha Stroheim. "Kahwa is Egyptian for café, or for coffee-house. Would you like tea? Or a game of dominoes?"

"We would like to be shown to our rooms," said Jackie Newhouse.

"Not me," said Zebediah T. Crawcrustle. "I'll sleep in the street. It's warm enough, and that doorstep over there looks mighty comfortable."

"I'll have coffee, please," said Augustus TwoFeathers McCoy.

"Of course."

"Do you have water?" asked Professor Mandalay.

"Who said that?" said Mustapha Stroheim. "Oh, it was you, little grey man. My mistake. When I first saw you I thought you were someone's shadow."

"I will have *ShaySokkar Bosta*," said Virginia Boote, which is a glass of hot tea with the sugar on the side. "And I will play backgammon with anyone who wishes to take me on. There's not a soul in Cairo I cannot beat at backgammon, if I can remember the rules."

Augustus Twofeathers McCoy was shown to his room. Professor Mandalay was shown to his room. Jackie Newhouse was shown to his room. This was not a lengthy procedure; they were all in the same room, after all. There was another room in the back where Virginia would sleep, and a third room for Mustapha Stroheim and his family.

"What's that you're writing?" asked Jackie Newhouse.

"It's the procedures, annals, and minutes of the Epicurean Club," said Professor Mandalay. He was writing in a large leather-bound book with a small black pen. "I have chronicled our journey here, and all the things that we have eaten on the way. I shall keep writing as we eat the Sunbird, to record for posterity all the tastes and textures, all the smells and the juices."

"Did Crawcrustle say how he was going to cook the Sunbird?" asked Jackie Newhouse.

"He did," said Augustus TwoFeathers McCoy. "He says that he will drain a beer can, so it is only a third full. And then he will add herbs and spices to the beer can. He will stand the bird up on the can, with the can in its inner cavity, and place it up on the barbecue to roast. He says it is the traditional way."

Jackie Newhouse sniffed. "It sounds suspiciously modern to me."

"Crawcrustle says it is the traditional method of cooking the Sunbird," repeated Augustus.

"Indeed I did," said Crawcrustle, coming up the stairs. It was a small building. The stairs weren't that far away, and the walls were not thick ones. "The oldest beer in the world is Egyptian Beer, and they've been cooking the Sunbird with it for over five thousand years now."

"But the beer can is a relatively modern invention," said Professor Mandalay, as Zebediah T. Crawcrustle came through the door. Crawcrustle was holding a cup of Turkish coffee, black as tar, which steamed like a kettle and bubbled like a tarpit.

"That coffee looks pretty hot," said Augustus TwoFeathers McCoy.

Crawcrustle knocked back the cup, draining half the contents. "Nah," he said. "Not really. And the beercan isn't really that new an invention. We used to make them out of an amalgam of copper and tin in the old days, sometimes with a little silver in there, sometimes not. It depended on the smith, and what he had to hand. You need something that would stand up to the heat. I see that you are all looking at me doubtfully. Gentlemen, consider: of course the Ancient Egyptians made beer cans; where else would they have kept their beer?"

From outside the window, at the tables in the street, came a wailing, in many voices. Virginia Boote had persuaded the locals to start playing backgammon for money, and she was cleaning them out. That woman was a backgammon shark.

Out back of Mustapha Stroheim's coffee-house there was a courtyard, containing a broken-down old barbecue, made of clay bricks and a half-melted metal grating, and an old wooden table. Crawcrustle spent the next day rebuilding the barbecue and cleaning it, oiling down the metal grille.

"That doesn't look like it's been used in forty years," said Virginia Boote. Nobody would play backgammon with her any longer, and her purse bulged with grubby piasters.

"Something like that," said Crawcrustle. "Maybe a little more. Here, Ginnie, make yourself useful. I've written a list of things I need from the market. It's mostly herbs and spices and wood chips. You can take one of the children of Mustapha Stroheim to translate for you."

"My pleasure, Crusty."

The other three members of the Epicurean Club were occupying themselves in their own way. Jackie Newhouse was making friends with many of the people of the area, who were attracted by his elegant suits and his skill at playing the violin. Augustus TwoFeathers McCoy went for long walks. Professor Mandalay spent time translating the hieroglyphics he had noticed were incised upon the clay bricks in the barbecue. He said that a foolish man might believe that they proved that the barbecue in Mustapha Stroheim's back yard was once sacred to the Sun. "But I, who am an intelligent man," he said, "I see immediately that what has happened is that bricks that were once, long ago, part of a temple, and have, over the millennia, been reused. I doubt that these people know the value of what they have here."

"Oh, they know all right," said Zebediah T. Crawcrustle. "And these bricks weren't part of any temple. They've been right here for five thousand years, since we built the barbecue. Before that we made do with stones."

Virginia Boote returned with a filled shopping basket. "Here," she said. "Red sandalwood and patchouli, vanilla beans, lavender twigs and sage and cinnamon leaves, whole nutmegs, garlic bulbs, cloves and rosemary: everything you wanted and more."

Zebediah T. Crawcrustle grinned with delight.

"The Sunbird will be so happy," he told her.

He spent the afternoon preparing a barbecue sauce. He said it was only respectful, and besides, the Sunbird's flesh was often slightly on the dry side.

The Epicureans spent that evening sitting at the wicker tables in the street out front, while Mustapha Stroheim and his family brought them tea and coffee and hot mint drinks. Zebediah T. Crawcrustle had told them that they would be having the Sunbird of Suntown for Sunday lunch, and that they might wish to avoid food the night before, to ensure that they had an appetite.

"I have a presentiment of doom upon me," said Augustus TwoFeathers McCoy that night, in a bed that was far too small for him, before he slept. "And I fear it shall come to us with barbecue sauce."

They were all so hungry the following morning. Zebediah T. Crawcrustle had a comedic apron on, with the words KISS THE COOK written upon it in violently green letters. He had already sprinkled the brandy-soaked raisins and grain beneath the stunted avocado tree behind the house, and he was arranging the scented woods, the herbs, and the spices on the bed of charcoal. Mustapha Stroheim and his family had gone to visit relatives on the other side of Cairo.

"Does anybody have a match?" Crawcrustle asked.

Jackie Newhouse pulled out a Zippo lighter, and passed it to Crawcrustle, who lit the dried cinnamon-leaves and dried laurel-leaves beneath the charcoal. The smoke drifted up into the noon air.

"The cinnamon and sandalwood smoke will bring the Sunbird," said Crawcrustle.

"Bring it from where?" asked Augustus TwoFeathers McCoy.

"From the Sun," said Crawcrustle. "That's where he sleeps."

Professor Mandalay coughed discreetly. He said, "The Earth is, at its closest, 91 million miles from the Sun. The fastest dive by a bird ever recorded is that of the peregrine falcon, at 273 miles per hour. Flying at that speed, from the Sun, it would take a bird a little over thirty-eight years to reach us — if it could fly through the dark and cold and vacuum of space, of course."

"Of course," agreed Zebediah T. Crawcrustle. He shaded his eyes and squinted and looked upward. "Here it comes," he said.

It looked almost as if the bird was flying out of the sun; but that could not have been the case. You could not look directly at the noonday sun, after all.

First it was a silhouette, black against the sun and against the blue sky, then the sunlight caught its feathers, and the watchers on the ground caught their breath. Yo have never seen anything like sunlight on the Sunbird's feathers; seeing something like that would take your breath away.

The Sunbird flapped its wide wings once, then it began to glide in ever-decreasing circles in the air above Mustapha Stroheim's coffee-house.

The bird landed in the avocado tree. Its feathers were golden, and purple, and silver. It was smaller than a turkey, larger than a rooster, and had the long legs and high head of a heron, though its head was more like the head of an eagle.

"It is very beautiful," said Virginia Boote. "Look at the two tall feathers on its head. Aren't they lovely?"

"It is indeed quite lovely," said Professor Mandalay.

"There is something familiar about that bird's headfeathers," said Augustus TwoFeathers McCoy.

"We pluck the headfeathers before we roast the bird," said Zebediah T Crawcrustle. "It's the way it's always done."

The Sunbird perched on a branch of the avocado tree, in a patch of sun. It seemed almost as if it were glowing, gently, in the sunlight, as if its feathers were made of sunlight, iridescent with purples and greens and golds. It preened itself, extending one wing in the sunlight, then it nibbled and stroked at the wing with its beak until all the feathers were in their correct position, and oiled. Then it extended the other wing, and repeated the process. Finally, the bird emitted a contented chirrup, and flew the short distance from the branch to the ground.

It strutted across the dried mud, peering from side to side short-sightedly.

"Look!" said Jackie Newhouse. "It's found the grain."

"It seemed almost that it was looking for it," said Augustus TwoFeathers McCoy. "That it was expecting the grain to be there."

"That's where I always leave it," said Zebediah T. Crawcrustle..

"It's so lovely," said Virginia Boote. "But now I see it closer, I can see that it's much older than I thought. Its eyes are cloudy and its legs are shaking. But it's still lovely."

"The Bennu bird is the loveliest of birds," said Zebediah T. Crawcrustle.

Virginia Boote spoke good restaurant Egyptian, but beyond that she was all at sea. "What's a Bennu Bird?" She asked. "Is that Egyptian for Sunbird?"

"The Bennu bird," said Professor Mandalay, "roosts in the Persea Tree. It has two feathers on its head. It is sometimes represented as being like a heron, and sometimes like an eagle. There is more, but it is too unlikely to bear repeating."

"It's eaten the grain and the raisins!" exclaimed Jackie Newhouse. "Now it's stumbling drunkenly from side to side — such majesty, even in its drunkenness!"

Zebediah T. Crawcrustle walked over to the Sunbird, which, with a great effort of will, was walking back and forth on the mud beneath the avocado tree, not tripping over its long legs. He stood directly in front of the bird, and then, very slowly, he bowed to it. He bent like a very old man, slowly and creakily, but still he bowed. And the Sunbird bowed back to him, then it toppled to the mud. Zebediah T Crawcrustle picked it up reverently, and placed it in his arms, carrying it as if one would carry a child, and he took it back to the plot of land behind Mustapha Stroheim's coffee-house, and the others followed him.

First he plucked the two majestic headfeathers, and set them aside.

And then, without plucking the bird, he gutted it, and placed the guts on the smoking twigs. He put the half-filled beercan inside the body cavity, and placed the bird upon the barbecue.

"Sunbird cooks fast," warned Crawcrustle. "Get your plates ready."

The beers of the ancient Egyptians were flavoured with cardamom and coriander, for the Egyptians had no hops; their beers were rich and flavoursome and thirst-quenching. You could build pyramids after drinking that beer, and sometimes people did. On the barbecue the beer steamed the inside of the Sunbird, keeping it moist. As the heat of the charcoal reached them, the feathers of the bird burned off, igniting with a flash like a magnesium flare, so bright that the Epicureans were forced to avert their eyes.

The smell of roast fowl filled the air, richer than peacock, lusher than duck. The mouths of the assembled Epicureans began to water. It seemed like it had been cooking for no time at all, but Zebediah lifted the Sunbird from the charcoal bed, and put it on the table. Then, with a carving knife, he sliced it up and placed the steaming meat on the plates. He poured a little barbecue sauce over each piece of meat. He placed the carcase directly onto the flames.

Each member of the Epicurean Club sat in the back of Mustapha Stroheim's coffee-house, sat around an elderly wooden table, and they ate with their fingers.

"Zebby, this is amazing!" said Virginia Boote, talking as she ate. "It melts in your mouth. It tastes like heaven."

"It tastes like the sun," said Augustus TwoFeathers McCoy, putting his food away as only a big man can. He had a leg in one hand, and some breast in the other. "It is the finest thing I have ever eaten, and I do not regret eating it, but I do believe that I shall miss my daughter."

"It is perfect," said Jackie Newhouse. "It tastes like love and fine music. It tastes like truth."

Professor Mandalay was scribbling in the bound annals of the Epicurean

Club. He was recording his reaction to the meat of the bird, and recording the reactions of the other Epicureans, and trying not to drip on the page while he wrote, for with the hand that was not writing he was holding a wing, and, fastidiously, he was nibbling the meat off it.

"It is strange," said Jackie Newhouse, "for as I eat it, it gets hotter and hotter in my mouth and in my stomach."

"Yup. It'll do that. It's best to prepare for it ahead of time," said Zebediah T. Crawcrustle. "Eat coals and flames and lightning bugs to get used to it. Otherwise it can be a trifle hard on the system."

Zebediah T. Crawcrustle was eating the head of the bird, crunching its bones and beak in his mouth. As he ate, the bones sparked small lightnings against his teeth. He just grinned and chewed the more.

The bones of the Sunbird's carcase burned orange on the barbeque, and then they began to burn white. There was a thick heat-haze in the courtyard at the back of Mustapha Stroheim's coffee-house, and in it everything shimmered, as if the people around the table were seeing the world through water or a dream.

"It is so good!" said Virginia Boote as she ate. "It is the best thing I have ever eaten. It tastes like my youth. It tastes like forever." She licked her fingers, then picked up the last slice of meat from her plate. "The Sunbird of Suntown," she said. "Does it have another name?"

"It is the Phoenix of Heliopolis," said Zebediah T. Crawcrustle. "It is the bird that dies in ashes and flame, and is reborn, generation after generation. It is the Bennu bird, which flew across the waters when all was dark. When its time is come it is burned on the fire of rare woods and spices and herbs, and in the ashes it is reborn, time after time, world without end."

"Fire!" exclaimed Professor Mandalay. "It feels as if my insides are burning up!" He sipped his water, but seemed no happier.

"My fingers," said Virginia Boote. "Look at my fingers." She held them up. They were glowing inside, as if lit with inner flames.

Now the air was so hot you could have baked an egg in it.

There was a spark and a sputter. The two yellow feathers in Augustus TwoFeathers McCoy's hair went up like sparklers. "Crawcrustle," said Jackie Newhouse, aflame, "answer me truly. How long have you been eating the Phoenix?"

"A little over ten thousand years," said Zebediah. "Give or take a few thousand. It's not hard, once you master the trick of it; it's just mastering the trick of it that's hard. But this is the best Phoenix I've ever prepared. Or do I mean, 'this is the best I've ever cooked this Phoenix'?"

"The years!" said Virginia Boote. "They are burning off you!"

"They do that," admitted Zebediah. "You've got to get used to the heat, though, before you eat it. Otherwise you can just burn away."

"Why did I not remember this?" said Augustus TwoFeathers McCoy, through the bright flames that surrounded him. "Why did I not remember that this was how my father went, and his father before him, that each of them went to Heliopolis to eat the Phoenix? And why do I only remember it now?"

"Because the years are burning off you," said Professor Mandalay. He had closed the leather book as soon as the page he had been writing on caught fire. The edges of the book were charred, but the rest of the book would be fine. "When the years burn, the memories of those years come back." He looked more solid now, through the wavering burning air, and he was smiling. None of them had ever seen Professor Mandalay smile before.

"Shall we burn away to nothing?" asked Virginia, now incandescent. "Or shall we burn back to childhood and burn back to ghosts and angels and then come forward again? It does not matter. Oh Crusty, this is all such *fun!*"

"Perhaps," said Jackie Newhouse through the fire, "there might have been a little more vinegar in the sauce. I feel a meat like this could have dealt with something more robust." And then he was gone, leaving only an after-image.

"*Chacun a son gout,*" said Zebediah T. Crawcrustle, which is French for "each to his own taste" and he licked his fingers and he shook his head. "Best it's ever been," he said, with enormous satisfaction.

"Goodbye, Crusty," said Virginia. She put her flame-white hand out, and held his dark hand tightly, for one moment, or perhaps for two.

And then there was nothing in the courtyard back of Mustapha Stroheim's *Kahwa* (or coffee-house) in Heliopolis (which was once the city of the Sun, and is now a suburb of Cairo) but white ash, which blew up in the momentary breeze, and settled like powdered sugar or like snow; and nobody there but a young man with dark, dark hair and even ivory-coloured teeth, wearing an apron that said KISS THE COOK.

A tiny golden-purple bird stirred in the thick bed of ashes on top of the clay bricks, as if it were waking for the first time. It made a high-pitched "peep!" and it looked directly into the sun, as an infant looks at a parent. It stretched its wings as if to dry them, and, eventually, when it was quite ready, it flew upward, toward the sun, and nobody watched it leave but the young man in the courtyard.

There were two long golden feathers at the young man's feet, beneath the ash that had once been a wooden table, and he gathered them up, and brushed the white ash from them and placed them, reverently, inside his jacket. Then he removed his apron, and he went upon his way.

Hollyberry TwoFeathers McCoy is a grown woman, with children of her own. There are silver hairs on her head, in there with the black, beneath the golden feathers in the bun at the back. You can see that once the feathers must have looked pretty special, but that would have been a long time ago. She is the President of the Epicurean Club — a rich and rowdy bunch — having inherited the position, many long years ago, from her father.

I hear that the Epicureans are beginning to grumble once again. They are saying that they have eaten everything.

(For HMG — a belated birthday present).

A Knot of Toads
Jane Yolen

Jane Yolen is the award-winning author of more than 200 books, mostly written for children. A talented composer, she is also a professional storyteller on the stage, the mother of three grown children, and a grandmother. Her best-known work, the critically acclaimed Owl Moon *(illustrated by John Schoenherr), won the prestigious Caldecott Medal for 1988. Her fiction has been awarded the Christopher Medal and the Nebula, World Fantasy, Society of Children's Book Writers, Mythopoeic Society's Aslan, Boy's Club Jr. Book, Garden State Children's Book, and Daedalus awards. Her works for adults include the powerful holocaust fantasy* Briar Rose, *and the "Great Alta" trilogy. Some of her short fiction has been collected in* Once Upon a Time (She Said).

"*March 1931: Late on Saturday night*," the old man had written, "*a toad came into my study and looked at me with goggled eyes, reflecting my candlelight back at me. It seemed utterly unafraid. Although nothing so far seems linked with this appearance, I have had enough formidable visitants to know this for a harbinger.*"

A harbinger of spring, I would have told him, but I arrived too late to tell him anything. I'd been summoned from my Cambridge rooms to his little white-washed stone house with its red pantile roof overlooking St. Monan's harbor. The summons had come from his housekeeper, Mrs. Marr, in a frantic early morning phone call. Hers was from the town's one hotel, to me in the porter's room which boasted the only telephone at our college.

I was a miserable ten hours getting there. All during the long train ride, though I tried to pray for him, I could not, having given up that sort of thing long before leaving Scotland. Loss of faith, lack of faith — that had been my real reason for going away from home. Taking up a place at Gerton College had only been an excuse.

What I had wanted to do this return was to mend our fences before it was too late to mend anything at all. Father and I had broken so many fences — stones, dykes, stiles, and all — that the mending would have taken more than the fortnight's holiday I had planned for later in the summer. But I'd been summoned home early this March because, as Mrs. Marr said, father had had a bad turn.

"A *verrry* bad turn," was what she'd actually said, before the line had gone dead, her r's rattling like a kettle on the boil. In her understated way, she might have meant anything from a twisted ankle to a major heart attack.

The wire that had followed, delivered by a man with a limp and a harelip, had been from my father's doctor, Ewan Kinnear. "Do not delay," it read. Still, there was no diagnosis.

Even so, I did not delay. We'd had no connection in ten years beside a holiday letter exchange. Me to him, not the other way round. But the old man was my only father. I was his only child.

He was dead by the time I got there, and Mrs. Marr stood at the doorway of the house wringing her hands, her black hair caught up in a net. She had not aged a day since I last saw her.

"So ye've left it too late, Janet," she cried. "And wearing green I see."

I looked down at my best dress, a soft green linen now badly creased with travel.

She shook her head at me, and only then did I remember. In St. Monans they always said, "After green comes grief."

"I didn't know he was that ill. I came as fast as I could."

But Mrs. Marr's face showed her disdain for my excuse. Her eyes narrowed and she didn't put out her hand. She'd always been on father's side, especially in the matter of my faith. "His old heart's burst in twa." She was of the old school in speech as well as faith.

"His heart was stone, Maggie, and well you know it." A widow, she'd waited twenty-seven years, since my mother died birthing me, for the old man to notice her. She must be old herself now.

"Stane can still feel pain," she cried.

"What pain?" I asked.

"Of your leaving."

What good would it have done to point out I'd left more than ten years earlier and he'd hardly noticed. He'd had a decade more of calcification, a decade more of poring over his bloody old books — the Latin texts of apostates and heretics. A decade more of filling notebooks with his crabbed script.

A decade more of ignoring his only child.

My God, I thought, meaning no appeal to a deity but a simple swear, *I am still furious with him. It's no wonder I've never married.* Though I'd had chances. Plenty of them. Well, two that were real enough.

I went into the house, and the smell of candle wax and fish and salt sea were as familiar to me as though I'd never left. But there was another smell, too.

Death.

And something more.

It was fear. But I was not to know that till later.

The study where evidently he'd died, sitting up in his chair, was a dark place, even when the curtains were drawn back, which had not been frequent in my childhood. Father liked the close, wood-paneled room, made closer by the ever-burning fire. I'd been allowed in there only when being punished, standing just inside the doorway, with my hands clasped behind me, to listen to my sins being counted. My sins were homey ones, like shouting in the hallway, walking too loudly by his door, or refusing to learn my verses from the Bible. I was far too innocent a child for more than that.

Even at five and six and seven I'd been an unbeliever. Not having a mother had made me so. How could I worship a God whom both Mrs. Marr and my father assured me had so wanted mother, He'd called her away. A selfish God, that, who had listened to his own desires and not mine. Such a God was not for me. Not then. Not now.

I had a sudden urge — me, a postgraduate in a prestigious university who should have known better — to clasp my hands behind me and await my punishment.

But, I thought, *the old punisher is dead. And — if he's to be believed — gone to his own punishment.* Though I was certain that the only place he had gone was to the upstairs bedroom where he was laid out, awaiting my instructions as to his burial.

I went into every other room of the house but that bedroom, memory like an old fishing line dragging me on. The smells, the dark moody smells, remained the same, though Mrs. Marr had a good wood fire burning in the grate, not peat, a wee change in this changeless place. But everything else was so much smaller than I remembered, my little bedroom at the back of the house the smallest of them all.

To my surprise, nothing in my bedroom had been removed. My bed, my toys — the little wooden doll with jointed arms and legs I called Annie, my ragged copy of *Rhymes and Tunes for Little Folks*, the boxed chess set just the size for little hands, my cloth bag filled with buttons — the rag rug, the over-worked sampler on the wall. All were the same. I was surprised to even find one of my old pinafores and black stockings in the wardrobe. I charged Mrs. Marr with more sentiment than sense. It was a shrine to the child that I'd been, not the young woman who had run off. It had to have been Mrs. Marr's idea. Father would never have countenanced false gods.

Staring out of the low window, I looked out toward the sea. A fog sat on the horizon, white and patchy. Below it the sea was a deep, solitary blue. Spring comes early to the East Neuk but summer stays away. I guessed that pussy willows had already appeared around the edges of the lochans, snowdrops and aconite decorating the inland gardens.

Once I'd loved to stare out at that sea, escaping the dark brooding house whenever I could, even in a cutting wind, the kind that could raise bruises. Down I'd go to the beach to play amongst the yawls hauled up on the high wooden trestles, ready for tarring. Once I'd dreamed of going off to sea with the fishermen, coming home to the harbor in the late summer light, and seeing the silver scales glinting on the beach. Though of course fishing was not a woman's job. Not then, not now. A woman in a boat was unthinkable even this far into the twentieth century. St. Monans is firmly eighteenth century and likely to remain so forever.

But I'd been sent off to school, away from the father who found me a loud and heretical discomfort. At first it was just a few towns away, to St. Leonard's in St. Andrews, but as I was a boarder — my father's one extravagance — it might as well have been across the country, or the ocean, as far as seeing my father was concerned. And there I'd fallen in love with words in books.

Words — not water, not wind.

In that way I showed myself to be my father's daughter. Only I never said so to him, nor he to me.

Making my way back down the stairs, I overheard several folk in the kitchen. They were speaking of those things St. Monan's folk always speak of, no matter their occupations: fish and weather.

"There's been nae herring in the firth this winter," came a light man's voice. "Nane." Doctor Kinnear.

"It's a bitter wind to keep the men at hame, the fish awa." Mrs. Marr agreed.

Weather and the fishing. Always the same.

But a third voice, one I didn't immediately recognize, a rumbling growl of a voice, added, "Does she know?"

"Do I know what?" I asked, coming into the room where the big black-leaded grate threw out enough heat to warm the entire house. "How Father died?"

I stared at the last speaker, a stranger I thought, but somehow familiar. He was tall for a St. Monans man, but dressed as one of the fisherfolk, in dark trousers, a heavy white sweater, thick white sea stockings. And he was sunburnt like them, too, with eyes the exact blue of the April sea, gathered round with laugh lines. A ginger mustache, thick and full, hung down the sides of his mouth like a parenthesis.

"By God, Alec Hughes," I said, startled to have remembered, surprised that I could have forgotten. He grinned.

When we'd been young — very young — Alec and I were inseparable. Never mind that boys and girls never played together in St. Monans. Boys from the Bass, girls from the May, the old folk wisdom went. The Bass Rock, the Isle of May, the original separation of the sexes. Apart at birth and ever after. Yet Alec and I had done everything together: messed about with the boats, played cards, built sand castles, fished with *pelns* — shore crabs about to cast their shells — and stolen jam pieces from his mother's kitchen to eat down by one of the gates in the drystone dykes. We'd even often hied off to the low cliff below the ruins of Andross Castle to look for *croupies*, fossils, though whether we ever found any I couldn't recall. When I'd been sent away to school, he'd stayed on in St. Monan's, going to Anstruther's Waid Academy in the next town but one, until he was old enough — I presumed — to join the fishing fleet, like his father before him. His father was a stern and dour soul, a Temperance man who used to preach in the open air.

Alec had been the first boy to kiss me, my back against the stone windmill down by the salt pans. And until I'd graduated from St. Leonard's, the only boy to do so, though I'd made up for that since.

"I thought, Jan," he said slowly, "that God was not in your vocabulary."

"Except as a swear," I retorted. "Good to see you, too, Alec."

Mrs. Marr's eyebrows both rose considerably, like fulmars over the green-grey sea of her eyes.

Alec laughed and it was astonishing how that laugh reminded me of the boy who'd stayed behind. "Yes," he said. "Do you know how your father died?"

"Heart attack, so Mrs. Marr told me."

I stared at the three of them. Mrs. Marr was wringing her hands again, an oddly old-fashioned motion at which she seemed well practiced. Dr. Kinnear polished his eyeglasses with a large white piece of cloth, his flyaway eyebrows proclaiming his advancing age. And Alec — had I remembered how blue his eyes were? Alec nibbled on the right end of his mustache.

"Did I say that?" Mrs. Marr asked. "Bless me, I didna."

And indeed, she hadn't. She'd been more poetic.

"*Burst in twa*, you said." I smiled, trying to apologize for mis-speaking. Not a good trait in a scholar.

"Indeed. Indeed." Mrs. Marr's wrangling hands began again. Any minute I supposed she would break out into a Psalm. I remembered how her one boast was that she'd learned them all by heart as a child and never forgot a one of them.

"A shock, I would have said," Alec said by way of elaborating.

"A fright," the doctor added.

"Really? Is that the medical term?" I asked. "What in St. Monans could my father possibly be frightened of?"

Astonishingly, Mrs. Marr began to wail then, a high, thin keening that went on and on till Alec put his arm around her and marched her over to the stone sink where he splashed her face with cold water and she quieted at once. Then she turned to the blackened kettle squalling on the grate and started to make us all tea.

I turned to the doctor who had his glasses on now, which made him look like a somewhat surprised barn owl. "What do you really mean, Dr. Kinnear?"

"Have you nae seen him yet?" he asked, his head gesturing towards the back stairs.

"I... I couldn't," I admitted. But I said no more. How could I tell this man I hardly knew that my father and I were virtual strangers. No — it was more than that. I was afraid of my father dead as I'd never been alive. Because now he knew for certain whether he was right or I was, about God and Heaven and the rest.

"Come," said Doctor Kinnear in a voice that seemed permanently gentle. He held out a hand and led me back up the stairs and down the hall to my father's room. Then he went in with me and stood by my side as I looked down.

My father was laid out on his bed, the Scottish double my mother had died in, the one he'd slept in every night of his adult life except the day she'd given birth, the day she died.

Like the house, he was much smaller than I remembered. His wild, white hair lay untamed around his head in a kind of corolla. The skin of his face was parchment stretched over bone. That great prow of a nose was, in death, strong enough to guide a ship in. Thankfully his eyes were shut. His hands were crossed on his chest. He was dressed in an old dark suit. I remembered it well.

"He doesn't look afraid," I said. Though he didn't look peaceful either. Just dead.

"Once he'd lost the stiffness, I smoothed his face a bit," the doctor told me. "Smoothed it out. Otherwise Mrs. Marr would no have settled."

"Settled?"

He nodded. "She found him at his desk, stone dead. Ran down the road screaming all the way to the pub. And lucky I was there, having a drink with friends. I came up to see yer father sitting up in his chair, with a face so full of fear, I looked around mysel' to discover the cause of it."

"And did you?"

His blank expression said it all. He simply handed me a pile of five notebooks. "These were on the desk in front of him. Some of the writing is in

Latin, which I have but little of. Perhaps ye can read it, being the scholar. Mrs. Marr has said that they should be thrown on the fire, or at least much of them scored out. But I told her that had to be yer decision and Alec agrees."

I took the notebooks, thinking that this was what had stolen my father from me and now was all I had of him. But I said none of that aloud. After glancing over at the old man again, I asked, "May I have a moment with him?" My voice cracked on the final word.

Dr. Kinnear nodded again and left the room.

I went over to the bed and looked down at the silent body. *The old dragon,* I thought, *has no teeth.* Then I heard a sound, something so tiny I scarcely registered it. Turning, I saw a toad by the bedfoot.

I bent down to pick it up. "Nothing for you here, puddock," I said, reverting to the old Scots word. Though I'd worked so hard to lose my accent and vocabulary, here in my father's house the old way of speech came flooding back. Shifting the books to one hand, I picked the toad up with the other. Then, I tiptoed out of the door as if my father would have minded the sound of my footsteps.

Once outside, I set the toad gently in the garden, or the remains of the garden, now so sadly neglected, its vines running rampant across what was once an arbor of white roses and red. I watched as it hopped under some large dock leaves and, quite effectively, disappeared.

Later that afternoon my father's body was taken away by three burly men for its chestening, being placed into its coffin and the lid screwed down. Then it would lie in the cold kirk till the funeral the next day.

Once he was gone from the house, I finally felt I could look in his journals. I might have sat comfortably in the study, but I'd never been welcomed there before, so didn't feel it my place now. The kitchen and sitting room were more Mrs. Marr's domain than mine. And if I never had to go back into the old man's bedroom, it would be years too soon for me.

So I lay in my childhood bed, the covers up to my chin, and read by the flickering lamplight. Mrs. Marr, bless her, had brought up a warming pan which she came twice to refill. And she brought up as well a pot of tea and jam pieces and several slabs of good honest cheddar.

"I didna think ye'd want a big supper."

She was right. Food was the last thing on my mind.

After she left the room, I took a silver hip flask from under my pillow where I'd hidden it, and then poured a hefty dram of whisky into the teapot. I would need more than Mrs. Marr's offerings to stay warm this night. Outside the sea moaned as it pushed past the skellies, on its way to the shore. I'd all but forgotten that sound. It made me smile.

I read the last part of the last journal first, where father talked about the toad, wondering briefly if it was the very same toad I had found at his bed-foot. But it was the bit right after, where he spoke of "formidable visitants" that riveted me. What had he meant? From the tone of it, I didn't think he meant any of our St. Monans neighbors.

The scholar in me asserted itself, and I turned to the first of the journals, marked 1926, some five years earlier. There was one book for each year. I started with that first notebook and read long into the night.

The journals were not easy to decipher for my father's handwriting was crabbed with age and, I expect, arthritis. The early works were splotchy and, in places, faded. Also he had inserted sketchy pictures and diagrams. Occasionally he'd written whole paragraphs in corrupted Latin, or at least in a dialect unknown to me.

What he seemed engaged upon was a study of a famous trial of local witches in 1590, supervised by King James VI himself. The VI of Scotland, for he was Mary Queen of Scots' own son, and Queen Elizabeth's heir.

The witches, some ninety in all according to my father's notes, had been accused of sailing over the Firth to North Berwick in riddles — sieves, I think he meant — to plot the death of the king by raising a storm when he sailed to Denmark. However, I stumbled so often over my Latin translations, I decided I needed a dictionary. And me a classics scholar.

So halfway through the night, I rose and, taking the lamp, made my way through the cold dark, tiptoeing so as not to wake Mrs. Marr. Nothing was unfamiliar beneath my bare feet. The kitchen stove would not have gone out completely, only filled with gathering coal and kept minimally warm. All those years of my childhood came rushing back. I could have gone into the study without the lamp, I suppose. But to find the book I needed, I'd have to have light.

And lucky indeed I took it, for in its light it I saw — gathered on the floor of my father's study — a group of toads throwing strange shadows up against the bookshelves. I shuddered to think what might have happened had I stepped barefooted amongst them.

But how had they gotten in? And was the toad I'd taken into the garden amongst them? Then I wondered aloud at what such a gathering should be called. I'd heard of a murder of crows, an exaltation of larks. Perhaps toads came in a congregation? For that is what they looked like, a squat congregation, huddled together, nodding their heads, and waiting on the minister in this most unlikely of kirks.

It was too dark even with the lamp, and far too late, for me to round them up. So I sidestepped them and, after much searching, found the Latin dictionary where it sat cracked open on my father's desk. I grabbed it up, avoided the congregation of toads, and went out the door. When I looked back, I could still see the odd shadows dancing along the walls.

I almost ran back to my bed, shutting the door carefully behind me. I didn't want that dark presbytery coming in, as if they could possibly hop up the stairs like the frog in the old tale, demanding to be taken to my little bed.

But the shock of my father's death and the long day of travel, another healthy swallow of my whisky, as well as that bizarre huddle of toads, all seemed to combine to put me into a deep sleep. If I dreamed, I didn't remember any of it. I woke to one of those dawn choruses of my childhood, comprised of blackbirds, song thrushes, gulls, rooks, and jackdaws, all arguing over who should wake me first.

For a moment I couldn't recall where I was. Eyes closed, I listened to the birds, so different from the softer, more lyrical sounds outside my Cambridge windows. But I woke fully in the knowledge that I was back in my childhood home, that my father was dead and to be buried that afternoon if possible, as I had requested of the doctor and Mrs. Marr, and I had only hours to make things tidy in my mind. Then I would be away from St. Monans and its small-mindedness, back to Cambridge where I truly belonged.

I got out of bed, washed, dressed in the simple black dress I always travel with, a black bandeaux on my fair hair, and went into the kitchen to make myself some tea.

Mrs. Marr was there before me, sitting on a hardback chair and knitting a navy blue guernsey sweater with its complicated patterning. She set the steel needles down and handed me a full cup, the tea nearly black even with its splash of milk. There was a heaping bowl of porridge, sprinkled generously with salt, plus bread slathered with golden syrup.

"Thank you," I said. It would have done no good to argue that I drank coffee now, nor did I like either oatmeal or treacle, and never ate till noon. Besides, I was suddenly ravenous. "What do you need me to do?" I asked between mouthfuls, stuffing them in the way I'd done as a youngster.

"'Tis all arranged," she said, taking up the needles again. No proper St. Monans woman was ever idle long. "Though sooner than is proper. But all to accommodate ye, he'll be in the kirkyard this afternoon. Lucky for ye it's a Sunday, or we couldna do it. The men are home from fishing." She was clearly not pleased with me. "Ye just need to be there at the service. Not that many will come. He was no generous with his company." By which she meant he had few friends. Nor relatives except me.

"Then I'm going to walk down by the water this morning," I told her. "Unless you have something that needs doing. I want to clear my head."

"Aye, ye would."

Was that condemnation or acceptance? Who could tell? Perhaps she meant I was still the thankless child she remembered. Or that I was like my father. Or that she wanted only to see the back of me, sweeping me from her domain so she could clean and bake without my worrying presence. I thanked her again for the meal, but she wanted me gone. As I had been for the past ten years. And I was as eager to be gone, as she was to have me. The funeral was not till mid afternoon.

"There are toads in the study," I said as I started out the door.

"Toads?" She looked startled. Or perhaps frightened.

"Puddocks. A congregation of them."

Her head cocked to one side. "Och, ye mean a knot. A knot of toads."

A knot. Of course. I should have remembered. "Shall I put them out?" At least I could do that for her.

She nodded. "Aye."

I found a paper sack and went into the study, but though I looked around for quite some time, I couldn't find the toads anywhere. If I hadn't still had the Latin dictionary in my bedroom, I would have thought my night visit amongst them and my scare from their shadows had been but a dream.

"All gone," I called to Mrs. Marr before slipping out through the front door and heading toward the strand.

Nowhere in St. Monans is far from the sea. I didn't realize how much the sound of it was in my bones until I moved to Cambridge. Or how much I'd missed that sound till I slept the night in my old room.

I found my way to the foot of the church walls where boats lay upturned, looking like beached dolphins. A few of the older men, past their fishing days, sat with their backs against the salted stone, smoking silently, and staring out to the gray slatey waters of the Forth. Nodding to them, I took off along the beach. Overhead gulls squabbled and far out, near the Bass Rock, I could see, gannets diving head-first into the water.

A large boat, some kind of yacht, had just passed the Bass and was sailing west majestically toward a mooring, probably in South Queensferry. I wondered who would be sailing these waters in such a ship.

But then I was interrupted by the wind sighing my name. Or so I thought at first. Then I looked back at the old kirk on the cliff above me. Someone was waving at me in the ancient kirkyard. It was Alec.

He signaled that he was coming down to walk with me and as I waited, I thought about what a handsome man he'd turned into. *But a fisherman,* I reminded myself, a bit of the old snobbery biting me on the back of the neck. St. Monans, like the other fishing villages of the East Neuk, were made up of three classes — fisher folk, farmers, and the shopkeepers and tradesmen.

My father being a scholar was outside of them all, which meant that as his daughter, I belonged to none of them either.

Still, in this place, where I was once so much a girl of the town — from the May — I felt my heart give a small stutter. I remembered that first kiss, so soft and sweet and innocent, the windmill hard against my back. My last serious relationship had been almost a year ago, and I was more than ready to fall in love again. Even at the foot of my father's grave. But not with a fisherman. Not in St. Monans.

Alec found his way down to the sand and came toward me. "Off to find croupies?" he called.

I laughed. "The only fossil I've found recently has been my father," I said, then bit my lower lip at his scowl.

"He was nae a bad man, Jan," he said, catching up to me. "Just undone by his reading."

I turned a glared at him. "Do you think reading an ailment then?"

He put up his hands palms towards me. "Whoa, lass. I'm a big reader myself. But what the old man had been reading lately had clearly unnerved him. He couldna put it into context. Mrs. Marr said as much before you came. These last few months he'd stayed away from the pub, from the kirk, from everyone who'd known him well. No one kenned what he'd been on about."

I wondered what sort of thing Alec would be reading. *The fishing report? The local paper?* Feeling out of sorts, I said sharply, "Well, I was going over his journals last night and what he's been on about are the old North Berwick witches."

Alec's lips pursed. "The ones who plotted to blow King James off the map." It was a statement, not a question.

"The very ones."

"Not a smart thing for the unprepared to tackle."

I wondered if Alec had become as hag-ridden and superstitious as any St. Monans' fisherman. Ready to turn home from his boat if he met a woman on the way. Or not daring to say "salmon" or "pig" and instead speaking of "red fish" and "curly tail," or shouting out "Cauld iron!" at any mention of them. All the East Neuk tip-leavings I was glad to be shed of.

He took the measure of my disapproving face, and laughed. "Ye take me for a gowk," he said. "But there are more things in heaven and earth, Janet, than are dreamt of in yer philosophy."

I laughed as Shakespeare tumbled from his lips. Alec could always make me laugh. "Pax," I said.

He reached over, took my hand, gave it a squeeze. "Pax." Then he dropped it again as we walked along the beach, a comfortable silence between us.

The tide had just turned and was heading out. Gulls, like satisfied house-wives, sat happily in the receding waves. One lone boat was on the horizon, a small fishing boat, not the yacht I had seen earlier, which must already be coming into its port. The sky was that wonderful spring blue, without a threatening cloud, not even the fluffy Babylonians, as the fishermen called them.

"Shouldn't you be out there?" I said, pointing at the boat as we passed by the smoky fish-curing sheds.

"I rarely get out there anymore," he answered, not looking at me but at the sea. "Too busy until summer. And why old man Sinclair is fishing when the last of the winter herring have been hauled in, I canna fathom."

I turned toward him. "Too busy with what?"

He laughed. "Och, Janet, yer so caught up in yer own preconceptions, ye canna see what's here before yer eyes."

I didn't answer right away, and the moment stretched between us, as the silence had before. Only this was not comfortable. At last I said, "Are you too busy to help me solve the mystery of my father's death?"

"Solve the mystery of his life first," he told me, "and the mystery of his death will inevitably be revealed." Then he touched his cap, nodded at me, and strolled away.

I was left to ponder what he said. Or what he meant. I certainly wasn't going to chase after him. I was too proud to do that. Instead, I went back to the house, changed my shoes, made myself a plate of bread and cheese. There was no wine in the house. Mrs. Marr was as Temperance as Alec's old father had been. But I found some miserable sherry hidden in my father's study. It smelled like turpentine, so I made do with fresh milk, taking the plate and glass up to my bedroom, to read some more of my father's journals until it was time to bury him.

It is not too broad a statement to say that Father was clearly out of his mind. For one, he was obsessed with local witches. For another, he seemed to believe in them. While he spared a few paragraphs for Christian Dote, St. Monans' homegrown witch of the 1640s, and a bit more about the various Anstruther, St. Andrews, and Crail trials — listing the hideous tortures, and executions of hundreds of poor old women in his journal entries — it was the earlier North Berwick crew who really seemed to capture his imagination. By the third year's journal, I could see that he obviously considered the North Berwick witchery evil real, whereas the others, a century later, he dismissed as deluded or senile old women, as deluded and senile as the men who hunted them.

Here is what he wrote about the Berwick corps: "*They were a scabrous bunch, these ninety greedy women and six men, wanting no more than what they considered their due: a king and his bride dead in the sea, a kingdom in ruins, themselves set up in high places."*

"Oh, Father," I whispered, "what a noble mind is here o'erthrown," For whatever problems I'd had with him — and they were many — I had always admired his intelligence.

He described the ceremonies they indulged in, and they were awful. In the small North Berwick church, fueled on wine and sex, the witches had begun a ritual to call up a wind that would turn over the royal ship and drown King James. First they'd christened a cat with the name of Hecate, while black candles flickered fitfully along the walls of the apse and nave. Then they tortured the poor creature by passing it back and forth across a flaming hearth. Its elf-knotted hair caught fire and burned slowly, and the little beastie screamed in agony. The smell must have been appalling, but he doesn't mention that. I once caught my hair on fire, bending over a stove on a cold night in Cambridge, and it was the smell that was the worst of it. It lingered in my room for days.

Then I thought of my own dear moggie at home, a sweet orange-colored puss who slept each night at my bedfoot. If anyone ever treated her the way the North Berwick witches had that poor cat, I'd be more than ready to kill. And not with any wind, either.

But there was worse yet, and I shuddered as I continued reading. One of the men, so Father reported, had dug up a corpse from the church cemetery, and with a companion had cut off the dead man's hands and feet. Then the witches attached the severed parts to the cat's paws. After this they attached the corpse's sex organs to the cat's. I could only hope the poor creature was dead by this point. After this desecration, they proceeded to a pier at the port of Leith where they flung the wee beastie into the sea.

Father wrote: "*A storm was summarily raised by this foul method, along with the more traditional knotted twine. The storm blackened the skies, with wild gales churning the sea. The howl of the wind could be heard all the way across the Firth to Fife. But the odious crew had made a deadly miscalculation. The squall caught a ship crossing from Kinghorn to Leith and smashed it to pieces all right, but it was not the king's ship. The magic lasted only long enough to kill a few innocent sailors on that first ship, and then blew itself out to sea. As for the king, he proceeded over calmer waters with his bride, arriving safely in Denmark and thence home again to write that great treatise on witchcraft, Demonology, and preside over a number of witch trials thereafter."*

I did not read quickly because, as I have said, parts of the journal were in a strange Latin and for those passages I needed the help of the diction-ary. I was like a girl at school with lines to translate by morning, frustrated, achingly close to comprehension, but somehow missing the point. In fact, I did not understand them completely until I read them aloud. And then suddenly, as a roiled liquid settles at last, all became clear. The passages were some sort of incantation, or invitation, to the witches and to the evil they so devoutly and hideously served.

I closed the journal and shook my head. Poor Father. He wrote as if the witchcraft were fact, not a coincidence of gales from the southeast that threw up vast quantities of seaweed on the shore, and the haverings of tortured old women. Put a scold's bridle on me, and I would probably admit to intercourse with the devil. Any devil. And describe him and his nether parts as well.

But Father's words, as wild and unbelievable as they were, held me in a kind of thrall. And I would have remained on my bed reading further if Mrs. Marr hadn't knocked on the door and summoned me to his funeral.

She looked me over carefully, but for once I seemed to pass muster, my smart black Cambridge dress suitable for the occasion. She handed me a black hat. "I didna think ye'd have thought to bring one." Her lips drew down into a thin, straight line.

Standing before me, her plain black dress covered at the top by a solemn dark shawl, and on her head an astonishing hat covered with artificial black flowers, she was clearly waiting for me to say something.

"Thank you," I said at last. And it was true, bringing a hat along hadn't occurred to me at all. I took off the bandeaux, and set the proffered hat on my head. It was a perfect fit, though made me look fifteen years older, with its masses of black feathers, or so the mirror told me.

Lips pursed, she nodded at me, then turned, saying over her shoulder, "Young Mary McDougall did for him."

It took me a moment to figure out what she meant. Then I remembered. Though she must be nearer sixty than thirty, Mary McDougall had been both midwife and dresser of the dead when I was a child. So it had been she and not Mrs. Marr who must have washed my father and put him into the clothes he'd be buried in. *So Mrs. Marr missed out on her last great opportunity to touch him*, I thought.

"What do I give her?" I asked to Mrs. Marr's ramrod back.

Without turning around again, she said, "We'll give her all yer father's old clothes. She'll be happy enough with that."

"But surely a fee..."

She walked out of the door.

It was clear to me then that nothing had changed since I'd left. It was still the nineteenth century. Or maybe the eighteenth. I longed for the burial to be over and done with, my father's meager possessions sorted, the house sold, and me back on a train heading south.

We walked to the kirk in silence, crossing over the burn which rushed along beneath the little bridge. St. Monans has always been justifiably proud of its ancient kirk and even in this dreary moment I could remark its beauty. Some of its stonework runs back in an unbroken line to the thirteenth century.

And some of its customs, I told myself without real bitterness.

When we entered the kirk proper, I was surprised to see that Mrs. Marr had been wrong. She'd said not many would come, but the church was overfull with visitants.

We walked down to the front. As the major mourners, we commanded the first pew, Mrs. Marr, the de facto wife, and me, the runaway daughter. There was a murmur when we sat down together, not quite of disapproval, but certainly of interest. Gossip in a town like St. Monans is everybody's business.

Behind us, Alex and Dr. Kinnear were already settled in. And three men sat beside them, men whose faces I recognized, friends of my father's, but grown so old. I turned, nodded at them with, I hope, a smile that thanked them for coming. They didn't smile back.

In the other pews were fishermen and shopkeepers and the few teachers I could put a name to. But behind them was a congregation of strangers who leaned forward with an avidity that one sees only in the faces of vultures at their feed. I knew none of them and wondered if they were newcomers to the town. Or if it was just that I hadn't been home in so long, even those families who'd been here forever were strangers to me now.

Father's pine box was set before the altar and I kept my eyes averted, watching instead an ettercap, a spider, slowly spinning her way from one edge of the pulpit to the other. No one in the town would have removed her, for it was considered bad luck. It kept me from sighing, it kept me from weeping.

The minister went on for nearly half an hour, lauding my father's graces, his intelligence, his dedication. If any of us wondered about whom he was talking, we didn't answer back. But when it was over, and six large fishermen, uneasy in their Sunday clothes, stood to shoulder the coffin, I leaped up with them. Putting my hand on the pine top, I whispered, "I forgive you, Father. Do you forgive me?"

There was an audible gasp from the congregation behind me, though I'd spoken so low, I doubted any of them — not even Alec — could have heard me. I sat down again, shaken and cold.

And then the fishermen took him off to the kirkyard, to a grave so recently and quickly carved out of the cold ground, its edges were jagged. As we stood there, a huge black cloud covered the sun. The tide was dead low and the bones of the sea, those dark grey rock skellies, showed in profusion like the spines of some prehistoric dragons.

As I held on to Mrs. Marr's arm, she suddenly started shaking so hard, I thought she would shake me off.

How she must have loved my father, I thought, and found myself momentarily jealous.

Then the coffin was lowered, and that stopped her shaking. As the first clods were shoveled into the gaping hole, she turned to me and said, "Well, that's it then."

So we walked back to the house where a half dozen people stopped in for a dram or three of whiskey — brought in by Alec despite Mrs. Marr's strong disapproval. "There's a Deil in every mouthful of whiskey," she muttered, setting out the fresh baked shortbread and sultana cakes with a pitcher of lemonade. To mollify her, I drank the lemonade, but I was the only one.

Soon I was taken aside by an old man — Jock was his name — and told that my father had been a great gentleman though late had turned peculiar. Another, bald and wrinkled, drink his whiskey down in a single gulp, before declaring loudly that my father had been "one for the books." He managed to make that sound like an affliction. One woman of a certain age who addressed me as "Mistress," added, apropos of nothing, "He needs a langshankit spoon that sups wi' the Deil." Even Alec, sounding like the drone on a bagpipes, said "Now you can get on with your own living, Jan," as if I hadn't been doing just that all along.

For a wake, it was most peculiar. No humorous anecdotes about the dearly departed, no toasts to his soul, only half-baked praise and a series of veiled warnings.

Thank goodness no one stayed long. After the last had gone, I insisted on doing the washing up, and this time Mrs. Marr let me. And then she, too, left. Where she went I wasn't to know. One minute she was there, and the next away.

I wondered at that. After all, this was her home, certainly more than mine. I was sure she'd loved my father who, God knows, was not particularly loveable, but she walked out the door clutching her big handbag, without a word more to me; not a goodbye or "I'll not be long," or anything. And suddenly, there I was, all alone in the house for the first time in years. It was an uncomfortable feeling. I am not afraid of ghosts, but that house fairly burst with ill will, dark and brooding. So as soon as I'd tidied away the dishes, I went out, too, though not before slipping the final journal into the pocket of my overcoat and winding a long woolen scarf twice around my neck to ward the chill.

The evening was drawing in slowly, but there was otherwise a soft feel in the air, unusual for the middle of March. The East Neuk is like that — one minute still and the next a flanny wind rising.

I headed east along the coastal path, my guide the stone head of the windmill with its narrow, ruined vanes lording it over the flat land. Perhaps sentiment was leading me there, the memory of that adolescent kiss that Alec had given me, so wonderfully innocent and full of desire at the same time. Perhaps I just wanted a short, pleasant walk to the old salt pans. I don't know why I went that way. It was almost as if I were being called there.

For a moment I turned back and looked at the town behind me which showed, from this side, how precariously the houses perch on the rocks, like gannets nesting on the Bass.

Then I turned again and took the walk slowly; it was still only ten or fifteen minutes to the windmill from the town. No boats sailed on the Firth today. I could not spot the large yacht so it must have been in its berth. And the air was so clear, I could see the Bass and the May with equal distinction. How often I'd come to this place as a child. I probably could still walk to it barefooted and without stumbling, even in the blackest night. The body has a memory of its own.

Halfway there, a solitary curlew flew up before me and as I watched it flap away, I thought how the townsfolk would have cringed at the sight, for the bird was thought to bring bad luck, carrying away the spirits of the wicked at nightfall.

"But I've not been wicked," I cried after it, and laughed. *Or at least not wicked for a year, more's the pity.*

At last I came to the windmill with its rough stones rising high above the land. Once it had been used for pumping seawater to extract the salt. Not a particularly easy operation, it took something like thirty-two tons of water to produce one ton of salt. We'd learned all about it in primary school, of course. But the days of the salt pans were a hundred years in the past, and the poor windmill had seen better times.

Even run down, though, it was still a lovely place, with its own memories. Settling back against the mill's stone wall, I nestled down and drew out the last journal from my coat pocket. Then I began to read it from the beginning as the light slowly faded around me.

Now, I am a focused reader, which is to say that once caught up in a book, I can barely swim back up to the surface of any other consciousness. The world dims around me. Time and space compress. Like a Wellsian hero, I am drawn into an elsewhere that becomes absolute and real. So as I read my Father's final journal, I was in his head and his madness so completely,

I heard nothing around me, not the raucous cry of gulls nor the wash of water onto the stones far below.

So it was, with a start that I came to the final page, with its mention of the goggle-eyed toad. Looking up, I found myself in the gray gloaming surrounded by nearly a hundred such toads, all staring at me with their horrid wide eyes, a hideous echo of my father's written words.

I stood up quickly, trying desperately not to squash any of the poor paddocks. They leaned forward like children trying to catch the warmth of a fire. Then their shadows lengthened and grew.

Please understand, there was no longer any sun and very little light. There was no moon overhead for the clouds crowded one on to the other, and the sky was completely curtained. So there should not have been any shadows at all. Yet, I state again — their shadows lengthened and grew. Shadows like and unlike the ones I had seen against my father's study walls. They grew into dark-caped creatures, almost as tall as humans yet with those goggly eyes.

I still held my father's journal in my left hand, but my right covered my mouth to keep myself from screaming. My sane mind knew it to be only a trick of the light, of the dark. It was the result of bad dreams and just having put my only living relative into the ground. But the primitive brain urged me to cry out with all my ancestors, "Cauld iron!" and run away in terror.

And still the horrid creatures grew until now they towered over me, pushing me back against the windmill, their shadowy fingers grabbing at both ends of my scarf.

Who are you? What are you? I mouthed, as the breath was forced from me. Then they pulled and pulled the scarf until they'd choked me into unconsciousness.

When I awoke, I was tied to a windmill vane, my hands bound high above me, the ropes too tight and well-knotted for any escape.

"Who are you?" I whispered aloud this time, my voice sounding froglike, raspy, hoarse. "What are you?" Though I feared I knew. "What do you want of me? Why are you here?"

In concert, their voices wailed back. "A wind! A wind!"

And then in horror all that Father had written — about the hands and feet and sex organs of the corpse being cut off and attached to the dead cat — bore down upon me. Were they about to dig poor father's corpse up? Was I to be the offering? Were we to be combined in some sort of desecration too disgusting to be named? I began to shudder within my bonds, both hot and cold. For a moment I couldn't breathe again, as if they were tugging on the scarf once more.

Then suddenly, finding some latent courage, I stood tall and screamed at them, "I'm not dead yet!" Not like my father whom they'd frightened into his grave.

They crowded around me, shadow folk with wide white eyes, laughing. "A wind! A wind!"

I kicked out at the closest one, caught my foot in its black cape, but connected with nothing more solid than air. Still that kick forced them back for a moment.

"Get away from me!" I screamed. But screaming only made my throat ache, for I'd been badly choked just moments earlier. I began to cough and it was as if a nail were being driven through my temples with each spasm.

The shadows crowded forward again, their fingers little breezes running over my face and hair, down my neck, touching my breasts.

I took a deep breath for another scream, another kick. But before I could deliver either, I heard a cry.

"Aroint, witches!"

Suddenly I distinguished the sound of running feet. Straining to see down the dark corridor that was the path to Pittenweem, I leaned against the cords that bound me. It was a voice I did and did not recognize.

The shadow folk turned as one and flowed along the path, hands before them as if they were blindly seeking the interrupter.

"Aroint, I say!"

Now I knew the voice. It was Mrs. Marr, in full cry. But her curse seemed little help and I feared that she, too, would soon be trussed up by my side.

But then, from the east, along the path nearer town, there came another call.

"Janet! Janet!" That voice I recognized at once.

"Alec..." I said between coughs.

The shadows turned from Mrs. Marr and flowed back, surrounding Alec, but he held something up in his hand. A bit of a gleam from a crossbar. His fisherman's knife.

The shadows fell away from him in confusion.

"Cauld iron!" he cried at them. "Cauld iron!"

So they turned to go back again towards Mrs. Marr, but she reached into her large handbag and pulled out her knitting needles. Holding them before her in the sign of a cross, she echoed Alec's cry. "Cauld iron." And then she added, her voice rising as she spoke, "Oh let the wickedness of the wicked come to an end; but establish the just: for the righteous God trieth the hearts and reigns."

I recognized it as part of a psalm, one of the many she'd presumably memorized as a child, but I could not have said which.

Then the two of them advanced on the witches, coming from east and west, forcing the awful crew to shrink down, as if melting, into dark pud-docks once again.

Step by careful step, Alec and Mrs. Marr herded the knot of toads off the path and over the cliff's edge.

Suddenly the clouds parted and a brilliant half moon shone down on us, its glare as strong as the lighthouse on Anster's pier. I watched as the entire knot of toads slid down the embankment, some falling onto the rocks and some into the water below.

Only when the last puddock was gone, did Alec turn to me. Holding the knife in his teeth, he reached above my head to my bound hands and began to untie the first knot.

A wind started to shake the vanes and for a second I was lifted off my feet as the mill tried to grind, though it had not done so for a century.

"Stop!" Mrs. Marr's voice held a note of desperation.

Alec turned. "Would ye leave her tied, woman? What if those shades come back again. I told ye what the witches had done before. It was all in the his journals."

"No, Alec," I cried, hating myself for trusting the old ways, but changed beyond caring. "They're elfknots. Don't untie them. Don't!" I shrank away from his touch.

"Aye," Mrs. Marr said, coming over and laying light fingers on Alec's arm. "The lass is still of St. Monan's though she talks like a Sassanach." She laughed. "It's no the drink and the carousing that brings the wind. That's just for fun. Nor the corpse and the cat. That's just for show. My man told me. It's the knots, he says."

"The knot of toads?" Alec asked hoarsely.

The wind was still blowing and it took Alec's hard arms around me to an-chor me fast or I would have gone right around, spinning with the vanes.

Mrs. Marr came close till they were eye to eye. "The knots in the rope, lad," she said. "One brings a wind, two bring a gale, and the third..." She shook her head. "Ye dinna want to know about the third."

"But —" Alec began.

"Och, but me know buts, my lad. Cut between," Mrs. Marr said. "Just dinna untie them or King George's yacht at South Queensferry will go down in a squall, with the king and queen aboard, and we'll all be to blame."

He nodded and slashed the ropes with his knife, between the knots, free-ing my hands. Then he lifted me down. I tried to take it all in: his arms, his breath on my cheek, the smell of him so close. I tried to understand what had happened here in the gloaming. I tried until I started to sob and he began stroking my hair, whispering, "There, lass, it's over. It's over."

"Not until we've had some tea and burned those journals," Mrs. Marr said.

"I told ye we should have done it before."

"And I told ye," he retorted, "that they are invaluable to historians."

"Burn them," I croaked, knowing at last that the invitation in Latin they contained was what had called the witches back. Knowing that my speaking the words aloud had brought them to our house again. Knowing that the witches were Father's "visitants" who had, in the end, frightened him to death. "Burn them. No historian worth his salt would touch them."

Alec laughed bitterly. "I would." He set me on my feet and walked away down the path toward town.

"Now ye've done it," Mrs. Marr told me. "Ye never were a lass to watch what ye say. Ye've injured his pride and broken his heart."

"But…" We were walking back along the path, her hand on my arm, leading me on. The wind had died and the sky was alert with stars. "But he's not an historian."

"Ye foolish lass, yon lad's nae fisherman, for all he dresses like one. He's a lecturer in history at the University, in St. Andrews," she said. "And the two of ye the glory of this village. Yer father and his father always talking about the pair of ye. Hoping to see ye married one day, when pride didna keep the two of ye apart. Scheming they were."

I could hardly take this in. Drawing my arm from her, I looked to see if she was making a joke. Though in all the years I'd known her, I'd never heard her laugh.

She glared ahead at the darkened path. "Yer father kept yer room the way it was when ye were a child, though I tried to make him see the foolishness of it. He said that someday yer own child would be glad of it."

"My father — "

"But then he went all queer in the head after Alec's father died. I think he believed that by uncovering all he could about the old witches, he might help Alec in his research. To bring ye together. though what he really fetched was too terrible to contemplate."

"Which do you think came first?" I asked slowly. "Father's summoning the witches, or the shadows sensing an opportunity?"

She gave a bob of her head to show she was thinking, then said at last, "Dinna mess with witches and weather, my man says..."

"Your man?" She'd said it before, but I thought she'd meant her dead husband. "Weren't you…I mean, I thought you were in love with my father."

She stopped dead in her tracks and turned to me. The half moon lit her face. "Yer father?" She stopped, considered, then began again. "Yer father had a heart only for two women in his life, yer mother and ye, Janet, though he had a hard time showing it.

And…" she laughed, "he was no a bonnie man."

I thought of him lying in his bed, his great prow of a nose dominating his face. No, he was not a bonnie man.

"Och, lass, I had promised yer mother on her deathbed to take care of him, and how could I go back on such a promise? I didna feel free to marry as long as he remained alive. Now my Pittenweem man and I have set a date, and it will be soon. We've wasted enough time already."

I had been wrong, so wrong, and in so many ways I could hardly comprehend them all. And didn't I understand about wasted time. But at least I could make one thing right again.

"I'll go after Alec, I'll..."

Mrs. Marr clapped her hands. "Then run, lass, run like the wind."

And untying the knot around my own pride, I ran.

For M. R. James

Boatman's Holiday
Jeffrey Ford

Jeffrey Ford is the author of six novels — Vanitas, World Fantasy Award *winner* The Physiognomy, Memoranda, The Beyond, The Portrait of Mrs Charbuque, *and* The Girl in the Glass — *and World Fantasy Award winning collection* The Fantasy Writer's Assistant and Other Stories. *His short fiction, which has appeared in* Fantasy & Science Fiction, SciFiction, Black Gate, The Green Man, Leviathan 3, The Dark, *and many year's best anthologies, has won the World Fantasy and Nebula Awards. He lives in South Jersey with his wife and two sons, and teaches Writing and Literature at Brookdale Community College in Monmouth County, New Jersey. A new collection,* The Empire of Ice Cream, *was published in early 2006.*

Beneath a blazing orange sun, he maneuvered his boat between the two petrified oaks that grew so high their tops were lost in violet clouds. The vast trunks and complexity of branches were bone white, as if hidden just below the surface of the murky water was a stag's head the size of a mountain. Thousands of crows, like black leaves, perched amidst the pale tangle, staring silently down. Feathers fell, spiraling in their descent with the slow grace of certain dreams, and he wondered how many of these journeys he'd made or if they were all, always, the same journey.

Beyond the oaks, the current grew stronger, and he entered a constantly shifting maze of whirlpools, some spinning clockwise, some counter, as if to negate the passage of time. Another boatman might have given in to panic and lost everything, but he was a master navigator and knew the river better than himself. Any other craft would have quickly succumbed to the seething waters, been ripped apart and its debris swallowed.

His boat was comprised of an inner structure of human bone lashed together with tendon and covered in flesh stitched by his own steady hand, employing a thorn needle and thread spun from sorrow. The lines of its contours lacked symmetry, meandered and went off on tangents. Along each side, worked into the gunwales well above the waterline, was a row of eyeless, tongueless faces — the empty sockets, the gaping lips, portals through which the craft breathed. Below, in the hold, there reverberated a heartbeat that fluttered randomly and died every minute only to be revived the next.

On deck, there were two long rows of benches fashioned from skulls for his passengers, and at the back, his seat at the tiller. In the shallows, he'd stand and use his long pole to guide the boat along. There was no need of a sail as the vessel moved slowly forward of its own volition with a simple command. On the trip out, the benches empty, he'd whisper, "There!" and on the journey back, carrying a full load, "Home!" and no river current could dissuade its progress. Still, it took a sure and fearless hand to hold the craft on course.

Charon's tall, wiry frame was slightly but irreparably bent from centuries hunched beside the tiller. His beard and tangled nest of snow-white hair, his complexion the color of ash, made him appear ancient. When in the throes of maneuvering around Felmian, the blue serpent, or in the heated rush along the shoals of the Island of Nothing, however, he'd toss one side of his scarlet cloak back over his shoulder, and the musculature of his chest, the coiled bulge of his bicep, the thick tendon in his forearm, gave evidence of the power hidden beneath his laconic façade. Woe to the passenger who mistook those outer signs of age for weakness and set some plan in motion, for then the boatman would wield his long shallows stick and shatter every bone in their body.

Each treacherous obstacle, the clutch of shifting boulders, the rapids, the waterfall that dropped into a bottomless star-filled space, was expertly avoided with a skill born of intuition. Eventually a vague but steady tone like the uninterrupted buzz of a mosquito came to him over the water; a sign that he drew close to his destination. He shaded his eyes against the brightness of the flaming sun and spotted the dark, thin edge of shoreline in the distance. As he advanced, that distant, whispered note grew steadily into a high keening, and then fractured to reveal itself a chorus of agony. A few more leagues and he could make out the legion of forms crowding the bank. When close enough to land, he left the tiller, stood, and used the pole to turn the boat so it came to rest sideways on the black sand. Laying down the pole, he stepped to his spot at the prow.

Two winged, toad-faced demons with talons for hands and hands for feet, Gesnil and Trinkthil, saw to the orderliness of the line of passengers that ran from the shore back a hundred yards into the writhing human continent of dead. Every day there were more travelers, and no matter how many trips Charon made, there was no hope of ever emptying the endless beach.

Brandishing a cat-o-nine-tails with barbed tips fashioned from incisors, the demons lashed the "tourists," as they called them, subduing those un-willing to go.

"Another load of the falsely accused, Charon," said Gesnil, puffing on a lit human finger jutting from the corner of his mouth.

"Watch this woman, third back, in the blue dress," said Trinkthil, "her blithering lamentations will bore you to sleep. You know, she never really meant to add belladonna to the recipe for her husband's gruel."

Charon shook his head.

"We've gotten word that there will be no voyages for a time," said Gesnil.

"Yes," said Charon, "I've been granted a respite by the Master. A holiday."

"A century's passed already?" said Gesnil. "My, my, it seemed no more than three. Time flies...."

"Traveling?" asked Trinkthil. "Or staying home?"

"There's an island I believe I'll visit," he said.

"Where's it located?" asked Gesnil.

Charon ignored the question and said, "Send them along."

The demons knew to obey, and they directed the first in line to move forward. A bald, overweight man in a cassock, some member of the clergy, stepped up. He was trembling so that his jowls shook. He'd waited on the shore in dire fear and anguish for centuries, milling about, fretting as to the ultimate nature of his fate.

"Payment," said Charon.

The man tilted his head back and opened his mouth. A round shiny object lay beneath his tongue. The boatman reached out and took the gold coin, putting it in the pocket of his cloak. "Next," called Charon as the man moved past him and took a seat on the bench of skulls.

Hell's orange sun screamed in its death throes every evening, a pandemonium sweeping down from above that made even the demons sweat and set the master's three-headed dog to cowering. That horrendous din worked its way into the rocks, the river, the petrified trees, and everything brimmed with misery. Slowly, it diminished as the starless, moonless dark came on, devouring every last shred of light. With that infernal night came a cool breeze whose initial tantalizing relief never failed to deceive the damned, though they be residents for a thousand years, with a false promise of Hope. That growing wind carried in it a catalyst for memory, and set all who it caressed to recalling in vivid detail their lost lives — a torture individually tailored, more effective than fire.

Charon sat in his home, the skull of a fallen god, on the crest of a high flint hill, overlooking the river. Through the left eye socket glazed with transparent lies, he could be seen sitting at a table, a glutton's-fat tallow burning, its flame guttering in the night breeze let in through the gap of a missing tooth. Laid out before him was a curling width of tattooed flesh skinned from the back of an ancient explorer who'd no doubt sold his soul for a sip from the Fountain of Youth. In the boatman's right hand was a compass and in his left a writing quill. His gaze traced along the strange parchment the course of his own river, Acheron, the River of Pain, to where it crossed paths with Pyriphlegethon, the River of Fire. That burning course was eventually quelled in cataracts of steam where it emptied into and became the Lethe, River of Forgetting.

He traced his next day's journey with the quill tip, gliding it an inch above the meandering line of vein blue. There, in the meager width of that last river's depiction, almost directly halfway between its origin and end in the mournful Cocytus, was a freckle. Anyone else would have thought it no more than a bodily blemish inked over by chance in the production of the map, but Charon was certain after centuries of overhearing whispered snatches of conversation from his unlucky passengers that it represented the legendary island of Oondeshai.

He put down his quill and compass and sat back in the chair, closing his eyes. Hanging from the center of the cathedral cranium above, the wind chime made of dangling bat bones clacked as the mischievous breeze that invaded his home lifted one corner of the map. He sighed at the touch of cool wind as its insidious effect reeled his memory into the past.

One night, he couldn't recall how many centuries before, he was lying in bed on the verge of sleep, when there came a pounding at the hinged door carved in the left side of the skull. "Who's there?" he called in the fearsome voice he used to silence passengers. There was no verbal answer, but another barrage of banging ensued. He rolled out of bed, put on his cloak and lit a tallow. Taking the candle with him, he went to the door and flung it open. A startled figure stepped back into the darkness. Charon thrust the light forward and beheld a cowed, trembling man, his naked flesh covered in oozing sores and wounds.

"Who are you?" asked the boatman.

The man stared up at him, holding out a hand.

"You've escaped from the pit, haven't you?"

The back side of the flint hill atop which his home sat overlooked the enormous pit, its circumference at the top a hundred miles across. Spiraling along its inner wall was a path that led down and down in ever decreasing arcs through the various levels of Hell to end at a pinpoint in the very mind of the Master. Even at night, if Charon were to go behind the skull and peer out over the rim, he could see a faint reddish glow and hear the distant echo of plaintive wails.

The man finally nodded.

"Come in," said Charon, and held the door as the stranger shuffled past him.

Later, after he'd been offered a chair, a spare cloak, and a cup of nettle tea, his broken visitor began to come around.

"You know," said Charon, "there's no escape from Hell."

"This I know," mumbled the man, making a great effort to speak, as if he'd forgotten the skill. "But there is an escape in Hell."

"What are you talking about? The dog will be here within the hour to fetch you back. He's less than gentle."

"I need to make the river," said the man.

"What's your name?" asked Charon.

"Wieroot," said the man with a grimace.

The boatman nodded. "This escape in Hell, where is it, what is it?"

"Oondeshai," said Wieroot, "an island in the River Lethe."

"Where did you hear of it?"

"I created it," he said, holding his head with both hands as if to remember. "Centuries ago, I wrote it into the fabric of the mythology of Hell."

"Mythology?" asked Charon. "I suppose those wounds on your body are merely a myth?"

"The suffering's real here, don't I know it, but the entire construction of Hell is, of course, man's own invention. The Pit, the three-headed dog, the rivers, you, if I may say so, all sprang from the mind of humanity, confabulated to punish itself."

"Hell has been here from the beginning," said Charon.

"Yes," said Wieroot, "in one form or another. But when, in the living world, something is added to the legend, some detail to better convince believers or convert new ones, here it leaps into existence with a ready-made history that instantly spreads back to the start and a guaranteed future that creeps inexorably forward." The escapee fell into a fit of coughing, smoke from the fires of the pit issuing in small clouds from his lungs.

"The heat's made you mad," said Charon. "You've had too much time to think."

"Both may be true," croaked Wieroot, wincing in pain, "but listen for a moment more. You appear to be a man, yet I'll wager you don't remember your youth. Where were you born? How did you become the boatman?"

Charon strained his memory, searching for an image of his past in the world of the living. All he saw was rows and rows of heads, tilting back, proffering the coin beneath the tongue. An image of him setting out across the river, passing between the giant oaks, repeated behind his eyes three dozen times in rapid succession.

"Nothing there, am I correct?"

Charon stared hard at his guest.

"I was a cleric, and in copying a sacred text describing the environs of Hell, I deviated from the disintegrating original and added the existence of Oondeshai. Over the course of years, decades, centuries, other scholars found my creation and added it to their own works and so, now, Oondeshai, though not as well known as yourself or your river, is an actuality in this desperate land."

From down along the riverbank came the approaching sound of Cerberus baying. Wieroot stood, sloughing off the cloak to let it drop into his chair. "I've got to get to the river," he said. "But consider this. You live in the skull of a fallen god. This space was once filled with a substance that directed the universe, no, was the universe. How does a god die?"

"You'll never get across," said Charon.

"I don't want to. I want to be caught in its flow."

"You'll drown."

"Yes, I'll drown, be bitten by the spiny eels, burned in the River of Fire, but I won't die, for I'm already dead. Some time ages hence, my body will wash up on the shore of Oondeshai, and I will have arrived home. The way I crafted the island, the moment you reach its shores and pull yourself from the River of Forgetting, you instantly remember everything."

"It sounds like a child's tale," Charon murmured.

"Thank you," said the stranger.

"What gave you cause to create this island?" asked the boatman.

Wieroot staggered toward the door. As he opened it and stepped out into the pitch black, he called back, "I knew I would eventually commit murder."

Charon followed out into the night and heard the man's feet pacing away down the flint hill toward the river. Seconds later, he heard the wheezing breath of the three-headed dog. Growling, barking, sounded in triplicate. There was silence for a time, and then finally...a splash, and in that moment, for the merest instant, an image of a beautiful island flashed behind the boatman's eyes.

He'd nearly been able to forget the incident with Wieroot as the centuries flowed on, their own River of Pain, until one day he heard one of his passengers whisper the word "Oondeshai" to another. Three or four times this happened, and then, only a half century past, a young woman, still radiant though dead, with shiny black hair and a curious red dot of a birthmark just below her left eye, was ushered onto his boat. He requested payment. When she tilted her head back, opened her mouth and lifted her tongue, there was no coin but instead a small, tightly folded package of flesh. Charon nearly lost his temper as he retrieved it from her mouth, but she whispered quickly, "A map to Oondeshai."

These words were like a slap to his face. He froze for the merest instant, but then thought quickly, and, nodding, stepped aside for her to take a seat. "Next," he yelled and the demons were none the wiser. Later that night, he unfolded the crudely cut rectangle of skin, and after a close inspection of the tattoo cursed himself for having been duped. He swept the map onto the floor and the night breeze blew it into a corner. Weeks later, after finding it had been blown back out from under the table into the middle of the floor, he lifted it and searched it again. This time he noticed the freckle in the length of Lethe's blue line and wondered.

He kept his boat in a small lagoon hidden by a thicket of black poplars. It was just after sunrise, and he'd already stowed his provisions in the hold below deck. After lashing them fast with lengths of hangman's rope cast off over the years by certain passengers, he turned around to face the chaotically beating heart of the craft. The large blood organ, having once resided in the chest of the Queen of Sirens, was suspended in the center of the hold by thick branch-like veins and arteries that grew into the sides of the boat. Its vasculature expanded and contracted, and the heart itself beat erratically, undulating and shivering, sweating red droplets.

Charon waited until after it died, lay still, and then was startled back to life by whatever immortal force pervaded it chambers. Once it was moving again, he gave a high-pitched whistle, a note that began at the bottom of the register and quickly rose to the top. At the sound of this signal, the wet red meat of the thing parted in a slit to reveal an eye. The orb swiveled to and fro, and the boatman stepped up close with a burning tallow in one hand and the map, opened, in the other. He back-lit the scrap of skin to let the eye read its tattoo. He'd circled the freckle that represented Oondeshai with his quill, so the destination was clearly marked. All he'd have to do is steer around the dangers, keep the keel in deep water and stay awake. Otherwise, the craft now knew the way to go.

Up on deck, he cast off the ropes, and instead of uttering the word "There," he spoke a command used less than once a century — "Away." The boat moved out of the lagoon and onto the river. Charon felt something close to joy at not having to steer between the giant white oaks. He glanced up to his left at the top of the flint hill and saw the huge skull, staring down at him. The day was hot and orange and all of Hell was busy at the work of suffering, but he, the boatman, was off on a holiday.

On the voyage out, he traveled with the flow of the river, so its current combined with the inherent, enchanted propulsion of the boat made for swift passage. There were the usual whirlpools, outcroppings of sulfur and brimstone to avoid, but these occasional obstacles were a welcome diversion. He'd never taken this route before when on holiday. Usually, he'd just stay home, resting, making minor repairs to the boat, playing knucklebones with some of the bat-winged demons from the pit on a brief break from the grueling work of torture.

Once, as a guest of the master during a holiday, he'd been invited into the bottommost reaches of the pit, transported in a winged chariot that glided down through the center of the great spiral. There, where the Czar of the Underworld kept a private palace made of frozen sighs, in a land of snow so cold one's breath fractured upon touching the air, he was led by an army of living marble statues, shaped like men but devoid of faces, down a tunnel that led to an enormous circle of clear ice. Through this transparent barrier he could look out on the realm of the living. Six days he spent transfixed between astonishment and fear at the sight of the world the way it was. That vacation left a splinter of ice in his heart that took three centuries to melt.

None of his previous getaways ever resulted in a tenth the sense of relief he already felt having gone but a few miles along the nautical route to Oondeshai. He repeated the name of the island again and again under his breath as he worked the tiller or manned the shallows pole, hoping to catch another glimpse of its image as he had the night Wieroot dove into the Acheron. As always, that mental picture refused to coalesce, but he'd learned to suffice with its absence, which had become a kind of solace in itself.

To avoid dangerous eddies and rocks in the middle flow of the river, Charon was occasionally forced to steer the boat in close to shore on the port side. There, he glimpsed the marvels of that remote, forgotten landscape — a distant string of smoldering volcanoes; a thundering herd of bloodless behemoths, sweeping like a white wave across the immensity of a fissured salt flat; a glittering forest of crystal trees alive with long-tailed monkeys made of lead. The distractions were many, but he struggled to put away his curiosity and concentrate for fear of running aground and ripping a hole in the hull.

He hoped to make the River of Fire before nightfall, so as to have light with which to navigate. To travel the Acheron blind would be sheer suicide, and unlike Wieroot, Charon was uncertain as to whether he was already dead or alive or merely a figment of Hell's imagination. There was the possibility of finding a natural harbor and dropping the anchor, but the land through which the river ran had shown him fierce and mysterious creatures stalking him along the banks and that made steering through the dark seem the fairer alternative.

As the day waned, and the sun began to whine with the pain of its gradual death, Charon peered ahead with a hand shading his sight in anticipation of a glimpse at the flames of Pyriphlegethon. During his visit to the palace of frozen sighs, the master had let slip that the liquid fire of those waters burned only sinners. Because the boat was a tool of Hell, made of Hell, he was fairly certain it could withstand the flames, but he wasn't sure if at some point in his distant past he had not sinned. If he were to blunder into suffering, though, he thought that he at least would learn some truth about himself.

In the last moments of light, he lit three candles and positioned them at the prow of the boat. They proved ineffectual against the night, casting their glow only a shallow pole-length ahead of the craft. Their glare wearied Charon's eyes and he grew fatigued. To distract himself from fatigue, he went below and brought back a dried, salted Harpy leg to chew on. In recent centuries the winged creatures had grown scrawny, almost thin enough to slip his snares. The meat was known to improve eyesight and exacerbate the mind. Its effect had nothing to do with clarity, merely a kind of agitation of thought that was, at this juncture, preferable to slumber. Sleep was the special benefit of the working class of Hell, and the boatman usually relished it. Dreams especially were an exotic escape from the routine of work. The sinners never slept, nor did the master.

Precisely at the center of the night Charon felt some urge, some pull of intuition to push the tiller hard to the left. As soon as he'd made the reckless maneuver, he heard from up ahead the loud gulping sound that meant a whirlpool lay in his path. The sound grew quickly to a deafening strength, and only when he was upon the swirling monster, riding its very lip around the right arc, was he able to see its immensity. The boat struggled to free itself from the draw, and instead of being propelled by its magic it seemed to be clawing its way forward, dragging its weight free of the hopeless descent. There was nothing he could do but hold the tiller firm and stare with widened eyes down the long, treacherous tunnel. Not a moment passed after he was finally free of it than the boat entered the turbulent waters where Acheron crossed the River of Fire.

He released his grip on the tiller and let the craft lead him with its knowledge of the map he'd shown it. His fingers gripped tightly into the eye holes of two of the skulls that formed his seat, and he held on so as not to be thrown overboard. Pyriphlegethon now blazed ahead of him, and the sight of its dancing flames, some flaring high into the night, made him scream, not with fear but exhilaration. The boat forged forward, cleaved the burning surface, and then was engulfed in a yellow-orange brightness that gave no heat. The frantic illumination dazed Charon, and he sat as in a trance, dreaming wide awake. He no longer felt the passage of Time, the urgency to reach his destination, the weight of all those things he'd fled on his holiday.

Eventually, after a prolonged bright trance, the blazing waters became turbulent, lost their fire, and a thick mist rose off them. That mist quickly became a fog so thick it seemed to have texture, brushing against his skin like a feather. He thought he might grab handfuls until it slipped through his fingers, leaked into his nostrils, and wrapped its tentacles around his memory.

When the boatman awoke to the daily birth cry of Hell's sun, he found himself lying naked upon his bed, staring up at the clutch of bat bones dangling from the cranial center of his skull home. He was startled at first, grasping awkwardly for a tiller that wasn't there, tightening his fist around the shaft of the absent shallows stick that instead rested at an angle against the doorway. As soon as the shock of discovery that he was home had abated, he sighed deeply and sat up on the edge of the bed. It struck him then that his entire journey, his holiday, had been for naught.

He frantically searched his thoughts for the slightest shred of a memory that he might have reached Oondeshai, but every trace had been forgotten. For the first time in centuries, tears came to his eyes, and the frustration of his predicament made him cry out. Eventually, he stood and found his cloak rolled into a ball on the floor at the foot of his bed. He dressed and without stopping to put on his boots or grab the shallows pole, he left his home.

With determination in his stride, he mounted the small rise that lay back behind the skull and stood at the rim of the enormous pit. Inching to the very edge, he peered down into the spiraled depths at the faint red glow. The screams of tortured sinners, the wailing laments of self-pity, sounded in his ears like distant voices in a dream. Beneath it all he could barely discern, like the buzzing of a fly, the sound of the master laughing uproariously, joyously, and that discordant strain seemed to lace itself subtly into everything.

Charon's anger and frustration slowly melted into a kind of numbness as cold as the hallways of Satan's palace, and he swayed to and fro, out over the edge and back, not so much wanting to jump as waiting to fall. Time passed, he was not aware how much, and then as suddenly as he had dressed and left his home, he turned away from the pit.

Once more inside the skull, he prepared to go to work. There was a great heaviness within him, as if his very organs were now made of lead, and each step was an effort, each exhalation a sigh. He found his eelskin ankle boots beneath the table at which he'd studied the flesh map at night. Upon lifting one, it turned in his hand, and a steady stream of blonde sand poured out onto the floor. The sight of it caught him off guard and for a moment he stopped breathing.

He fell to his knees to inspect the little pile that had formed. Carefully, he lifted the other boot, turned it over and emptied that one into its own neat little pile next to the other. He reached toward these twin wonders, initially wanting to feel the grains run through his fingers, but their stark proof that he had been to Oondeshai and could not recall a moment of it ultimately defeated his will and he never touched them. Instead, he stood, took up the shallows pole, and left the skull for his boat.

As he guided the boat between the two giant oaks, he no longer wondered if all his journeys across the Acheron were always the same journey. With a dull aspect, he performed his duties as the boatman. His muscles, educated in the task over countless centuries, knew exactly how to avoid the blue serpent and skirt the whirlpools without need of a single thought. No doubt it was these same unconscious processes that had brought Charon and his craft back safely from Oondeshai.

Gesnil and Trinkthil inquired with great anticipation about his vacation when he met them on the far shore. For the demons, who knew no respite from the drudgery of herding sinners, even a few words about a holiday away would have been like some rare confection, but he told them nothing. From the look on Charon's face, they knew not to prod him and merely sent the travelers forward to offer coins and take their places on the benches.

During the return trip that morning, a large fellow sitting among the passengers had a last-second attack of nerves in the face of an impending eternity of suffering. He screamed incoherently, and Charon ordered him to silence. When the man stood up and began pacing back and forth, the boatman ordered him to return to his seat. The man persisted moving about, his body jerking with spasms of fear, and it was obvious his antics were spooking the other sinners. Fearing the man would spread mutiny, Charon came forth with the shallows stick and bringing it around like a club, split the poor fellow's head. That was usually all the incentive a recalcitrant passenger needed to return to the bench, but this one was now insane with the horror of his plight.

The boatman waded in and beat him wildly, striking him again and again. With each blow, Charon felt some infinitesimal measure of relief from his own frustration. When he was finished, the agitator lay in a heap on deck, nothing more than a flesh bag full of broken bones, and the other passengers shuffled their feet sideways so as not to touch his corpse.

Only later, after he had docked his boat in the lagoon and the winged demons had flown out of the pit to lead the damned up the flint hill and down along the spiral path to their eternal destinies, did the boatman regret his rage. As he lifted the sac of flesh that had been his charge and dumped it like a bale of chum over the side, he realized that the man's hysteria had been one and the same thing as his own frustration.

The sun sounded its death cry as it sank into a pool of blood that was the horizon and then Hell's twilight came on. Charon dragged himself up the hill and went inside his home. Before pure night closed its fist on the riverbank, he kicked off his boots, gnawed on a haunch of Harpy flesh, and lit the tallow that sat in its holder on the table. Taking his seat there he stared into the flame, thinking of it as the future that constantly drew him forward through years, decades, centuries, eons, as the past disappeared behind him. "I am nothing but a moment," he said aloud and his words echoed around the empty skull.

Some time later, still sitting at his chair at the table, he noticed the candle flame twitch. His eyes shifted for the first time in hours to follow its movement. Then the fire began to dance, the sheets of flesh parchment lifted slightly at their corners, the bat bones clacked quietly overhead. Hell's deceptive wind of memory had begun to blow. He heard it whistling in through the space in his home's grin, felt its coolness sweep around him. This most complex and exquisite torture that brought back to sinners the times of their lives now worked on the boatman. He moved his bare feet beneath the table and realized the piles of sand lay beneath them.

The image began in his mind no more than a dot of blue and then rapidly unfolded in every direction to reveal a sky and crystal water. The sun there in Oondeshai had been yellow and it gave true warmth. This he remembered clearly. He'd sat high on a hill of blond sand, staring out across the endless vista of sparkling water. Next to him on the left was Wieroot, legs crossed, dressed in a black robe and sporting a beard to hide the healing scars that riddled his face. On the right was the young woman with the shining black hair and the red dot of a birthmark beneath her left eye.

"...And you created this all by writing it in the other world?" asked Charon. There was a breeze blowing and the boatman felt a certain lightness inside as if he'd eaten of one of the white clouds floating across the sky.

"I'll tell you a secret," said Wieroot, "although it's a shame you'll never get a chance to put it to use."

"Tell me," said the boatman.

"God made the world with words," he said in a whisper.

Charon remembered that he didn't understand. He furrowed his brow and turned to look at the young woman to see if she was laughing. Instead she was also nodding along with Wieroot. She put her hand on the boatman's shoulder and said, "And man made God with words."

Charon's memory of the beach on Oondeshai suddenly gave violent birth to another memory from his holiday. He was sitting in a small structure with no door, facing out into a night scene of tall trees whose leaves were blowing in a strong wind. Although it was night, it was not the utter darkness he knew from his quadrant of Hell. High in the black sky there shone a bright disk, which cast its beams down onto the island. Their glow had seeped into the small home behind him and fell upon the forms of Wieroot and the woman, Shara was her name, where they slept upon a bed of reeds. Beneath the sound of the wind, the calls of night birds, the whirr of insects, he heard the steady breathing of the sleeping couple.

And one last memory followed. Charon recalled Wieroot drawing near to him as he was about to board his boat for the return journey.

"You told me you committed murder," said the boatman.

"I did," said Wieroot.

"Who?"

"The god whose skull you live in," came the words which grew faint and then disappeared as the night wind of Hell ceased blowing. The memories faded and Charon looked up to see the candle flame again at rest. He reached across the table and drew his writing quill and a sheaf of parchment toward him. Dipping the pen nib into the pot of blood that was his ink, he scratched out two words at the top of the page. My Story, he wrote, and then set about remembering the future. The words came, slowly at first, reluctantly, dragging their imagery behind them, but after a short while their numbers grew to equal the number of sinners awaiting a journey to the distant shore. He ferried them methodically, expertly, from his mind to the page, scratching away long into the dark night of Hell until down at the bottom of the spiral pit, in his palace of frozen sighs, Satan suddenly stopped laughing.

The Language of Moths
Christopher Barzak

Christopher Barzak was born in rural Ohio, and lived in California and Michigan before returning to Ohio, where he completed a Master's Degree in English at Youngstown State University. He has had short fiction published in Trampoline, Lady Churchill's Rosebud Wristlet, Nerve, Rabid Transit, Realms of Fantasy, The Year's Best Fantasy and Horror, *and* The Mammoth Book of Best New Horror. *He has finished a first novel,* One for Sorrow, *and is working on a second set in Japan. He was awarded The Speculative Literature Foundation's Travel Grant for Writers and is currently living and working near Tokyo, Japan.*

1. Swallowing Bubbles

The four of them had been traveling for what seemed like forever, the two in the front seat rattling maps like they did newspapers on Sunday mornings. They rode in the wagon, her favorite car, the one with the wood paneling on its doors. The wagon wound through the twisty backroads of the mountains, leaving behind it clouds of dust through which sunlight passed, making the air shimmer like liquid gold. The girl wanted the wagon to stop so she could jump out and run through the golden light behind her. She climbed halfway over the back seat and pushed her face against the rear window, trying to get a better look.

The little old man beside her shouted, "No! No! No! Sit down, you're slobbering all over the glass. Sit down this instant!" He grabbed her around her waist and pulled her back into a sitting position. He pulled a strap across her chest, locking it with a decisive click. The little old man narrowed his eyes; he waved a finger in the girl's face. He said things at her. But as his words left his lips, they became bubbles. Large silver bubbles that shimmied and wobbled in the air. The bubbles filled the car in mere moments. So many words all at once! The girl laughed delightedly. She popped some of the bubbles between her fingers. Others she plucked from the air and swallowed like grapes. She let them sit sweetly on her tongue for a while, before taking them all the way in for good. When the bubbles reached her stomach, they burst into music. The sound of them echoed through her body, reverberating. She rang like a bell. One day, when she swallowed enough bubbles, she might understand what the little old man beside her was saying. All of the time, not just now and then. Maybe she'd even be able to say things back to him. She wondered if her own words would taste as sweet. Like honey, maybe. Or like flowers.

2. *Being Selfish*

Eliot is watching his mother hang bed sheets from a cord of clothesline she's tied off at two walls facing opposite of each other in their cabin. "To give us all a sense of personal space," she explains. Eliot tells his mother that this cabin is so small, hanging up bed sheets to section off rooms is a futile activity. "Where did you learn that word," his mother asks. "Futile. Who taught you that?"

"At school," Eliot says, paging through an *X-Men* comic book, not bothering to look up.

His mother makes a face that looks impressed. "Maybe public school isn't so bad after all," she says. "Your father was right, as usual."

Eliot doesn't know if his father is right, or even if his father is usually right, as his mother seems to imagine. After all, here they are in the Allegheny Mountains, in Pennsylvania, for God's sake, hundreds of miles away from home. Away from Boston. And for what? For a figment of his father's imagination. For a so-called undiscovered moth his father claims to have seen when he was Eliot's age, fourteen, camping right here in this very cabin. Eliot doesn't believe his father could remember anything that far back, and even if he could, his memory of the event could be completely fictional at this point, an indulgence in nostalgia for a time when his life still seemed open in all directions, flat as a map, unexplored and waiting for him.

Eliot's father is an entomologist. His specialty is lepidoptera, moths and butterflies and what Eliot thinks of as creepy-crawlies, things that spin cocoons around themselves when they're unhappy with their present circumstances and wait inside their shells until either they've changed or the world has, before coming out. Eliot's father is forty-three years old, a once-celebrated researcher on the mating habits of moths found in the Appalachian Mountains. He is also a liar. He lied to his grant committee at the college, telling them in his proposal that he required the funds for this expedition to research the habits of a certain species of moth with which they were all familiar. He didn't mention his undiscovered moth, the one that glowed orange and pink, as he once told Eliot during a reverie, with his eyes looking at something unimaginably distant while he spoke of it. Maybe, Eliot thinks, an absurd adventure like this one is a scientist's version of a mid-life crisis. Instead of chasing after other women, Eliot's father is chasing after a moth that, let's face it, he probably imagined.

"There now, isn't that better?" Eliot's mother stands in the center of the cabin, which she has finished sectioning into four rooms. The cabin is a perfect square with clothesline bisecting the center in both directions, like a plus sign. Eliot owns one corner, and Dawn, his sister, has the one next to his: That makes up one half of the cabin. The other half has been divided into the kitchen and his parents' space. The sheet separating Eliot's corner from his sister's is patterned with blue flowers and tiny teacups. These sheets are Dawn's favorites, and secretly, Eliot's too.

Eliot's mother glances around, smiling vaguely, wiping sweat off of her brow. She's obviously happy with her achievement. After all, she's an academic, a philosopher, unaccustomed to cleaning house and rigging up clotheslines and bed linen. The maid back in Boston—back home, Eliot thinks—Marcy, she helps around the house with domestic things like that. Usually Eliot's mother uses her mind to speculate on how the mind works; not just her own mind—but *the* mind—the idea of what a mind is. Now she finds herself using her mental prowess to tidy up a ramshackle cabin. Who would have guessed she'd be so capable? So *practical*? Not Eliot. Certainly not herself.

The door to the cabin swings open, flooding the room with bright sunlight that makes Eliot squint. He shields his eyes with one hand, like an officer saluting, to witness the shadowy figure of his father's body filling the doorframe, and his sister Dawn trailing behind.

Dawn is more excited than usual, which has made this trip something less than a vacation. For Eliot's father, Dr. Carroll, it was never a vacation; that was a well-known fact. For Dr. Carroll, this was an expedition, possibly his last chance to inscribe his name in History. But the rest of the family was supposed to "take things easy and enjoy themselves." When Dr. Carroll said that, Eliot had snorted. Dr. Carroll had placed his hands on his hips and glowered. "Why the attitude, Eliot?" he'd asked.

"Take it *easy*?" Eliot repeated in a squeaky-scratchy voice that never failed to surface when he most needed to appear justified and righteous. "How can you expect us to do that with Dawn around?"

Dr. Carroll had stalked away, not answering, which didn't surprise Eliot at all. For most of his life, this is what Eliot has seen whenever he questions his father: his father's back, walking away, leaving a room full of silence.

Dawn pushes past Dr. Carroll and runs over to Eliot's cot. She jumps on the mattress, which squeals on old coils, and throws her arms across the moth-eaten pink quilt. The quilt smells of mold and mildew and something a little like mothballs, as if it had been stored in a cedar chest for a long time. Dawn turns to Eliot, her wide blue eyes set in a face as white and smooth as porcelain, and smiles at him, her blonde hair fanning out on the pillow. Eliot considers her over the top of his comic book, pretending not to have noticed her.

Dawn is autistic. She's seventeen years old, three years older than Eliot. But when she's around, Eliot feels as if he's already an old man, forced into an early maturity, responsible for things no fourteen year old boy should have to think about. He blames this all on his parents, who often encourage him when he pays attention to Dawn, who often scold him when he wants something for himself. "Being selfish," is what his mother calls that, leaving Eliot dashed to pieces on the rocks of guilt. He feels guilty even now, trying to read the last page of his comic book instead of paying attention to Dawn.

"I'm leaving," Dr. Carroll announces. He's wearing khaki pants with pockets all over them, and a wide-brimmed hat with mosquito netting pulled down over his face. A backpack and sleeping bag are slung on his back. He lifts the mosquito netting and kisses Eliot's mother on her cheek and calls her Dr. Carroll affectionately, then looks at Eliot and says, "You take care of Dawn while I'm away, Eliot. Stay out of trouble."

He walks outside, and all of them—Eliot, Dawn and their mother—move to the doorway. As if magnetized by Dr. Carroll's absence, they try to fill the space he's left. They watch him become smaller and smaller, a shadow, until he reaches the trail that will take him farther into the graying mountains, where his moth awaits.

"Good luck," Eliot's mother whispers, waving goodbye to his back, his nets and pockets. She closes her eyes and says, "Please," to something she cannot name, even though she no longer believes in higher powers, ghosts or gods of any sort.

3. First Words

It was strange for the girl in this place; she hadn't been prepared for it. Suddenly the wagon had come to a stop and they all spilled out. The mother and the father, they seemed so excited. They smiled so hard, their faces split in half. The little old man kept scowling; he was so funny. She patted him on his shoulder and he opened his mouth to make room for one huge silver bubble to escape. She grabbed hold of its silky surface and almost left the ground as it floated upwards, towards the clouds. But it popped, and she rocked back on her heels, laughing. When the bubble popped, it shouted, "Get off!"

The father left soon after. The girl was a little frightened at first. Like maybe the father would never come back? Did the father still love her? These thoughts frightened her more than anything else. But then she watched the little old man chop wood for the fire, his skinny arms struggling each time he lifted the axe above his head, which made her laugh, sweeping the fear out of her like the mother sweeping dirt off the front porch. Swish! Goodbye, fear! Good riddance! She forgot the father because the little old man made her laugh so much.

There were so many trees here, the girl thought she'd break her neck from tilting her head back to see their swaying tops. Also, strange sounds burrowed into her skin, and she shivered a lot. Birds singing, crickets creeking. This little thing no bigger than the nail of her pinky—it had transparent wings and hovered by her ear, buzzing a nasty song. She swatted at it, but it kept returning. It followed her wherever she went. Finally the mother saw it and squashed it in a Kleenex. But as it died, it told the girl, "You've made a horrible mistake. I am not the enemy." Then it coughed, sputtered, and was dead.

The girl thought of the wagon. It was still one of her favorite things in the world. But now she was thinking she wasn't so sure. Maybe there were other things just as special as riding in the wagon with the mother, the father and the little old man. She wished the mother wouldn't have killed the winged creature so quick. She wanted it to tell her more things, but now it was dead and its last words still rang in her ears. When the winged creature spoke, no bubbles came out of its mouth. Words, pure and clear, like cold water, filled her up. The winged creature had more words for her, she just knew it. She knew this without knowing why, and she didn't care. She only cared that the bubbles didn't come between her and the words when the creature spoke to her. One drink of that and she wanted more.

4. *The Scream*

Before Eliot's father left, he placed him in charge of Dawn, and his mother seems more than willing to follow her husband's orders to the letter, leaving Eliot to look after Dawn while she sits on the front porch of the cabin, or in the kitchen, and writes. Eliot finds his mother's loyalty to his father's declarations an annoying trait, as if she had no say-so about anything when it comes to her children; she simply goes along with whatever his father says. He's watched Dawn every day since his father left, which has been for an entire week. He's taken her on the trails that are clearly marked; they've stared into the shallow depths of a creek where the water was as dark as tea, where red and blue crayfish skittered for cover under rocks. He's introduced Dawn to grasshoppers, which she loved immediately and, to Eliot's amazement, coaxed into a perfect line, making them leap in time together, like figure skaters. He was proud of Dawn for that, and could tell she was too; she looked up at him after the synchronized leap went off without a hitch and clapped her hands for a full minute.

Each day they pick wildflowers together, which, when they return in the late afternoons, hang tattered and limp in Dawn's grip. Still, their mother takes them from Dawn gratefully when they're offered. "Oh, they're beautiful," she says, and puts the ragged daisies and buttercups in empty Coke bottles, filling the cabin with their bittersweet scent.

Eliot never gives his mother flowers. He leaves that pleasure for Dawn. And anyway, he knows something Dawn doesn't: his mother doesn't even like flowers, and Dr. Carroll doesn't even give them to her for Valentine's day or for their wedding anniversary. Eliot has to admit that his mother's graciousness in the face of receiving a gift she doesn't like is a mark of her tact and love for Dawn. He couldn't ever be so nice. He watches his mother and Dawn find "just the right place" for the flowers and thinks, I am a bad person. He thinks this because he's imagined himself far away, not from his present location in the mountains, but far away from his family itself. He's imagined himself in a place of his own, with furniture and a TV set and his own books. In none of these fantasies does his mother or father appear, except for the occasional phone call. He never misses them and he wonders if this means he's a wrong person somehow. Shouldn't children love their parents enough to call every once in a while? Apparently in these fantasies, parents aren't that important.

Dawn isn't a part of these fantasies either. Eliot doesn't even imagine phone calls from her because, really, what would be the use? At most, Dawn might latch onto a phrase and ask him it over and over. She might say, like she once did at his twelfth birthday party, "How old is your cat?" sending all of his friends into fits of laughter.

Eliot doesn't have a cat.

Eliot's mother has begun a new essay, and during the day, she spends her time reading essays and books written by other philosophers and scientists who she thinks has something to say on the subject she's considering. "This one," she tells Eliot one morning, "will be a feminist revision of *Walden*. I think it has great potential."

She's packed her Thoreau, Eliot realizes, irritation suddenly tingling at the base of his neck. He's beginning to suspect that, this summer, he has become the victim of a conspiracy got up by his parents, a conspiracy that will leave him the sole caretaker of Dawn. Within the frame of a few seconds he's turned red and his skin has started to itch. He's close to yelling at his mother. He wants to accuse her of this conspiracy, to call her out, so to speak. To scold her for being selfish. I could do that, he thinks. Scold his parents. He's done it before and he'll do it again. He finds nothing wrong with that; sometimes they deserve to be reprimanded. Why does everyone think that because someone gives birth to you and is older, they inherently deserve your respect? Eliot decided a long time ago that he wouldn't respect his parents unless they respected him. Sometimes this becomes a problem.

Before he unleashes his penned-up tensions, though, his mother stops scribbling and lifts her face from her notebook. She smiles at Eliot and says, "Why don't you go into that village we passed on the way in and make some friends? You've been doing so well with your sister, You deserve a break."

She gives Eliot ten dollars from her purse, which he crumples into a wad in his front pocket. She's releasing him for the day, and though he's still fuming over the conspiracy, he runs at this window of chance. He grabs his bike and trots with it at his side for a minute, before leaping onto its sun-warmed seat. Then he peddles away, down the mountain.

When he thinks he's far enough away, Eliot screams at the top of his lungs, an indecipherable noise that echoes and echoes in this silent, wooded place. The scream hangs over the mountainside like a cloud of black smoke, a stain on the clear sky, following Eliot for the rest of the day. Like some homeless mutt he's been nice to without thinking about the consequences, the scream will follow him forever now, seeking more affection, wanting to be a permanent part of his life.

5. The Butterfly's Question

The girl found the butterflies by accident. They were swarming in a small green field splashed yellow and white and orange from their wings. She ran out to meet them, stretched out her fingertips to touch them, and they flitted onto her arms, dusted her face with pollen, kissed her forehead and said,

"Child, where have you been?"

The butterfly that spoke to her was large, and its wings were a burnt orange color, spider-webbed with black veins. It floated unsteadily in front of her face, cocking its head back and forth as if examining her. No silver bubbles came out of its mouth when it spoke, just like the first winged creature, just like the grasshoppers who performed their leaps, their little tricks just for her pleasure.

"Well?" The butterfly circled her head once.

"I don't know," Dawn said. "It's hard to explain. But there are these people. They take care of me really nice."

"I would expect nothing less," said the butterfly, coming to rest on the back of her wrist. It stayed there for a while, its wings moving back and forth slowly, fanning itself. Finally, it crawled up the length of the girl's arm and came to rest on her shoulder. It whispered in her ear, "Why now? Why have they brought you too us now, so late in your life?"

The girl didn't know how to answer the butterfly. She simply looked down at her bare feet in the high grass and shrugged. "I don't know," she told the butterfly, and nearly started crying. But the butterfly brushed her cheek with its wings and said, "No, no. Don't cry, my love. Everything in its own time. Everything in its own time. Now isn't that right?"

6. *Centipede*

When Eliot rode into the village his first thought was: What a dump. When they passed through it a week ago, they had driven through without stopping, and he figured his father must have been speeding because he hadn't noticed how sad this so-called village is. It has one miserable main street running through the center, a general store called Mac's, a gas station that serves ice cream inside, and a bar called Murdock's Place. Other than that, the rest of the town is made up of family cemeteries and ramshackle farms. The Amish have a community just a few miles out of town, and the occasional horse-drawn buggy *clop-clops* it way down the main street, carrying inside its bonnet girls wearing dark blue dresses and men with bushy beards and straw hats.

Inside Mac's general store, Eliot is playing *Centipede*, an incredibly archaic arcade game from the 1980s. He has to play the game with an old trackball, which is virtually extinct in the arcade world, and it only has one button to push for laser beam attacks. Ridiculous, thinks Eliot. Uncivilized. This is the end of the world, he thinks, imagining the world to be flat, like the first explorers described it, where, in the furthest outposts of undiscovered country, the natives play *Centipede* and sell ice cream in gas stations, traveling from home to school in horse-drawn buggies. He misses his computer in Boston, which offers far more sophisticated diversions. Games where you actually have to think, he thinks.

The front screen door to Mac's squeals open then bangs shut. Mac, the man behind the counter with the brown wart on his nose and the receding hairline, couldn't have oiled the hinges for ages. Probably not since the place was first built. Eliot looks over his shoulder to catch a glimpse of the tall town boy who just entered, standing at the front counter, talking to Mac. He's pale as milk in the gloom of Mac's dusty store, and his hair looks almost colorless. More like fiber optics than hair, Eliot thinks, clear as plastic filaments. Mac calls the boy Roy, and rings up a tin of chewing tobacco on the cash register. Another piece of pre-history, Eliot thinks. This place doesn't even have price scanners, which have been around for how long? Like more than twenty years at least.

Eliot turns back to his game to find he's been killed because of his carelessness. That's okay, though, because he still has one life left to lose and, anyway, he doesn't have to feel like a failure because the game is so absurd that he doesn't even care anymore. He starts playing again anyway, spinning the trackball in its orbit, but suddenly he feels someone breathing on the back of his neck. He stops moving the trackball. He looks over his shoulder to find Roy standing behind him.

"Watch out!" Roy says, pointing a grease-stained finger at the video screen. Eliot turns back and saves himself by the skin of his teeth. "You almost bought it there," says Roy in a congratulatory manner, as if Eliot has passed some sort of manhood rite in which near-death experiences are a standard. Roy sends a stream of brown spit splashing against the back corner of the arcade game, and Eliot grins without knowing why. He's thinking this kid Roy is a real loser, trashy and yet somehow brave to spit on Mac's property when Mac is only a few steps away. Guys like this are enigmas to Eliot. They frighten him, piss him off for how easy-going they act, fire his imagination in ways that embarrass him. He abhors them; he wants to be more like them; he wants them to want to be more like him; he wants them to tell him they want to be more like him, so he can admit to his own desire for aspects of their own personalities. Shit, he thinks. What the hell is wrong with me? Why do I think these things?

After another minute, Eliot crashes yet another life, and the arcade game bleeps wearily, asking for another quarter for another chance. Eliot turns to Roy and asks, "You want a turn?"

Up close, he can see Roy's eyes are green, and his hair is brown, not colorless. In fact, Eliot decides, in the right light, Roy's hair may even be auburn, reddish-brown, like leaves in autumn.

Roy gives Eliot this dirty grin that makes him appear like he's onto Eliot about something. His lips curl back from his teeth. His nostrils flare, then retract. He's caught the scent of something. "No," he tells Eliot, still grinning. "Why don't we do something else instead?"

Eliot is already nodding. He doesn't know what he's agreed to, but he's willing to sign on the dotted line without reading the small print. It doesn't matter, he's thinking. He's only wondering what Roy's hair will look like outside, out of the dark of Mac's store, out in the sunlight.

7. Do You Understand Me?

The mother came out of nowhere, and the girl looked frantically around the field for a place to hide, as if she'd been caught doing something bad, or was naked, like that man and woman in the garden with the snake. Sometimes, the grandma who babysitted for the mother and the father would tell the girl that story and say, "Dear, you are wiser than all of us. You did not bite that apple." The grandma would pet the girl's hair, as if she were a dog or a cat.

The mother said, "Dawn! What are you doing so far away? I've been looking for you everywhere! You know you're not supposed to wander." The mother was suddenly upon the girl then, and she grabbed hold of her wrist, tight. "Come on," said the mother. "Let's go back to the cabin. I've got work to do. You can't run off like this. Do you understand me? Dawn! Understand?"

The mother and father were always talking about work. The girl didn't know what work was, but she thought it was probably something like when she had to go to the special school, where the Mrs. Albert made her say, "B is for book, B. B is for bat, B. B is for butterfly, B. Buh, buh, buh." It was a little annoying. But the girl was given a piece of candy each time she repeated the Mrs. Albert correctly. The candy made the buh, buh, buhs worth saying.

The mother tugged on the girl's wrist and they left the field together. The girl struggled against her mother's grip, but could not break it. Behind her, the butterflies all waved their wings goodbye, winking in the high grass and yellow-white flowers like stars in the sky at night. The girl waved back with her free hand, and the butterflies started to fly towards her, as if she'd issued them a command. They ushered the mother and girl out of their field, flapping behind the girl like a banner.

When they reached the cabin, the girl saw that the little old man was back again. Something was funny about him now, but it wasn't the kind of funny that usually made her laugh. Something was different. He didn't look so old anymore maybe, as if all the adulthood had drained out of his normally pinched-looking face. He didn't even scold her when she ran up to him and squealed at him, pointing out the difference to him, in case he hadn't noticed it himself. The little old man didn't seem to be bothered by anything now, not the girl, nor the mother. His eyes looked always somewhere else, far away, like the father's. Off in the distance. The mother asked the little old man, "How was your day?" and the little old man replied, "Great."

This was a shock for the girl. The little old man *never* sounded so happy. He went into the cabin to take a nap. The girl was curious, so she climbed onto the porch and peered through the window that looked down on the little old man's cot. He was lying on his back, arms crossed behind his head, staring at the ceiling. His face suddenly broke into a smile, and the girl cocked her head, wondering why he would ever do that. Then she realized: He'd found something like she had with the insects, and it made her happy for them both.

The little old man stopped staring at the ceiling. He stared at the girl, his eyes warning signals to keep her distance, but he didn't yell like he usually did. The girl nodded, then backed away from the window slowly. She didn't want to ruin his happiness.

8. Life in the Present Tense

Eliot and Roy are sitting in the rusted-out shell of a 1969 Corvette, once painted red, now rotted away to the browns of rust. The corvette rests in the back of a scrap metal junkyard on the edge of town, which Roy's uncle owns. His uncle closes the place down every afternoon at five o'clock sharp. Now it's nine o'clock at night, and the only light available comes from the moon, and from the orange glow on the cherry of Roy's cigarette.

Eliot is holding a fifth of Jim Beam whiskey in his right hand. The bottle is half empty. He lifts it to his lips and drinks. The whiskey slides down his throat, warm and bitter, and explodes in his stomach, heating his body, flushing his skin bright red. He and Roy started drinking over an hour ago, taking shots, daring each other to take another, then another, until they were both good and drunk. It's the first time for Eliot.

"We need to find something to do," Roy says, exhaling a plume of smoke. "Jeez, this'd be better if we'd at least have a radio or something."

"It's all right," Eliot says, trying to calm Roy down before he works himself up. He and Roy have been hanging out together relentlessly for the past few weeks. Here's one thing Eliot's discovered about Roy: He gets angry over little things fast. Things that aren't really problems. Like not having music in the junkyard while they drink. Roy's never satisfied with what's available. His mind constantly seeks out what could make each moment better than it is, rather than focusing on the moment itself. Roy lives in the future imperfect, Eliot's realized, while Eliot mainly lives in the present tense.

"I hate this town," Roy says, taking the bottle from Eliot. He sips some of the whiskey, then takes a fast and hard gulp. "Ahh," he hisses. He turns to Eliot and smiles, all teeth. His smile is almost perfect, except for one of his front teeth is pushed out a little further than the other, slightly crooked. But it suits him somehow, Eliot thinks.

"I don't know," Eliot shrugs. "I kind of like it here. It's better than being up on that stupid mountain with my parents. They're enough to drive you up a wall."

"Or to drink," says Roy, lifting the bottle again, and they both laugh.

"Yeah," Eliot says, smiling back at Roy. He leans back to rest his head against the seat and looks up through the rusted-out roof of the Corvette, where the stars pour through, reeling and circling above them, as though some invisible force is stirring them up. "It's not like this in Boston," Eliot says. "Most of the time you can't even see the stars because of the city lights."

"In Boston," Roy mimics, his voice whiney and filled with a slight sneer. "All you talk about is Boston. You know, Boston isn't everything. It's the not the only place in the world."

"I know," Eliot says. "I was just trying to say exactly that. You know, how

I can't see the stars there like I can here?"

"Oh," Roy says, and looks down into his lap.

Eliot pats him on the shoulder and tells him not to get all sad. "We're having fun," Eliot says. "Everything's great."

Roy agrees and then Eliot goes back to staring at the stars above them. The night air feels cold on his whiskey-warmed skin, and he closes his eyes for a moment to feel the slight breeze on his face. Then he suddenly feels hands cupping his cheeks, the skin rough and grainy, and when Eliot opens his eyes, Roy's face floats before him, serious and intent. Roy leans in and they're lips meet briefly. Something electric uncoils through Eliot's body, like a live wire, dangerous and intense. He feels as if all the gaps and cracks in his being are stretching out to the horizon, filling up with light.

"Are you all right?" Roy asks, and Eliot realizes that he's shaking.

"Yes," Eliot says, so softly and quietly that the word evaporates before it can be heard. He nods instead and, before they kiss again, Roy brushes his thumb over Eliot's cheek and says, "Don't worry. We're friends. It's nothing to worry about, right?"

Eliot can't help but begin worrying, though. He already knows some of the things that will come to pass because of this. He will contemplate suicide, he will contemplate murder, he will hate himself for more reasons than usual—not just because he doesn't want to be away from his family, but because he has turned out to be the sort of boy who kisses other boys, and who wants a son like that? Everything seems like a dream right now, though, so sudden, and maybe it is a dream, nothing more than that. Eliot is prepared to continue sleepwalking.

He nods to answer again, his voice no longer functioning properly. Then Roy presses close again, his breath thick with whiskey and smoke. His body above Eliot blocks out the light from the stars.

9. Sad Alone

In the woods at night, the girl danced to the songs of frogs throating, crickets chirring, wind snaking through leaves, the gurgle of the nearby creek. A happy marriage these sounds made, so the girl danced, surrounded by fireflies and moths.

She could still see the fire through the spaces between the trees, her family's campsite near the cabin, so she was safe. She wasn't doing anything wrong—she was following the rules—so the mother shouldn't come running to pull her back to the fire to sit with her and the father. He was back again, but he didn't seem to be there. Not *really* there, that is. He didn't look at the girl during dinner, only stared into the fire before him, slouching. He didn't open his mouth for any bubbles to come out.

Now that it was night, the little old man was back again. This had become a regular event. In the early evening, after dinner, the little old man would leave, promising to be back before sunset at nine-thirty, or else he'd spend the night with his new friend. This time, though, the little old man had come back with his new friend riding along on a bike beside him, saying, "This is Roy. He'll be spending the night."

The girl missed the little old man when he was gone now, but she didn't dwell on this too much. The little old man no longer glowered at her, no longer gripped her hand too tight like the mother did; he no longer looked angry all the time, so she forgave his absence. He was happy, the girl realized, and in realizing the little old man's happiness and the distance between them that went along with it, she realized her own happiness as well. She didn't miss him enough to be sad about his absence, unlike the father, who made the mother sad when he was gone, who made everyone miss him in a way that made them want to cry or shout in his face.

This moth, the girl thought, stopping her dance for the moment. If she could find this moth, the moth that the father was looking for, perhaps he would come back and be happy, and make the mother happy, and then everyone could be happy together, instead of sad alone. She smiled, proud of her idea, and turned to the fireflies and moths that surrounded her to ask the question:

"Can anyone help me?"

To which the insects all responded at once, their voices a chorus, asking, "What can we do? Are you all right? What? What?"

So the girl began to speak.

10. *Each in their Own Place*

Dr. Carroll is sitting by the campfire, staring at his two booted feet. Eliot's mother is saying, "This week it will happen. You can't get down on yourself. It's only been a month. You have the rest of the summer still. Don't worry."

Eliot's mother is cooking barbecued beans in a pot over the campfire. The flames lick at the bottom of the pan. Dr. Carroll shakes his head, looking distraught. There are new wrinkles in his forehead, and also around his mouth.

This has been a regular event over the past few weeks, Eliot's father returning briefly for supplies and rest, looking depressed and slightly damaged, growing older-looking before Eliot's eyes. Eliot feels bad for his father, but he'd also like to say, I told you so. That's just too mean, though, he's decided. The Old Eliot would have said that, the New Eliot won't.

The New Eliot is a recent change he's been experiencing, and it's because of Roy. Roy's changed him somehow without trying, and probably without even wanting to make Eliot into someone new in the first place. Eliot supposes this is what happens when you meet a person with whom you can truly communicate. The New Eliot will always try to be nice and not so world-weary. He will not say mean things to his parents or sister. He will love them and think about their needs, because his no longer seem so bad off.

Roy says, "Is it always like this?" He and Eliot are sitting on the swing in the cabin's front porch. The swing's chains squeal above their heads as they rock. This is Roy's first visit to the place. Eliot's tried to keep him away from his family, because even though he's made the choice to be nice, he's still embarrassed by them a little. Also, he'd rather have Roy to himself.

That's another thing that's come between them. It happened a couple of weeks back. Roy and Eliot had been hanging out together, getting into minor trouble. They'd spray-painted their names on an overpass; egged Roy's neighbor's car; toilet-papered the high school Roy attends; drank whiskey until they've puked. It's been a crazy summer, the best Eliot can remember really, and he doesn't want it to ever stop. Usually he goes to computer camp or just sits in front of the TV playing video games until school starts back up. Besides the vandalism and the drunken bouts, Eliot thinks he has fallen in love. Something like that. He and Roy have become like a couple, without using those words, without telling anyone else.

"My father's like Sisyphus," Eliot says, and Roy gives him this puzzled look.

"What did you say?"

"Sisyphus," Eliot repeats. "He was this guy from myth who was doomed by the gods to roll a rock up a mountain, but it keeps rolling back down when he gets to the top, so he has to roll it up again, over and over. Camus says it's the definition of the human condition, that myth. My mother teaches a class on it."

"Oh." Roy shakes his head. "Well, whatever."

That *whatever* is another thing that's come between them. Lately Roy says it whenever he doesn't understand Eliot, and doesn't care to try. It makes Eliot want to punch Roy right in the face. Eliot has taken to saying it as well, to see if it pisses off Roy as much, but whenever he says, "Whatever," Roy doesn't seem to give a damn. He just keeps on talking without noticing Eliot's attempts to make him angry.

The fireflies have come out for the evening, glowing on and off in the night mist. Crickets chirp, rubbing their legs together. An owl calls out its own name in the distance. Dawn is running between trees, her figure a silhouette briefly illuminated by the green glow of the fireflies, a shadow in the woods. Eliot still hasn't introduced her to Roy, and Roy hasn't asked why she acts so strangely, which makes Eliot think maybe he should explain before Roy says something mean about her, not understanding her condition. Dawn irritates Eliot, but he still doesn't want other people saying nasty things about her.

"She's autistic," Eliot says all of a sudden, pre-empting Roy's remarks. He pushes against the porch floorboards to make them swing faster, so Roy can't get off this ride too quick.

Roy doesn't seem shocked, though, or even interested in Dawn's erratic behavior. And why should he be? Eliot thinks. Roy himself has told Eliot much weirder things about his family. He told Eliot that first day, over an ice cream at the gas station, that he lived with his grandparents because his mother was an alcoholic, and his father was who-knows-where. That his mother would fight anyone in town, even Roy when she was drunk. That his grandfather was a member of the Ku Klux Klan, that he had found the white robes and the pointy hood in his grandfather's closet. That his grandmother used to sit him down at night before bed and read to him for a half an hour out of the Bible, and that afterwards she'd tell him he was born in sin, and should pray for forgiveness. It frightens Eliot a little, and makes him shiver, thinking of what it must be like to be Roy. He only hopes Roy's secret-sharing doesn't require an admission of his own private weirdnesses. He's not ready for that.

"Let's go inside," Roy says, putting his feet down flat on the porch. The swing suddenly comes to a halt. Roy stands and Eliot follows him into the cabin, already knowing what's going to happen. It's a vice of Roy's, fooling around in places where they might get caught.

We won't get caught here, Eliot thinks. His parents are outside by the heat of the fire, involved in their own problems. They won't bother to come inside the cabin now. Roy leads Eliot to the pink-quilted cot and they lay down together, and begin to kiss.

Roy's lips are larger than Eliot's. Eliot feels like his lips aren't big enough. They're too thin and soft, like rose petals. Roy, he thinks, would probably like his lips bigger and rougher, chapped even. He can feel the cracks in Roy's lips, can taste Roy's cigarettes. Roy's stubble scratches Eliot's cheeks in this way that makes him crazy. Then Roy is pulling off Eliot's shirt, kissing Eliot's stomach, unbuttoning Eliot's shorts. Eliot closes his eyes. He mouths the words, *Someone is in love with me.* He is in the habit of mouthing sentences silently when he wants what he is saying to be true.

He feels his shorts being tugged down, then his breath catches in his throat, and he is off, off, off. Far away, his parents argue and his sister runs through the wilderness like a woodland creature, a nymph. Each of them in their private spaces, like the sections his mother made of the cabin when they first arrived. Each of them in their own place.

11. *What the Firefly Said*

"So," said the firefly, "you're looking for a moth."

The girl nodded. "Yes," she said. "Actually, it's for my father. He's been searching for over a month."

"And what does it look like?" the firefly said, floating in front of her face. "You know, a moth is a moth is a moth. But that's just my opinion."

"This one glows," she said. "An orangey-pink. It has brown and gold streaks on its back, and also it only comes out at night."

"Hmm," said the firefly. "I see. Wait here a moment."

The firefly flew off. The girl watched it for a while, then lost it among the other greenish blips. She sighed, sat down on the ground beneath a pine tree, picking up a few needles covered in sticky sap.

"I'm back," said the firefly, and the girl looked up. It had brought a friend, and they both landed on her lap.

"I know who you're looking for," the other firefly said.

The girl felt a rush of excitement churl in her stomach. Her face flushed with heat. "Really?" she said. "Oh, please, you must help me find it."

"This moth, though," the firefly said, "it's a bit of a loner. There are a few of them I know of, but they don't even talk amongst themselves. I don't understand them. You know, we fireflies, we like to have a good time. We like to party." It chuckled softly and nudged its friend.

"I'll do anything," the girl said. "Please, if only it would make my father happier. He looks paler and thinner each time he comes back."

"Well," the firefly said. "Let me see what I can make happen. I have a lot of connections. We'll see what turns up."

"Thank you," said the girl, "Oh, thank you, thank you."

The fireflies both floated off. She sat under the tree for a while longer, thinking everything would be good now. Her whole family would be happy for once.

Then the mother and the father were calling her name, loud, over and over. She saw them coming towards her, running. The mother pulled her up from the ground and said, "I was so worried, so worried." The father grunted and led them back to the cabin, where the little old man and his new friend were sitting by the campfire.

"I can't do this anymore," said the mother. "I can't keep her in one place. She's always wandering off."

"Just a little longer," said the father. "I can't go back without it. I've been teaching the same classes to an endless stream of students. I can't go back without this."

The mother nodded and rubbed her temples. "I know," she said. "I know."

Then the little old man told his friend, "This is my sister. Her name is Dawn. She doesn't talk much."

The little old man's friend stared at her for a moment. His eyes grew wide; he smiled at her. The little old man's friend said, "Your sister's beautiful," as if he couldn't believe it himself.

12. *Your Sister's Beautiful*

Your sister's beautiful.
Your sister's beautiful.
Your sister's beautiful.

Lying on his cot, staring at the bare rafters of the cabin, imagining Roy hanging by his neck from one of the rafters, his face blue in death, Eliot cannot force Roy's words out of his mind. He's been hearing them over and over since Roy—stupid idiotic trashy no-good thoughtless bastard—said them three nights ago.

Your sister's beautiful.

And me? Eliot thinks. What about me? Why couldn't Roy have said the same thing about Eliot, with whom he's much more involved and supposedly loves enough to take to bed? Eliot is thinking, I should kill him. I should be like one of those people on talk shows, or in novels. I should commit a crime of passion that anyone could understand.

Outside somewhere, Roy is hanging out with Dawn. He's been with Eliot for over a month and never once cared to come up to the cabin until Eliot brought him himself. Now he's come up everyday since that first night, and Eliot has been ignoring him defiantly, walking away when Roy starts to speak, finding opportunities to make Roy feel stupid, talking to his mother about high-minded philosophical things in front of Roy. Even if Eliot himself doesn't understand some of the things that comes out of his mother's mouth, he's been around her long enough to pretend like he knows what he's talking about; he knows enough catch-phrases to get by. Whatever works, he's thinking, to make that jerk go away or feel sorry.

Eliot notices that everything is strangely quiet, both inside the cabin and out. He sits up in bed and looks out the window. The campfire is a pile of ashes, still glowing orange and red from last night. His mother is nowhere to be seen, and both Roy and Dawn aren't around either. His father, he thinks, is who-knows-where.

Eliot goes outside and looks around back of the cabin.

Nothing but weeds and a few scrub bushes and saplings grow here.

He walks to the edge of the woods, to where the trails begin, and starts to worry. Dawn. He hasn't been in a state of mind to watch her, and his mother has proved ineffectual at the task. He mouths the words, *My sister is safe and around that tree there, playing with a caterpillar,* and then he goes to check.

Dawn's not behind the tree, and there are no caterpillars in sight. Eliot suddenly clenches his teeth. He hears, somewhere close by, Roy's voice. He can't make out what Roy is saying, but he's talking to someone in that voice of his—the idiotic stupid no-good trashy bastard voice.

Eliot walks in the direction of the voice. He follows a trail until it narrows and dips down into a ravine. There's the creek where he and Dawn watched crayfish for hours. The way water moves, the way it sparkles under light, and reflects the things around it, the trees and Eliot's and Dawn's own faces, can entrance Dawn for hours. The creek holds the image of the world on its surface, the trees and clouds and a sun pinned like a jewel on its narrow, rippled neck. Beneath the creek, under the water, is another world, full of crayfish and snakes and fish no bigger than fingers. Eliot wonders if his mother has included something philosophical about the creek in her feminist revision of *Walden*. He wonders if she's noticed the same things that he notices.

Roy's voice fades, then reappears, like a trick or a prank, and soon Eliot sees him sitting under a tree with Dawn. Roy's talking to her real sweet. Eliot recognizes that voice. He's playing with Dawn's hand, which she keeps pulling away from him. Roy doesn't know Dawn hates to be touched. The only thing she can stand is a tight embrace, and then she won't ever let go. It's a symptom, her doctor has told the family, of her autism.

Now Roy is leaning into Dawn, trying to kiss her, and Dawn pulls her head back. She stands up and starts walking towards the creek. Eliot feels his hands clench, becoming fists. Roy stands up and follows Dawn. He walks in front of her and she squeals in his face. A high-pitched banshee squeal. The squeal, Eliot thinks, of death.

Eliot finds he is running towards them, his fists ready to pummel Roy. He wonders if he can actually do it, he hasn't ever used them before, not like this. Can I do it, he wonders, as Roy turns with a surprised expression on his face.

Yes, he can.

His first punch lands on Roy's cheekbone, right under Roy's eye. The second one glances blandly off of Roy's stomach, making Roy double up and expel a gasp of breath. Then Eliot is screaming at the top of his lungs, "Get out! Get the hell out! Get the hell out!" His voice turns hoarser each time he screams, but he keeps screaming anyway. Roy looks up at Eliot with a red mark on his face. It's already darkening into a bruise that Eliot wishes he could take a picture of and frame. He'd like to hang it on his wall and keep it forever. A reminder of his ignorance.

Roy says, "Whatever. Fucking faggot," and starts to walk away, back up the trail. When he reaches the top of the ravine and walks over it, he disappears from Eliot's sight, and from Eliot's life, forever.

Eliot is breathing heavily, ready to hit Roy again. He's a little surprised at how easy it was, that he has a space inside him that harbors violence. At the same time, he's impressed with himself. He's not sure if he should feel afraid or proud of his actions. He's not sure if he has room for both.

Dawn stands beside him, looking into his face. She's quiet and still for once in her life. She smoothes down the wrinkles in her shorts with the flats of her hands, over and over. He's most likely disturbed her. Or Roy has. Or both of them did. Eliot says, "Come on, let's go back." He doesn't yell at her or yank her wrist. And Dawn follows him up the trail, out of the ravine, back to the cabin.

13. *The Assignation*

Something woke her late in the night. *Tap, tap, tap.* Something kept tapping, and so she sat up in bed and looked around her. The mother and father were asleep on their cots, the little old man slept on the other side of the sheet separating them. None of them were tapping.

Then she heard it again, and looked over her shoulder. In the window square, two fireflies hovered, blinking out a message. *Outside. Five minutes.*

The girl quietly got out of her cot and stepped into her sandals. She pulled a piece of hair out of her mouth. Peaking around the corner of the sheet, she watched the little old man for a while, his chest rising and falling in steady rhythms of sleep. Earlier that evening, she and the little old man had sat in their respective corners, on their respective cots, and by the light of a lantern, they had made shadow creatures appear on the sheet separating their rooms. Bats and butterflies, and even a dog's head that could open its mouth and bark. She loved the little old man, and wished she could tell him as much.

Then she tiptoed out of the cabin, closing the door behind her carefully. The two fireflies were waiting for her by the smoldering campfire.

"What's the matter?" the girl asked. "Has something happened?"

The fireflies nodded together. One of them said, "We've found your moth. The one you asked about. Orangey-pink glow, gold and brown streaks on its wings? We found him."

"Oh, thank you so much," she told them. "How can I repay you?" "Wait," the fireflies both said. "He isn't here with us. You'll have to wait. He was busy. A real snob, if you want our opinions. But he said he would drop by tomorrow evening. He asked why you wanted to meet him. We said you were a new fixture here, and wanted to meet all the neighbors."

"That's wonderful," the girl said, liking the idea of her being a fixture here, of being a part of the natural surroundings.

She told the fireflies she would be waiting by the campfire the next evening, and that they could bring the moth to her there. "Won't my father be surprised!" she told the fireflies, and they both shrugged, saying, "It's just a moth, I mean really! What's so special about that?"

You have no idea, she wanted to tell them. But she simply told them thank you, and crept back into the cabin to sleep.

14. *Why Now?*

When Dr. Carroll returned from his latest outing, he looked ready to fold up and die on the spot. Eliot and Dawn hung back in the shadows of the porch, swinging a little, while their mother sat at the campfire with their father and tried her best to comfort him. There was still no moth, he told her, and he was ready to face up to the possibility that this summer has been a total waste, that his memory of something unique that no one else had ever discovered was probably false.

Eliot decided to make himself and Dawn scarce, so he took her inside the cabin and, lighting a lantern, entertained her with hand shadows thrown against the sheet separating their cots. They fell asleep after a while, and when Eliot wakes the next morning, he finds his mother and father already outside, cooking breakfast over the fire.

"We're going to leave tomorrow," Eliot's father tells him, whisking eggs in a stainless steel bowl.

"Good," says Eliot, rubbing sleep out of his eyes. He yawns, and takes a glass of orange juice his mother offers him. She's been to town already, and has brought back some fresh food and drinks from Mac's. He takes a sip of the orange juice and holds it in his mouth for a moment, savoring the taste.

"Well, I for one have got a lot of work to do when we get back," Eliot's mother says. "A whole summer spent camping, and I haven't prepared anything for my fall classes yet."

Eliot looks at Dawn, who sits on a log on the other side of the fire, eating sausage links with her fingers. He smiles at her, and gives her a wink. Dawn, to his surprise, smiles and winks back.

The day passes with all of them making preparations to leave the next day. They pack the wagon full of their clothes and camping equipment, and then retire at dusk to the fire, where their faces flush yellow and orange from the flames. All four of them stare at each other, or stare at the last pot of beans cooking on the fire. They're tired, all of them. Puffy gray sacs of flesh hang under their eyes. They are a family, Eliot thinks, of zombies. The walking dead. Faces gray, eyes distant, mouths closed. No one speaks.

Soon after they're finished eating, Dawn gets up from her seat and wanders away from the fire. But not so far that her mother and father can't see where she has gone. Finally, when the fireflies have come to life, filling the night air with an apple green glow, Eliot spots it, his father's moth, pinwheeling through the air around Dawn, surrounded by an orangey-pink halo.

"Dad," he says, "Dad, look." And Dr. Carroll turns to see where Eliot is pointing. A strange little noise comes out of his mouth. Almost a squeak. He heaves himself off the log he's crouched on, and stumbles towards Dawn and the moth.

There it is, thinks Eliot. Why now? Why has it decided to make an appearance after all this time, after all this pain? Why now? he wonders, wanting answers that perhaps don't exist. He suspects Dawn has something to do with it, the same way Dawn made the grasshoppers line up together and do synchronized leaps.

Dr. Carroll shouts, "Keep an eye on it, don't let it get away!" and he rushes to the car to dig through the back for a net or a box. He comes jogging back with a clear plastic box that has a screen fitted into the lid and vents on the sides. A few twigs and leafs wait inside of it. He opens the lid, scoops up the moth, and snaps the box shut.

But then Dawn is squealing. She runs over to her father and tries to pry the box out of his hands. What is she doing? Eliot can't understand why she'd do a thing like that. She's beating at her father's chest, saying—what?—saying, "No! No! No! You can't lock it up like that!"

What? Eliot's thinking. He's thinking, What's happening here?

His mother steps between Dawn and Dr. Carroll, grabbing Dawn around her shoulders to pull her in for a hug. Dawn is sobbing now, her shoulders heaving, and she leans into her mother for the hug, and doesn't let go for fifteen minutes at least. Eliot stays by the fire, afraid of what's going on in front of him. He doesn't know what to do or say.

Dr. Carroll says, "What's wrong with her? I can't believe she tried to do that."

Eliot's mother says, "Leave her alone. Just leave her alone, why don't you? Can't you see she's upset?"

Dr. Carroll walks away from them, holding his box with the moth inside it close to his chest. It glows still. The box lights up like a faery lantern. The smile on his father's face tells Eliot exactly what he is holding. This box, says Eliot's father's smile, contains my youth.

15. *The Message*

It is late now, so late that Eliot has fallen asleep for several hours and then, inexplicably, woke in the night. He doesn't have to pee, and he doesn't feel too hot, or sick. But something is wrong, and it makes him sit up and look around the cabin. His parents are asleep on their cots. The cabin is quiet except for their breathing. He gets out of bed, and once again, the coils of the cot squeal as he removes his weight from them. He pulls back a corner of the sheet separating his room from Dawn's and finds that she is not in her bed. She's not in the cabin at all.

Eliot runs out of the cabin in his bare feet. The grass is dewy, wetting his feet. He doesn't look behind the cabin, or by the fire, or in the nearby field. He runs down the trail to the ravine where he hit Roy, and finds Dawn there, standing by the creek. Mist and fog hover over the water. Dawn stands in the mist surrounded by a swarm of fireflies. She looks like a human Christmas tree with all of those lights blinking around her. She looks like a magic creature. Like a woodland spirit, Eliot thinks.

"Dawn," he says when he reaches her. But Dawn holds out her hand and raises one of her fingers. Wait, she is asking. One moment. Wait.

Eliot stands before her, and suddenly the fireflies drop from the air as if they have all had sudden heart attacks, their lights extinguished. They lay at his feet, crawling around in the grasses. Then, all at the same time, their lights flicker on again, and Eliot finds they have arranged themselves into letters. Spelled out in the grass, glowing green, are the words *Love You, Eliot.*

Eliot looks up to find Dawn's face shining with tears, and he feels his own eyes filling. He steps around the fireflies and hugs Dawn, and whispers that he loves her, too. They stay there for a while, hugging, until Eliot takes Dawn's hand and leads her back to the cabin before their parents wake up.

16. *Now*

When the Carroll's return home from Pennsylvania, they do their best to return to their lives as they once knew them. Eliot's father, uncanny specimen in hand, sets to work on his new research. His mother resumes classes in the Fall and publishes an essay called "Woman, Nature, Words" in a feminist philosophy journal.

On Mondays, Wednesdays and Fridays, Dawn attends school—she has learned how to say "My name is Dawn Carroll, I am seventeen years old, Thank you, You're Welcome, Goodbye, Goodbye, Goodbye." Goodbye is her favorite new word. She sometimes shouts it at the top of her lungs, and

Goodbye floats up to the vaulted ceilings at home, spinning this direction and that, searching for an escape route, a way out of the confines of walls and floors and ceilings. Eventually it bursts, and bits of Goodbye, wet and soapy, fall back down onto her face.

Eliot returns to school as well, to high school, where he learns to slouch and to not look up from his feet, and how to evade talking to other people as much as possible. He begins to dress in black clothes and to listen to depressing music—"Is that what they mean by Gothic?" his mother asks him—but he doesn't dignify her question with an answer. His grades flag and falter. "Needs to work harder," his teachers report. Mr. and Mrs. Carroll send him to a psychologist, a Dr. Emery, who sits behind her desk and doesn't say much of anything. She waits in the long silences for Eliot to begin speaking, and once he starts talking, it's difficult to stop.

Eliot tells her everything that happened over the summer, and Dr. Emery nods a lot and continues to offer little in the way of conversation. Dr. Emery advises Eliot to tell his parents whatever he feels he needs to, and that she will try to help them understand. But Eliot isn't ready, not yet at least, and now that he's told someone else what happened, he wants to think about other things for a while. Video games, music, television, even his schoolwork. Things that are comforting and easy. For now it's enough to have Dr. Emery to talk to, someone safe and understanding. For now.

This is the first in a series of people that Eliot finds he can actually talk to. The others will come to him, friends and lovers, scattered throughout the rest of his life. In a few years he won't even be thinking that no one can understand him. He will be leaning back on his pillows and staring at the neon plastic stars he's pasted to his ceiling, in his own apartment a few blocks from where he attends college, and he will be thinking about that night in the ravine, by the creek. He'll remember Dawn lit up by fireflies, and how they arranged themselves into glowing green letters, like the constellation of glowing stars above him, like the stars he watched through the roof of the rusted-out corvette with Roy. He'll think about his sister and how she learned to speak the language of moths, the language of fireflies and crickets. How he had learned the language of love and betrayal, the language of self-hate and mistrust. How much more his sister knew, he realizes later, than he ever did.

When he thinks about Dawn's message, Eliot will be in love with someone who loves him back. This boy that he'll love will be asleep beside him while Eliot stays awake, staring at the stars above, thinking about Dawn's message.

Love You, Eliot, she had instructed the fireflies to spell out.

At the time, Eliot had interpreted Dawn's message to mean she loved him, and of course there's that, too. But when he thinks about it now, in the future, he's not so sure. The "I" of her message was mysteriously missing, but its absence might only have been an informal gesture on Dawn's part. He wonders now if Dawn was saying something entirely different that night. Has he misunderstood her message, or only understood half of it? Meaning is always lost, at least partially, in translation, he thinks.

Love You, Eliot, she had told him, the letters glowing like green embers in the grass.

Now, in the future, this future that he imagined so many years ago, the future in which he lived in his own apartment, with his own television and his own books, the future in which he goes to college and finds himself not as wrong or as weird as he once thought he was, in this future he wonders if Dawn was also giving him a piece of advice.

Love You, Eliot, she had told him.

And he does that. He knows how to do that.

Now.

ANYWAY
M. RICKERT

Mary Rickert grew up in Fredonia, Wisconsin. When she was eighteen she moved to California where she worked at Disneyland. She still has fond memories of selling balloons there. After many years (and through the sort of "odd series of events" that describe much of her life), she got a job as a kindergarten teacher in a small private school for gifted children. She worked there for almost a decade, then left to pursue her life as a writer.

She has had many stories published by The Magazine of Fantasy & Science Fiction, *a few of which have been reprinted in various Year's Best anthologies. Her collection,* Map of Dreams, *is due to be published later this year.*

"What if you could save the world? What if all you had to do was sacrifice your son's life, Tony's for instance, and there would be no more war, would you do it?"

"Robbie's the name of my son," I say. "Remember, Mom? Tony is your son. You remember Tony, don't you?"

I reach into the cabinet where I've stored the photograph album. I page through it until I find the picture I want, Tony and me by his VW just before he left on the Kerouac-inspired road trip from which he never returned. We stand, leaning into each other, his long hair pulled into a ponytail, and mine finally grown out of the pixie cut I'd had throughout my single-digit years. He has on bell-bottom jeans and a tie-dyed T-shirt. I have on cut-offs and a simple cotton short-sleeved button-down blouse and, hard to see but I know they are there, a string of tiny wooden beads, which Tony had, only seconds before, given to me. I am looking up at him with absolute adoration and love.

"See, Mom," I point to Tony's face. She looks at the picture and then at me. She smiles.

"Well, hello," she says, "when did you get here?"

I close the book, slide it into the cabinet, kiss her forehead, pick up my purse, and walk out of the room. I learned some time ago that there is no need for explanation. She sits there in the old recliner we brought from her house, staring vacantly at nothing, as if I have never been there, not today, or ever.

I stop at the nurse's station, hoping to find my favorite nurse, Anna Vinn. I don't even remember the name of the nurse who looks up at me and smiles. I glance at her name tag.

"Charlotte?"

"Yes?"

"My mother asked me the strangest question today."

Charlotte nods.

"Do the patients ever, you know, snap out of it? Have you ever heard of that happening?"

Charlotte rests her face in her hand, two fingers under the rim of her glasses, rubbing her temple. She sighs and appraises me with a kind look. "Sometimes, but you know, they..."

"Snap right back again?"

"Would you like to talk to the social worker?"

I shake my head, tap the counter with my fingertips before I wave, breezy, unconcerned.

Once outside I look at my watch. I still have to get the groceries for tomorrow's dinner. It's my father's birthday and he wants, of all things, pot roast. Luckily, my son, Robbie, has agreed to cook it. I've been a vegetarian for eighteen years and now I have to go buy a pot roast.

"What if you could save the world?" I remember my mother asking the question, so clearly, as if she were really present — in her skin and in her mind — in a way she hasn't been for years.

"Mom," I say, as I unlock the car door, "I can't even save this cow."

That's when I realize that a man I've seen inside the home, but who I don't know by name, stands between my car and his (I assume). He stares at me for a moment and then, with a polite smile, turns away.

I start to speak, to offer some explanation for what he's overheard, but he is walking away from me, toward the nursing home, his shoulders hunched as if under a weight, or walking against a wind, though it is early autumn and the weather is mild.

On Sunday, my dad and Robbie sit in the kitchen drinking beer while the pot roast cooks, talking about war. I have pleaded with my father for years not to talk to Robbie this way, but he has always dismissed my concerns. "This is men talk," he'd say, elbowing Robbie in the ribs, tousling his hair while Robbie, gap-toothed and freckled and so obviously not a man, grinned up at me. But now Robbie is nineteen. He drinks a beer and rubs his long fingers over the stubble of his chin. "Don't get me wrong," my dad says, "it's a terrible thing, okay? There's mud and snakes and bugs, and we didn't take a shower for three months." He glances at me and nods. I know that this is meant as a gesture on his part, a sort of offering to me and my peacenik ways.

The smell of pot roast drives me from the kitchen to the backyard. It's cooler today than yesterday, and the sky has a grayish cast. Most of the leaves have fallen, the yard littered with the muted red, gold, and green. I sit on the back step. "Didn't take a shower for three months," my father says again, loudly. I hear him through the kitchen windows that I had cracked open, trying to alleviate the odor of cooked meat.

I listen to the murmur of Robbie's voice.

"Oh, but it was a beautiful thing," my dad says. "It was the right thing to do. Nobody questioned it back then. We were saving the world."

For dessert we have birthday cake, naturally. My dad's favorite, chocolate with banana filling and chocolate chip-studded chocolate frosting. I feel quite queasy by this point, the leftover pot roast congealing in the roaster on top of the stove, Robbie's and my father's plates gleaming with a light gray coating — it was all I could do to eat my salad. "Why don't we have our cake in the living room?" I say.

"Aw, no," my father says. "You don't have to get all fancy for me."

But Robbie sees something in my face that causes him to stand up quickly. "Come on, Pops," he says, and, as my father begins to rise, "you and mom go in the living room and talk. I'll bring out the cake."

I try not to notice the despair that flits over my father's face. I take him by the elbow and steer him into the living room, helping him into the recliner I bought (though he does not know this) for him.

"I saw Mom today," I say.

He nods, scratches the inside of his ear, glances longingly at the kitchen.

I steel myself against the resentment. I'm happy about the relationship he's developed with Robbie. But some small part of me, some little girl who, in spite of my forty-five years, resides in me and will not go away, longs for my father's attention and yes, even after all these years, approval.

"She asked me the strangest question."

My father grunts. Raises his eyebrows. It is obvious that he thinks there is nothing particularly fascinating about my mother asking a strange question.

"One time," he says, "she asked me where her dogs were. I said, 'Meldy, you know you never had any dogs.' So she starts arguing with me about how of course she's always had dogs, what kind of woman do I think she is? So, later that day I'm getting ice out of the freezer, and what do you think I find in there but her underwear, and I say, 'Meldy, what the hell is your underwear doing in the freezer?' So she grabs them from me and says, 'My dogs!'"

"Ha-a-appy Birrrrrthday to youuuu." Robbie comes in, carrying the cake blazing with candles. I join in the singing. My father sits through it with an odd expression on his face. I wonder if he's enjoying any of this.

Later, when I drive him home while Robbie does the dishes, I say, "Dad, listen, today Mom, for just a few seconds, she was like her old self again. Something you said tonight, to Robbie, reminded me of it. Remember how you said that during the war it was like you were saving the world?" I glance at him. He sits, staring straight ahead, his profile composed of sharp shadows. "Anyway, Mom looked right at me, you know, the way she used to have that look, right, and she said, 'What if you could save the world? What if all you had to do was sacrifice one life and there would be no more war, would you do it?'"

My father shakes his head and mumbles something.

"What is it, Dad?"

"Well, that was the beginning, you know."

"The beginning?"

"Yeah, the beginning of the Alzheimer's. 'Course, I didn't know it then. I thought she was just going a little bit nuts." He shrugs. "It happened. Lots of women used to go crazy back then."

"Dad, what are you talking about?"

"All that business with Tony." His voice cracks on the name. After all these years he can still not say my brother's name without breaking under the grief.

"Forget it, Dad. Never mind."

"She almost drove me nuts, asking it all the time."

"Okay, let's just forget about it."

"All those fights we had about the draft and Vietnam, and then he went and got killed anyway. You were just a girl then, so you probably don't remember, it almost tore us apart."

"We don't have to talk about this, Dad."

I turn into the driveway. My father stares straight ahead. I wait a few seconds and then open my car door; he leans to open his. When I walk beside him to guide him by the elbow, he steps away from me. "I'm not an invalid," he says. He reaches in his pocket and pulls out his keys. Together we walk to the door, which he unlocks with shaking hands. I step inside and flick on the light switch. It is the living room of a lonely old man, the ancient plaid couch and recliner, family photographs gathering dust, fake ivy.

"Satisfied?" he says, turning toward me.

I shake my head, shrug. I'm not sure what he's talking about.

"No boogeymen are here stealing all your inheritance, all right?"

"Dad, I — "

"The jewels are safe."

He laughs at that. I smile weakly. "Happy Birthday, Dad," I say.

But he has already turned and headed into the bedroom. "Wait, let me check on the jewels."

My father, the smart aleck.

"Okay, Dad," I say, loudly, so he can hear me over the sound of drawers being opened and closed. "I get the point. I'm leaving."

"No, no. The jewels."

Suddenly I am struck by my fear, so sharp I gasp. He's got it too, I think, and he's going to come out with his socks or underwear and he's going to call them jewels and —

"Ah, here they are. I honest to God almost thought I lost them."

I sit down on the threadbare couch I have offered to replace a dozen times. He comes into the living room, grinning like an elf, carrying something. I can't bear to look.

"What's the matter with you?" he asks and thrusts a shoebox onto my lap.

"Oh my God."

"These are yours now."

I take a deep breath. I can handle this, I think. I've handled a lot already; my brother's murder, my husband's abandonment, my mother's Alzheimer's. I lift the lid. The box is filled with stones, green with spots of red on them. I pick one up. "Dad, where did you get these? Is that blood?"

He sits in the recliner. "They were in the bedroom. They're your responsibility now."

"Are these — "

"Bloodstone, it's called. At least that's what your mother said, but you know, like I told you, she was already getting the Alzheimer's back then."

"Bloodstone? Where did she — "

"I already told you." He looks at me, squinty-eyed, and I almost laugh when I realize he is trying to decide if I have Alzheimer's now. "She wouldn't stop. She almost drove me crazy with her nonsense. She kept saying it, all the time, 'Why'd he have to die anyway?' You get that? 'Anyway,' that's what she said, 'Why'd he have to die anyway,' like there was a choice or something. Finally one day I just lost it and I guess I hollered at her real bad and she goes, 'What if you could save the world? What if all you had to do was sacrifice one life, not your own, but, oh, let's say, Tony's, and there would be no more war, would you do it?' I reminded her that our Tony — " His voice cracks. He reaches for the remote control and turns the TV on but leaves the sound off. "She says, 'I know he's dead anyway, but I mean before he died, what would you have done?'"

"And I told her, 'The world can go to hell.'" He looks at me, the colors from the TV screen flickering across his face. "The whole world can just go to hell if I could have him back for even one more day, one more god-damned hour." For a moment I think he might cry, but he moves his mouth as if he's sucking on something sour and continues. "And she says, 'That's what I decided. But then he died anyway.'"

I look at the red spots on the stones. My father makes an odd noise, a sort of rasping gasp. I look up to the shock of his teary eyes.

"So she tells me that these stones were given to her by her mother. You remember Grandma Helen, don't you?"

"No, she died before — "

"Well, she went nuts too. So you see, it runs in the women of the family. You should probably watch out for that. Anyway, your mother tells me that her mother gave her these stones when she got married. There's one for every generation of Mackeys, that was your mother's name before she married me. There's a stone for her mother and her mother's mother, and so on, and so on, since before time began I guess. They weren't all Mackeys, naturally, and anyhow, every daughter gets them."

"But why?"

"Well, see this is the part that just shows how nuts she was. She tells me, she says, that all the women in her family got to decide. If they send their son to war and, you know, agree to the sacrifice, they are supposed to bury the stones in the garden. Under a full moon or some nonsense like that. Then the boy will die in the war, but that would be it, okay? There would never be another war again in the whole world."

"What a fantastic story."

"But if they didn't agree to this sacrifice, the mother just kept the stones, you know, and the son went to war and didn't die there, he was like protected from dying in the war but, you know, the wars just kept happening. Other people's sons would die instead."

"Are you saying that Mom thought she could have saved the world if Tony had died in Vietnam?"

"Yep."

"But Dad, that's just — "

"I know. Alzheimer's. We didn't know it back then, of course. She really believed this nonsense too, let me tell you. She told me if she had just let Tony die in Vietnam at least she could have saved everyone else's sons. There weren't girl soldiers then, like there are now, you know. Course he just died anyway."

"Tony didn't want to go to Vietnam."

"Well, she was sure she could have convinced him." He waves his hand as though brushing away a fly. "She was nuts, what can I say? Take those things out of here. Take the box of them. I never want to see them again."

When I get home the kitchen is, well, not gleaming, but devoid of pot roast. Robbie left a note scrawled in black marker on the magnetic board on the refrigerator. "Out. Back later." I stare at it while I convince myself that he is fine. He will be back, unlike Tony who died or Robbie's father who left me when I was six months' pregnant because, he said, he realized he had to pursue his first love, figure skating.

I light the birch candle to help get rid of the cooked meat smell, which still lingers in the air, sweep the floor, wipe the counters and the table. Then I make myself a cup of decaf tea. While it steeps, I change into my pajamas. Finally, I sit on the couch in front of the TV, the shoebox of stones on the coffee table in front of me. I sip my tea and watch the news, right from the start so I see all the gruesome stuff, the latest suicide bombing, people with ravaged-grief faces carrying bloody bodies, a weeping mother in robes, and then, a special report, an interview with the mother of a suicide bomber, clutching the picture of her dead son and saying, "He is saving the world."

I turn off the TV, put the cup of tea down, and pick up the shoebox of stones. They rattle in there, like bones, I think, remembering the box that held Tony's ashes after he was cremated. I tuck the shoebox under my arm, blow out the candle in the kitchen, check that the doors are locked, and go to bed. But it is the oddest thing: the whole time I am doing these tasks, I am thinking about taking one of those stones and putting it into my mouth, sucking it like a lozenge. It makes no sense, a strange impulse, I think, a weird synapse in my brain, a reaction to today's stress. I shove the shoebox under my bed, lick my lips and move my mouth as though sucking on something sour. Then, just as my head hits the pillow, I sit straight up, remembering.

It was after Tony's memorial, after everyone had left our house. There was an odd smell in the air, the scent of strange perfumes and flowers (I remember a bouquet of white flowers already dropping petals in the heat) mingled with the odor of unusual foods, casseroles and cakes, which had begun arriving within hours after we learned of Tony's death. There was also a new silence, a different kind of silence than any I had ever experienced before in my eleven years. It was a heavy silence and oddly, it had an odor all its own, sweaty and sour. I felt achingly alone as I walked through the rooms, looking for my parents, wondering if they, too, had died. Finally, I found my father sitting on the front porch, weeping. It was too terrible to watch. Following the faint noises I heard coming from there, I next went to the kitchen. And that's when I saw my mother sitting at the table, picking stones out of a shoebox and shoving them into her mouth. My brother was dead. My father was weeping on the porch and my mother was sitting in the kitchen, sucking on stones. I couldn't think of what to do about any of it. Without saying anything, I turned around and went to bed.

It is so strange, what we remember, what we forget. I try to remember everything I can about Tony. It is not very much, and some of it is suspect. For instance, I think I remember us standing next to the Volkswagen while my dad took that photograph, but I'm not even sure that I really remember it because when I picture it in my mind, I see us the way we are in the photograph, as though I am looking at us through a lens, and that is not the way I would have experienced it. Then I try to remember Robbie's father, and I find very little. Scraps of memory, almost like the sensation when you can hear a song in your head but can't get it to the part of your brain where you can actually sing it. I decide it isn't fair to try this with Robbie's father because I had worked so hard to forget everything about him.

I wonder if all my mother has really lost is the ability to fake it anymore. To pretend, the way we all do, to be living a memory-rich life. Then I decide that as a sort of homage to her, I will try to remember her, not as she is now, in the nursing home, curled in her bed into the shape of a comma, but how she used to be. I remember her making me a soft-boiled egg, which I colored with a face before she dropped it into the water, and I remember her sitting at the sewing machine with pins in her mouth and once, in the park, while Tony and I play in the sandbox, she sits on a bench, wearing her blue coat and her Sunday hat, the one with the feathers, her gloved hands in her lap, talking to some man and laughing, and I remember her sitting at the kitchen table sucking on stones. And that's it. That's all I can remember, over and over again, as though my mind is a flip book and the pages have gotten stuck. It seems there should be more, but as hard as I look, I can't find any. Finally, I fall asleep.

Two weeks after my father's birthday, Robbie tells me that he has enlisted in the Marines. Basically, I completely freak out, and thus discover that a person can be completely freaked out while appearing only slightly so.

"Don't be upset, Mom," Robbie says after his announcement.

"It doesn't work like that. You can't do this and then tell me not to be upset. I'm upset."

"It's just, I don't know, I've always felt like I wanted to be a soldier, ever since I was a little kid. You know, like when people say they 'got a calling'? I always felt like I had a calling to be a soldier. You know, like dad with figure skating."

"Hm."

"Don't just sit there, Mom, say something, okay?"

"When are you leaving?"

He pulls out the contract he signed, and the brochures and the list of supplies he needs to buy. I read everything and nod and ask questions, and I am completely freaked out. That's when I begin to wonder if I have been fooling myself about this for my whole adult life, even longer. Now that I think about it, I think maybe I've been completely freaked out ever since my mother came into my room and said that Tony's body had been found in a dumpster in Berkeley.

I start to get suspicious of everyone: the newscaster, with her wide, placid face reading the reports of the suicide bombings and the number killed since the war began; my friend, Shelly, who's a doctor, smiling as she nurses her baby (the very vulnerability of which she knows so intimately); even strangers in the mall, in the grocery store, not exactly smiling or looking peaceful, generally, but also not freaking out, and I think, oh, but they are. Everybody is freaking out and just pretending that they aren't.

I take up smoking again. Even though I quit twenty years ago, I find it amazingly easy to pick right back up. But it doesn't take away the strange hunger I've developed, and so far resisted, for the bloodstones safely stored in the shoebox under my bed.

When I visit my mother it is with an invigorated sense of dread. Though I grill her several times, I cannot get her to say anything that makes sense. This leaves me with only my dad.

"Now, let me get this right, Mom believed that if she buried the bloodstones — are you supposed to bury just one, or all of them? — then that meant Tony would die, right, and there would never be another war?"

"He had to die over there, see? In Vietnam. He had to be a soldier. It didn't matter when he died in California; that didn't have anything to do with it, see?"

"But why not?"

"How should I know?" He taps the side of his head with a crooked finger. "She was nuts already way back then. Want my opinion? It was his dying that did it to her, like the walnut tree."

"What's a walnut tree have to do with — "

"You remember that tree in front of our house. That was one magnificent tree. But then the blight came, and you know what caused it? Just this little invisible fungus, but it killed that giant. You see what I'm talking about?"

"No, Dad, I really don't."

"It's like what happened with ... It was bad, all right? But when you look at a whole entire life, day after day and hour after hour, minute after minute we were having a good life, me and your mom and you kids. Then this one thing happened and, bam, there goes the walnut tree."

That night I dream that my mother is a tree or at least I am talking to a tree in the backyard and calling it Mom. Bombs are exploding all around me. Tony goes by on a bicycle. Robbie walks past, dressed like a soldier but wearing ice-skates. I wake up, my heart beating wildly. The first thing I think is, What if it's true? I lean over the side of the bed and pull out the shoebox, which rattles with stones. I lick my lips. What if I could save the world?

I open the lid, reach in, and pick up a stone, turning it in my fingers and thumb, enjoying the sensation of smooth. Then I let it drop back into the box, put the lid on, shove it under the bed, and turn on the bedside lamp. For the first time in my entire life, I smoke in bed, using a water glass as an ashtray. Smoking in bed is extremely unwise, but, I reason, at least it's not nuts. At least I'm not sitting here sucking on stones. That would be nuts.

While I smoke, I consider the options, in theory. Send my son to war and bury the stones? Did my father say under a full moon? I make a mental note to check that and then, after a few more puffs, get out of bed and start rummaging in my purse until I find my checkbook, with the pen tucked inside. I tear off a check and write on the back of it, "Find out if stones have to be buried under full moon or not." Satisfied, I crawl back into bed, being very careful with my lit cigarette.

There's a knock on my bedroom door. "Mom? Are you all right?"

"Just couldn't sleep."

"Can I come in?"

"Sure, honey."

Robbie opens the door and stands there, his brown curls in a shock of confusion on his forehead, the way they get after he's been wearing a hat. He still has his jacket on and exudes cool air. "Are you smoking?"

I don't find this something necessary to respond to. I take a puff. I mean, obviously I am. I squint at him. "You know, people are dying over there."

"Mom."

"I'm just saying. I want to make sure you know what you're getting into. It's not like you're home in the evenings watching the news. I just want to make sure you know what's going on."

"I don't think you should smoke in bed. Jesus, Mom, it really stinks in here. I'm not going to die over there, okay?"

"How do you know?"

"I just do."

"Don't be ridiculous. Nobody knows something like that."

"I have to go to bed, Mom. Don't fall asleep with that cigarette, okay?"

"I'm not a child. Robbie?"

"Yeah?"

"Would it be worth it to you?"

"What?"

"Well, your life? I mean, are you willing to give it up for this?"

I bring the cigarette to my lips. I am just about to inhale when I realize I can hear him breathing. I hold my own breath so I can listen to the faint but beautiful sound of my son breathing. He sighs. "Yeah, Mom."

"All right then. Good night, Robbie."

"Good night, Mom." He shuts the door, gently, not like a boy at all, but like a man trying not to disturb the dreams of a child.

The next day's news is particularly grim: six soldiers are killed and a school is bombed. It's a mistake, of course, and everyone is upset about it.

Without even having to look at the note I wrote to myself on the back of the check, I call my father and ask him if the stones are supposed to be buried when there's a full moon. I also make sure he's certain of the correlations, bury stones, son dies but all wars end, don't bury stones and son lives but the wars continue.

My father has a little fit about answering my questions but eventually he tells me, yes, the stones have to be buried under a full moon (and he isn't sure if it's one stone or all of them) and yes, I have the correlations right.

"Is there something about sucking them?"

"What's that?"

"Did mom ever say anything about sucking the stones?"

"This thing with Robbie has really knocked the squirrel out of your tree, hasn't it?"

I tell him that it is perfectly rational that I be upset about my son going off to fight in a war.

He says, "Well, the nut sure doesn't fall far from the tree."

"The fruit," I say.

"What's that?"

"That expression. It isn't the nut doesn't fall far from the tree, it's the fruit."

The day before Robbie is to leave, I visit my mother at the nursing home. I bring the shoebox of stones with me.

"Listen, Mom," I hiss into the soft shell of her ear. "I really need you to do everything you can to give me some signal. Robbie's joined the Marines. Robbie, my son. He's going to go to war. I need to know what I should do."

She stares straight ahead. Actually, staring isn't quite the right description. The aides tell me that she is not blind, but the expression in her eyes is that of a blind woman. Exasperated, I begin to rearrange the untouched things on her dresser: a little vase with a dried flower in it; some photographs of her and dad, me and Robbie; a hairbrush. Without giving it much thought, I pick up the shoebox. "Remember these," I say, lifting the lid. I shake the box under her face. I pick up one of the stones. "Remember?"

I pry open her mouth. She resists, for some reason, but I pry her lips and teeth apart and shove the stone in, banging it against the plate of her false teeth. She stares straight ahead but makes a funny noise. I keep her mouth open and, practically sitting now, almost on the arm of the chair, grab a handful of stones and begin shoving them into her mouth. Her arms flap up, she jerks her head. "Come on," I say, "you remember, don't you?"

Wildly, her eyes roll, until finally they lock on mine, a faint flicker of recognition, and I am tackled from behind, pulled away from her. There's a flurry of white pant cuffs near my face, and one white shoe comes dangerously close to stepping on me.

"Jesus Christ, they're stones. They're stones."

"Well, get them out."

"Those are my stones," I say, pushing against the floor. A hand presses my back, holding me down.

"Just stay there," says a voice I recognize as belonging to my favorite nurse, Anna Vinn.

Later, in her office, Anna says, "We're not going to press charges. But you need to stay away for a while. And you should consider some kind of counseling."

She hands me the shoebox.

"I'm sure I was trying to get the stones out of her mouth."

She shakes her head. "Are you going to be okay? Driving home?"

"Of course," I say, unintentionally shaking the shoebox. "I'm fine."

When I get outside I take a deep breath of the fresh air. It is a cold, gray day, but I am immediately struck by the beauty of it, the beauty of the gray clouds, the beauty of the blackbirds arcing across the sky, the beauty of the air on my face and neck. I think: *I cannot save him.* Then I see a familiar-looking man. "Excuse me?" I say. He continues, head bent, shoulders hunched, toward the nursing home. "Excuse me?"

He stops and turns, slightly distracted, perhaps skeptical, as if worried I might ask for spare change.

"Don't we know each other?"

He glances at the nursing home, I think longingly, but that can't possibly be correct. Nobody longs to go in there. He shakes his head.

"Are you sure? Anyway, I have a question. Let's say you could save the world by sacrificing your son's life, would you do it?"

"I don't have a son. Or a daughter. I don't have any children."

"But hypothetically?"

"Is this, are you..." He thrusts his hands into his pockets. "Is this some kind of religious thing? 'Cause I'm not looking to convert."

"Are you sure we don't know each other?"

"I've seen you before." He glances over his shoulder. For a moment I'm sure he's going to say something important, but instead he turns away and hurries to the nursing home.

I walk to the car with my box of stones. I have to decide. Robbie leaves in the morning. It's time to stop fooling around.

This, I think, is like a Zen koan. What is the sound of one hand clapping? The secret for these things is not to be too clever. The fact that I am aware of this puts me at risk of being too clever. Okay, focus, I think as I carefully stop at a green light, realize what I've done and accelerate as the light changes to yellow. It's really very simple. Do I bury the stones? Or not? Glancing at the box, I lick my lips.

When I get home, Robbie is there with several of his friends. They are in his room, laughing and cursing. I knock on his door and ask him if he'll be home for dinner. He opens it and says, "Mom, are you all right?"

"I was just trying to get the stones out of her mouth."

He shakes his head. "What are you talking about?" His eyes are the same color as the stones, without the red spots, of course. "You remember about the party, right?"

"The party?"

"Remember? Len? He's having a party for me? Tonight?"

I remember none of this, but I nod. It's apparently the right thing to do. There's some rustling going on behind him and a sharp bang against the wall, punctuated by masculine giggles. Robbie turns around. "Guys, be quiet for a minute." He turns back to me and smiles, bravely I think. "Hey, I don't have to go."

"It's your party. Go. I want you to."

He's relieved, I can tell. I carry the shoebox of stones into my bedroom, where I crawl into bed and fall asleep. When I wake up, feeling sweaty and stinky, creased by the seams of my clothing, it is like waking from a fever. The full moon sheds a cool glow into the room and throughout the house as I walk through it aimlessly. In the kitchen I see that Robbie amended the note on the magnetic board on the refrigerator. "Gone. Back later. Love."

I go to the bedroom to get the box of stones. I drop them onto the kitchen table. They make a lovely noise, like playing with marbles or checkers when I was young and Tony was young too and alive. I pick up a stone, pop it into my mouth, and see, almost like a memory but clearer (and certainly this is not my life), the life of a young man, a Roman, I think. I don't know how long this process takes, because there is a strange, circular feeling to it, as though I have experienced this person's entire life, not in the elongated way we live hours and days and years but rather as something spherical. I see him as a young boy, playing in a stream, and I see him with his parents, eating at some sort of feast, I see him kiss a girl, and I see him go to battle. The battle scenes are very gruesome but I don't spit out the stone because I have to know how it turns out. I see him return home, I see his old mother's tearful face but not his father's, because his father was killed in the war, but then there are many happy scenes, a wedding, children, he lives a good life and dies in a field one day, all alone under a bright sun, clutching wet blades of grass with one hand, his heart with the other. I pick up another stone and see the life of another boy, and another, and another. Each stone carries the whole life of a son. Now, without stopping to spit them out, I shove stones into my mouth, swirling through centuries of births and wars and dying until at last I find Tony's, from the blossomed pains of his birth, through his death in Berkeley, stabbed by a boy not much older than he was, the last thing he saw, this horrified boy saying, "Oh, shit." I shove stones into my mouth, dizzy with the lives and deaths and the ever-repeating endless cycle of war. When my mouth is too full, I spit them out and start again. At last I find Robbie's, watching every moment of his birth and growing years while the cacophony of other lives continues around me, until I see him in a bedroom, the noise of loud music, laughter, and voices coming through the crack under the door. He is naked and in bed with a blond girl. I spit out the stones. Then, carefully, I pick up the wet stones one at a time until I again find Robbie's and Tony's. These I put next to the little Buddha in the hallway. The rest I put into the box, which I shove under my bed.

The next day, I drive Robbie to the bus depot.

"I don't want you worrying about me. I'm going to be fine," he says.

I smile, not falsely. The bus is late, of course. While we wait we meet two other families whose children are making the same trip as Robbie is. Steve, a blue-eyed boy with the good looks of a model, and Sondra, whose skin is smooth and brown, lustrous like stone. I shake their hands and try to say the right things, but I do not look into those young bright faces for long. I cannot bear to. When their parents try to make small talk, I can only murmur my replies. Nobody seems to blame me. It is expected that I act this way, upset and confused. Certainly nobody suspects the truth about me, that I am a murderer, that I have bargained their children's lives for my son's.

When it comes time to say good-bye, I kiss him on the cheek. Oh, the wonderful warmth of his skin! The wonderful certainty that he will survive!

I stand and wave as the bus pulls away. I wave and wave even though I can't see his face, and I have no idea if he can see mine, I wave until somebody, Sondra's dad, I think, tries to get me to stop, then, mumbling, walks away. I stand here waving even after there is no bus on the road. People walk in wide circles around me as if somehow they know that I am the destroyer of the world. They are completely freaked out but act like they're not, because, after all, what can they do about it, anyway?

THE EMPEROR OF GONDWANALAND
PAUL DI FILIPPO

Paul Di Filippo sold his first story in 1977. Since then he's had nearly 150 sto-
ries published, the majority of them collected in his ten short story collections.
He has written nine novels, including Fuzzy Dice *and* Spondulix. *New novel*
Time's Black Lagoon, *featuring the Creature from the Black Lagoon, and new*
collection, Shuteye for the Timebroker, *are both due in early 2006. Di Filippo*
has also begun scripting comics of late, with his first major project being a se-
quel to Alan Moore's Top 10. *He lives in his native state, Rhode Island, amidst*
eldritch Lovecraftian surroundings, with his mate of thirty years, Deborah
Newton, a chocolate cocker spaniel named Brownie, and a three-colored cat
named Penny Century.

"Hey, Mutt! It's playtime, let's go!"

Mutt Spindler raised his gaze above the flatscreen monitor
that dominated his desk. The screen displayed Pagemaker
layouts for next month's issue of *PharmaNotes*, a trade publication for the
drug industry. Mutt had the cankerous misfortune to be assistant editor of
PharmaNotes, a job he had held for the last three quietly miserable years.

In the entrance to his cubicle stood Gifford, Cody, and Melba, three of
Matt's co-workers. Gifford sported a giant foam finger avowing his allegiance
to whatever sports team was currently high in the standings of whatever
season it chanced to be. Cody had a silver hip flask raised to her lips, imbib-
ing a liquid that Mutt could be fairly certain did not issue from the Poland
Springs cooler. Melba had already undone her formerly decorous shirt
several buttons upward from the hem and knotted it, exposing a belly that
reminded Mutt of a slab of Godiva chocolate.

Mutt pictured with facile vividness the events of the evening that would
ensue, should he choose to accept Gifford's invitation. His projections were
based on numerous past such experiences. Heavy alcohol consumption and
possible ingestion of illicit stimulants, followed by slurred, senseless conversation conducted at eardrum- piercing volume to overcome whatever jagged
ambient noise was passing itself off as music these days. Some hypnagogic,
sensory-impaired dancing with one strange woman or another, leading in all

likelihood to a meaningless hookup, the details of which would be impossible to recall in the morning, resulting in hypochondriacal worries and vacillating committments to get one kind of STD test or another. And of course the leftover brain damage and fraying of neurological wiring would ensure that the demands of the office would be transformed from their usual simple hellishness to torture of an excruciating variety undreamed of by even, say, a team of Catholic school nuns and the unlamented Uday Hussein.

Gifford could sense his cautious friend wavering toward abstinence. "C'mon, Mutt! We're gonna hit Slamdunk's first, then Black Rainbow. And we'll finish up at Captains Curvaceous."

Mention of the last-named club, a strip joint where Mutt had once managed to drop over five hundred dollars of his tiny Christmas bonus while simultaneously acquiring a black eye and a chipped tooth, caused a shiver to surf his spine.

"Uh, thanks, guys, for thinking of me. But I just can't swing it. If I don't get this special ad section squared away by tonight, we'll miss the printer's deadlines."

Cody pocketed her flask and grabbed Gifford's arm. "Oh, leave the little drudge alone, Giff. It's obvious he's so in love with his job. Haven't you seen his lip-prints on the screen?"

Mutt was hurt and insulted. Was it his fault that he had been promoted to assistant editor over Cody? He wanted to say something in his defense, but couldn't think of a comeback that wouldn't sound whiny. And then the window closed on any possible repartee.

Gifford unselfconsciously scratched his butt with his foam finger. "Okay, pal, maybe next time. Let's shake a tail, ladies."

Melba winked at Mutt as she walked away. "Gonna miss you, loverboy."

Then the trio was gone.

Mutt hung his head in his hands. Why had he ever slept with Melba? Sleeping with co-workers was insane. Yet he had done it. The affair was over now, but the awkward repercussions lingered. Another black mark on his karma.

Refocusing on the screen, Mutt tried hard to proof the text floating before him. "Epigenetix-brand sequencers guarantee faster throughput..." The words and pictures blurred into a jittery multicolored fog like a mosh pit full of amoebas. Was he crying? For Christ's sake, why the hell was he crying? Just because he had to hold down a suck-ass job he hated just to pay his grad-school loans, had no steady woman, hadn't been snow-boarding in two years, had put on five pounds since the summer, and experienced an undeniable yet shameful thrill when contemplating the purchase of a new *necktie*?

Mutt knuckled the moisture from his eyes and mentally kicked his own ass for being a big baby. This wasn't a bad life, and plenty of people had it worse. Time to pull up his socks and buckle down and all that other self-improvement shit.

But not right now. Right now, Mutt needed a break. He hadn't lied to Gifford and the others, he had to finish this job tonight. But he could take fifteen minutes to websurf his way to some amusing site that would lift his spirits.

And that was how Mutt discovered Gondwanaland.

In retrospect, after the passage of time had erased his computer's logs, the exact chain of links leading to Gondwanaland was hard to reconfigure. He had started looking for new recordings by his favorite group, Dead End Universe. That had led somehow to a history of pirate radio stations. And from there it was a short jump to micronations.

Fascinated, Mutt lost all track of time as he read about this concept that was totally new to him.

Micronations — also known as cybernations, fantasy countries, or ephemeral states — were odd blends of real-world rebellious politics, virtual artsy-fartsy projects and elaborate spoofs. Essentially, a micronation was any assemblage of persons regarding themselves as a sovereign country, yet not recognized by international entities such as the United Nations. Sometimes micronations were associated with real physical territory. The Cocos Islands had once been ruled as a fiefdom by the Clunies-Ross family. Sarawak was once the province of the White Rajas, as the Brooke clan had styled themselves.

With the advent of the internet, the number of micronations had exploded. There were now dozens of imaginary online countries predicated on different philosophies, exemplifying scores of different governmental systems, each of them more or less seriously arguing that they were totally within their rights to issue passports, currency and stamps, and to designate ministers, nobility and bureaucratic minions.

Mutt had always enjoyed fantasy sports in college. Imaginary leagues, imaginary rosters, imaginary games — Something about being totally in charge of a small universe had appealed to him, as an antidote to his lack of control over the important factors and forces that batted his own life around. He had spent a lot of time playing Sims too. The concept of cybernations seemed like a logical extension of those pursuits, an appealing refuge from the harsh realities of career and relationships.

The site Mutt had ended up on was a gateway to a whole host of online countries. The Aerican Empire, the Kingdom of Talossa, the Global State of Waveland, the Kingdom of Redonda, Lizbekistan —

And Gondwanaland.

Memories of an introductory geoscience course came back to Mutt. Gondwanaland was the super-continent that had existed hundreds of millions of years ago, before splitting and drifting apart into the configuration of separate continental landforms familiar today.

Mutt clicked on the Gondwanaland button.

The page built itself rapidly on his screen. The animated image of a spinning globe dominated. Sure enough, the globe featured only a single huge continent, marked with interior divisions into states and featuring the weird names of cities.

Mutt was about to scan some of the text on the page when his eye fell on the blinking time readout in the corner of the screen.

Holy shit! Nine-thirty! He'd be here till midnight unless he busted his ass.

Reluctantly abandoning the Gondwanaland page and its impossible globe, Mutt returned to his work.

Which still sucked.

Maybe worse.

The next day Mutt was almost as tired as if he had gone out with Gifford and the gang. But at least his head wasn't throbbing and his mouth didn't taste as if he had french-kissed a hyena. Proofing the advertorial section had taken until eleven-forty-five, and by the time he had ridden the subway home, eaten some leftover General Gao's chicken, watched Letterman's Top Ten and fallen asleep, it had been well into the small hours of the morning. When his alarm went off at seven-thirty, he had thrashed about in confusion like a drowning man, dragged from some engrossing dream that instantly evaporated out of memory.

Once in the office, Mutt booted up his machine. He had been doing something interesting last evening, hadn't he? Oh, yeah, that Gondwanaland thing —

Before his butt hit the chair, someone was IMing him. Oh, shit, Kicklighter wanted to see him in his office. Mutt got up to visit his boss.

He ran into Gifford in the hall. Unrepentant yet visibly hurting, Gifford managed a sickly grin. "Missed a swinging time last night, my friend. After her fifth jello shot, Cody got up on stage at Captains. Took two bouncers to get her down, but not before she managed to earn over a hundred bucks."

Mutt winced. This was more information than he needed about the extra-curricular activities of his jealous co-worker. How would it be possible now to work on projects side-by-side with her, without conjuring up visions of her drunkenly shedding her clothing?

Suddenly this hip young urban wastrel shtick, the whole life-is-fucked-so-let's-get-fucked-up playacting that Mutt and his friends had been indulging in for so long looked incredibly boring and tedious and counterproductive, possibly even the greased chute delivering one's ass to eternal damnation. Mutt knew with absurd certainty that he could no longer indulge in such a wasteful lifestyle. Something inside him had shifted irrevocably, some emotional tipping point had been reached.

But what was he going to do with his life instead?

Making a half-hearted neutral comment to Gifford — no point in turning into some kind of zealous lecturing missionary asshole Gifford would tune out anyway — Mutt continued through the cube-farm.

Dan Kicklighter, the middle-aged editor of *PharmaNotes*, resembled the captain of a lobster trawler, bearded, burly and generally disheveled, as if continually battling some invisible Perfect Storm. He had worked at a dozen magazines in his career, everything from *Atlantic Monthly* to *Screw*. A gambling habit that oscillated from moderate — a dozen scratch-ticket purchases a day — to severe — funding an Atlantic City spree with money the bank rightly regarded as a year's worth of mortgage payments — had determined the jagged progression of his resumé. Right now, after some serious rehab, he occupied one of the higher posts of his career.

"Matthew, come in. I just want you to know that I'm going to be away for the next four days. Big industry conference in Boston. With a little detour to Foxwoods Casino on either side. But that's just between you and me."

Kicklighter was upfront about his addiction, at least with his subordinates, and claimed that he was now cured to the point where he could indulge himself recreationally, like any casual bettor.

"I'm putting you in charge while I'm gone. I know it's a lot of responsibility, but I think you're up to it. This is a crucial week, and I'm counting on you to produce an issue we can all be proud of."

There were three assistant editors at *PharmaNotes*, so this advancement was not insignificant. But Mutt cringed at the temporary promotion. He just wanted to stay in his little miserable niche and not have anybody notice him. Yet what could he do? Deny the assignment? Wasn't such an honor the kind of thing he was supposed to be shooting for, next step up the ladder and all that shit? Cody would've killed for such a nomination.

"Uh, fine, Dan. Thank you. I'll do my best."

"That's what I'm counting on. Here, take this list of targets you need to hit before Monday. It's broken down into ten-minute activity blocks. Say, have you heard the odds on the Knicks game this weekend?"

Back in his cube, Mutt threw down the heavy sheaf of paper with disgust. He just knew he'd have to work through the weekend.

Before he had gotten through the tasks associated with the first ten-minute block, Cody appeared.

"So, all your ass-kissing finally paid off. Well, I want you to know that you haven't fooled everyone here. Not by a long shot."

Before Mutt could protest his lack of ambition, Cody was gone. Her angry strut conjured up images of pole-dancing in Mutt's traitorous imagination.

A short time later, Melba sauntered in and poised one haunch on the corner of Mutt's desk.

"Hey, big guy, got any plans for Friday night?"

"Yeah. Thanks to Kicklighter, I'll be ruining my eyesight right here at my desk."

Melba did not seem put off by Mutt's sour brusqueness. "Well, that's too bad. But I'm sure there'll be some other night we can, ah, hook up."

Once Melba left, Mutt tried to resume work. But he just couldn't focus. So he brought up the Gondwanaland page.

Who was going to tell him he couldn't? Kicklighter was probably already out the office and halfway to the roulette wheels.

Below the spinning foreign globe was a block of text followed by some hot-button links: IMPERIAL LINEAGE, CUSTOMS, NATURAL HISTORY, POLITICAL HISTORY, ART, FORUMS, and so forth. Mutt began to read the main text.

> For the past ten thousand years of recorded history, Gondwanaland's imperial plurocracy has insured the material well-being as well as the physical, spiritual and intellectual freedom of its citizens. Since the immemorial era of Fergasse I, when the walled communities of the Only Land — prominently, Lyskander, Port Shallow, Vybergum and Turnbuckle — emerged from the state of siege imposed by the roving packs of scalewargs and amphidonts, banding together into a network of trade and discourse, right up until the current reign of Golusty IV, the ascent of the united peoples of Gondwanaland has been unimpeded by war or dissent, despite a profusion of beliefs, creeds, philosophical paradigms and social arrangements. A steady accumulation of scientific knowledge from the perspicacious and diligent researchers at our many technotoria, combined with the practical entrepreneurship of the ingeniator class, has led to a mastery of the forces of nature, resulting in such now-essential inventions as the strato-carriage, storm-dispeller, object-box and meta-palp.
>
> The grateful citizens of Gondwanaland can assume — with a

surety they feel when they contemplate the regular rising of the Innermost Moon — that the future will only continue this happy progression...

Fascinated, Mutt continued to scan the introductory text on the main page, before beginning to bop around the site. What he discovered on these dependent pages were numerous intriguing photos of exotic scenes — cities, people, buildings, landscapes, artworks — and many more descriptive and explanatory passages that amounted to a self-consistent and utterly convincing portrait of an alien world.

The Defeat of the Last 'Warg; a recipe for bluebunny with groundnut sauce; *The Adventures of Calinok Cannikin*, by Ahleucha Mamarosa; Jibril III's tornado-struck coronation; the deadly glacier apes; the first landing on the Outermost Moon; the Immaculate Epidemic; the Street of Lanternmoths in Scordatura; the voices of children singing the songs of Mourners Day; the Teetering Needle in the Broken Desert; sunlight on the slate roofs of Saurelle; the latest fashion photographs of Yardley Legg —

Mutt's head was spinning and the clock icon on his screen read noon. Man, people thought Tolkien was an obsessive perfectionist dreamer! Whoever had put this site together was a goddamn fantasy genius! The backstory to Gondwanaland possessed the kind of organic cohesiveness that admitted of the random and contradictory. Why hadn't the citizens of Balamuth ever realized that they were sitting on a vein of pure allurium until a sheepherder named Thunn Pumpelly fell into that sinkhole? They just hadn't! A hundred other circumstantial incidents and anecdotes contributed to the warp and woof of Gondwanaland, until in Mutt's mind the whole invention assumed the heft and sheen of a length of richly embroidered silk.

Mutt wondered momentarily if the whole elaborate hoax was the work of a single creator, or a group effort. Perhaps the name or names of the perps was hidden in some kind of Easter Egg —

The one link Mutt hadn't yet explored led to the FORUMS. Now he went there.

He faced a choice of dozens of boards on different topics, all listing thousands of archived posts. He arbitrarily chose one — IMPERIAL NEWS — and read a few recent posts in chronological order.

Anybody heard any reports since Restday from the Liminal Palace on G4's health?
— IceApe13

The last update from the Remediator General said G4 was

still in serious condition. Something about not responding to the
infusion of nurse-hemomites.
    — LenaFromBamford

Looks like we could be having an Imperial Search soon then. I
hope the Cabal of Assessors has their equipment in good working
order. When was the last IS? 9950, right?
    — Gillyflower87

Aren't we all being a little premature? Golusty IV isn't dead
yet!
    — IlonaG

Mutt was baffled, even somehow a little pissed off, by the intensity of the
roleplaying on display here. These people — assuming the posts indeed
originated from disparate individuals — were really into this micronation
game, more like Renaissance Faire headcases and Civil War reenactors than
the art-student goofballs Mutt had envisioned as the people responsible for
the Gondwanaland site. Still, their fervent loyalty to their fantasy world offered Mutt a wistful, appealing alternative to his own anomie.

Impulsively, Mutt launched his own post.

From everything I've seen, Golusty IV seems like a very fine
Emperor and a good person. I hope he gets better.
    — MuttsterPrime

He quit his browser and brought up his word-processor.

Then he resumed trying to fit his life into ten-minute boxes.

Kicklighter returned from the Boston trip looking as if he had spent the
entire time wrestling rabid tigers. Evidently, his cure had not been totally
effective. His vaunted invulnerability to the seductions of Native-Ameri-
can-sponsored games of chance plainly featured chinks. An office pool was
immediately begun centered on his probable date of firing by the publisher,
Henry Huntsman. Ironically, Kicklighter himself placed a wager.

But all these waves of office scandal washed over Mutt without leaving
any impression at all. Likewise, his dealings with his former friends and
rivals had no impact on his abstracted equilbrium. Gifford's unceasing
invitations to get wasted, Cody's sneers and jibes, Melba's purring attempts
at seduction — None of these registered. Oh, Mutt continued to perform
his job in a semi-competent, off-handed way. But most of the time his head

was in Gondwanaland.

With his new best IM buddy, Ilona Grobes.

Ilona Grobes — IlonaG — had posted the well-mannered, respectful comment about not hastening Golusty IV into his grave. Upon reading Mutt's similarly themed post, she had contacted him directly.

> *MuttsterPrime, that was a sensitive and compassionate senti-*
> *ment. I'm glad you're not so thrilled by the prospect of an IS like*
> *most of these vark-heads that you forget the human dimension of*
> *this drama. I don't recognize your name from any of the boards.*
> *What clade do you belong to?*
> *— Ilona G*

That question left Mutt scratching his head. He debated telling Ilona to cut the fantasy crap and just talk straight to him. But in the end he decided to go along with the play-acting.

> *Ilona, is my clade really so important? I'd like to think that we*
> *can relate to each other on an interpersonal level without such*
> *official designations coming between us.*
> *— MuttsterPrime*

When Ilona's reply came, Mutt was relieved to see that his strategy of conforming to her game-playing had paid off.

> *How true! I never thought to hear from another Sloatist on this*
> *board! I only asked because I didn't want to give offense if you*
> *were an ultra-Yersinian. But it's so refreshing to dispense with*
> *such outdated formalities. Tell me some more about yourself.*
> *— IlonaG*

> *Not much to tell really. I'm an assistant editor at a magazine,*
> *and it sucks.*
> *— MuttsterPrime*

> *I'm afraid you've lost me there, Muttster. Why would a reposi-*
> *tory for excess grain need even one professional scurrilator, much*
> *less an assistant? And how can a condition or inanimate object*
> *"suck"? Where do you live? It must be someplace rather isolated,*
> *with its own dialect. Perhaps the Ludovici Flats?*
> *— IlonaG*

Mutt stood up a moment and looked toward the distant window in the far-off wall of the cube-farm, seeing a slice of the towers of Manhattan and thereby confirming the reality of his surroundings. This woman was playing some serious games with his head. He sat back down.

> *Oh, my home town is no place you've ever heard of. Just a dreary backwater. But enough about my boring life. Tell me about yours!*
> — *MuttsterPrime*

Ilona was happy to comply. Over the next several weeks, she spilled her life story, along with a freight of fascinating details about life in Gondwanaland.

Ilona had been born on a farm in the Ragovoy Swales district. Her parents raised moas. She grew up loving the books of Idanell Swonk and the antic-tableaus (were these movies?) featuring Roseway Partridge. She broke her arm when she was eleven, competing in the annual running of the aurochs. After finishing her schooling, earning an advanced instrumentality in cognitive combinatorics, she had moved to the big city of Tlun, where she had gotten a job with the Cabal of Higher Heuristics. (Best as Mutt could figure, her job had something to do with writing the software for artificial mineral-harvesting deep-sea fish.) Every Breathday Ilona and a bunch of girlfriends — fellow geeks, Mutt conjectured — would participate in *zymurgy*, a kind of public chess match where the pieces were represented by living people and the action took place in a three-dimensional labyrinth. She liked to relax with a glass of cloudberry wine and the music of Clay Zelta. (She sent Mutt a sample when he said he wasn't familiar with that artist. It sounded like punk polkas with a dash of tango.)

The more Mutt learned about Ilona, the more he liked her. She might be crazy, living in this fantasy world of hers, but it was an attractive neurosis. The world she and her fellow hoaxers had built was so much saner and exotic than the one Mutt inhabited. Why wouldn't anyone want to pretend they lived in such a place?

As for the larger outlines of Gondwanalandian society and its finer details, Mutt learned much that appealed to him. For instance, the role of Emperor or Empress was not an inherited one, or restricted to any particular class of citizen. Upon the death of the reigning monarch — whose powers were limited yet essential in the day-to-day functioning of the plurocracy — the Cabal of Assessors began a continent-wide search for a psychic heir. At death, the holy spirit of the ruler — not exactly that individual's unique soul, but something like free-floating semi-divine mojo — was believed to detach and descend on a destined individual, whose altered status could be confirmed by subtle detection apparatus. And then there was that eminently sensible business about every citizen receiving a lifetime stipend that rendered work not a necessity but a dedicated choice. Not to mention such attractions as the regular state-sanctioned orgies in such cities as Swannack, Harsh Deep, and Camp Collard that apparently made Mardi Gras look like the Macy's Thanksgiving Day Parade.

As for the crisis of Golusty IV's impending death, the boards remained full of speculation and chatter. The remediators were trying all sorts of new treatments, and the Emperor's health chart resembled Earth's stock market's gyrations, one minute up and the next way down.

Earth's stock market? Mutt was shocked to find himself so convinced of Gondwanaland's reality that he needed to distinguish between the two worlds.

With some judicious self-censorship and liberal use of generalities, Mutt was able to convey something of his life and character to Ilona as well, without baffling her further. He made up a lot of stuff too, incidents and anecdotes that dovetailed with Gondwanalandian parameters. Her messages began to assume an intimate tone. As did Mutt's.

By the time Ilona sent him her picture, Mutt realized he was in love. The photograph clinched it. (It was too painful for Mutt even to dare to think the image might be a fake, the Photoshop ruse of some thirteen-year-old male dweeb.) Ilona Grobes was a dark-haired, dark-eyed beauty with a charming mole above quirked lips. If all cognitive combinatorics experts looked like this, Gondwanaland had proved itself superior in the geek department as well. With the photo was a message:

> *Dear Mutt, don't you think it's time we met in the flesh? The Emperor can't live much longer, and of course all non-essential work and other activities will be suspended during the moratorium of the Imperial Search, for however long that may take. We could use those leisurely days to really get to know each other better.*
> *— IlonaG*

Finally, here was the moment when all charades would collapse, for good or ill. After some deliberation, Mutt attached his own photo and wrote back:

> *Getting together would be really great, Ilona. Just tell me where you live, and I'll be right there!*

— MuttsterPrime

You're such a joker, Mutt! You know perfectly well that I live at Number 39 Badgerway in the Funes district of Tlun! When can you get here? The aerial tramway service to Tlun is extensive, no matter where you live. Here's a pointer to the online schedules. Try not to keep me waiting too long! And I think your auroch-lick hairstyle is charming!
— IlonaG

Mutt felt his spirits slump. He was in love with a clinically insane person, one so mired in her delusions that she could not break out even when offered genuine human contact. Should he cut things off right here and now? No, he couldn't bring himself to.

Let me check those schedules and tidy up some loose ends here, Ilona. Then I'll get right back to you.
— MuttsterPrime

Mutt was still sitting in a motionless, uninspired funk half an hour later when Kicklighter called him into his office.

All the editor's photos were off the walls and in cardboard boxes, along with his other personal possessions. The hairy, rumpled man looked relieved.

"I'm outta here as of this minute, kid. Security's coming to escort me to the front door. But I wanted to let you know that I put in a good word for you to take over my job. Huntsman might not like my extracurricular activities too much, but he's a good publisher and realizes I know my stuff when it comes to getting a magazine out. He trusts me on matters of personnel. So you've got a lock on the job, if you want it. And who wouldn't? But you've got to get your head out of your ass. I don't know where you've been the past few weeks, but it hasn't been here."

All Mutt could do was stare at Kicklighter without responding. Scurrilator, he thought. Why would I want to be head scurrilator?

After another awkward minute, Mutt managed to mumble some thanks and good-luck wishes, then left.

He dropped in to Gifford's cubicle. Maybe his friend could offer some advice.

Gifford looked like shit. His tie was askew, his face pale and bedewed with sweat. There was a white crust around his nostrils like the rim of Old Faithful. He smiled wanly when he saw Mutt.

"Hey, pal, I'd love to talk to you right now, but I don't feel so good. Little touch of stomach trouble. In fact, I gotta hit the john pronto."

Gifford bulled past Mutt. He smelled like spoiled yogurt.

Mutt wandered purposelessly through the cube-farm. He found himself at Cody's box. She glared at him and said, "If you're here like the rest of them to gloat, you can just get in line."

"Gloat? About what?"

"Oh, come on, don't pretend you haven't heard about the layoffs."

"No — no, I haven't, really. I'm — I'm sorry, Cody."

Cody just snorted and turned away.

Melba wasn't in her cube. Mutt learned why from an official notice on the bulletin board near the coffee-maker.

> *If any employee is contacted by any member of the media regarding the sexual discrimination suit lodged by Ms. Melba Keefe, who is on extended leave until litigation is settled, he or she will refrain from commenting upon penalty of dismissal....*

Back in his cubicle, Mutt brought up the Gondwanaland web page. The coastline of Gondwanaland bore unmistakeable resemblances to the geography Mutt knew, the way an assembled jigsaw puzzle recalled the individual lonely pieces. As far as he could make out, Tlun was located where Buenos Aires was on Earth.

> *Ilona, I'm going to try to reach you somehow. I'm setting out today. Wish me luck.*
> *MuttsterPrime*

Mutt left his cheap hotel — roaches the size of bite-sized Snickers bars, obese hookers smoking unfiltered cigarettes and trolling the corridors 24/7 — for the fifth time that day. He carried a twofold map. Before he had left the US, he had printed off a detailed street map of Tlun. He had found a similar map for Buenos Aires and transferred it to a transparent sheet. Using certain duplicate, unvarying physical features such as rivers and the shape of the bay, he had aligned the two. This cartographic construction was what he was using to search for Number 39 Badgerway.

Of course, Buenos Aires featured no such street in its official atlas. And the neighborhood that Ilona supposedly lived in was of such a rough nature as to preclude much questioning of the shifty-eyed residents — even if Mutt's Spanish had been better than the "¿Que pasa, amigo?" variety. Watched suspiciously by glue-huffing, gutter-crawling juveniles and their felonious elders hanging out at nameless bars, Mutt could only risk a cursory inspection of the Badgerway environs.

After checking out the most relevant district, Mutt was reduced to wandering the city's boulevards and alleys, parks and promenades, looking for any other traces of a hidden, subterranean, alternative city that plainly didn't exist anywhere outside the fevered imagination of a handful of online losers, praying for a glimpse of an unforgotten female face graced by a small mole. Maybe Ilona was some Argentinian hacker-girl who had been subliminally trying to overcome her own reluctance to divulge her real whereabouts by giving him all these clues.

But even if that were the case, Mutt met with no success.

He had now been in Argentina for ten days. All costs, from expensively impromptu airline tickets to meals and lodging, had been put on plastic. He had turned his last paycheck into local currency for small purchases, but Mutt's loan payments had left him no nestegg. And the upper limits on his lone credit card weren't infinite. Pretty soon he'd have to admit defeat, return the New York, and try to pick up the shambles of his life.

But for the next few days anyhow, he would continue to look for Tlun and Ilona.

Returning today to the neighborhood labeled Funes on the Tlun map, Mutt entered a small café he had come to patronize only because it was marginally less filthy than any other. He ordered a coffee and a pastry. Spreading his map on the scarred countertop he scratched his stubble and pondered the arrangement of streets. Had he explored every possible niche — ?

A finger tapped Mutt's shoulder. He turned to confront a weasly individual whose insincere yet broad smile revealed more gaps than teeth. The fellow wore a ratty Von Dutch t-shirt that proclaimed I KISS BETTER THAN YOU.

"*Señor*, what is it you look for? Perhaps I can help. I know this district like the breast of my own mother."

Mutt realized that this guy must be some kind of con-artist. But even so, he represented the best local informant Mutt had yet encountered, the only person who had deigned to speak with him.

Pointing to the map, Mutt said, "I'm looking for this street. Do you know it?"

"*Si, seguro!* I will take you there without delay!"

Experiencing a spark of hope, Mutt followed the guide outside.

They came to a dank *calle* Mutt was half-sure he had visited once before. The guide gestured to a shadowy cross-street that was more of a channel between buildings, only large enough for pedestrian traffic. A few yards along, the street transformed into a steep flight of greasy twilit stairs.

"Right down here, *señor*, you will find *exactamente* what you are looking for."

Mutt tried to banish all fear from his heart and head. He summoned up into his mind's eye Ilona's smiling face. He advanced tentatively into the claustrophobic cattle-chute.

He heard the blow coming before he felt it. Determined not to lose his focus on Ilona, he still could not help flinching. The blow sent him reeling, blackness seeping over Ilona's face like spilled tar, until only her smile, Cheshire-cat-like, remained, then faded.

Sunlight poured through lacy curtains, illuminating a small cheerful room. On the wall hung a painting which Mutt recognized as one of Sigalit's studies for his *Skydancer* series. Mutt saw a vase filled with strange flowers on a nearby small table. Next to the flowers sat a box labeled LIBERTO'S ECLECTIC PASTILLES and a book whose spine bore the legend:

Ancient Caprices, by Idanell Swonk

Mutt lay in what was obviously a hospital bed, judging by the peripheral gadgetry around him, including an object-box and a pair of meta-palps. The blanket covering him diffused an odd yet not unpleasant odor, as if woven from the hairs of an unknown beast. He saw what looked like a call button and he buzzed it.

A nurse hurried into the room, all starched calm business in her traditional tricornered hat and life-saving medals.

Behind her strode Ilona Grobes.

Ilona hung back smiling only until the nurse assured herself that Mutt was doing fine and left. Then Ilona flung herself on Mutt. They hugged wordlessly for minutes before she stood up and found a seat for herself.

"Oh, Mutt, what *happened* to you? A Junior Effectuator found you unconscious a few feet from my door and brought you here. I was at work. The first thing I knew about your troubles was when I saw your picture on the evening propaedeutic. 'Unknown citizen hospitalized.' I rushed right here, but the remediators told me not to wake you. You slept for over thirty hours, right from Fishday to Satyrsday!"

Mutt grabbed Ilona's hand. "Let's just say I had kind of a hard time getting to Tlun."

Ilona giggled. "What a funny accent you have! That's one thing that doesn't come across online."

"And you — you're more beautiful than any photo. And you smell like — like vanilla ice cream."

Ilona looked shyly away, then back. "I'm sure that's a compliment, whatever vanilla ice cream may be. But look — I brought you some candy, and one of my favorite books."

"Thank you. Thank you very much for being here."

No ice cream, Mutt thought. He'd be a millionaire by this time next year.

They talked for several hours more, until the sounds of some kind of commotion out in the hall made them pause.

The door to Mutt's room opened and three men walked in. They were clad in elaborately stitched ceremonial robes and miters, and carried among them several pieces of equipment.

Seeing Mutt's puzzlement, Ilona explained. "It's just a team of Assessors. Golusty died yesterday, shortly after your arrival. The Imperial Search has begun."

One Assessor addressed Ilona. "Citizen Grobes, your testing will take place at your residence. But we need to assess this stranger now."

"Of course," Ilona said.

The Assessors approached Mutt's bedside. "With your permission, citizen — "

Mutt nodded, and they placed a cage of wires studded with glowing lights and delicate sensors on his head like a crown.

THE PIRATE'S TRUE LOVE
SEANA GRAHAM

Seana Graham lives in Santa Cruz, California, where she has worked for many years in a large, independent bookstore. She has admired the work of great fantasy writers ever since she first stumbled across the novels of E. Nesbit and Edward Eager in childhood, and is continually amazed by the vitality and diversity of the genre today. Although her writing, like her reading, tends to be all over the map, fantasy holds a special place in her heart. Her stories have appeared or are forthcoming in Red Wheelbarrow Literary Magazine, Eclipse, *and* Lady Churchill's Rosebud Wristlet, *where this story first appeared. She is currently working on a fantasy novel called* The Birdwatchers.

It was a fine spring morning as the pirate sat with his true love before sailing out to sea. She was wearing a long purple dress, and her cheeks were red with crying. The pirate held her hand and promised her jewels and fine clothes, but nothing helped. She would much rather have sat with the pirate till the end of time, and watched her purple dress turn to rags and then to dust than to have him sail off and find her the finest jewels in all the world. But she did not say this aloud, because she knew that the pirate would not want to sit holding her hand until the end of time, even if her dress did turn to dust. For the pirate's heart would always be with her, but his mind would be always on treasure. So, though she cried till her cheeks were red, she did not beg him to stay.

The pirate sailed away that spring morning and gave himself over to plundering and looting. He was good at his work, and lucky, and if that work involved a certain amount of anti-social behavior, well, it was what he was born to do. He was not a terribly analytical person, for he never stopped to ask himself why he needed to go around plundering and looting the high seas when all he'd ever really wanted was his ship and his men and the heart of his true love waiting back by the bay at home. Of course, he did have to pay somehow for the costly garments of satin and silk and lace he wore. True, these were not really necessary for plundering, but they did rather seem to go with the job.

After he left, the pirate's true love walked to the cliffs every day and looked out over the water. Sometimes, if she stood and stared long enough, she seemed to see the smoke of a great battle going on far out at sea. (Of course, her pirate love was by this time many leagues away, so this was either eyestrain or imagination.) And, after looking a great while, she would sigh and walk sadly back to her humble home. It might have helped pass the time if the pirate had left her some plunder to sort, or some loot to tidy, but the fact was gold and jewels had a way of slipping through pirate fingers like so much water. By the time the pirate sailed out on his next adventure, there was never much left but the pirate's mess to clean up, which she somehow could not find altogether romantic.

It was one day late in August when the pirate's true love turned from her lonely vigil on the cliffs, sighing because her humble home was now entirely too neat and tidy, now that the pirate's mess had long been cleared away — and realized that she was not alone. The truth was she never had been alone, but had just become too far-sighted to notice. But now — if she squinted — she could see that there were many other pirates' true loves standing on the cliff, sighing and straining their eyes over the all-too-empty waters. And she had to admit that, sad though it was, it was also just a little bit silly. After all, the pirates never came home before October. Now the pirate's true love — and let us call her May, since that was her name and we do not want to lose her in the anxious throng of other true loves there on the cliff — May could be a rather enterprising young woman when she saw the need, and right away she saw the need for a Pirate Women's Auxiliary. For there is such a thing as too much looking out over the water.

The Pirate Women's Auxiliary flourished quite handsomely for awhile. For one thing, with organization, only one true love needed to go and stand anxious and brooding above the cliffs on behalf of all the rest, and though at first they would quarrel among themselves for their turns, after awhile they began to devote themselves to the group's new task — fundraising. For there was quite enough wealth in the town — after all those years of relieving pirates of their treasure — to support any number of bake sales and raffles and charity balls. (Though it is true that, during these latter events, the pirates' true loves would have to bravely blink back the tears as they thought of their bold buccaneers out looting and pillaging and not knowing what they were missing. And sadly but also truly, there was more than one pirate's true love who suddenly noticed that there were some not-too-shabby looking farmers and blacksmiths and shopkeepers around . . . but that is not our story.)

The *true* true loves remained loyal, but a problem began to arise. For when the brave pirates returned that fall (in November, and very soggy), they found that their true loves were not oohing and ahhing over the heaps of treasure they had brought back with quite the enthusiasm the pirates were accustomed to arousing. The truth of the matter is, the fundraising had gone a little too well, and the pirates' true loves had managed to amass pretty much all the gold and jewels and fine clothes they could ever desire — and these did not slip through their fingers like water at all. Oh, they did try to summon up the right note of gratitude at being showered with diamonds and rubies, but it was hard, as they were all secretly dying to get back to their carpentry lessons. For they had unanimously voted to use whatever excess earnings were lying around to build a nice warm tea house on top of the cliffs in time for spring, so that the lonely cliff vigil would not be quite so cold and, well, tedious. By now, even the most steadfast of pirate true loves had begun to look for excuses to avoid her shift.

So the pirates were a little dismayed and the true loves were a little distracted, but if the jewels failed to excite, the handholding was still nice, and all went well through the winter. The pirates' treasure troves slowly dwindled (and, unbeknownst to them, came back by indirect routes to their true loves' coffers), and at last the spring day came when the pirates needs must sail to replenish their pirate hoards. So the pirates held hands with their true loves, and the true loves' cheeks were red with crying, although noticeably less red than the year before (and some might even have been justly accused of cosmetic deception). And though their true hearts ached to see the pirate ship fade from view on the treacherous sea, they all hurried home to get the pirates' mess cleaned up, because they were anxious to start working on a ship of their very own.

For certainly it is understandable that, after you stand, year in and year out, watching a fine pirate ship fade from view on the treacherous sea, you might get some hankering to go and find out what all the fuss is about. Because it couldn't be just about the treasure, could it? (As we have seen, the pirates' true loves had grown a little jaded by gold, jewels, etc.) So the handiest true loves built a sturdy little vessel and the sharpest true loves studied navigation, and one warm day in August, they were ready to sail. They christened the ship the True Love (of course), and they ran up a flag made from May's purple dress (which was a much better use for it than letting it turn to rags), emblazoned with a picture of two hands clasped, and they left the now-thriving tea shop in the care of their faithful friends, who were now farmers' true loves and blacksmiths' true loves and shopkeepers' true loves. And they faded slowly away from view on the treacherous sea.

When the brave pirates returned to their home by the bay (in early December and even soggier than the year before), their ship rode more lightly on the water than it had in many a year, for, truth to tell, their plundering had not come to much these last few months. Since August, in fact, they had not managed to get aboard a single fat galleon, or even raid one silent, sleeping coastal town. For just as they came within firing range of some ship or shoreline, a jaunty little ship with a purple flag (they could never get close enough to quite make out its logo, and what some of them *thought* they saw was too ridiculous to be believed) would race into view and warn them off with a furious blast of cannons and muskets. And though the pirates fought very bravely and fiercely, inevitably they would eventually have to make their escape, hidden by the walls of billowing smoke all around them. They were bold and fearless, but they were not stupid. They knew when they had met their match. Curiously, none of this great bombardment ever seemed to actually hit their ship, and some of the pirates swore that the enemy was purposely missing. But the other pirates only laughed at this, for the Pirates' Code made this unthinkable. Besides, some of that musket shot had come close enough to singe the whiskers of their gorgeous pirate beards.

So now, as the brave pirates alit from their ship, each walked to his humble home a little more slowly, a little less boisterously, a little less certainly than he had the previous year. (Though actually they should have been walking faster, for the treasure chests they carried were quite a bit lighter than they had been then.) They were not too sure that their true loves would love them quite so truly when they noticed that the customary shower of gold and jewels lasted for a conspicuously shorter period of time. The pirates, all in all, were a little ashamed.

But what was shame when compared to the wonder that filled each pirate's heart as he approached his true love's door — and found it locked and bolted? And what was shame compared to his consternation as he peered through a (dirty) window, and could make out no warm and glowing fire, no true love waiting next to it? And what, above all, was shame compared to the terror that seized each pirate as he stood alone in the cold, damp night and thought that some farmer . . . or blacksmith . . . or shopkeeper . . . might well be happy in his place tonight?

Now, as each pirate was beginning to consider that treasure was a rather paltry thing compared to some other things that could be won — or lost — a pinprick of light appeared on the crest of a hill above. And it was followed by another. And another. And another. Until finally a torchlight procession could be seen wending its way swiftly down the hillside. And every pirate's heart leapt suddenly with a terrible, yearning hope that sent him running to the center of town, where the hillside road would end.

And the pirates' true loves (after a long tramp from a secret lagoon, where a certain ship lay safely berthed for the winter) came rushing down to meet them, chattering vaguely of some Pirate Women's Auxiliary project which had unavoidably detained them. If any pirate recalled at that moment a purple flag on a distant sea, he made up his mind to forget it. For all hearts present felt, though silently, that this reunion was something rather more than the usual shower of gold and jewels.

One fine spring morning in the following year, the pirates once again sat holding hands with their true loves (none of whose cheeks were red at all, but all of whose eyes glowed beautifully). And then, a little reluctantly this time, the pirates boarded their fine ship, which soon faded from view on the treacherous sea.

And one warm day in August (for pirates are pirates, and should never be thwarted completely), the True Love sailed out after them. And so it sailed for many an August to come.

INTELLIGENT DESIGN
ELLEN KLAGES

Ellen Klages won the Nebula Award in 2005 for her novelette, "Basement Magic." Her short fiction has appeared in Bending the Landscape, Fantasy and Science Fiction, Black Gate, *and* Strange Horizons, *and has been short-listed for the Hugo, Nebula, Tiptree, and Spectrum awards. Klages has also written four books of hands-on science activities for children for the Exploratorium museum in San Francisco, one of which,* The Science Explorer Out and About, *was honored with Scientific American's Young Readers Book Award. She was a finalist for the John W. Campbell Award, and is a graduate of the Clarion South writing workshop. She is also a member of the Motherboard of the James Tiptree, Jr. Award, and is the auctioneer/entertainment for its benefit auctions. When she's not writing fiction, she sells old toys on eBay, and collects lead civilians. She lives in Cleveland, Ohio, surrounded by lots of very odd objects. Her first novel,* The Green Glass Sea, *will be published in 2006.*

> *"If one could conclude as to the nature of the Creator from a study of creation, it would appear that God has an inordinate fondness for stars and beetles."*
> — *J.B.S. Haldane, 1951*

God cocked his thumb and aimed his index finger at the firmament.

Ka-pow! Pow! Pow! A line of three perfect glowing pinpoints of light appeared in the black void. He squeezed his eyes almost shut and let off a single shot. Ping! The pinprick of light at the far edge of the firmament, just where it touched the rim of the Earth, glowed faintly red.

God got bored. Ratatatatatatat! He peppered one corner of the sky with tiny specks of light clustered tight together. Each one glowed steadily. God lay down on his back and looked up at what he'd created. It was okay.

He blinked. The lights flickered in and out. He blinked again. Flicker. Flicker. Flicker. God lay on his back and thought hard for a tiny bit of time, then stopped blinking. The lights continued to shimmer and twinkle up in the firmament. God smiled. That was better.

God's grandmother — she who was before the before, she who created dust out of nothing and the universe out of dust, sculptor of the clay of the world, creator and destroyer — was baking. She peered through the thickening mist that separated that which *is* from that which is becoming, and sighed.

"God," she called out. "Don't you think that's enough of those?" She had thought the night should remain in darkness. It was getting quite light in the firmament.

"Just a couple more?" God said.

"All right. But only a few. Then I need you to come in and help with the animals."

Nanadeus rolled out a sheet of clay while she waited for God to come in out of the void. Now that there was fire, there was much to be done. Systems and cycles and chains of being to set in place. And the oceans, which had turned out to be a little tricky.

The waters had been gathered together, separate from the dry land, and that was fine. But they weren't moving. They just lay there, wet and placid and still. She'd gone out and shifted them back and forth, and they did move, but then they slowed down and lay still again, and that just wouldn't do. They had to keep moving, and she didn't have the time to go out and shake them twice a day. Besides, they were too heavy for her to be lifting all the time. Maybe she had made the deep *too* deep? Where was God? If he could help make some of the simpler creatures, she'd have time to deal with the oceans.

God lay on the Earth, watching the twinkling stars, spraying random corners of the firmament with his outstretched finger, filling in the parts that seemed a little empty. Pow! Powpowpowpow! KAPOW! Ooops. He pursed his lips and drew in a breath, sucking a bit of light from that spot, then another, and another, until there were a few holes in the midst of the stars, blacker than the black of the void.

He sat up and examined a small muddy pebble clinging to his right knee. He put it on the palm of his hand and flicked it with his first finger, as hard as he could. The pebble shot far up into the firmament. God waited for it to fall down again, but it didn't. It wobbled a little, then just hung there. God made a POP! sound with his lips and the pebble began to glow with a bright white light. He grinned and reached for another pebble.

"God. I need you. Now," called Nanadeus.

God dropped the pebble and went in. "What're you making? Can I help?"

Nanadeus smiled and rumpled his hair. "Yes, you can. You can be a big help right now. Watch what I do."

She pulled a tray of tiny brown ovals from the oven. "You need to decorate them while they're still soft," she said, putting one on the counter. She reached into one of the bins that lined the counter. LEGS, said one. WINGS. ANTENNAE.

She stretched the oval a little, added two hair-like feelers and six legs, daubed it with a bit of green pigment and added two multicolored wings. She held out her palm. The little bug was perfect in every detail, except it was just clay. Its tiny eyes were blank and featureless and it lay still.

"Pay attention," she said. "This is important." She picked up another soft, baked lump and added identical legs and antennae and wings, stretching it in the same way. "You have to make two of each. They can be different colors, if you want, but the very same creature. Okay, God?"

He nodded slowly, his eyes wide and curious.

"Good. Now watch." She pinched a bit of bluish sparkling dust from a stone vat on the counter and sprinkled it over the dark shapes. "This is the fun part." She leaned over the clay figures and breathed on them gently. "Butterfly," she said.

The butterflies' wings quivered, then slowly beat together and out again. They flew onto the edge of the tray, to God's shoulder, and out into the void.

"Wow!" God clapped his hands in delight. "Can I try?"

His grandmother scooped two clay dots from the tray. God stuck his tongue in the corner of his mouth and very carefully put five tiny legs into the warm clay. "Can I make them red?" he asked.

"Yes," laughed Nanadeus. "We'll need a lot of insects, and you may decorate them in any colors you want. Do try for symmetry, though, won't you dear?"

God nodded solemnly and added a sixth leg and two little wings. He painted the round bugs bright red, and after a moment's thought, added some tiny black spots. He held them out to Nanadeus.

"Very nice," she said. She sprinkled and blew onto them. "Ladybug," she said, and they flew away.

"What other kind of bugs can I make?" God asked.

"Use your imagination," she said. "Just don't get carried away. Keep them small."

"Yay!" said God.

"But — " she held up her finger in warning. "Remember. Only two of each kind. They will make more of themselves."

"Okay," said God. He made two red ants, and two tiny green aphids, and a pair of flies with fuzzy flocked legs. Nanadeus had just breathed onto the second fly when there was a shudder, and then silence.

"Oh, God, the seas have stopped," she sighed. "Will you be all right by yourself? I need to start them up. Again."

He nodded. "I like making bugs," he said.

"I thought you might," Nanadeus smiled. "Have fun, but don't sprinkle them. We'll name them all when I come back." She patted him on the cheek and went out to deal with still waters.

God made two brown ants, and a different kind of aphid. Then he looked to make certain that his grandmother was gone, and opened all the other bins.

FANGS. PINCERS. HORNS. ARMOR. STINGERS.

"Cool," said God. He took one of the larger mounds and outfitted it with fierce claws and long fuzzy antennae, painting it bright, bright green. Then he made three hundred dozen dozen more, each more fearsome and garish than the last. Horns, claws, stripes, spots, bristling legs and armored carapaces blazed in every iridescent hue.

Bugs everywhere. God wanted to make even more, but he had run out of counter space. Where could he move them to? Move . . . ? God looked at the vat of shimmering dust. Nanadeus had said to wait for her, but . . .

He took a handful of the dust and flung it over the trays of inanimate insects.

"Well," said Nanadeus from out in the void. "That was easier than I'd feared." Her voice was small and distant. "The rock you put up there really did the trick. Moon. Tides. Now why didn't I think of that ages ago. . . ."

She was getting closer. God could hear her sensible shoes tramping across the face of the Earth.

He looked at the shimmering trays of bugs and blew, hard, over all of them at once. God whispered, as fast as he could:

"Scarab. Scarab, scarab, scarab. Weevil. Tiger beetle. Leaf beetle. Weevil. Weevil. Weevil. Click beetle. Harlequin, palm borer, leaf miner. Firefly. Weevil, weevil, weevil. Jewel beetle. Blister beetle. Bark beetle. Flour beetle. Stag beetle. Potato beetle. Stink beet — "

"God? How are you coming with those insects?" Nanadeus asked from just beyond.

God looked over his shoulder, then quickly back at the last pair of un-moving creatures on the tray. "*DUNG* beetle," he said with a grin. And it was so.

Then he leaned back and began to whistle as if he hadn't done anything at all. Creeping things covered every surface, legs and claws and pincers scuttling and skittering. God saw them and smiled.

They were good.

PIP AND THE FAIRIES
THEODORA GOSS

Theodora Goss was born in Hungary and now lives in Boston with her husband, daughter, and four cats in an apartment that contains the history of English literature, from Beowulf *to* Octavia E. Butler. *She is currently completing a PhD in English literature, learning Hungarian and looking for dragons. Her fiction, which has been nominated for the World Fantasy Award, has appeared in* Realms of Fantasy, Alchemy, Strange Horizons, Polyphony, *and* The Year's Best Fantasy and Horror, *and she has won the Rhysling Award for speculative poetry. Goss's first collection,* In the Forest of Forgetting, *was published in 2006.*

"Why, you're Pip!"

She has gotten used to this, since the documentary. She could have refused to be interviewed, she supposes. But it would have seemed — ungrateful, ungracious, particularly after the funeral.

"Susan Lawson," read the obituary, "beloved author of *Pip and the Fairies, Pip Meets the Thorn King, Pip Makes Three Wishes,* and other Pip books, of ovarian cancer. Ms. Lawson, who was sixty-four, is survived by a daughter, Philippa. In lieu of flowers, donations should be sent to the Susan Lawson Cancer Research Fund." Anne had written that.

"Would you like me to sign something?" she asks.

White hair, reading glasses on a chain around her neck — too old to be a mother. Perhaps a librarian? Let her be a librarian, thinks Philippa. Once, a collector asked her to sign the entire series, from *Pip and the Fairies* to *Pip Says Goodbye.*

"That would be so kind of you. For my granddaughter Emily." A grandmother, holding out *Pip Learns to Fish* and *Under the Hawthorns.* She signs them both "To Emily, may she find her own fairyland. From Philippa Lawson (Pip)."

This is the sort of thing people like: the implication that, despite their minivans and microwaves, if they found the door in the wall, they too could enter fairyland.

"So," the interviewer asked her, smiling indulgently, the way parents smile at their children's beliefs in Santa Claus, "did you really meet the Thorn King? Do you think you could get me an interview?"

And she answered as he, and the parents who had purchased the boxed set, were expecting. "I'm afraid the Thorn King is a very private person. But I'll mention that you were interested." Being Pip, after all these years.

Maintaining the persona.

Her mother never actually called her Pip. It was Pipsqueak, as in, "Go play outside, Pipsqueak. Can't you see Mommy's trying to finish this chapter? Mommy's publisher wants to see something by Friday, and we're a month behind on the rent." When they finally moved away from Payton, they were almost a year behind. Her mother sent Mrs. Payne a check from California, from royalties she had received for the after-school special.

Philippa buys a scone and a cup of coffee. There was no café when she used to come to this bookstore, while her mother shopped at the food co-op down the street, which is now a yoga studio. Mrs. Archer used to let her sit in a corner and read the books. Then she realizes there is no cup holder in the rental car. She drinks the coffee quickly. She's tired, after the long flight from Los Angeles, the long drive from Boston. But not much farther now. Payton has stayed essentially the same, she thinks, despite the yoga studio. She imagines a planning board, a historical society, the long and difficult process of obtaining permits, like in all these New England towns.

As she passes the fire station, the rain begins, not heavy, and intermittent. She turns on the windshield wipers.

There is Sutton's dairy, where her mother bought milk with cream floating on top, before anyone else cared about pesticides in the food chain. She is driving through the country, through farms that have managed to hold on despite the rocky soil. In the distance she sees cows, and once a herd of alpacas. There are patches too rocky for farms, where the road runs between cliffs covered with ivy, and birches, their leaves glistening with rain, spring up from the shallow soil.

Then forest. The rain is heavier, pattering on the leaves overhead. She drives with one hand, holding the scone in the other (her pants are getting covered with crumbs), beneath the oaks and evergreens, thinking about the funeral.

It was not large: her mother's co-workers from the Children's Network, and Anne. It was only after the documentary that people began driving to the cemetery in the hills, leaving hyacinths by the grave. Her fault, she supposes.

The interviewer leaned forward, as though expecting an intimate detail. "How did she come up with Hyacinth? Was the character based on anyone she knew?"

"Oh, hyacinths were my mother's favorite flower."

And letters, even contributions to the Susan Lawson Cancer Research Fund. Everyone, it seems, had read *Pip and the Fairies*. Then the books had gone out of print and been forgotten. But after the funeral and the documentary, everyone suddenly remembered, the way they remembered their childhoods. Suddenly, Susan Lawson was indeed "beloved."

Philippa asked Anne to drive up once a week, to clear away the letters and flowers, to take care of the checks. And she signed over the house. Anne was too old to be a secretary for anyone neater than Susan Lawson had been. In one corner of the living room, Philippa found a pile of hospital bills, covered with dust. She remembers Anne at the funeral, so pale and pinched. It is good, she supposes, that her mother found someone at last. With the house and her social security, Anne will be all right.

Three miles to Payne House. Almost there, then. It had been raining too, on that first day.

"Look," her mother said, pointing as the Beetle swerved erratically. If she looked down, she could see the road though the holes in the floor, where the metal had rusted away. Is that why she has rented one of the new Beetles? Either nostalgia, or an effort to, somehow, rewrite the past. "There's Payne House. It burned down in the 1930s. The Paynes used to own the mills at the edge of town," now converted into condominiums, Mrs. Archer's successor, a woman with graying hair and a pierced nostril, told her, "and one night the millworkers set the stables on fire. They said the Paynes took better care of their horses than of their workers."

"What happened to the horses?" She can see the house from the road, its outer walls burned above the first story, trees growing in some of the rooms. She can see it through both sets of eyes, the young Philippa's and the old one's. Not really old of course, but — how should she describe it? — tired. She blames the documentary. Remembering all this, the road running through the soaked remains of what was once a garden, its hedges overgrown and a rosebush growing through the front door. She can see it through young eyes, only a few weeks after her father's funeral, the coffin draped with an American flag and the minister saying "fallen in the service of his country" although really it was an accident that could have happened if he had been driving to the grocery store. And through old eyes, noticing that the rosebush has spread over the front steps.

As if, driving down this road, she were traveling into the past. She felt this also, sitting beside the hospital bed, holding one pale hand, the skin dry as paper, on which the veins were raised like the roots of an oak tree. Listening to the mother she had not spoken to in years.

"I have to support us now, Pipsqueak. So we're going to live here. Mrs. Payne's going to rent us the housekeeper's cottage, and I'm going to write books."

"What kind of books?"

"Oh, I don't know. I guess I'll have to start writing and see what comes out."

How did it begin? Did she begin it, by telling her mother, over her milk and the oatmeal cookies from the food co-op that tasted like baked sawdust, what she had been doing that day? Or did her mother begin it, by writing the stories? Did she imagine them, Hyacinth, the Thorn King, the Carp in the pond who dreamed, so he said, the future, and the May Queen herself? And, she thinks, pulling into the drive that leads to the housekeeper's cottage, what about Jack Feather? Or did her mother imagine them? And did their imaginations bring them into being, or were they always there to be found?

She slams the car door and brushes crumbs from her pants. Here it is, all here, for what it is worth, the housekeeper's cottage, with its three small rooms, and the ruins of Payne House. The rain has almost stopped, although she can feel a drop run down the back of her neck. And, not for the first time, she has doubts.

"One room was my mother's, one was mine, and one was the kitchen, where we took our baths in a plastic tub. We had a toaster oven and a Crockpot to make soup, and a small refrigerator, the kind you see in hotels. One day, I remember having soup for breakfast, lunch, and dinner. Of course, when the electricity was turned off, none of them worked. Once, we lived for a week on oatmeal cookies." The interviewer laughed, and she laughed with him. When they moved to California, she went to school. Why doesn't she remember going to school in Payton? She bought lunch every day, meatloaf and mashed potatoes and soggy green beans. Sometimes the principal gave her lunch money. She was happier than when the Thorn King had crowned her with honeysuckle. "Young Pip," he had said, "I pronounce you a Maid of the May. Serve the May Queen well."

That was in *Pip Meets the May Queen*. And then she stops — standing at the edge of the pond — because the time has come to think about what she has done.

What she has done is give up *The Pendletons*, every weekday at two o'clock, Eastern Standard Time, before the afternoon talk shows. She has given up being Jessica Pendleton, the scheming daughter of Bruce Pendleton, whose attractive but troublesome family dominates the social and criminal worlds of Pinehurst.

"How did your mother influence your acting career?"

She did not answer, "By teaching me the importance of money." Last week, even a fan of *The Pendletons* recognized her as Pip.

She has given up the house in the hills, with a pool in the backyard. Given up Edward, but then he gave her up first, for a producer. He wanted, so badly, to do prime time. A cop show or even a sitcom, respectable television. "I hope you understand, Phil," he said. And she did understand, somehow. Has she ever been in love with anyone — except Jack Feather?

What has she gained? She remembers her mother's cold hand pulling her down, so she can hear her whisper, in a voice like sandpaper, "I always knew they were real."

But does she, Philippa, know it? That is why she has come back, why she has bought Payne House from the Payne who inherited it, a Manhattan lawyer with no use for the family estate. Why she is standing here now, by the pond, where the irises are about to bloom. So she can remember.

The moment when, in *Pip and the Fairies*, she trips over something lying on the ground.

> *"Oh," said a voice. When Pip looked up she saw a girl, about her own age, in a white dress, with hair as green as grass. "You've found it, and now it's yours, and I'll never be able to return it before he finds out!"*
>
> *"What is it?" asked Pip, holding up what she had tripped over: a piece of brown leather, rather like a purse.*
>
> *"It's Jack Feather's Wallet of Dreams, which he doesn't know I've taken. I was just going to look at the dreams — their wings are so lovely in the sunlight — and then return it. But 'What You Find You May Keep.' That's the law." And the girl wept bitterly into her hands.*
>
> *"But I don't want it," said Pip. "I'd like to look at the dreams, if they're as nice as you say they are, but I certainly don't want to keep them. Who is Jack Feather, and how can we return his wallet?"*
>
> *"How considerate you are," said the girl. "Let me kiss you on both cheeks — that's the fairy way. Then you'll be able to walk through the door in the wall, and we'll return the wallet together. You can call me Hyacinth."*
>
> *Why couldn't she walk through the door by herself? Pip wondered. It seemed an ordinary enough door, opening from one of the overgrown rooms to another. And what was the fairy way? She was just starting to wonder why the girl in the white dress had green hair when Hyacinth opened the door and pulled her*

through.

On the other side was a country she had never seen before. A forest stretched away into the distance, until it reached a river that shone like a snake in the sunlight, and then again until it reached the mountains.

Standing under the trees at the edge of the forest was a boy, not much taller than she was, in trousers made of gray fur, with a birch-bark hat on his head. As soon as he saw them, he said, "Hyacinth, if you don't give me my Wallet of Dreams in the clap of a hummingbird's wing, I'll turn you into a snail and present you to Mother Hedgehog, who'll stick you into her supper pot!"

— *From Pip and the Fairies, by Susan Lawson*

How clearly the memories are coming back to her now, of fishing at night with Jack Feather, searching for the Wishing Stone with Hyacinth and Thimble, listening to stories at Mother Hedgehog's house while eating her toadstool omelet. There was always an emphasis on food, perhaps a reflection of the toaster and Crock-pot that so invariably turned out toast and soup. The May Queen's cake, for example, or Jeremy Toad's cricket cutlets, which neither she nor Hyacinth could bear to eat.

"I hope you like crickets," said Jeremy Toad. Pip and Hyacinth looked at one another in distress. "Eat What You Are Offered," was the Thorn King's law. Would they dare to break it? That was in *Jeremy Toad's Birthday Party.*

She can see, really, where it all came from.

"I think the feud between the Thorn King and the May Queen represented her anger at my father's death. It was an accident, of course. But she blamed him for leaving her, for going to Vietnam. She wanted him to be a conscientious objector. Especially with no money and a daughter to care for. I don't think she ever got over that anger."

"But the Thorn King and the May Queen were reconciled."

"Only by one of Pip's wishes. The other — let me see if I remember. It was a fine wool shawl for Thimble so she would never be cold again."

"Weren't there three? What was the third wish?"

"Oh, that was the one Pip kept for herself. I don't think my mother ever revealed it. Probably something to do with Jack Feather. She — I — was rather in love with him, you know."

The third wish had been about the electric bill, and it had come true several days later when the advance from the publisher arrived.

Here it is, the room where she found Jack Feather's wallet. Once, in *Pip Meets the Thorn King,* he allowed her to look into it. She saw herself, but considerably older, in a dress that sparkled like stars. Years later, she recognized it as the dress she would wear to the Daytime Emmys.

And now what? Because there is the door, and after all the Carp did tell her, in *Pip Says Goodbye*, "You will come back some day."

But if she opens the door now, will she see the fields behind Payne House, which are mown for hay in September? That is the question around which everything revolves. Has she been a fool, to give up California, and the house with the pool, and a steady paycheck?

"What happened, Pip?" her mother asked her, lying in the hospital bed, her head wrapped in the scarf without which it looked as fragile as an egg-shell. "You were such an imaginative child. What made you care so much about money?"

"You did," she wanted to and could not say. And now she has taken that money out of the bank to buy Payne House.

If she opens the door and sees only the unmown fields, it will have been for nothing. No, not nothing. There is Payne House, after all. And her memories. What will she do, now she is no longer Jessica Pendleton? Perhaps she will write, like her mother. There is a certain irony in that.

The rain on the grass begins to soak through her shoes. She should remember not to wear city shoes in the country.

But it's no use standing here. That is, she has always told herself, the difference between her and her mother: she can face facts.

Philippa grasps the doorknob, breathes in once, quickly, and opens the door.

> "I've been waiting forever and a day," said Hyacinth, yawning. She had fallen asleep beneath an oak tree, and while she slept the squirrels who lived in the tree had made her a blanket of leaves.
>
> "I promised I would come back if I could," said Pip, "and now I have."
>
> "I'm as glad as can be," said Hyacinth. "The Thorn King's been so sad since you went away. When I tell him you're back, he'll prepare a feast just for you."
>
> "Will Jack Feather be there?" asked Pip.
>
> "I don't know," said Hyacinth, looking uncomfortable. "He went away to the mountains, and hasn't come back. I didn't want to tell you yet, but — the May Queen's disappeared! Jack Feather went to look for her with Jeremy Toad, and now they've disappeared too."
>
> "Then we'll have to go find them," said Pip.
>
> — From *Pip Returns to Fairyland*, by Philippa Lawson

LEVIATHAN
SIMON BROWN

Simon Brown lives on the south coast of New South Wales, Australia, with his wife Alison and children Edlyn and Fynn. He is the author of two science fiction novels, Privateer *and* Winter, *and the five fantasy novels to date that make up the Keys of Power and Chronicles of Kydan fantasy trilogies. His latest novel is fantasy* Rival's Son. *Brown's short fiction, which has twice won the Aurealis Award, has been collected in* Cannibals of the Fine Light. *A new collection,* Troy, *was published in early 2006.*

L ike all fish stories, this one's a whopper. Unlike all other fish stories, this one starts thirty-five thousand feet in the air.

Gerard Francis McVitty

Over the Pacific Ocean, a Boeing 707 en route to Honolulu from Sydney, just past the Gilbert Islands and a whisker short of the International Date Line, suddenly encountered the sort of engine trouble an engineer would call "catastrophic."

Not too many minutes later, bits of 707 and people and suitcases and loose clothing were floating down onto the ocean like confetti at a wedding. One of those bits comprised a large man's overcoat, puffed out like a parachute, and Gerard Francis McVitty, ten years old, hanging onto the coat's arms and tail for dear life.

Looking down between his feet, Gerard saw blue — dimpled, sun-reflecting — and precious little else.

Except.

Except for a splodge of something darker near his left ankle; he tugged experimentally on the overcoat with his right hand and the splodge shifted to between his feet. As Gerard descended it developed into a round island, green-topped and surrounded by rippling circles of waves.

He was saved.

It turned out to be a very wet island, and slippery as all out, but there was fresh water and what looked like figs and Gerard figured he could fix up a fishing rod, although he'd have to give some thought to making a hook;

there were bits of metal from the 707 around, and he figured he could rig something from that. The island wasn't big as islands went, but at least it was solid land and he wasn't going to die from hunger or thirst, and as far as he could see he was the only big animal on it. He had been secretly worried about the possibility of tigers on his way down, but there was nothing more aggressive here than a couple of hungry mosquitoes.

He gave some thought to attracting any rescue craft that might come by; he was sure someone would send out search parties once the 707 didn't arrive in Honolulu. It was too wet to start a signal fire, and anyway he wasn't sure he knew how to start one without matches. He hit upon the idea of writing something out on the fringe of the island using palm leaves, his name for example.

But that could wait, for after his near miss with death and his exploration of his island, he was exhausted. He found a relatively dry, mossy spot near a shallow pool of rain water, and used for a pillow the overcoat that had saved his life. He felt warm and safe, and in no time was fast asleep.

When he woke what felt like many hours later, Gerard searched the island looking for palm leaves that had dropped to the ground, but he didn't find any. He figured they must have blown away. Then he tried climbing up one of the palm trees, but it was too slippery and rubbery and all he could do was clamber up to his height before sliding down. He wondered how else he might make a sign for any searchers, but didn't come up with any ideas. Then he remembered the overcoat. He searched the pockets and found a pocket knife on the end of a key chain. The biggest blade was no longer than his little finger, but it was better than nothing at all.

He picked the thinnest palm tree, steadied the trunk with one hand, and then started sawing away. Almost immediately the ground beneath him shook. Gerard figured it was an earthquake and dropped the knife to hold onto the palm tree with both hands, but both of his hands slipped right off as if they were greased and his head bounced off the trunk.

The earth stopped moving.

For a moment he didn't do anything. Then he remembered his head *bounced* off the trunk. He automatically felt his skull. It seemed hard enough, but there was blood on his hands.

Gerard panicked. He frantically wiped his head with his forearm to see where the blood was coming from, but nothing rubbed off. He whipped off all his clothes and searched his body — the bits he could see — for any wound.

Nothing.

Drip. He looked up. The palm tree was bleeding. His little island lurched again. Gerard fell heavily, bouncing on the ground as if it was made from a trampoline. He opened his mouth automatically to say "ouch" but he was so surprised nothing came out. He was scrabbling to his feet when the ground moved beneath him again, and he had the nauseating sensation of rising into the sky. He just had time to grasp onto the bleeding palm tree when the island tipped over and started sinking. His body slipped sideways and dangled precariously over the ocean, then he was in it, salty, caustic, gulping, drowning...

...and out again. He gasped, coughed for breath, then was underneath a second time. The surface of the ocean was above him, glittering bright, the sky refracted. Water flooded up his nose and he sneezed, drank more of the ocean...

...was dangling, legs kicking, in the sky. White water spumed over him and it stank.

The island leveled off and, miraculously still gripping the palm, he levered himself to his feet. He was moving.

In fact, the whole island was moving.

Diggety

"You got a nickname?"

"Um," Gerard said.

The doctor smiled. "I thought all kids had nicknames these days." He used his hands to press the boy's stomach; Gerard was supposed to tell him if it hurt.

"Sometimes the kids at school call me Diggety." There was a twinge in his stomach and he flinched.

The doctor progressed to his ribcage. "Diggety? Why do they call you that?"

"Hot diggety dog. I got sunburned at the swimming carnival."

The doctor turned Gerard around and started pressing his back, especially along his spine. A couple of times the boy flinched.

"How long ago was that?"

"February." Gerard said it like the doctor should have known. When else did schools hold their swimming carnivals?

"Did you win anything?"

"Got a ribbon for the relay. My house came second."

"Oh, that's good."

Gerard didn't say anything, but he didn't think coming second any good. He was flinching more as the doctor explored his lower back.

"Okay, you can put your shirt on."

As Gerard dressed the doctor turned to his parents and sighed. "I'd really like to get some X-rays."

"Where do we go for them?" Mrs. McVitty asked.

"The base hospital. I'll give you a referral. Go as soon as you can, then come back here next week."

The drive back to the family's cattle station took longer than expected. A storm came out of the north — thunderheads the size of cities — and dumped the best part of the district's annual rainfall in less than an hour. Gidgee Gidgee Creek flash-flooded and Gerard and his parents were stuck on the wrong side of the road.

"Mum's gonna kill us," Mr. McVitty said. "She didn't want to baby-sit the kids in the first place."

"Nothin' we can do about it," Mrs. McVitty said flatly, as if being killed by Gerard's grandmother was a danger she faced every day.

An hour and a half later the rain had stopped but the creek was still up. Gerard's parents were walking around the car, heads bent down in earnest talk they didn't want their son to hear. Gerard stayed in the car, head resting against a side window. It was hot, and his clothes stuck to his skin, but he didn't have the energy to get out.

They didn't know it, but Gerard knew they were talking about him. They didn't look at him at all, that's how he could tell. Maybe when they looked at him they couldn't forget how sick he was. Not that anybody would tell him he was sick. But he wasn't stupid.

A couple of weeks later it felt like fire when he pissed, and when he tried to shit all he could do was bleed. Gerard was too embarrassed to tell his dad, so he told his mother when Mr. McVitty left to do a boundary ride. She listened attentively, then looked out over the station, her big brown eyes narrowing for a second. Gerard saw his mother swallow once, then twice, then heard her clear her throat.

"We've been kinda expecting it," she said slowly, drawing out the words. "I'm sorry it hurts. I wished to God it didn't, but there you go." She reached out suddenly and took Gerard's hand in her own. "We'll tell your dad when he gets back." She cleared her throat again. "You go and play now."

"Don't feel like playing much," Gerard said.

Mrs. McVitty nodded. "Guess not."

"What's for tea tonight?"

"Corned beef. Same as always on Tuesday. Would you like something special?"

"We got any ice cream?"

"We'll see about that. I gotta go to town later, so I might get some then."

"What's in town?"

"Your grandma," Mrs. McVitty said, almost disinterested. Then she smiled down at her son. "And ice cream, of course."

Gerard Francis McVitty

The monster had a sing-song voice that seemed too thin and too high for something so big, and it came from its spout — what Gerard had first thought was a pool — and not its mouth. And when it spoke the water in top of the spout bubbled so it sounded like it was talking under water all the time.

"Don't go cutting me again or I'll drown you."

"I thought you were an island."

"That's my lure. I get sailors landing on me all the time, then I drown them and swallow them and eat their ship."

Gerard, who had survived a 35,000 foot drop from a busted 707 and was filled with so much cancer he was almost all tumor and no boy, found he was still afraid of dying. He did not want to be eaten alive.

"I wouldn't have landed on you if I'd known you were a..." Gerard thought, but couldn't come up with the name. "You gotta be almost as big as a blue whale. I've seen pictures of them. They're a hundred feet long."

"No. Bigger than any whale. I'm Leviathan. I'm in the Bible. You read your Bible?"

"Don't have one. Read my mum's now and then. So you gonna eat me now?"

"Thinking about it. You very big? I can't see you way up there."

"I'm just a boy. I wouldn't be bigger'n one of your teeth. I'm as little as a mouse."

"If you slipped down a little so I could see you I could tell you if I was gonna eat you or not."

"I don't think that's a good idea."

"I'm not hungry or anything. I just want to see you. Climb down next to one of my eyes."

"I don't wanna. I like it up here just fine."

"Well, alright," Leviathan said, sort of easy.

But Gerard wasn't trusting the monster, and it was just as well, because next second it was heaving and curving and Gerard was holding his breath again. He thought he was going to die this time for sure, but then he was gasping for air and water was running off Leviathan in waterfalls. He didn't think he'd last another one, he was so tired and scared, but when he saw the blow hole spray hot steam in the air, and heard air getting sucked back in, he got an idea.

"So, slip down and show yourself," Leviathan said, almost teasing.

"Still don't think that's a good idea," Gerard said as casually as he could, and let go of his grasp on the palm tree or whatever it was to collect a long piece of 707 with a flash of red kangaroo on it, then scrambled back to the tree.

"Well, okay. I hate to do it this way. I like swallowing my prey whole and quick so nothing suffers. But you had a choice."

"I had a choice," Gerard admitted.

"So," Leviathan said, and started his dive again.

But this time Gerard was ready for him. As they went under, he used the metal to dig around in the pool until he found the actual blow hole in the bottom and wedged it open. They came up so fast Gerard thought they would launch into the sky, and the sound from the blow hole was a scream so high, so piercing, he could feel his brain go all fuzzy around the edges.

When the scream was finished, Leviathan sucked in a few acres of air and said, "We gotta talk about this."

Diggety

It wasn't just the hospital that convinced Gerard he was really sick — like so sick he might not be coming home; it was the way everyone smiled at him and told him he would be discharged in no time at all. That and the pain, which never really went away. He was getting morphine through a drip, and although it made bearable that small wafer of life still left to him, the pain lurked beneath like a shark under a wave.

The worst thing was the vomiting, especially when there was blood in the sputum, red traces of it in the phlegm. That was when he really wanted everyone to tell him he was going to be alright, but whenever it happened he could see the skin on his parents' faces go as white as the bark on a dead gum tree.

His mum stayed by his bed almost the whole time, but his dad had to go home to look after the station and his brothers and sisters. Grandma was not up to babysitting full time. His mum always bought him comic books: Casper the Ghost, and Wendy the Witch, and Archie, and best of all Classics Illustrated: Gerard's favourite was Sinbad the Sailor. He liked the look of the Arabian dhows with their fore-and-aft sails like white triangles, the garish brightness of tropical lands in seas too blue to be true, the rocs and whales and the sword fighting with saifs and tulwars...

But instead of white sails he had white sheets, instead of a steel sword he had a cold bedpan, and instead of the currents and tides of the Indian Ocean he had the currents and tides of pain that swirled through his little body in eddies and whirlpools.

A priest came to talk to him. Gerard first saw him talking with his parents, their voices low, the priest with one hand on his father's shoulder and another on his mother's. Then he sat down next to Gerard's bed and smiled in the way a lot of adults smiled at children, as if to prove they were not really adults at all but just kids with big hands.

"So, skipping school, eh?" The priest winked.

Gerard stared at him.

"My name is Father Walsh. I wanted to come in and see how you were going."

"Why?"

Walsh pursed his lips. "Because I look after Catholics who are staying in the hospital." He winked again. "You're part of my flock."

Gerard had a quick mental image of being a sheep.

"A good shepherd always looks after his flock," Walsh continued. "That is something our lord Jesus Christ taught us, through his example."

"Jesus will look after me?"

"He will," Walsh said with certainty.

"Will he make me get better?"

"He may. Or..." Walsh swallowed. "Or he may call you to him."

Gerard knew what that meant, and in that moment knew why the priest was here. He glanced over Walsh's shoulder and saw his parents looking at him like he was already half-ghost. Somehow it made what he already knew was going to happen to him more than concrete; his sickness was becoming an execution. Suddenly anger swirled through him.

"I piss blood," he said to the priest. "Will Jesus still love me?"

"Especially," Walsh said softly.

And the anger ebbed away as quickly as it had come.

Gerard Francis McVitty

Despite saying he wanted to talk, Leviathan said nothing for a long time. Gerard shivered as he dried, and at first did not notice the wake. When he did he looked up, saw the sky setting ahead, and knew they were heading west. He was hungry and tired and still scared.

"Where are we going?" he asked.

"Sinbad's Sea."

"Where's that?"

"A way. You going to let me see you, little mouse?"

"Haven't changed my mind."

"That thing in my blowhole is hurting. Take it out? Won't dive if you do."

"Won't dive for sure if I leave it in," Gerard said, more to himself. "Is there anything I can eat up here? I'm betting those figs aren't real figs."

"Why should I help you? If you starve to death you'll just drop off one day and then I can eat you."

"If I die that metal in your blowhole will never come out."

"Don't matter to me."

Gerard snorted in disbelief. He was ten — hell, almost eleven! — and could play that game better than any monster. "Don't matter to me, either," he said nonchalantly, and meant it.

"I can float on the surface for years and years, my little mouse, and not worry about it."

"Sure."

There was a long pause, and then Leviathan said, "Mussels."

Automatically, like he was playing Connections with his mum, Gerard said, "Bones."

"No, not muscles. Mussels like shellfish. You eat shellfish?"

Gerard frowned. "I come from the middle of Australia. We don't get much shellfish there."

"Don't know where Australia is, but if you look in the pool, you'll see mussels and barnacles and things stuck to my skin. Try and eat them."

Gerard put his hand over the lip of the pool and felt under the rim. There were some hard shells there and he pulled one off. It looked like a stone mouth with a wispy beard.

"What do I do with it?"

"Open it and eat the animal inside."

Gerard looked around for something to open it with. He regretted losing the pen knife, but he had been hanging on for dear life at the time and it was gone and there was nothing he could do about it. Then he remembered the metal plug in the blowhole, and he worked a part of the top of it loose, bending it this way and then that until he had a jagged piece about the size and shape of a carving knife. With some effort, and a cut finger, he opened the shellfish and, without looking too closely at the white soft thing inside, swallowed the contents in one gulp. It tasted fishy and gritty and slimy all the way down, and Gerard almost gagged, but his stomach liked having something inside it, and he quickly scavenged another one.

Diggety

He had never tasted piss, but Gerard reckoned the medicine he had to take every four hours would probably be close to it. It made his whole face screw up and his tongue hang out looking for relief. Afterwards he always got an orange cordial, double strength so it was real sweet, but even that did not get rid of the grungy-piss taste at the back of his throat. The taste lasted until he had a hot meal.

In the confined space he inhabited, with the repetitive routine that became for Gerard as predictable and boring as the plains back on the station, that medicine was the only highlight in the whole day. He had been in the hospital so long that when his mum visited they had ran out of things to say. And his dad, on the rare occasion he made it in, uttered barely a half dozen words and stared at his son almost balefully, as if it was his fault he was sick, as if he had planned to get cancer all along; Gerard wanted to stare defiantly back at his dad, but it was like looking at car lights on high beam and he could not do it.

Other than the medicine, the only other bump in the routine happened once a week when Father Walsh came in. They played cards a lot, first it was whist, but then Walsh taught him how to play poker and what a suicide king was and just how much fun you could have when jokers were wild. They used matchsticks for stakes.

"You gotta bet with poker, otherwise there's no point and it's just cards," Walsh told Gerard. "Might as well stick with whist."

Eventually the conversation would get off one-eyed jacks and onto cancer and dying and God. Gerard was getting the idea that all three were inextricably linked. You could not have cancer without God, and you could not have God without dying coming into it somewhere, and he wondered what role Walsh fulfilled in the whole deal.

"You been a priest your whole life?" he asked Walsh one day.

Walsh was studying his hand. "Not yet."

"I mean, you go straight into it from school?"

Walsh shook his head. "I was a teacher first. Wasn't enough for me." He put some cards down and held up two fingers. Gerard passed him two from the top of the deck. "My mother said I should be a priest. So I thought about it and figured she was right. And here I am." He grinned widely and lay down two pair. "Kings over tens."

"And here I am," Gerard said, smiling slyly, and lay down a full house. He won an awful lot of matches.

"Does it make you closer to God?"

Walsh pursed his lips. "Not that I've noticed. But I rely on him a lot more than I used to. I've gotten to understand some of His ways."

"What about dying. Gotten to understand that yet?"

Walsh paused in shuffling the cards. At first he did not meet Gerard's gaze. "Well, not really. My mother died last year, and I reckon it was as hard for me as a priest as it would have been if I was a teacher. One thing I've learned, maybe, is that not everything has an answer, at least not an answer we want to hear."

Gerard thought death was like one of those great summer storms that came every couple of years from the north, with huge dense banks of curving darkness, and no matter how long you looked it just seemed to stay where it was, but once you looked away it rushed in and next thing you know the wind's ripping off your tin roof and cattle are being blown over and the rain's so heavy it turns the whole plain into a river as wide as the state of Queensland. Gerard didn't want to be surprised like that by death, so he kept on staring at it, and it just stayed there on the horizon, coming no closer, as big as the sky.

Gerard Francis McVitty

Over the next few days, Gerard saw islands slide by as Leviathan made his way west. These were real islands, with people and beaches on them, and sometimes the people ran away when they saw Leviathan, and sometimes they just stood still and stared at the monster. The first time it happened Gerard called for help, but he did not know if anyone saw him — just a dot up near the blowhole — let alone heard him over the whooshing sound of the sea parting before them, white walls of water jetting up either side of Leviathan's maw.

"Cut your caterwauling," Leviathan told him. "It's hurting my ears."

Gerard shut up.

Leviathan must have been moving at close to fifty or sixty miles an hour, and the wind chaffed and burned Gerard's face if he stood up all the time, like he was sticking his head out of a car window. He found he could get quite comfortable sitting against one of the growths that looked like a palm tree and with his feet in the blowhole. Although the back of the beast was as wide and big as an island itself, at night Gerard tied himself to the tree with the overcoat he'd used as a parachute because he was afraid of slipping off.

"Do you always travel so close to land?" he asked Leviathan on the morning of the third day after he fell from the sky.

"Sure, it's how I navigate, but I'm usually underwater so nobody knows I'm around." The blowhole made a sound like a disappointing hiss. "But since that isn't possible right now, I'm forced to do it on the surface. No thanks to you, and no telling what will happen because of it."

Gerard found out soon enough. It was almost evening of the third day, and the sun was a bloated yellow balloon on the horizon, cool enough to look at, when a flash in the darkening sky to their left drew their attention. They saw a thin white line curve into the sky and then droop towards them. Without hesitation, Leviathan smashed his great tail in the ocean, sending up a waterspout over a hundred feet high, and shouted, "Hang on, little mouse!" and made a quick and violent turn to port.

Gerard didn't hang on quite quick enough and his feet slipped out from underneath him. He slid about three yards before he could get up, and he scrambled for the overcoat, still tied to its palm tree, and held on to it for dear life.

If Gerard thought the monster was going fast before, it was nothing to the burst of speed it put on now. The sea rainbowed above him, drenching him. Fish smacked down next to him, flapping uselessly, some spilling into the blowhole. Gerard felt Leviathan surge above the surface of the ocean then splash back down with a huge crack that sounded like a cannon shot, then surge forward and up again.

"Food!" Leviathan shouted with glee, and Gerard pulled himself to his feet to see what it was Leviathan had sighted.

About halfway to the horizon was a grey ship, not much bigger than a ferry. It had a single gun near the bow which fired, pom-pom-pom, sending tracer overhead. The distance between them closed quicker than Gerard would have thought possible, and when it seemed they were about to collide Leviathan arched into the sky and came down, maw open, straight onto the ship. There was sound of twisting, crunching metal, flames shot out the side of Leviathan's jaws and Gerard thought he heard the squeal of someone impaled on a giant tooth.

And then calm, absurd and sudden.

Gerard peered over the side and saw a slight oil slick, shiny blue, floating on the surface, and then they left it behind.

Leviathan's stomach rumbled. "Delicious," the monster said.

Diggety

His mother came in smiling like she had good news, and she was holding her arms out straight.

"Wings," she said.

Gerard smiled back. "Aeroplane."

"Jet."

"Boeing 707."

She plumped down next to him on the bed and shook her arms out.

"Red Skelton," he said.

Her mum looked confused. "What?"

"On television. He comes on stage shaking his arms and says, 'I've just flown in from Albuquerque and boy! are my arms tired.'"

His mum laughed. "I've got good news."

"I'm getting out of hospital and going home," Gerard said, feeling hope rise in him like mercury in a thermometer.

For a fraction of a second, Gerard saw his mum's face collapse, and underneath got a glimpse of desolation. Then it all came right, smile perfect, and she said, "Almost! You're going to Disneyland."

Gerard was still seeing the desolation, though, and his brain did not understand the words.

"You hear that, sweetheart? You're getting out of hospital and going to Disneyland!"

His brain caught up, and he said, vaguely, "But that's in America."

She put her arms out again and made pathetic engine sounds, and Gerard understood at last. "I'm going on a 707? All the way to America?"

His mother nodded. "There's a group in Sydney who give very sick kids special favours. We asked if you could go to Disneyland, and they're going to pay for you and me to go."

"Wow."

"But," his mother said, straightening his bed clothes with one hand, "you have to get a bit better first. Just a bit, just enough to let you travel. Can you do that for me, honey?"

Gerard nodded eagerly. "Oh, yeah."

Gerard Francis McVitty

Leviathan went after the big, round, red-hulled ships the most. They plumped like metal sausages in the sea, smoky, rusty, white-masted ships, and he would chase them down from astern then raise himself in the sky like a tidal wave and fall on them, smashing them, swallowing them, flipping people in the air with his tongue and gobbling them like cocktail frankfurters. Squishy sounds, rending metal sounds, explosions when the oil caught fire and whooshed up the monster's sides, singing Gerard's eyebrows. Then off again, fast as the wind, throwing the sea up in long curtains of glistening water.

"This is Sinbad's Sea, little mouse," Leviathan told him. "This is where the ocean is warmest, where the meat is sweetest, where the ships always travel the same lanes, following the coastlines that captains have been navigating for thousands of years."

"Is that how old you are?"

"Older. I am as old as the sea. As long as sailors have existed, they've remembered me. I am their first nightmare, and sometimes their last one." He laughed his funny, air-blowing laugh, almost a whistle. "I am adventure. Without me all sailors have to fear is storms and drowning, and that's not enough. Imagination's way to big for storms and drowning, and needs me to fill it up."

Gerard felt cold suddenly. "You're death," he said.

"Nothing so fancy," Leviathan said, his levity gone, and then more lightly, "Look, there's an old-time dhow. See how the sail's rigged? Arabs been using that kind of boat for three thousand years or more."

"You going to eat it?"

"I'm Leviathan. What do you think?"

At night Leviathan would slow down. He didn't have to rush through the sea to find ships because they had their lights on and he could see them from quite some distance. Then he would ease up and take them broadside, snapping the hull in two with one bite, then obliterating everything left with a smack of his giant tail. When the monster wasn't rushing after food, Gerard would sometimes lay on his back and look at the stars, making sure one arm of the overcoat was tied to his leg, and another tied to one of the fake palm trees. He was still afraid of slipping off and just disappearing into the sea, splash, and sinking so deep he would scrunch up like a prune. To while away the hours he would talk with the monster. Leviathan liked talking, because he didn't get much chance to do it.

"How many stars can you count?" Leviathan asked once.

"I dunno. Too many to count. Must be millions."

"Thousands of millions," Leviathan said. "I've counted them. Sometimes, more in the past than now, I used to float on the surface at night, just like now, and do nothing but count the stars. My eyes are better than yours, so I can see in the abyss below, and I can see so far into space that sometimes I think there's no end to it."

"You've counted them all?"

"And named them. Every one. There's Opal, blue and bright, above us right now. And over east is Pearl. That red one we're heading towards is — "

"Ruby," Gerard said.

"Now how did you know that?"

"They're all gems. Must be more stars than gems, though."

"Oh, sure. Then I use words like Wind, and Gabriel, and — "

"Must be more stars than words," Gerard pointed out.

"Then I say Red Gabriel and Blue Sunfish. I'll never run out of words."

"What else do you see?"

"Remember Pearl?"

"Oh, yeah. Big white one in the east."

"Six planets. Two have life on them, and one of those has singing crabs, size of houses."

"Really?"

"You laying down?"

Gerard nodded, then remembered Leviathan could not see him. "Yup."

"Look real close at Pearl. Don't take your eyes off it. Then you'll see for yourself."

After an hour or two of staring, Gerard was surprised to learn that Leviathan was right.

Diggety

His dad came without his mum, but at first his vision was so blurred he couldn't be sure. Then he heard his dad's voice, kind of tight. "Does it hurt?"

To his surprise the pain wasn't too bad, and he said so, but vaguely because his attention was drawn to the spots of blackness that floated around his field of vision. He was surprised that when the spots came it was with a flash, like small explosions, but explosions of darkness, not light.

"Doctor says you're getting better soon," his dad went on, but Gerard knew he was lying.

He felt the bed lean when his dad sat down on it. His big, rough calloused hand rested on his chest, which was heaving up and down like a water pump with mud in the pipe. "Oh, Jesus, Gerard."

That brought Gerard up. His dad had never called him by his name before. It had always been "mate" or "son," or if he was in trouble "you." Never Gerard.

That's me, he thought. Gerard Francis McVitty.

He wanted to sit up, but did not have the strength. He settled for tying to move his arm, but there was a tube in it and the arm seemed to be as heavy as iron.

"Your mum's at mass," his dad said. "She's prayin' all day long for you. Wish I could, but she's doin' enough for the both of us."

"You don't have to go to mass to pray," Gerard said. "Father Walsh told me that. I pray all the time. I want to go to Disneyland. So I pray to get better. God listens."

"I guess it's true." His father's face loomed over him. "How are you, Gerard? Really?"

Gerard Francis McVitty

"Tired."

"What are you doing, little mouse?" Leviathan asked, munching the last, flat top bit of an aircraft carrier. Little jets screamed all around the air, looking for someplace to land. Sometimes they zoomed right over Leviathan, firing little bullets that bounced off his skin with a pneumatic phut-phut-phut sound. One bullet came so close to Gerard's head it made his hair wave and he could smell something acrid and metal.

He was busy pulling the bit of airliner out of Leviathan's blowhole.

"I'm tired of hanging on," he said. "I'm tired of being afraid."

The plug went "pop!" and air hissed after it. Gerard heard Leviathan sigh like a steam train coming to rest.

"You want to see me now?"

There was a long pause before Leviathan said, "I know what you look like, little mouse. We've been talking and talking for so long now, I can see you as clearly as Azhur's Mako, way out near the end of the universe, a blue star as big as the solar system. I can see your face as clearly as I can see the snails at the bottom of the sea."

Gerard didn't care about blue stars or little snails. His eyes wanted to close. He undid the arm of the overcoat from around his leg and from around the palm tree and lay down not caring if he dropped into the ocean.

A great lethargy overtook him, like an enormous silence, and he could no longer hear his own breathing.

"Well, you sleep," Leviathan said gently, "and I'll just turn around and take you home."

THE DENIAL
BRUCE STERLING

Bruce Sterling was born in Texas in 1954, and received a BA in Journalism from the University of Texas in 1976. His first short story, "Man Made Self", appeared the same year. His first two novels, Involution Ocean *and* The Artificial Kid, *were far-future adventures, the latter presaging the cyberpunk movement he is credited with creating. Sterling edited cyberpunk anthology* Mirrorshades, *considered the definitive representation of the sub-genre, and his near-future thriller* Islands in the Net *won the John W. Campbell Memorial Award. In 1990 he collaborated with William Gibson on alternate history novel* The Difference Engine. *Future history novel* Schismatrix *introduced his Shaper-Mechanist universe, which pits bio-engineering against mathematics, also the setting of some of the stories in collection* Crystal Express. *After writing the non-fiction book* The Hacker Crackdown, *he returned to fiction with near-future, high-tech scenarios in* Heavy Weather, Holy Fire, *Arthur C. Clarke Award winner* Distraction, *and* The Zenith Angle.

Sterling has produced a large and influential body of short fiction, much of which have been collected in Crystal Express, Globalhead, *and* A Good Old-Fashioned Future. *His novelette "Bicycle Repairman" won the Hugo Award and novelette "Taklamakan" won the Hugo and the Locus Award. Sterling's nonfiction has appeared in* The New York Times, Wired, Nature, Newsday, *and* Time Digital. *A new collection,* Visionary in Residence, *was published in early 2006. Upcoming is a major career retrospective,* Ascendancies: The Best of Bruce Sterling.*

Yusuf climbed the town's ramshackle bridge. There he joined an excited crowd: gypsies, unmarried apprentices, the village idiot, and three ne'er-do-wells with a big jug of plum brandy. The revelers had brought along a blind man with a fiddle.

The river was the soul of the town, but the heavy spring rains had been hard on her. She was rising from her bed in a rage. Tumbling branches clawed through her foam like the mutilated hands of thieves.

The crowd tore splinters from the bridge, tossed them in the roiling water, and made bets. The blind musician scraped his bow on his instrument's

191

single string. He wailed out a noble old lament about crops washed away, drowned herds, hunger, sickness, poverty, and grief.

Yusuf listened with pleasure and studied the rising water with care. Suddenly a half-submerged log struck a piling. The bridge quivered like a sobbing violin. All at once, without a word, the crowd took to their heels.

Yusuf turned and gripped the singer's ragged shoulder. "You'd better come with me."

"I much prefer it here with my jolly audience, thank you, sir!"

"They all ran off. The river's turning ugly, this is dangerous."

"No, no, such kind folk would not neglect me!"

Yusuf pressed a coin into the fiddler's palm.

The fiddler carefully rubbed the coin with his callused fingertips. "A copper penny! What magnificence! I kiss your hand!"

Yusuf was the village cooper. When his barrel trade turned lean, he sometimes patched pots. "See here, fellow, I'm no rich man to keep concubines and fiddlers!"

The fiddler stiffened. "I sing the old songs of your heritage, as the living voice of the dead! The devil's crows will peck the eyeballs of the stingy!"

"Stop trying to curse me and get off this stupid bridge! I'm buying your life with that penny!"

The fiddler spat. At last he tottered toward the far riverbank.

Yusuf abandoned the bridge for the solid cobbles of the marketplace. Here he found more reasonable men: the town's kadi, the wealthy beys, and the seasoned hadjis. These local notables wore handsome woolen cloaks and embroidered jackets. The town's Orthodox priest had somehow been allowed to join their circle.

Yusuf smoothed his vest and cummerbund. Public speech was not his place, but he was at least allowed to listen to his betters. He heard the patriarchs trade the old proverbs. Then they launched light-hearted quips at one another, as jolly as if their town had nothing to lose. They were terrified.

Yusuf hurried home to his wife.

"Wake and dress the boy and girl," he commanded. "I'm off to rouse my uncle. We're leaving the house tonight."

"Oh, no, we can't stay with your uncle," his wife protested.

"Uncle Mehmet lives on high ground."

"Can't this wait till morning? You know how grumpy he gets!"

"Yes, my Uncle Mehmet has a temper," said Yusuf, rolling his eyes. "It's also late, and it's dark. It will rain on us. It's hard work to move our possessions. This may all be for nothing. Then I'll be a fool, and I'm sure you'll let me know that."

Yusuf roused his apprentice from his sleeping nook in the workshop.

He ordered the boy to assemble the tools and wrap them with care against damp. Yusuf gathered all the shop's dinars and put them inside his wife's jewelry box, which he wrapped in their best rug. He tucked that bundle into both his arms.

Yusuf carried his bundle uphill, pattered on by rain. He pounded the old man's door, and, as usual, his uncle Mehmet made a loud fuss over nothing. This delayed Yusuf's return. When he finally reached his home again, back down the crooked, muddy lanes, the night sky was split to pieces by lightning. The river was rioting out of her banks.

His wife was keening, wringing her hands, and cursing her unhappy fate. Nevertheless, she had briskly dressed the children and packed a stout cloth sack with the household's precious things. The stupid apprentice had disobeyed Yusuf's orders and run to the river to gawk; naturally, there was no sign of him.

Yusuf could carry two burdens uphill to his uncle's, but to carry his son, his daughter, and his cooper's tools was beyond his strength.

He'd inherited those precious tools from his late master. The means of his livelihood would be bitterly hard to replace.

He scooped the little girl into his arms. "Girl, be still! My son, cling to my back for dear life! Wife, bring your baggage!"

Black water burst over their sill as he opened the door. Their alley had become a long, ugly brook.

They staggered uphill as best they could, squelching through dark, crooked streets. His wife bent almost double with the heavy sack on her shoulders. They sloshed their way to higher ground. She screeched at him as thunder split the air.

"What now?" Yusuf shouted, unable to wipe his dripping eyes.

"My trousseau!" she mourned. "My grandmother's best things!"

"Well, I left my precious tools there!" he shouted. "So what? We have to live!"

She threw her heavy bag down. "I must go back or it will be too late!"

Yusuf's wife came from a good family. Her grandmother had been a landowner's fine lady, with nothing more to do than knit and embroider all day. The grandam had left fancy garments that Yusuf's wife never bothered to wear, but she dearly treasured them anyway. "All right, we'll go back together!" he lied to her. "But first, save our children!"

Yusuf led the way uphill. The skies and waters roared. The children wept and wriggled hard in their terror, making his burden much worse. Exhausted, he set them on their feet and dragged them by the hands to his uncle's door.

Yusuf's wife had vanished. When he hastened back downhill, he found her heavy bag around a streetcorner. She had disobeyed him, and run back downhill in the darkness.

The river had risen and swallowed the streets. Yusuf ventured two steps into the black, racing flood and was tumbled off his feet and smashed into the wall of a bakery. Stunned and drenched, he retreated, found his wife's abandoned bag, and threw that over his aching shoulders.

At his uncle's house, Mehmet was doubling the woes of his motherless children by giving them a good scolding.

As soon as it grew light enough to see again, Yusuf returned to the wreck of his home. Half the straw roof was gone, along with one wall of his shop. Black mud squished ankle-deep across his floor. All the seasoned wood for his barrels had floated away. By some minor quirk of the river's fury, his precious tools were still there, in mud-stained wrappings.

Yusuf went downstream. The riverbanks were thick with driftwood and bits of smashed homes. Corpses floated, tangled in debris. Some were children.

He found his wife past the bridge, around the riverbend. She was lodged in a muddy sandbar, along with many drowned goats and many dead chickens.

Her skirt, her apron, her pretty belt and her needleworked vest had all been torn from her body by the raging waters. Only her headdress, her pride and joy, was still left to her. Her long hair was tangled in that sodden cloth like river weed.

He had never seen her body nude in daylight. He pried her from the defiling mud, as gently as if she were still living and in need of a husband's help. Shivering with tenderness, he tore the shirt from his wet torso and wrapped her in it, then made her a makeshift skirt from his sash. He lifted her wet, sagging body in his arms. Grief and shame gave him strength. He staggered with her halfway to town.

Excited townsfolk were gathering the dead in carts. When they saw him, they ran to gawk.

Once this happened, his wife suddenly sneezed, lifted her head and, quick as a serpent, hopped down from his grip.

"Look, the cooper is alive!" the neighbors exulted. "God is great!"

"Stop staring like fools," his wife told them. "My man lost his shirt in the flood. You there, lend him your cloak."

They wrapped him up, chafed his cheeks, and embraced him.

The damage was grave in Yusuf's neighborhood, and worse yet on the opposite bank of the river, where the Catholics lived. The stricken people searched the filthy streets for their lost possessions and missing kin. There was much mourning, tumult, and despair. The townsfolk caught two looters, pilfering in the wreckage. The kadi had them beheaded. Their severed heads were publicly exposed on the bridge. Yusuf knew the headless thieves by sight; unlike the others, those rascals wouldn't be missed much.

It took two days for the suffering people to gather their wits about them, but common sense prevailed at last, and they pitched in to rebuild. Wounds were bound up and families reunited. Neighborhood women made soup for everyone in big cooking pots. Alms were gathered and distributed by the dignitaries. Shelter was found for the homeless in the mosques, the temple, and the churches. The dead were retrieved from the sullen river and buried properly by their respective faiths.

The Vizier sent troops from Travnik to keep order. The useless troopers thundered through town on horseback, fired their guns, stole and roasted sheep, and caroused all night with the gypsies. Moslems, Orthodox, and Catholics alike waited anxiously for the marauders to ride home and leave them in peace.

Yusuf's wife and the children stayed at his uncle's while Yusuf put another roof on his house. The apprentice had stupidly broken his leg in the flood — so he had to stay snug with his own family, where he ate well and did no work, much as usual.

Once the damaged bridge was safe for carts again, fresh-cut lumber became available. In the gathering work of reconstruction, Yusuf found his own trade picking up. With a makeshift tent up in lieu of his straw roof, Yusuf had to meet frantic demands for new buckets, casks, and water-barrels. Price was no object, and no one was picky about quality.

Sensing opportunity, the Jews lent money to all the craftsmen of standing, whether their homes were damaged or not. Gold coins appeared in circulation, precious Ottoman sultani from the royal mint in distant Istanbul. Yusuf schemed hard to gain and keep a few.

When he went to fetch his family back home, Yusuf found his wife with a changed spirit. She had put old Mehmet's place fully into order: she'd aired the old man's stuffy cottage, beaten his moldy carpet, scrubbed his floors, banished the mice, and chased the spiders into hiding. His uncle's dingy vest and sash were clean and darned. Old Mehmet had never looked so jolly. When Yusuf's lively children left his home, Mehmet even wept a little.

His wife flung her arms around Yusuf's neck. When the family returned to her wrecked, muddy home, she was as proud as a new bride. She made cleaning up the mud into an exciting game for the children. She cast the spoilt food from her drowned larder. She borrowed flour, bought eggs, conjured up salt, found milk from heaven, and made fresh bread.

Neighbors came to her door with soup and cabbage rolls. Enchanted by her charming gratitude, they helped her to clean. As she worked, his wife sang like a lark. Everyone's spirits rose, despite all the trials, or maybe even because of the trials, because they gave people so much to gripe about. Yusuf said little and watched his wife with raw disbelief. With all her cheerful talk and singing, she ate almost nothing. That which she chewed, she did not swallow.

When he climbed reluctantly into their narrow bed, she was bright-eyed and willing. He told her that he was tired. She obediently put her cool, damp head into the hollow of his shoulder and passed the night as quiet as carved ivory: never a twitch, kick, or snore.

Yusuf knew for a fact that his wife had been swept away and murderously tumbled down a stony riverbank for a distance of some twenty arshin. Yet her pale skin showed no bruising anywhere. He finally found hidden wounds on the soles of her feet. She had struggled hard for her footing as the angry waters dragged her to her death.

In the morning she spoke sweet words of encouragement to him. His hard work would bring them sure reward. Adversity was refining his character. The neighbors admired his cheerful fortitude. His son was learning valuable lessons by his manly example. All this wifely praise seemed plausible enough to Yusuf, and no more than he deserved, but he knew with a black flood of occult certainty that this was not the woman given him in marriage. Where were her dry, acidic remarks? Her balky backtalk? Her black, sour jokes? Her customary heartbreaking sighs, which mutely suggested that every chance of happiness was lost forever?

Yusuf fled to the market, bought a flask of fiery rakija and sat down to drink hard in midday.

Somehow, in the cunning pretext of "repairing" their flood-damaged church, the Orthodox had installed a bronze bell in their church tower. Its clangor now brazenly competed with the muezzin's holy cries. It was entirely indecent that this wicked contraption of the Serfish Slaves (the Orthodox were also called "Slavish Serfs," for dialects varied) should be casting an ungodly racket over the stricken town. Yusuf felt as if that great bronze barrel and its banging tongue had been hung inside his own chest.

The infidels were ringing bells, but he was living with a corpse.

Yusuf drank, thought slowly and heavily, then drank some more. He might go to the kadi for help in his crisis, but the pious judge would recommend what he always suggested to any man troubled by scandal — the long pilgrimage to Mecca. For a man of Yusuf's slender means, a trip to Arabia was out of the question. Besides, word would likely spread that he had sought public counsel about his own wife. His own wife, and from such a good family, too.

That wasn't the sort of thing that a man of standing would do.

The Orthodox priest was an impressive figure, with a big carved staff and a great black towering hat. Yusuf had a grudging respect for the Orthodox. Look how they'd gotten their way with that bell tower of theirs, against all sense and despite every obstacle. They were rebellious and sly, and they clung to their pernicious way of life despite being taxed, fined, scourged, beheaded, and impaled. Their priest — he might well have some dark, occult knowledge that could help in Yusuf's situation.

But what if, in their low cunning, the peasants laughed at him and took advantage somehow? Unthinkable!

The Catholics were fewer than the Orthodox, a simple people, somewhat more peaceable. But the Catholics had Franciscan monks. Franciscan monks were sorcerers who had come from Austria with picture books. The monks recited spells in Latin from their gold-crowned Pope in Rome. They boasted that their Austrian troops could beat the Sultan's janissaries. Yusuf had seen a lot of Austrians. Austrians were rich, crafty, and insolent. They knew bizarre and incredible things. Bookkeeping, for instance.

Could he trust Franciscan monks to deal with a wife who refused to be dead? Those celibate monks didn't even know what a woman was for! The scheme was absurd.

Yusuf was not a drinking man, so the rakija lifted his imagination to great heights. When the local rabbi passed by chance, Yusuf found himself on his feet, stumbling after the Jew. The rabbi noticed this and confronted him. Yusuf, suddenly thick of tongue, blurted out something of his woes.

The rabbi wanted no part of Yusuf's troubles. However, he was a courteous man, and he had a wise suggestion.

There were people of the Bogomil faith within two days' journey. These Bogomils had once been the Christian masters of the land, generations ago, before the Ottoman Turks brought order to the valleys and mountains. Both Catholics and Orthodox considered the Bogomils to be sinister heretics. They thought this for good reason, for the Bogomils (who were also known as "Cathars" and "Patarines"), were particularly skilled in the conjuration and banishment of spirits.

So said the rabbi. The local Christians believed that the last Bogomils had been killed or assimilated long ago, but a Jew, naturally, knew better than this. The rabbi alleged that a small clan of the Old Believers still lurked in the trackless hills. Jewish peddlers sometimes met the Bogomils, to do a little business: the Bogomils were bewhiskered clansmen with goiters the size of fists, who ambushed the Sultan's tax men, ripped up roads, ate meat raw on Fridays, and married their own nieces.

Next day, when Yusuf recovered from his hangover, he told his wife that he needed to go on pilgrimage into the hills for a few days. She should have pointed out that their house was still half-wrecked and his business was very pressing. Instead she smiled sweetly, packed him four days of home-cooked provisions, darned his leggings, and borrowed him a stout donkey.

No one could find the eerie Bogomil village without many anxious moments, but Yusuf did find it. This was a dour place where an ancient people of faith were finally perishing from the Earth. The meager village clustered in the battered ruin of a hillside fort. The poorly thatched hovels were patched up from tumbledown bits of rock. Thick nettles infested the rye fields. The goats were scabby, and the donkeys knock-kneed. The plum orchard buzzed with swarms of vicious yellow wasps. There was not a child to be seen.

The locals spoke a Slavish dialect so thick and archaic that it sounded as if they were chewing stale bread. They did have a tiny church of sorts, and in there, slowly dipping holy candles in a stinking yellow mix of lard and beeswax, was their elderly, half-starved pastor, the man they called their "Djed."

The Bogomil Djed wore the patched rags of black ecclesiastical robes. He had a walleye, and a river of beard tumbling past his waist.

With difficulty, Yusuf confessed.

"I like you, Moslem boy," said the Bogomil priest, with a wink or a tic of his bloodshot walleye. "It takes an honest man to tell such a dark story. I can help you."

"Thank you! Thank you! How?"

"By baptizing you in the gnostic faith, as revealed in the Palcyaf Bible. A dreadful thing has happened to you, but I can clarify your suffering, so hearken to me. God, the Good God, did not create this wicked world. This evil place, this sinful world we must endure, was created by God's elder archangel, Satanail the Demiurge. The Demiurge created all the Earth, and also some bits of the lower heavens. Then Satanail tried to create Man in the image of God, but he succeeded only in creating the flesh of Man. That is why it was easy for Satanail to confound and mislead Adam, and all of Adam's heritage, through the fleshly weakness of our clay."

"I never heard that word, 'Demiurge.' There's only one God."

"No, my boy, there are two Gods: the bad God, who is always with us, and the good God, who is unknowable. Now I will tell you all about the dual human and divine nature of Jesus Christ. This is the most wonderful of gnostic gospels; it involves the Holy Dove, the Archangel Michael, Satanail the Creator, and the Clay Hierographon."

"But my wife is not a Christian at all! I told you, she comes from a nice family."

"Your wife is dead."

A chill gripped Yusuf. He struggled for something to say.

"My boy, is your woman nosferatu? You can tell me."

"I don't know that word either."

"Does she hate and fear the light of the sun?"

"My wife loves sunlight! She loves flowers, birds, pretty clothes, she likes everything nice."

"Does she suck the blood of your children?"

Yusuf shook his head and wiped at his tears.

The priest shrugged reluctantly. "Well, no matter — you can still behead her and impale her through the heart! Those measures always settle things!"

Yusuf was scandalized. "What would I tell the neighbors?"

The old man sighed. "She's dead and yet she walks the Earth, my boy. You do need to do something."

"How could a woman be dead and not know she's dead?"

"In her woman's heart she suspects it. But she's too stubborn to admit it. She died rashly and foolishly, disobeying her lord and master, and she left her woman's body lying naked in some mud. Imagine the shame to her spirit! This young wife with a house and small children, she left her life's duties undone! Her failure was more than her spirit could admit. So, she does not live, but she stubbornly persists." The priest slowly dipped a bare white string into his pot of wax. "'A man may work from sun to sun, but a woman's work is never done.'"

Yusuf put his head in his hands and wept. The Djed had convinced him. Yusuf was sure that he had found the best source of advice on his troubles, short of a long trip to Mecca. "What's to become of me now? What's to become of my poor children?"

"Do you know what a succubus is?" said the priest.

"No, I never heard that word."

"If your dead wife had become a succubus, you wouldn't need any words. Never mind that. I will prophesy to you of what comes next. Her dead flesh and immortal spirit must part sometimes, for that is their dual nature. So sometimes you will find that her spirit is there, while her flesh is not there. You will hear her voice and turn to speak; but there will be no one. The pillow will have the dent of her head, but no head lying there. The pot might move from the stove to the table, with no woman's hands to move it."

"Oh," said Yusuf. There were no possible words for such calamities.

"There will also be moments when the spirit retreats and her body remains. I mean the rotten body of a woman who drowned in the mud. If you are lucky you might not see that rotten body. You will smell it."

"I'm accursed! How long can such torments go on?"

"Some exorcist must persuade her that she met with death and her time on Earth is over. She has to be confronted with the deceit that her spirit calls 'truth.' She has to admit that her life is a lie."

"Well, that will never happen," said Yusuf. "I never knew her to admit to a mistake since the day her father gave her to me."

"Impale her heart while she sleeps!" demanded the Djed. "I can sell you the proper wood for the sharpened stake — it is the wood of life, *lignum vitae*, I found it growing in the dead shrine of the dead God Mithras, for that is the ruin of a failed resurrection.... The wood of life has a great herbal virtue in all matters of spirit and flesh."

Yusuf's heart rebelled. "I can't stab the mother of my children between her breasts with a stick of wood!"

"You are a cooper," said the Djed, "so you do have a hammer."

"I mean that I'll cast myself into the river before I do any such thing!"

The Djed hung his candle from a small iron rod. "To drown one's self is a great calamity."

"Is there nothing better to do?"

"There is another way. The black way of sorcery." The Djed picked at his long beard. "A magic talisman can trap her spirit inside her dead body. Then her spirit cannot slip free from the flesh. She will be trapped in her transition from life to death, a dark and ghostly existence."

"What kind of talisman does that?"

"It's a fetter. The handcuff of a slave. You can tell her it's a bracelet, a woman's bangle. Fix that fetter, carved from the wood of life, firmly around her dead wrist. Within that wooden bracelet, a great curse is written: the curse that bound the children of Adam to till the soil, as the serfs of Satanail, ruler and creator of the Earth. So her soul will not be able to escape her clay, any more than Adam, Cain, and Abel, with their bodies made of clay by Satanail, could escape the clay of the fields and pastures. She will have to abide by that untruth she tells herself, for as long as that cuff clings to her flesh."

"Forever, then? Forever and ever?"

"No, boy, listen. I told you 'as long as that cuff clings to her flesh.' You will have to see to it that she wears it always. This is necromancy."

Yusuf pondered the matter, weeping. Peaceably, the Bogomil dipped his candles.

"But that's all?" Yusuf said at last. "I don't have to stab her with a stick? I don't have to bury her, or behead her? My wife just wears a bracelet on her arm, with some painted words! Then I go home."

"She's dead, my boy. You are trapping a human soul within the outward show of rotten form. She will have no hope of salvation. She will be the hopeless slave of earthly clay and the chattel of her circumstances. For you to do that to another human soul is a mortal sin. You will have to answer for that on the Day of Judgment." The Djed adjusted his sleeves. "But, you are Moslem, so you are damned already. All the more so for your woman, so...." The Djed spread his waxy hands.

The rabbi had warned Yusuf about the need for ready cash.

When Yusuf and his borrowed donkey returned home, footsore and hungry after five days of risky travel, he found his place hung with the neighbors' laundry. It was as festive as a set of flags. All the rugs and garments soiled by the flood needed boiling and bleaching. So his wife had made herself the bustling center of this lively activity.

Yusuf's smashed straw roof was being replaced with sturdy tiles. The village tiler and his wife had both died in the flood. The tiler's boy, a sullen, skinny teen, had lived, but his loss left him blank-eyed and silent.

Yusuf's wife had found this boy, haunted, shivering, and starving. She had fed him, clothed him, and sent him to collect loose tiles. There were many tiles scattered in the wrecked streets, and the boy knew how to lay a roof, so, somehow, without anything being said, the boy had become Yusuf's new apprentice. The new apprentice didn't eat much. He never said much. As an orphan, he was in no position to demand any wages or to talk back. So, although he knew nothing about making barrels, he was the ideal addition to the shop.

Yusuf's home, once rather well known for ruckus, had become a model of sociable charm. Neighbors were in and out of the place all the time, bringing sweets, borrowing flour and salt, swapping recipes, leaving children to be baby-sat. Seeing the empty barrels around, his wife had started brewing beer as a profitable sideline. She also stored red paprikas in wooden kegs of olive oil. People started leaving things at her house to sell. She was planning on building a shed to retail groceries.

There was never a private moment safe from friendly interruption, so Yusuf took his wife across the river, to the Turkish graveyard, for a talk. She wasn't reluctant to go, since she was of good birth and her long-established family occupied a fine, exclusive quarter of the cemetery.

"We never come here enough, husband," she chirped. "With all the rain, there's so much moss and mildew on Great-grandfather's stone! Let's fetch a big bucket and give him a good wash!"

There were fresh graves, due to the flood, and one ugly wooden coffin, still abandoned above ground. Moslems didn't favor wooden boxes for their dead — this was a Christian fetish — but they'd overlooked that minor matter when they'd had to inter the swollen, oozing bodies of the flood victims. Luckily, rumor had outpaced the need for such boxes. So a spare coffin was still on the site, half full of rainwater and humming with spring mosquitoes.

Yusuf took his wife's hand. Despite all her housework — she was busy as an ant — her damp hands were soft and smooth.

"I don't know how to tell you this," he said.

She blinked her limpid eyes and bit her lip. "What is it you have to complain about, husband? Have I failed to please you in some way?"

"There is one matter...a difficult matter.... Well, you see, there's more to the marriage of a man and woman than just keeping house and making money."

"Yes, yes," she nodded, "being respectable!"

"No, I don't mean that part."

"The children, then?" she said.

"Well, not the boy and girl, but...," he said. "Well, yes, children! Chil-dren, of course! It's God's will that man and woman should bring children into the world! And, well, that's not something you and I can do anymore."

"Why not?"

Yusuf shuddered from head to foot. "Do I have to say that? I don't want to."

"What is it you want from me, Yusuf? Spit it out!"

"Well, the house is as neat as a pin. We're making a profit. The neighbors love you. I can't complain about that. You know I never complain. But if you stubbornly refuse to die, well, I can't go on living. Wife, I need a mi-losnica."

"You want to take a concubine?"

"Yes. Just a maidservant. Nobody fancy. Maybe a teenager. She could help around the house."

"You want me to shelter your stupid concubine inside my own house?"

"Where else could I put a milosnica? I'm a cooper, I'm not a bey or an aga."

Demonic light lit his wife's eyes. "You think of nothing but money and your shop! You never give me a second glance! You work all day like a gelded ox! Then you go on a pilgrimage in the middle of everything, and now you tell me you want a concubine? Oh, you eunuch, you pig, you big talker! I work, I slave, I suffer, I do everything to please you, and now your favor turns to another!" She raised her voice and screeched across the graveyard. "Do you see this, Grandmother? Do you see what's becoming of me?"

"Don't make me angry," said Yusuf. "I've thought this through and it's reasonable. I'm not a cold fish. I'm living with a dead woman. Can't I have one live woman, just to warm my bones?"

"I'd warm your bones. Why can't I warm your bones?"

"Because you drowned in the river, girl. Your flesh is cold."

She said nothing.

"You don't believe me? Take off those shoes," he said wearily. "Look at those wounds on the bottoms of your feet. Your wounds never heal. They can't heal." Yusuf tried to put some warmth and color into his voice. "You have pretty feet, you have the prettiest feet in town. I always loved your feet, but, well, you never show them to me, since you drowned in that river."

She shook her head. "It was *you* who drowned in the river."

"What?"

"What about that huge wound in your back? Do you think I never noticed that great black ugly wound under your shoulder? That's why you never take your vest off anymore!"

Yusuf no longer dared to remove his clothes while his wife was around, so, although he tried a sudden, frightened glance back over his own shoulder, he saw nothing there but embroidered cloth. "Do I really have a scar on my back? I'm not dead, though."

"Yes, husband, you are dead," his wife said bluntly. "You ran back for your stupid tools, even though I begged you to stay with me and comfort me. I saw you fall. You drowned in the street. I found your body washed down the river."

This mad assertion of hers was completely senseless. "No, that can't be true," he told her. "You abandoned me and the children, against my direct word to you, and you went back for your grandmother's useless trousseau, and you drowned, and I found you sprawling naked in the mud."

"'Naked in the mud,'" she scoffed. "In your dreams!" She pointed. "You see that coffin? Go lie down in that coffin, stupid. That coffin's for you."

"That's your coffin, my dear. That's certainly not my coffin."

"Go lie down in there, you big hot stallion for concubines. You won't rise up again, I can promise you."

Yusuf gazed at the splintery wooden hulk. That coffin was a sorry piece of woodworking; he could have built a far better coffin himself. Out of nowhere, black disbelief washed over him. Could he possibly be in this much trouble? Was this what his life had come to? Him, a man of circumspection, a devout man, honest, a hard worker, devoted to his children? It simply could not be! It wasn't true! It was impossible.

He should have been in an almighty rage at his wife's stinging taunts, but somehow, his skin remained cool; he couldn't get a flush to his cheeks. He knew only troubled despair. "You really want to put me down in the earth, in such a cheap coffin, so badly built? The way you carry on at me, I'm tempted to lie down in there, I really am."

"Admit it, you don't need any concubine. You just want me out of your way. And after all I did for you, and gave to you! How could you pretend to live without me at your side, you big fool? I deserved much better than you, but I never left you, I was always there for you."

Part of that lament at least was true. Even when their temperaments had clashed, she'd always been somehow willing to jam herself into their narrow bed. She might be angry, yes, sullen, yes, impossible, yes, but she remained with him. "This is a pretty good fight we're having today," he said, "this is kind of like our old times."

"I always knew you'd murder me and bury me someday."

"Would you get over that, please? It's just vulgar." Yusuf reached inside the wrappings of his cummerbund. "If I wanted to kill you, would I be putting this on your hand?"

She brightened at once. "Oh! What's that you brought me? Pretty!"

"I got it on pilgrimage. It's a magic charm."

"Oh how sweet! Do let me have it, you haven't bought me jewelry in ages."

On a sudden impulse, Yusuf jammed his own hand through the wooden cuff. In an instant, memory pierced him. The truth ran through his flesh like a rusty sword. He remembered losing his temper, cursing like a madman, rushing back to his collapsing shop, in his lust and pride for some meaningless clutter of tools.... He could taste that deadly rush of water, see a blackness befouling his eyes, the chill of death filling his lungs —

He yanked his arm from the cuff, trembling from head to foot. "That never happened!" he shouted. "I never did any such thing! I won't stand for such insults! If they tell me the truth, I'll kill them."

"What are you babbling on about? Give me my pretty jewelry."

He handed it over.

She slid her hand through with an eager smile, then pried the deadly thing off her wrist as if it were red-hot iron. "You made me do that!" she screeched. "You made me run into the ugly flood! I was your victim! Nothing I did was ever my fault."

Yusuf bent at the waist and picked up the dropped bangle between his thumb and forefinger. "Thank God this dreadful thing comes off our flesh so easily!"

His wife rubbed the skin of her wrist. There was a new black bruise there. "Look, your gift hurt me. It's terrible!"

"Yes, it's very magical."

"Did you pay a lot of money for that?"

"Oh yes. I paid a lot of money. To a wizard."

"You're hopeless."

"Wife of mine, we're both hopeless. Because the truth is, our lives are over. We've failed. Why did we stumble off to our own destruction? We completely lost our heads!"

His wife squared her shoulders. "All right, fine! So you make mistakes! So you're not perfect!"

"Me? Why is it me all the time? What about you?"

"Yes, I know, I could be a lot better, but well, I'm stuck with you. That's why I'm no good. So, I don't forgive you, and I never will! But, anyway, I don't think we ought to talk about this anymore."

"Would you reel that snake's tongue of yours back into your head? Listen to me for once! We're all over, woman! We drowned, we both died together in a big disaster!"

"Yusuf, if we're dead, how can you be scolding me? See, you're talking nonsense! I want us to put this behind us once and for all. We just won't talk about this matter anymore. Not one more word. We have to protect the children. Children can't understand such grown-up things. So we'll never breathe a word to anyone. All right?"

Black temptation seized him. "Look, honey, let's just get in that coffin together. We'll never make a go of a situation like this, it can't be done. That coffin's not so bad. It's got as much room as our bed does."

"I won't go in there," she said. "I won't vanish from the Earth. I just won't, because I can't believe what you believe, and you can't make me." She suddenly snatched the bangle from his hand and threw it into the coffin. "There, get inside there with that nasty thing, if you're so eager."

"Now you've gone and spoiled it," he said sadly. "Why do you always have to do that, just to be spiteful? One of these days I'm really going to have to smack you around."

"When our children are ready to bury us, then they will bury us."

That was the wisest thing she had ever said. Yusuf rubbed the words over his dead tongue. It was almost a proverb. "Let the children bury us." There was a bliss to that, like a verse in a very old song. It meant that there were no decisions to be made. The time was still unripe. Nothing useful could be done. Justice, faith, hope and charity, life and death, they were all smashed and in a muddle, far beyond his repair and his retrieval. So just let it all be secret, let that go unspoken. Let the next generation look after all of that. Or the generation after that. Or after that. Or after that.

That was their heritage.

THE FARMER'S CAT
JEFF VANDERMEER

Jeff VanderMeer was born in Pennsylvania and grew up in New York, Florida, and the Fiji Islands. He attended the University of Florida where he studied journalism, English and history. VanderMeer founded The Ministry of Whimsy Press in 1984, began publishing stories in 1985, and attended Clarion in 1992. He is best known for his "Ambergris" series of stories (including the Sturgeon Memorial Award finalist "Dradin, in Love" and World Fantasy Award winner "The Transformation of Martin Lake"), which have been collected in City of Saints and Madmen: The Book of Ambergris. *His most recent novel,* Veniss Underground, *was nominated for the World Fantasy Award. Other recent books include major retrospective collection* Secret Life, *and non-fiction collection* Why Should I Cut Your Throat? *VanderMeer is also a respected editor and anthologist. His "Leviathan" series of anthologies have won the World Fantasy Award, while* The Thackery T. Lambshead Pocket Guide to Eccentric & Discredited Diseases *was nominated for both the Hugo and World Fantasy Awards. A major new novel set in Ambergris,* Shriek: An Afterword, *was published in early 2006. He is currently working on a new collection and a new "Leviathan" anthology.*

A long time ago, in Norway, a farmer found he had a big problem with trolls. Every winter, the trolls would smash down the door to his house and make themselves at home for a month. Short or tall, fat or thin, hairy or hairless, it didn't matter — every last one of these trolls was a disaster for the farmer. They ate all of his food, drank all of the water from his well, guzzled down all of his milk (often right from the cow!), broke his furniture, and farted whenever they felt like it.

The farmer could do nothing about this — there were too many trolls. Besides, the leader of the trolls, who went by the name of Mobhead, was a big brute of a troll with enormous claws who emitted a foul smell from all of the creatures he'd eaten raw over the years. Mobhead had a huge, gnarled head that seemed green in one kind of light and purple in another. Next to his head, his body looked shrunken and thin, but despite the way they looked his legs were strong as steel; they had to be or his head would have long since fallen off of his neck.

"Don't you think you'd be more comfortable somewhere else?" the farmer asked Mobhead during the second winter. His wife and children had left him for less troll-infested climes. He had lost a lot of his hair from stress.

"Oh, I don't think so," Mobhead said, cleaning his fangs with a toothpick made from a sharpened chair leg. The chair in question had been made by the farmer's father many years before.

"No," Mobhead said. "We like it here just fine." And farted to punctuate his point.

Behind him, one of the other trolls devoured the family cat, and belched.

The farmer sighed. It was getting hard to keep help, even in the summers, when the trolls kept to their lairs and caves far to the north. The farm's reputation had begun to suffer. A few more years of this and he would have to sell the farm, if any of it was left to sell.

Behind him, one of the trolls attacked a smaller troll. There was a splatter of blood against the far wall, a smell oddly like violets, and then the severed head of the smaller troll rolled to a stop at the farmer's feet. The look on the dead troll's face revealed no hint of surprise.

Nor was there a look of surprise on the farmer's face.

All spring and summer, the farmer thought about what he should do. Whether fairly or unfairly, he was known in those parts for thinking his way out of every problem that had arisen during twenty years of running the farm. But he couldn't fight off the trolls by himself. He couldn't bribe them to leave. It worried him almost as much as the lack of rain in July.

Then, in late summer, a traveling merchant came by the farm. He stopped by twice a year, once with pots, pans, and dried goods and once with livestock and pets. This time, he brought a big, lurching wooden wagon full of animals, pulled by ten of the biggest, strongest horses the farmer had ever seen.

Usually, the farmer bought chickens from the tall, mute merchant, and maybe a goat or two. But this time, the merchant pointed to a cage that held seven squirming, chirping balls of fur. The farmer looked at them for a second, looked away, then looked again, more closely, raising his eyebrows.

"Do you mean to say..." the farmer said, looking at the tall, mute merchant. "Are you telling me..."

The mute man nodded. The frown of his mouth became, for a moment, a mischievous smile.

The farmer smiled. "I'll take one. One should be enough."

The mute man's smile grew wide and deep.

That winter, the trolls came again, in strength — rowdy, smelly, raucous, and looking for trouble. They pulled out a barrel of his best beer and drank it all down in a matter of minutes. They set fire to his attic and snuffed it only when Mobhead bawled them out for "crapping where you eat, you idiots!"

They noticed the little ball of fur curled up in a basket about an hour after they had smashed down the front door.

"Ere now," said one of the trolls, a foreign troll from England, "Wot's this, wot?"

One of the other trolls — a deformed troll, with a third eye protruding like a tube from its forehead — prodded the ball of fur with one of its big clawed toes. "It's a cat, I think. Just like the last one. Another juicy, lovely cat."

A third troll said, "Save it for later. We've got plenty of time."

The farmer, who had been watching all of this, said to the trolls, "Yes, this is our new cat. But I'd ask that you not eat him. I need him around to catch mice in the summer or when you come back next time, I won't have any grain, and no grain means no beer. It also means lots of other things won't be around for you to eat, like that homemade bread you seem to enjoy so much. In fact, I might not even be around, then, for without grain this farm cannot survive."

The misshapen troll sneered. "A pretty speech, farmer. But don't worry about the mice. We'll eat them all before we leave."

So the farmer went to Mobhead and made Mobhead promise that he and his trolls would leave the cat alone.

"Remember what you said to the trolls who tried to set my attic on fire, O Mighty Mobhead," the farmer said, in the best tradition of flatterers everywhere.

Mobhead thought about it for a second, then said, "Hmmm. I must admit I've grown fond of you, farmer, in the way a wolf is fond of a lamb. And I do want our winter resort to be in good order next time we come charging down out of the frozen north. Therefore, although I have this nagging feeling I might regret this, I will let you keep the cat. But everything else we're going to eat, drink, ruin, or fart on. I just want to make that clear."

The farmer said, "That's fine, so long as I get to keep the cat."

Mobhead said he promised on his dead mothers' eyeteeth, and then he called the other trolls around and told them that the cat was off limits. "You are not to eat the cat. You are not to taunt the cat. You must leave the cat alone."

The farmer smiled a deep and mysterious smile. It was the first smile for him in quite some time. A troll who swore on the eyeteeth of his mothers could never break that promise, no matter what.

And so the farmer got to keep his cat. The next year, when the trolls came barging in, they were well into their rampage before they even saw the cat. When they did, they were a little surprised at how big it had grown. Why, it was almost as big as a dog. And it had such big teeth, too.

"It's one of those Northern cats," the farmer told them. "They grow them big up there. You must know that, since you come from up there. Surely you know that much?"

"Yes, yes," Mobhead said, nodding absent-mindedly, "we know that, farmer," and promptly dove face-first into a large bucket of offal.

But the farmer noticed that the cat made the other trolls nervous. For one thing, it met their gaze and held it, almost as if it weren't an animal, or thought itself their equal. And it didn't really look like a cat, even a Northern cat, to them. Still, the farmer could tell that the other trolls didn't want to say anything to their leader. Mobhead liked to eat the smaller trolls because they were, under all the hair, so succulent, and none of them wanted to give him an excuse for a hasty dinner.

Another year went by. Spring gave on to the long days of summer, and the farmer found some solace in the growth of not only his crops but also his cat. The farmer and his cat would take long walks through the fields, the farmer teaching the cat as much about the farm as possible. And he believed that the cat even appreciated some of it.

Once more, too, fall froze into winter, and once more the trolls came tumbling into the farmer's house, led by Mobhead. Once again, they trashed the place as thoroughly as if they were roadies for some drunken band of Scandanavian lute players.

They had begun their second trashing of the house, pulling down the cabinets, splintering the chairs, when suddenly they heard a growl that turned their blood to ice and set them to gibbering, and at their rear there came the sound of bones being crunched, and as they turned to look and see what was happening, they were met by the sight of some of their friends being hurled at them with great force.

The farmer just stood off to the side, smoking his pipe and chuckling from time to time as his cat took care of the trolls. Sharp were his fangs! Long were his claws! Huge was his frame!

Finally, Mobhead walked up alongside the farmer. He was so shaken, he could hardly hold up his enormous head.

"I could eat you right now, farmer," Mobhead snarled. "That is the largest cat I have ever seen — and it is trying to kill my trolls! Only *I* get to kill my trolls!"

"Nonsense," the farmer said. "My cat only eats mice. Your trolls aren't mice, are they?"

"I eat farmers sometimes," Mobhead said. "How would you like that?"

The farmer took the pipe out of his mouth and frowned. "It really isn't up to me. I don't think Mob-Eater would like that, though."

"Mob-Eater?"

"Yes — that's my name for my cat."

As much as a hairy troll can blanch, Mobhead blanched exactly that much and no more.

"Very well, I won't eat you. But I *will* eat your hideous cat," Mobhead said, although not in a very convincing tone.

The farmer smiled. "Remember your promise."

Mobhead scowled. The farmer knew the creature was thinking about breaking his promise. But if he did, Mobhead would be tormented by nightmares in which his mothers tortured him with words and with deeds. He would lose all taste for food. He would starve. Even his mighty head would shrivel up. Within a month, Mobhead would be dead...

Mobhead snarled in frustration. "We'll be back when your cat is gone, farmer," he said. "And then you'll pay!"

If he'd had a cape instead of a dirty pelt of fur-hair, Mobhead would have whirled it around him as he left, trailing the remains of his thoroughly beaten and half-digested trolls behind him.

"You haven't heard the last of me!" Mobhead yowled as he disappeared into the snow, now red with the pearling of troll blood.

The next winter, Mobhead and his troll band stopped a few feet from the farmer's front door.

"Hey, farmer, are you there?!" Mobhead shouted.

After a moment, the door opened wide and there stood the farmer, a smile on his face.

"Why, Mobhead. How nice to see you. What can I do for you?"

"You can tell me if you still have that damn cat. I've been looking forward to our winter get-away."

The farmer smiled even more, and behind him rose a huge shadow with large yellow eyes and rippling muscles under a thick brown pelt. The claws on the shadow were big as carving knives, and the fangs almost as large.

"Why, yes," the farmer said, "as it so happens I still have Mob-Eater. He's a very good mouser."

Mobhead's shoulders slumped.

It would be a long hard slog back to the frozen north, and only troll to eat along the way. As he turned to go, he kicked a small troll out of his way.

"We'll be back next year," he said over his shoulder. "We'll be back every year until that damn cat is gone."

"Suit yourself," the farmer said, and closed the door.

Once inside, the farmer and the bear laughed.

"Thanks, Mob-Eater," the farmer said. "You looked really fierce."

The bear huffed a deep bear belly laugh, sitting back on its haunches in a huge comfy chair the farmer had made for him.

"I am really fierce, father," the bear said. "But you should have let me chase them. I don't like the taste of troll all that much, but, oh, I do love to chase them."

"Maybe next year," the farmer said. "Maybe next year. But for now, we have chores to do. I need to teach you to milk the cows, for one thing."

"But I hate to milk the cows," the bear said. "You know that."

"Yes, but you still need to know how to do it, son."

"Very well. If you say so."

They waited for a few minutes until the trolls were out of sight, and then they went outside and started doing the farm chores for the day.

Soon, the farmer thought, his wife and children would come home, and everything would be as it was before. Except that now they had a huge talking bear living in their house.

Sometimes folktales didn't end quite the way you thought they would. But they *did* end.

There's a Hole in the City
Richard Bowes

Richard Bowes was born in Boston in 1944, where he studied creative writing with Mark Eisenstein at Hofstra University, and has lived in New York City since 1966. His first novels, Warchild, Feral Cell, *and* Goblin Market *were published in the late 1980s. He has written several sequences of stories which have later been published as mosaic novels, books "created, as a visual mosaic is, out of bits of glass, of tiles, of colored stones." The first of these,* Minions of the Moon, *was a sequence of semi-autobiographical stories that included World Fantasy Award winner "Streetcar Dreams" which won the Lambda Literary Award in 2000. The second, a series of stories that tell of the "cops who patrol the Time Stream, and the gods, Apollo, Diana, Mercury and the rest, whom they serve and with whom they struggle" was published in 2005 as* From the Files of the Time Rangers. *His short fiction has been collected in* Transfigured Night and Other Stories. *Upcoming is a new collection,* Streetcar Dreams, *and a new story cycle tentatively called "Dust Devils on a Quiet Street".*

WEDNESDAY 9/12

On the evening of the day after the towers fell, I was waiting by the barricades on Houston Street and LaGuardia Place for my friend Mags to come up from Soho and have dinner with me. On the skyline, not two miles to the south, the pillars of smoke wavered slightly. But the creepily beautiful weather of September 11 still held, and the wind blew in from the northeast. In Greenwich Village the air was crisp and clean, with just a touch of fall about it.

I'd spent the last day and a half looking at pictures of burning towers. One of the frustrations of that time was that there was so little most of us could do about anything or for anyone.

Downtown streets were empty of all traffic except emergency vehicles. The West and East Villages from Fourteenth Street to Houston were their own separate zone. Pedestrians needed identification proving they lived or worked there in order to enter.

The barricades consisted of blue wooden police horses and a couple of unmarked vans thrown across LaGuardia Place. Behind them were a couple of cops, a few auxiliary police and one or two guys in civilian clothes with ID's of some kind pinned to their shirts. All of them looked tired, subdued by events.

At the barricades was a small crowd: ones like me waiting for friends from neighborhoods to the south; ones without proper identification waiting for confirmation so that they could continue on into Soho; people who just wanted to be outside near other people in those days of sunshine and shock. Once in a while, each of us would look up at the columns of smoke that hung in the downtown sky then look away again.

A family approached a middle-aged cop behind the barricade. The group consisted of a man, a woman, a little girl being led by the hand, a child being carried. All were blondish and wore shorts and casual tops. The parents seemed pleasant but serious people in their early thirties, professionals. They could have been tourists. But that day the city was empty of tourists.

The man said something, and I heard the cop say loudly, "You want to go where?"

"Down there," the man gestured at the columns. He indicated the children. "We want them to see." It sounded as if he couldn't imagine this appeal not working.

Everyone stared at the family. "No ID, no passage," said the cop and turned his back on them. The pleasant expressions on the parents' faces faded. They looked indignant, like a maitre d' had lost their reservations. She led one kid, he carried the other as they turned west, probably headed for another checkpoint.

"They wanted those little kids to see Ground Zero!" a woman who knew the cop said. "Are they out of their minds?"

"Looters," he replied. "That's my guess." He picked up his walkie-talkie to call the checkpoints ahead of them.

Mags appeared just then, looking a bit frayed. When you've known someone for as long as I've known her, the tendency is not to see the changes, to think you both look about the same as when you were kids.

But kids don't have gray hair, and their bodies aren't thick the way bodies get in their late fifties. Their kisses aren't perfunctory. Their conversation doesn't include curt little nods that indicate something is understood.

We walked in the middle of the streets because we could. "Couldn't sleep much last night," I said.

"Because of the quiet," she said. "No planes. I kept listening for them. I haven't been sleeping anyway. I was supposed to be in housing court today. But the courts are shut until further notice."

I said, "Notice how with only the ones who live here allowed in, the South

Village is all Italians and hippies?"

"Like 1965 all over again."

She and I had been in contact more in the past few months than we had in a while. Memories of love and indifference that we shared had made close friendship an on-and-off thing for the last thirty-something years.

Earlier in 2001, at the end of an affair, I'd surrendered a rent-stabilized apartment for a cash settlement and bought a tiny co-op in the South Village. Mags lived as she had for years in a run-down building on the fringes of Soho.

So we saw each other again. I write, obviously, but she never read anything I publish, which bothered me. On the other hand, she worked off and on for various activist leftist foundations, and I was mostly uninterested in that.

Mags was in the midst of classic New York work and housing trouble. Currently she was on unemployment and her landlord wanted to get her out of her apartment so he could co-op her building. The money offer he'd made wasn't bad, but she wanted things to stay as they were. It struck me that what was youthful about her was that she had never settled into her life, still stood on the edge.

Lots of the Village restaurants weren't opened. The owners couldn't or wouldn't come into the city. Angelina's on Thompson Street was, though, because Angelina lives just a couple of doors down from her place. She was busy serving tables herself since the waiters couldn't get in from where they lived.

Later, I had reason to try and remember. The place was full but very quiet. People murmured to each other as Mags and I did. Nobody I knew was there. In the background Resphigi's *Ancient Airs and Dances* played.

"Like the Blitz," someone said.

"Never the same again," said a person at another table.

"There isn't even anyplace to volunteer to help," a third person said.

I don't drink anymore. But Mags, as I remember, had a carafe of wine. Phone service had been spotty, but we had managed to exchange bits of what we had seen.

"Mrs. Pirelli," I said. "The Italian lady upstairs from me. I told you she had a heart attack watching the smoke and flames on television. Her son worked in the World Trade Center and she was sure he had burned to death.

"Getting an ambulance wasn't possible yesterday morning. But the guys at that little fire barn around the corner were there. Waiting to be called, I guess. They took her to St. Vincent's in the chief's car. Right about then, her son came up the street, his pinstripe suit with a hole burned in the shoulder, soot on his face, wild-eyed. But alive. Today they say she's doing fine."

I waited, spearing clams, twirling linguine. Mags had a deeper and darker story to tell; a dip into the subconscious. Before I'd known her and afterward, Mags had a few rough brushes with mental disturbance. Back in college, where we first met, I envied her that, wished I had something as dramatic to talk about.

"I've been thinking about what happened last night." She'd already told me some of this. "The downstairs bell rang, which scared me. But with phone service being bad, it could have been a friend, someone who needed to talk. I looked out the window. The street was empty, dead like I'd never seen it.

"Nothing but papers blowing down the street. You know how every time you see a scrap of paper now you think it's from the Trade Center? For a minute I thought I saw something move, but when I looked again there was nothing.

"I didn't ring the buzzer, but it seemed someone upstairs did because I heard this noise, a rustling in the hall.

"When I went to the door and lifted the spy hole, this figure stood there on the landing. Looking around like she was lost. She wore a dress, long and torn. And a blouse, what I realized was a shirtwaist. Turn-of-the-century clothes. When she turned toward my door, I saw her face. It was bloody, smashed. Like she had taken a big jump or fall. I gasped, and then she was gone."

"And you woke up?"

"No, I tried to call you. But the phones were all fucked up. She had fallen, but not from a hundred stories. Anyway, she wasn't from here and now."

Mags had emptied the carafe. I remember that she'd just ordered a salad and didn't eat that. But Angelina brought a fresh carafe. I told Mags about the family at the barricades.

"There's a hole in the city," said Mags.

That night, after we had parted, I lay in bed watching but not seeing some old movie on TV, avoiding any channel with any kind of news, when the buzzer sounded. I jumped up and went to the view screen. On the empty street downstairs a man, wild-eyed, disheveled, glared directly into the camera.

Phone service was not reliable. Cops were not in evidence in the neighborhood right then. I froze and didn't buzz him in. But, as in Mags's building, someone else did. I bolted my door, watched at the spy hole, listened to the footsteps, slow, uncertain. When he came into sight on the second floor landing he looked around and said in a hoarse voice, "Hello? Sorry, but I can't find my mom's front-door key."

Only then did I unlock the door, open it, and ask her exhausted son how Mrs. Pirelli was doing.

"Fine," he said. "Getting great treatment. St. Vincent was geared up for thousands of casualties. Instead." He shrugged. "Anyway, she thanks all of you. Me too."

In fact, I hadn't done much. We said good night, and he shuffled on upstairs to where he was crashing in his mother's place.

THURSDAY 9/13

By September of 2001 I had worked an information desk in the university library for almost thirty years. I live right around the corner from Washington Square, and just before 10 a.m. on Thursday, I set out for work. The Moslem-run souvlaki stand across the street was still closed, its owner and workers gone since Tuesday morning. All the little falafel shops in the South Village were shut and dark.

On my way to work I saw a three-legged rat running not too quickly down the middle of MacDougal Street. I decided not to think about portents and symbolism.

The big TVs set up in the library atrium still showed the towers falling again and again. But now they also showed workers digging in the flaming wreckage at Ground Zero.

Like the day before, I was the only one in my department who'd made it in. The librarians lived too far away. Even Marco, the student assistant, wasn't around.

Marco lived in a dorm downtown right near the World Trade Center. They'd been evacuated with nothing more than a few books and the clothes they were wearing. Tuesday, he'd been very upset. I'd given him Kleenex, made him take deep breaths, got him to call his mother back in California. I'd even walked him over to the gym, where the university was putting up the displaced students.

Thursday morning, all of the computer stations around the information desk were occupied. Students sat furiously typing e-mail and devouring incoming messages, but the intensity had slackened since 9/11. The girls no longer sniffed and dabbed at tears as they read. The boys didn't jump up and come back from the restrooms red-eyed and saying they had allergies.

I said good morning and sat down. The kids hadn't spoken much to me in the last few days, had no questions to ask. But all of them from time to time would turn and look to make sure I was still there. If I got up to leave the desk, they'd ask when I was coming back.

Some of the back windows had a downtown view. The pillar of smoke wavered. The wind was changing.

The phone rang. Reception had improved. Most calls went through. When I answered, a voice, tight and tense, blurted out, "Jennie Levine was who I saw. She was nineteen years old in 1911 when the Triangle Shirtwaist Factory burned. She lived in my building with her family ninety years ago. Her spirit found its way home. But the inside of my building has changed so much that she didn't recognize it."

"Hi, Mags," I said. "You want to come up here and have lunch?"

A couple of hours later, we were in a small dining hall normally used by faculty on the west side of the Square. The university, with food on hand and not enough people to eat it, had thrown open its cafeterias and dining halls to anybody with a university identification. We could even bring a friend if we cared to.

Now that I looked, Mags had tension lines around her eyes and hair that could have used some tending. But we were all of us a little ragged in those days of sun and horror. People kept glancing downtown, even if they were inside and not near a window.

The Indian lady who ran the facility greeted us, thanked us for coming. I had a really nice gumbo, fresh avocado salad, a soothing pudding. The place was half-empty, and conversations again were muted. I told Mags about Mrs. Pirelli's son the night before.

She looked up from her plate, unsmiling, said, "I did not imagine Jennie Levine," and closed that subject.

Afterward, she and I stood on Washington Place before the university building that had once housed the sweatshop called the Triangle Shirtwaist Factory. At the end of the block, a long convoy of olive green army trucks rolled silently down Broadway.

Mags said, "On the afternoon of March 25, 1911, one hundred and forty-six young women burned to death on this site. Fire broke out in a pile of rags. The door to the roof was locked. The fire ladders couldn't reach the eighth floor. The girls burned."

Her voice tightened as she said, "They jumped and were smashed on the sidewalk. Many of them, most of them, lived right around here. In the renovated tenements we live in now. It's like those planes blew a hole in the city and Jennie Levine returned through it."

"Easy, honey. The university has grief counseling available. I think I'm going. You want me to see if I can get you in?" It sounded idiotic even as I said it. We had walked back to the library.

"There are others," she said. "Kids all blackened and bloated and wearing old-fashioned clothes. I woke up early this morning and couldn't go back to sleep. I got up and walked around here and over in the East Village."

"Jesus!" I said.

"Geoffrey has come back too. I know it."

"Mags! Don't!" This was something we hadn't talked about in a long time. Once we were three, and Geoffrey was the third. He was younger than either of us by a couple of years at a time of life when that still seemed a major difference.

We called him Lord Geoff because he said we were all a bit better than the world around us. We joked that he was our child. A little family cemented by desire and drugs.

The three of us were all so young, just out of school and in the city. Then jealousy and the hard realities of addiction began to tear us apart. Each had to find his or her own survival. Mags and I made it. As it turned out, Geoff wasn't built for the long haul. He was twenty-one. We were all just kids, ignorant and reckless.

As I made excuses in my mind, Mags gripped my arm. "He'll want to find us," she said. Chilled, I watched her walk away and wondered how long she had been coming apart and why I hadn't noticed.

Back at work, Marco waited for me. He was part Filipino, a bit of a little wiseass who dressed in downtown black. But that was the week before. Today, he was a woebegone refugee in oversized flip-flops, wearing a magenta sweatshirt and gym shorts, both of which had been made for someone bigger and more buff.

"How's it going?"

"It sucks! My stuff is all downtown where I don't know if I can ever get it. They have these crates in the gym, toothbrushes, bras, Bic razors, but never what you need, everything from boxer shorts on out, and nothing is ever the right size. I gave my clothes in to be cleaned, and they didn't bring them back. Now I look like a clown.

"They have us all sleeping on cots on the basketball courts. I lay there all last night staring up at the ceiling, with a hundred other guys. Some of them snore. One was yelling in his sleep. And I don't want to take a shower with a bunch of guys staring at me."

He told me all this while not looking my way, but I understood what he was asking. I expected this was going to be a pain. But, given that I couldn't seem to do much for Mags, I thought maybe it would be a distraction to do what I could for someone else.

"You want to take a shower at my place, crash on my couch?"

"Could I, please?"

So I took a break, brought him around the corner to my apartment, put sheets on the daybed. He was in the shower when I went back to work.

That evening when I got home, he woke up. When I went out to take a walk, he tagged along. We stood at the police barricades at Houston Street and Sixth Avenue and watched the traffic coming up from the World Trade Center site. An ambulance with one side smashed and a squad car with its roof crushed were hauled up Sixth Avenue on the back of a huge flatbed truck. NYPD buses were full of guys returning from Ground Zero, hollow-eyed, filthy.

Crowds of Greenwich Villagers gathered on the sidewalks clapped and cheered, yelled, "We love our firemen! We love our cops!"

The firehouse on Sixth Avenue had taken a lot of casualties when the towers fell. The place was locked and empty. We looked at the flowers and the wreaths on the doors, the signs with faces of the firefighters who hadn't returned, and the messages, "To the brave men of these companies who gave their lives defending us."

The plume of smoke downtown rolled in the twilight, buffeted about by shifting winds. The breeze brought with it for the first time the acrid smoke that would be with us for weeks afterward.

Officials said it was the stench of burning concrete. I believed, as did everyone else, that part of what we breathed was the ashes of the ones who had burned to death that Tuesday.

It started to drizzle. Marco stuck close to me as we walked back. Hip twenty-year-olds do not normally hang out with guys almost three times their age. This kid was very scared.

Bleecker Street looked semiabandoned, with lots of the stores and restaurants still closed. The ones that were open were mostly empty at nine in the evening.

"If I buy you a six-pack, you promise to drink all of it?" He indicated he would.

At home, Marco asked to use the phone. He called people he knew on campus, looking for a spare dorm room, and spoke in whispers to a girl named Eloise. In between calls, he worked the computer.

I played a little Lady Day, some Ray Charles, a bit of Haydn, stared at the TV screen. The president had pulled out of his funk and was coming to New York the next day.

In the next room, the phone rang. "No. My name's Marco," I heard him say. "He's letting me stay here." I knew who it was before he came in and whispered, "She asked if I was Lord Geoff."

"Hi, Mags," I said. She was calling from somewhere with walkie-talkies and sirens in the background.

"Those kids I saw in Astor Place?" she said, her voice clear and crazed. "The ones all burned and drowned? They were on the *General Slocum* when it caught fire."

"The kids you saw in Astor Place all burned and drowned?" I asked. Then I remembered our conversation earlier.

"On June 15, 1904. The biggest disaster in New York City history. Until now. The East Village was once called Little Germany. Tens of thousands of Germans with their own meeting halls, churches, beer gardens.

"They had a Sunday excursion, mainly for the kids, on a steamship, the *General Slocum,* a floating firetrap. When it burst into flames, there were no lifeboats. The crew and the captain panicked. By the time they got to a dock, over a thousand were dead. Burned, drowned. When a hole got blown in the city, they came back looking for their homes."

The connection started to dissolve into static.

"Where are you, Mags?"

"Ground Zero. It smells like burning sulfur. Have you seen Geoffrey yet?" she shouted into her phone.

"Geoffrey is dead, Mags. It's all the horror and tension that's doing this to you. There's no hole..."

"Cops and firemen and brokers all smashed and charred are walking around down here." At that point sirens screamed in the background. Men were yelling. The connection faded.

"Mags, give me your number. Call me back," I yelled. Then there was nothing but static, followed by a weak dial tone. I hung up and waited for the phone to ring again.

After a while, I realized Marco was standing looking at me, slugging down beer. "She saw those kids? I saw them too. Tuesday night I was too jumpy to even lie down on the fucking cot. I snuck out with my friend Terry. We walked around. The kids were there. In old, historical clothes. Covered with mud and seaweed and their faces all black and gone. It's why I couldn't sleep last night."

"You talk to the counselors?" I asked.

He drained the bottle. "Yeah, but they don't want to hear what I wanted to talk about."

"But with me..."

"You're crazy. You understand."

The silence outside was broken by a jet engine. We both flinched. No planes had flown over Manhattan since the ones that had smashed the towers on Tuesday morning.

Then I realized what it was. "The Air Force," I said. "Making sure it's safe for Mr. Bush's visit."

"Who's Mags? Who's Lord Geoff?"

So I told him a bit of what had gone on in that strange lost country, the 1960's, the naïveté that led to meth and junk. I described the wonder of that unknown land, the three-way union. "Our problem, I guess, was that instead of a real ménage, each member was obsessed with only one of the others."

"Okay," he said. "You're alive. Mags is alive. What happened to Geoff?

"When things were breaking up, Geoff got caught in a drug sweep and was being hauled downtown in the back of a police van. He cut his wrists and bled to death in the dark before anyone noticed."

This did for me what speaking about the dead kids had maybe done for him. Each of us got to talk about what bothered him without having to think much about what the other said.

FRIDAY 9/14

Friday morning two queens walked by with their little dogs as Marco and I came out the door of my building. One said, "There isn't a fresh croissant in the entire Village. It's like the Siege of Paris. We'll all be reduced to eating rats."

I murmured, "He's getting a little ahead of the story. Maybe first he should think about having an English muffin."

"Or eating his yappy dog," said Marco.

At that moment, the authorities opened the East and West Villages, between Fourteenth and Houston Streets, to outside traffic. All the people whose cars had been stranded since Tuesday began to come into the neighborhood and drive them away. Delivery trucks started to appear on the narrow streets.

In the library, the huge TV screens showed the activity at Ground Zero, the preparations for the president's visit. An elevator door opened and revealed a couple of refugee kids in their surplus gym clothes clasped in a passion clinch.

The computers around my information desk were still fully occupied, but the tension level had fallen. There was even a question or two about books and databases. I tried repeatedly to call Mags. All I got was the chilling message on her answering machine.

In a staccato voice, it said, "This is Mags McConnell. There's a hole in the city, and I've turned this into a center for information about the victims Jennie Levine and Geoffrey Holbrun. Anyone with information concerning the whereabouts of these two young people, please speak after the beep."

I left a message asking her to call. Then I called every half hour or so, hoping she'd pick up. I phoned mutual friends. Some were absent or unavailable. A couple were nursing grief of their own. No one had seen her recently.

That evening in the growing dark, lights flickered in Washington Square. Candles were given out; candles were lighted with matches and Bics and wick to wick. Various priests, ministers, rabbis, and shamans led flower-bearing, candlelit congregations down the streets and into the park, where they joined the gathering vigil crowd.

Marco had come by with his friend Terry, a kind of elfin kid who'd also had to stay at the gym. We went to this 9/11 vigil together. People addressed the crowd, gave impromptu elegies. There were prayers and a few songs. Then by instinct or some plan I hadn't heard about, everyone started to move out of the park and flow in groups through the streets.

We paused at streetlamps that bore signs with pictures of pajama-clad families in suburban rec rooms on Christmas mornings. One face would be circled in red, and there would be a message like, "This is James Bolton, husband of Susan, father of Jimmy, Anna, and Sue, last seen leaving his home in Far Rockaway at 7:30 a.m. on 9/11." This was followed by the name of the company, the floor of the Trade Center tower where he worked, phone and fax numbers, the e-mail address, and the words, "If you have any information about where he is, please contact us."

At each sign someone would leave a lighted candle on a tin plate. Someone else would leave flowers.

The door of the little neighborhood Fire Rescue station was open; the truck and command car were gone. The place was manned by retired fire-fighters with faces like old Irish and Italian character actors. A big picture of a fireman who had died was hung up beside the door. He was young, maybe thirty. He and his wife, or maybe his girlfriend, smiled in front of a ski lodge. The picture was framed with children's drawings of firemen and fire trucks and fires, with condolences and novena cards.

As we walked and the night progressed, the crowd got stretched out. We'd see clumps of candles ahead of us on the streets. It was on Great Jones Street and the Bowery that suddenly there was just the three of us and no traffic to speak of. When I turned to say maybe we should go home, I saw for a moment a tall guy staggering down the street with his face purple and his eyes bulging out.

Then he was gone. Either Marco or Terry whispered, "Shit, he killed himself." And none of us said anything more.

At some point in the evening, I had said Terry could spend the night in my apartment. He couldn't take his eyes off Marco, though Marco seemed not to notice. On our way home, way east on Bleecker Street, outside a bar that had been old even when I'd hung out there as a kid, I saw the poster.

It was like a dozen others I'd seen that night. Except it was in old-time black and white and showed three kids with lots of hair and bad attitude: Mags and Geoffrey and me.

Geoff's face was circled and under it was written, "This is Geoffrey Hol-brun, if you have seen him since Tuesday 9/11 please contact." And Mags had left her name and numbers.

Even in the photo, I looked toward Geoffrey, who looked toward Mags, who looked toward me. I stared for just a moment before going on, but I knew that Marco had noticed.

SATURDAY 9/15

My tiny apartment was a crowded mess Saturday morning. Every towel I owned was wet, every glass and mug was dirty. It smelled like a zoo. There were pizza crusts in the sink and a bag of beer cans at the front door. The night before, none of us had talked about the ghosts. Marco and Terry had seriously discussed whether they would be drafted or would enlist. The idea of them in the army did not make me feel any safer.

Saturday is a work day for me. Getting ready, I reminded myself that this would soon be over. The university had found all the refugee kids dorm rooms on campus.

Then the bell rang and a young lady with a nose ring and bright red ringlets of hair appeared. Eloise was another refugee, though a much better-organized one. She had brought bagels and my guests' laundry. Marco seemed delighted to see her.

That morning all the restaurants and bars, the tattoo shops and massage parlors, were opening up. Even the Arab falafel shop owners had risked insults and death threats to ride the subways in from Queens and open their doors for business.

At the library, the huge screens in the lobby were being taken down. A couple of students were borrowing books. One or two even had in-depth reference questions for me. When I finally worked up the courage to call Mags, all I got was the same message as before.

Marco appeared dressed in his own clothes and clearly feeling better. He hugged me. "You were great to take me in."

"It helped me even more," I told him.

He paused then asked, "That was you on that poster last night, wasn't it? You and Mags and Geoffrey?" The kid was a bit uncanny.

When I nodded, he said. "Thanks for talking about that."

I was in a hurry when I went off duty Saturday evening. A friend had called and invited me to an impromptu "Survivors' Party." In the days of the French Revolution, The Terror, that's what they called the soirees at which people danced and drank all night then went out at dawn to see which of their names were on the list of those to be guillotined.

On Sixth Avenue a bakery that had very special cupcakes with devastating frosting was open again. The avenue was clogged with honking, creeping traffic. A huge chunk of Lower Manhattan had been declared open that afternoon, and people were able to get the cars that had been stranded down there.

The bakery was across the street from a Catholic church. And that afternoon in that place, a wedding was being held. As I came out with my cupcakes, the bride and groom, not real young, not very glamorous, but obviously happy, came out the door and posed on the steps for pictures.

Traffic was at a standstill. People beeped "Here Comes the Bride," leaned out their windows, applauded and cheered, all of us relieved to find this ordinary, normal thing taking place.

Then I saw her on the other side of Sixth Avenue. Mags was tramping along, staring straight ahead, a poster with a black and white photo hanging from a string around her neck. The crowd in front of the church parted for her. Mourners were sacred at that moment.

I yelled her name and started to cross the street. But the tie-up had eased; traffic started to flow. I tried to keep pace with her on my side of the street. I wanted to invite her to the party. The hosts knew her from way back. But the sidewalks on both sides were crowded. When I did get across Sixth, she was gone.

AFTERMATH

That night I came home from the party and found the place completely cleaned up, with a thank-you note on the fridge signed by all three kids. And I felt relieved but also lost.

The Survivors' Party was on the Lower East Side. On my way back, I had gone by the East Village, walked up to Tenth Street between B and C. People were out and about. Bars were doing business. But there was still almost no vehicle traffic, and the block was very quiet.

The building where we three had lived in increasing squalor and tension thirty-five years before was refinished, gentrified. I stood across the street looking. Maybe I willed his appearance.

Geoff was there in the corner of my eye, his face dead white, staring up, unblinking, at the light in what had been our windows. I turned toward him and he disappeared. I looked aside and he was there again, so lost and alone, the arms of his jacket soaked in blood.

And I remembered us sitting around with the syringes and all of us making a pledge in blood to stick together as long as we lived. To which Geoff added, "And even after." And I remembered how I had looked at him staring at Mags and knew she was looking at me. Three sides of a triangle.

The next day, Sunday, I went down to Mags's building, wanting very badly to talk to her. I rang the bell again and again. There was no response. I rang the super's apartment.

She was a neighborhood lady, a lesbian around my age. I asked her about Mags.

"She disappeared. Last time anybody saw her was Sunday, 9/9. People in the building checked to make sure everyone was okay. No sign of her. I put a tape across her keyhole Wednesday. It's still there."

"I saw her just yesterday."

"Yeah?" She looked skeptical. "Well, there's a World Trade Center list of potentially missing persons, and her name's on it. You need to talk to them."

This sounded to me like the landlord trying to get rid of her. For the next week, I called Mags a couple of times a day. At some point, the answering machine stopped coming on. I checked out her building regularly. No sign of her. I asked Angelina if she remembered the two of us having dinner in her place on Wednesday, 9/12.

"I was too busy, staying busy so I wouldn't scream. I remember you, and I guess you were with somebody. But no, honey, I don't remember."

Then I asked Marco if he remembered the phone call. And he did but was much too involved by then with Terry and Eloise to be really interested.

Around that time, I saw the couple who had wanted to take their kids down to Ground Zero. They were walking up Sixth Avenue, the kids cranky and tired, the parents looking disappointed. Like the amusement park had turned out to be a rip-off.

Life closed in around me. A short-story collection of mine was being published at that very inopportune moment, and I needed to do some publicity work. I began seeing an old lover when he came back to New York as a consultant for a company that had lost its offices and a big chunk of its staff when the north tower fell.

Mrs. Pirelli did not come home from the hospital but went to live with her son in Connecticut. I made it a point to go by each of the Arab shops and listen to the owners say how awful they felt about what had happened and smile when they showed me pictures of their kids in Yankee caps and shirts.

It was the next weekend that I saw Mags again. The university had gotten permission for the students to go back to the downtown dorms and get their stuff out. Marco, Terry, and Eloise came by the library and asked me to go with them. So I went over to University Transportation and volunteered my services.

Around noon on Sunday, 9/23, a couple of dozen kids and I piled into a university bus driven by Roger, a Jamaican guy who has worked for the university for as long as I have.

"The day before 9/11 these kids didn't much want old farts keeping them company," Roger had said to me. "Then they all wanted their daddy." He led a convoy of jitneys and vans down the FDR Drive, then through quiet Sunday streets, and then past trucks and construction vehicles.

We stopped at a police checkpoint. A cop looked inside and waved us through.

At the dorm, another cop told the kids they had an hour to get what they could and get out. "Be ready to leave at a moment's notice if we tell you to," he said.

Roger and I as the senior members stayed with the vehicles. The air was filthy. Our eyes watered. A few hundred feet up the street, a cloud of smoke still hovered over the ruins of the World Trade Center. Piles of rubble smoldered. Between the pit and us was a line of fire trucks and police cars with cherry tops flashing. Behind us the kids hurried out of the dorm carrying boxes. I made them write their names on their boxes and noted in which van the boxes got stowed. I was surprised, touched even, at the number of stuffed animals that were being rescued.

"Over the years we've done some weird things to earn our pensions," I said to Roger.

"Like volunteering to come to the gates of hell?"

As he said that, flames sprouted from the rubble. Police and firefighters shouted and began to fall back. A fire department chemical tanker turned around, and the crew began unwinding hoses.

Among the uniforms, I saw a civilian, a middle-aged woman in a sweater and jeans and carrying a sign. Mags walked toward the flames. I wanted to run to her. I wanted to shout, "Stop her." Then I realized that none of the cops and firefighters seemed aware of her even as she walked right past them.

As she did, I saw another figure, thin, pale, in a suede jacket and bell-bottom pants. He held out his bloody hands, and together they walked through the smoke and flames into the hole in the city.

"Was that them?" Marco had been standing beside me.

I turned to him. Terry was back by the bus watching Marco's every move. Eloise was gazing at Terry.

"Be smarter than we were," I said.

And Marco said, "Sure," with all the confidence in the world.

MONSTER
KELLY LINK

Kelly Link was born in Miami, Florida and grew up on the East Coast. She attended Columbia University in New York and the University of North Carolina, Greensboro. She sold her first story, "Water Off a Black Dog's Back", just before attending Clarion in 1995. Her later stories have won or been nominated for the James Tiptree Jr., World Fantasy, and Nebula Awards. Link's stories have been collected in Stranger Things Happen *and* Magic for Beginners. *She has edited the anthology* Trampoline, *co-edits* The Year's Best Fantasy and Horror *with husband Gavin J. Grant and Ellen Datlow, and co-edits the 'zine* Lady Churchill's Rosebud Wristlet *with Grant.*

No one in Bungalow 6 wanted to go camping. It was raining, which meant that you had to wear garbage bags over your backpacks and around the sleeping bags, and even that wouldn't help. The sleeping bags would still get wet. Some of the wet sleeping bags would then smell like pee, and the tents already smelled like mildew, and even if they got the tents up, water would collect on the ground cloths. There would be three boys to a tent, and only the boy in the middle would stay dry. The other two would inevitably end up squashed against the sides of the tent, and wherever you touched the nylon, water would come through from the outside.

Besides, someone in Bungalow 4 had seen a monster in the woods. Bungalow 4 had been telling stories ever since they got back. It was a no-win situation for Bungalow 6. If Bungalow 6 didn't see the monster, Bungalow 4 would keep the upper hand that fate had dealt them. If Bungalow 6 did see a monster — but who wanted to see a monster, even if it meant that you got to tell everyone about it? Not anyone in Bungalow 6, except for James Lorbick, who thought that monsters were awesome. But James Lorbick was a geek and from Chicago and he had a condition that made his feet smell terrible. That was another thing about camping. Someone would have to share a tent with James Lorbick and his smelly feet.

And even if Bungalow 6 did see the monster, well, Bungalow 4 had seen it first, so there was nothing special about that, seeing a monster after Bungalow 4 went and saw it first. And maybe Bungalow 4 had pissed off that monster. Maybe that monster was just waiting for more kids to show up at the Honor Lookout where all the pine trees leaned backwards in a circle around the bald hump of the hill in a way that made you feel dizzy when you lay around the fire at night and looked up at them.

"There wasn't any monster," Bryan Jones said, "and anyway if there was a monster, I bet it ran away when it saw Bungalow 4." Everybody nodded. What Bryan Jones said made sense. Everybody knew that the kids in Bungalow 4 were so mean that they had made their counselor cry like a girl. The Bungalow 4 counselor was a twenty-year-old college student named Eric who had terrible acne and wrote poems about the local girls who worked in the kitchen and how their breasts looked lonely but also beautiful, like melted ice cream. The kids in Bungalow 4 had found the poetry and read it out loud at morning assembly in front of everybody, including some of the kitchen girls.

Bungalow 4 had sprayed a bat with insect spray and then set fire to it and almost burned down the whole bungalow.

And there were worse stories about Bungalow 4.

Everyone said that the kids in Bungalow 4 were so mean that their parents sent them off to camp just so they wouldn't have to see them for a few weeks.

"I heard that the monster had big black wings," Colin Simpson said. "Like a vampire. It flapped around and it had these long fingernails."

"I heard it had lots of teeth."

"I heard it bit Barnhard."

"I heard he tasted so bad that the monster puked after it bit him."

"I saw Barnhard last night at dinner," Colin Simpson's twin brother said. Or maybe it was Colin Simpson who said that and the kid who was talking about flapping and fingernails was the other twin. Everybody had a hard time telling them apart. "He had a Band-Aid on the inside of his arm. He looked kind of weird. Kind of pale."

"Guys," their counselor said. "Hey guys. Enough talk. Let's pack up and get going." The Bungalow 6 counselor was named Terence, but he was pretty cool. All of the kitchen girls hung around Bungalow 6 to talk to Terence, even though he was already going out with a girl from Ohio who was six-feet-two and played basketball. Sometimes before he turned out the lights, Terence would read them letters that the girl from Ohio had written. There was a picture over Terence's camp bed of this girl sitting on an elephant in Thailand. The girl's name was Darlene. Nobody knew the elephant's name.

"We can't just sit here all day," Terence said. "Chop chop."

Everyone started complaining.

"I know it's raining," Terence said. "But there are only three more days of camp left and if we want our overnight badges, this is our last chance. Besides it could stop raining. And not that you should care, but everyone in Bungalow 4 will say that you got scared and that's why you didn't want to go. And I don't want everyone to think that Bungalow 6 is afraid of some stupid Bungalow 4 story about some stupid monster."

It didn't stop raining. Bungalow 6 didn't exactly hike; they waded. They splashed. They slid down hills. The rain came down in clammy, cold, sticky sheets. One of the Simpson twins put his foot down at the bottom of a trail and the mud went up all the way to his knee and pulled his tennis shoe right off with a loud sucking noise. So they had to stop while Terence lay down in the mud and stuck his arm down, fishing for the Simpson twin's shoe.

Bryan Jones stood next to Terence and held out his shirt so the rain wouldn't fall in Terence's ear. Bryan Jones was from North Carolina. He was a big tall kid with a friendly face, who liked paint guns and BB guns and laser guns and pulling down his pants and mooning people and putting hot sauce on toothbrushes.

Sometimes he'd sit on top of James Lorbick's head and fart, but everybody knew it was just Bryan being funny, except for James Lorbick. James Lorbick was from Chicago. James Lorbick hated Bryan even more than he hated the kids in Bungalow 4. Sometimes James pretended that Bryan Jones's parents died in some weird accident while camp was still going on and that no one knew what to say to Bryan and so they avoided him until James came up to Bryan and said exactly the right thing and made Bryan feel better, although of course he wouldn't really feel better, he'd just appreciate what James had said to him, whatever it was that James had said. And of course then Bryan would feel bad about sitting on James's head all those times. And then they'd be friends. Everybody wanted to be friends with Bryan Jones, even James Lorbick.

The first thing that Terence pulled up out of the mud wasn't the Simpson twin's shoe. It was long and round and knobby. When Terence knocked it against the ground, some of the mud slid off.

"Hey. Wow," James Lorbick said. "That looks like a bone."

Everybody stood in the rain and looked at the bone.

"What is that?"

"Is it human?"

"Maybe it's a dinosaur," James Lorbick said. "Like a fossil."

"Probably a cow bone," Terence said. He poked the bone back in the mud and fished around until it got stuck in something that turned out to be the lost shoe. The Simpson twin took the shoe as if he didn't really want it back. He turned it upside down and mud oozed out like lonely, melting soft-squeeze ice cream.

Half of Terence was now covered in mud, although at least, thanks to Bryan Jones, he didn't have water in his ear. He held the dubious bone as if he was going to toss it off in the bushes, but then he stopped and looked at it again. He put it in the pocket of his rain jacket instead. Half of it stuck out. It didn't look like a cow bone.

By the time they got to Honor Lookout, the rain had stopped. "See?" Terence said. "I told you." He said it as if now they were fine. Now everything would be fine. Water plopped off the needles of the pitiful pine trees that leaned eternally away from the campground on Honor Lookout.

Bungalow 6 gathered wood that would be too wet to use for a fire. They unpacked their tents and tent poles, and tent pegs, which descended into the sucking mud and disappeared forever. They laid out their tents on top of ground cloths on top of the sucking, quivering, nearly-animate mud. It was like putting a tent up over chocolate pudding. The floor of the tents sank below the level of the mud when they crawled inside. It was hard to imagine sleeping in the tents. You might just keep on sinking.

"Hey," Bryan Jones said, "look out! Snowball fight!" He lobbed a brown mudball which hit James Lorbick just under the chin and splashed up on James's glasses. Then everyone was throwing mudballs, even Terence. James Lorbick even threw one. There was nothing else to do.

When they got hungry, they ate cold hot dogs for lunch while the mud dried and cracked and fell off their arms and legs and faces. They ate graham crackers with marshmallows and chocolate squares and Terence even toasted the marshmallows with a cigarette lighter for anyone who wanted. Since they couldn't make a fire, they made mud sculptures instead. Terence sculpted an elephant and a girl on top. The elephant even looked like an elephant. But then one of the Simpson twins sculpted an atom bomb and dropped it on Terence's elephant and Terence's girlfriend.

"That's okay," Terence said. "That's cool." But it wasn't cool. He went and sat on a muddy rock and looked at his bone.

The twins had made a whole stockpile of atom bombs out of mud. They decided to make a whole city with walls and buildings and everything. Some of the other kids from Bungalow 6 helped with the city so that the twins could bomb the city before it got too dark.

Bryan Jones had put mud in his hair and twisted it up in muddy spikes. There was mud in his eyebrows. He looked like an idiot, but that didn't matter, because he was Bryan Jones and anything that Bryan Jones did wasn't stupid. It was cool. "Hey man," he said to James. "Come and see what I stole off the clothes line at camp."

James Lorbick was muddy and tired and maybe his feet did smell bad, but he was smarter than most of the kids in Bungalow 6. "Why?" he said.

"Just come on," Bryan said. "I don't want anyone else to see this yet."

"Okay," James said.

It was a dress. It had big blue flowers on it and James Lorbick got a bad feeling.

"Why did you steal a dress?" he said.

Bryan shrugged. He was smiling as if the whole idea of a dress made him happy. It was big, happy, contagious smile, but James Lorbick didn't smile back. "Because it will be funny," Bryan said. "Put it on and we'll go show everybody."

"No way," James said. He folded his muddy arms over his muddy chest to show he was serious.

"I dare you," Bryan said. "Come on, James, before everybody comes over here and sees it. Everybody will laugh."

"I know they will," James said. "No."

"Look, I'd put it on, I swear, but it wouldn't fit me. No way would it fit. So you've got to do it. Just do it, James."

"No," James said.

James Lorbick wasn't sure why his parents had sent him off to a camp in North Carolina. He hadn't wanted to go. It wasn't as if there weren't trees in Chicago. It wasn't as if James didn't have friends in Chicago. Camp just seemed to be one of those things parents could make you do, like violin lessons, or karate, except that camp lasted a whole month. Plus, he was supposed to be thankful about it, like his parents had done him a big favor. Camp cost money.

So he made leather wallets in arts and crafts, and went swimming every other day, even though the lake smelled funny and the swim instructor was kind of weird and liked to make the campers stand on the high diving board with their eyes closed. Then he'd creep up and push them into the water. Not that you didn't know he was creeping up. You could feel the board wobbling.

He didn't make friends. But that wasn't true, exactly. He was friendly, but nobody in Bungalow 6 was friendly back. Sometimes right after Terence turned out the lights, someone would say, "James, oh, James, your hair looked really excellent today" or "James, James Lorbick, I wish I were as good at archery as you" or "James, will you let me borrow your water canteen tomorrow?" and then everyone would laugh while James pretended to be asleep, until Terence would flick on the lights and say, "Leave James alone – go to sleep or I'll give everyone five demerits."

James Lorbick knew it could have been worse. He could have been in

Bungalow 4 instead of Bungalow 6.

At least the dress wasn't muddy. Bryan let him keep his jeans and T-shirt on. "Let me do your hair," Bryan said. He picked up a handful of mud pushed it around on James's head until James had sticky mud hair just like Bryan's.

"Come on," Bryan said.

"Why do I have to do this?" James said. He held his hands out to the side so that he wouldn't have to touch the dress. He looked ridiculous. He felt worse than ridiculous. He felt terrible. He felt so terrible that he didn't even care anymore that he was wearing a dress.

"You didn't have to do this," Bryan said. He sounded like he thought it was a big joke, which it was. "I didn't make you do it, James."

One of the Simpson twins was running around, dropping atom bombs on the sagging, wrinkled tents. He skidded to a stop in front of Bryan and James. "Why are you wearing a dress?" the Simpson twin said. "Hey, James is wearing a dress!"

Bryan gave James a shove. Not hard, but he left a muddy handprint on the dress. "Come on," he said. "Pretend that you're a zombie. Like you're a kitchen girl zombie who's come back to eat the brains of everybody from Bungalow 6, because you're still angry about that time we had the rice pudding fight with Bungalow 4 out on the porch of the dining room. Like you just crawled out of the mud. I'll be a zombie too. Let's go chase people."

"Okay," James Lorbick said. The terrible feeling went away at the thought of being a zombie and suddenly the flowered dress seemed magical to him. It gave him the strength of a zombie, only faster. He staggered with Bryan along toward the rest of Bungalow 6, holding out his arms. Kids said things like, "Hey, look at James! James is wearing a DRESS!" as if they were making fun of him, but then they got the idea. They realized that James and Bryan were zombies and they ran away. Even Terence.

After a while, everybody had become a zombie. So they went for a swim. Everybody except for James Lorbick, because when he started to take off the dress, Bryan Jones stopped him. Bryan said, "No, wait. Keep it on. I dare you to wear that dress until we get back to camp tomorrow. I dare you. We'll show up at breakfast and say that we saw a monster and it's chasing us, and then you come in the dining room and it will be awesome. You look completely spooky with that dress and all the mud."

"I'll get my sleeping bag all muddy," James said. "I don't want to sleep in a dress. It's dumb."

Everybody in the lake began to yell things.

"Come on, James, wear the dress, okay?"

"Keep the dress on! Do it, James!"

"I dare you," said Bryan.

"I dare *you*," James said.

"What?" Bryan said. "What do you dare me to do?"

James thought for a moment. Nothing came to him. "I don't know."

Terence was floating on his back. He lifted his head. "You tell him, James. Don't let Bryan talk you into anything you don't want to do."

"Come on," Bryan said. "It will be so cool. Come on."

So everybody in Bungalow 6 went swimming except for James Lorbick. They splashed around and washed off all the mud and came out of the pond and James Lorbick was the only kid in Bungalow 6 who was still covered in crusty mud. James Lorbick was the only one who still had mud spikes in his hair. James Lorbick was the only one wearing a dress.

The sun was going down. They sat on the ground around the campfire that wouldn't catch. They ate the rest of the hotdogs and the peanut butter sandwiches that the kitchen girls always made up when bungalows went on overnight hikes. They talked about how cool it would be in the morning, when James Lorbick came running into the dining room back at camp, pretending to be a monster.

It got darker. They talked about the monster.

"Maybe it's a werewolf."

"Or a were-skunk."

"Maybe it's from outer space."

"Maybe it's just really lonely," James Lorbick said. He was sitting between Bryan Jones and one of the Simpson twins, and he felt really good, like he was really part of Bungalow 6 at last, and also kind of itchy, because of the mud.

"So how come nobody's ever seen it before?"

"Maybe some people have, but they died and so they couldn't tell anybody."

"No way. They wouldn't let us camp here if somebody died."

"Maybe the camp doesn't want anybody to know about the monster, so they don't say anything."

"You're so paranoid. The monster didn't do anything to Bungalow 4. Besides, Bungalow 4 is a bunch of liars."

"Wait a minute, do you hear that?"

They were quiet, listening. Bryan Jones farted. It was a sinister, brassy fart.

"Oh, man. That's disgusting, Bryan."

"What? It wasn't me."

"If the monster comes, we'll just aim Bryan at it."

"Wait, what's that?"

Something was ringing. "No way," Terence said. "That's my cell phone. No way does it get reception out here. Hello? Hey, Darlene. What's up?" He turned on his flashlight and shone it at Bungalow 6. "Guys. I've gotta go down the hill for a sec. She sounds upset. Something about her car and a chihuahua."

"That's cool."

"Be careful. Don't let the monster sneak up on you."

"Tell Darlene she's too good for you."

They watched Terence pick his way down the muddy path in a little circle of light. The light got smaller and smaller, farther and farther away, until they couldn't see it any more.

"What if it isn't really Darlene?" a kid named Timothy Ferber said.

"What?"

"Like what if it's the monster?"

"No way. That's stupid. How would the monster know Terence's cell phone number?"

"Are there any marshmallows left?"

"No. Just graham crackers."

They ate the graham crackers. Terence didn't come back. They couldn't even hear his voice. They told ghost stories.

"And she puts her hand down and her dog licks it and she thinks everything is okay. Except that then, in the morning, when she looks in the bathtub, her dog is in there and he's dead and there's lots of blood and somebody has written HA HA I REALLY FOOLED YOU with the blood."

"One time my sister was babysitting and this weird guy called and wanted to know if Satan was there and she got really freaked out."

"One time my grandfather was riding on a train and he saw a naked woman standing out in a field."

"Was she a ghost?"

"I don't know. He used to like to tell that story a lot."

"Were there cows in the field?"

"I don't know, how should I know if there were cows?"

"Do you think Terence is going to come back soon?"

"Why? Are you scared?"

"What time is it?"

"It's not even 10:30. Maybe we could try lighting the fire again."

"It's still too wet. It's not going to catch. Besides, if there was a monster and if the monster was out there and we got the fire lit, then the monster could see us."

"We don't have any marshmallows anyway."

"Wait, I think I know how to get it started. Like Bungalow 4 did with the bat. If I spray it with insecticide, and then—"

Bungalow 6 fell reverently silent.

"Wow. That's awesome, Bryan. They should have a special merit badge for that."

"Yeah, to go with the badge for toxic farts."

"It smells funny," James Lorbick said. But it was nice to have a fire going. It made the darkness seem less dark. Which is what fires are supposed to do, of course.

"You look really weird in the firelight, James. That dress and all the mud. It's kind of funny and kind of creepy."

"Thanks."

"Yeah, James Lorbick should always wear dresses. He's so hot."

"James Lorbick, I think you are so hot. Not."

"Leave James alone," Bryan Jones said.

"I had this weird dream last year," Danny Anderson said. Danny Anderson was from Terre Haute, Indiana. He was taller than anyone else in Bungalow 6 except for Terence. "I dreamed that I came home from school one day and nobody was there except this man. He was sitting in the living room watching TV and so I said, 'Who are you? What are you doing here?' And he looked up and smiled this creepy smile at me and he said, 'Hey, Danny, I'm Angelina Jolie. I'm your new dad.'"

"No way. You dreamed your dad was Angelina Jolie?"

"No," Danny Anderson said. "Shut up. My parents aren't divorced or anything. My dad's got the same name as me. This guy said he was my *new* dad. He *said* he was Angelina Jolie. But he was just some guy."

"That's a dumb dream."

"I know it is," Danny Anderson said. "But I kept having it, like, every night. This guy is always hanging out in the kitchen and talking to me about what we're going to do now that I'm his kid. He's really creepy. And the thing is, I just got a phone call from my mom, and she says that she and my dad are getting divorced and I think maybe she's got a new boyfriend."

"Hey, man. That's tough."

Danny Anderson looked as if he might be about to cry. He said, "So what if this boyfriend turns out to be my new dad? Like in the dream?"

"My stepdad's pretty cool. Sometimes I get along with him better than I get along with my mom."

"One time I had a dream James Lorbick was wearing a dress."

"What's that noise?"

"I didn't hear anything."

"Terence has been gone a long time."

"Maybe he went back to camp. Maybe he left us out here."

"The fire smells really bad."

"It reeks."

"Isn't insect stuff poisonous?"

"Of course not. Otherwise they wouldn't be able to sell it. Because you put it on your skin. They wouldn't let you put poison on your skin."

"Hey, look up. I think I saw a shooting star."

"Maybe it was a space ship."

They all looked up at the sky. The sky was black and clear and full of bright stars. It was like that for a moment and then they noticed how clouds were racing across the blackness, spilling across the sky. The stars disappeared. Maybe if they hadn't looked, the sky would have stayed clear. But they did look. Then snow started to fall, lightly at first, just dusting the muddy ground and the campfire and Bungalow 6 and then there was more snow falling. It fell quietly and thickly. It was going to be the thirteenth of June tomorrow, the next-to-last day of camp, the day that James Lorbick wearing a dress and a lot of mud was going to show up and scare everyone in the dining room.

The snow was the weirdest thing that had ever happened to Bungalow 6.

One of the Simpson twins said, "Hey, it's snowing!"

Bryan Jones started laughing. "This is awesome," he said. "Awesome!"

James Lorbick looked up at the sky, which had been so clear a minute ago. Fat snowflakes fell on his upturned face. He wrapped his crumbly mud-covered arms around himself. "*Awesome*," he repeated.

"Terence! Hey Terence! It's snowing!"

"Nobody is going to believe us."

"Maybe we should go get in our sleeping bags."

"We could build a snow fort."

"No, seriously. What if it gets really cold and we freeze to death? All I brought is my windbreaker."

"No way. It's going to melt right away. It's summer. This is just some kind of weather event. We should take a picture so we can show everybody."

So far they had taken pictures of mud, of people pretending to be mud-covered zombies, of James Lorbick pretending to be a mud-haired, dress-wearing monster. Terence had taken a picture of the bone that wasn't a cow bone. One of the Simpson twins had put a dozen marshmallows in his mouth and someone took a picture of that. Someone had a digital photo of Bryan Jones's big naked butt.

"So why didn't anyone from Bungalow 4 take a picture of the monster?"

"They did. But you couldn't see anything."

"Snow is cooler anyway."

"No way. A monster is way better."

"I think it's weird that Terence hasn't come back up yet."

"Hey, Terence! Terence!"

They all yelled for Terence for a few minutes. The snow kept falling. They did little dances in the snow to keep warm. The fire got thinner and thinner and started to go out. But before it went out, the monster came up the muddy, snowy path. It smiled at them and it came up the path and Danny Anderson shone his flashlight at it and they could all see it was a monster and not Terence pretending to be a monster. No one in Bungalow 4 had ever seen a monster before, but they all knew that a monster was what it was. It had a white face and its hands were red and dripping. It moved very fast.

You can learn a lot of stuff at camp. You learn how to wiggle an arrow so that it comes out of a straw target without the metal tip coming off. You learn how to make something out of yarn and twigs called a skycatcher, because there's a lot of extra yarn and twigs in the world, and someone had to come up with something to do with it. You learn how to jam your feet up into the mattress of the bunk above you, while someone is leaning out of it, so that they fall out of bed. You learn that if you are riding a horse and the horse sees a snake on the trail, the horse will stand on its hind legs. Horses don't like snakes. You find out that tennis rackets are good for chasing bats. You find out what happens if you leave your wet clothes in your trunk for a few days. You learn how to make rockets and you learn how to pretend not to care when someone takes your rocket and stomps on it. You learn to pretend to be asleep when people make fun of you. You learn how to be lonely.

The snow came down and people ran around Honor Lookout. They screamed and waved their arms around and fell down. The monster chased them. It moved so quickly that sometimes it seemed to fly. It was laughing like this was an excellent fun game. The snow was still coming down and it was dark which made it hard to see what the monster did when it caught people. James Lorbick sat still. He pretended that he was asleep or not there. He pretended that he was writing a letter to his best friend in Chicago who was spending the summer playing video games and hanging out at the library and writing and illustrating his own comic book. *Dear Alec, how are you? Camp is almost over, and I am so glad. This has been the worst summer ever. We went on a hike and it rained and my counselor found a bone. This kid made me put on a dress. There was a monster which ate everybody. How is your comic book coming? Did you put in the part I wrote about the superhero who can only fly when he's asleep?*

The monster had one Simpson twin under each arm. The twins were screaming. The monster threw them down the path. Then it bent over Bryan Jones, who was lying half inside one of the tents, half in the snow. There were slurping noises. After a minute it stood up again. It looked back and saw James Lorbick. It waved.

James Lorbick shut his eyes. When he opened them again, the monster was standing over him. It had red eyes. It smelled like rotting fish and kerosene. It wasn't actually all that tall, the way you'd expect a monster to be tall. Except for that, it was even worse than Bungalow 4 had said.

The monster stood and looked down and grinned. "You," it said. It had a voice like a dead tree full of bees: sweet and dripping and buzzing. It poked James on the shoulder with a long black nail. "What are you?"

"I'm James Lorbick," James said. "From Chicago."

The monster laughed. Its teeth were pointed and terrible. There was a smear of red on the dress where it had touched James. "You're the craziest thing I've ever seen. Look at that dress. Look at your hair. It's standing straight up. Is that mud? Why are you covered in mud?"

"I was going to be a monster," James said. He swallowed. "No offense."

"None taken," the monster said. "Wow, maybe I should go visit Chicago. I've never seen anything as funny as you. I could look at you for hours and hours. Whenever I needed a laugh. You've really made my day, James Lorbick."

The snow was still falling. James shivered and shivered. His teeth were clicking together so loudly he thought they might break. "What are you doing here?" he said. "Where's Terence? Did you do something to him?"

"Was he the guy who was down at the bottom of the hill? Talking on a cell phone?"

"Yeah," James said. "Is he okay?"

"He was talking to some girl named Darlene," the monster said. "I tried to talk to her, but she started screaming and it hurt my ears so I hung up. Do you happen to know where she lives?

"Somewhere in Ohio," James said.

"Thanks," the monster said. He took out a little black notebook and wrote something down.

"What are you?" James said. "Who are you?"

"I'm Angelina Jolie," the monster said. It blinked.

James's heart almost stopped beating. "Really?" he said. "Like in Danny Anderson's dream?"

"No," the monster said. "Just kidding."

"Oh," James said. They sat in silence. The monster used one long fingernail to dig something out between its teeth. It belched a foul, greasy belch. James thought of Bryan. Bryan probably would have belched right back, if he still had a head.

"Are you the monster that Bungalow 4 saw?" James said.

"Were those the kids who were here a few days ago?"

"Yeah," James said.

"We hung out for a while," the monster said. "Were they friends of yours?"

"No," James said. "Those kids are real jerks. Nobody likes them."

"That's a shame," the monster said. Even when it wasn't belching, it smelled worse than anything James had ever smelled before. Fish and kerosene and rotting maple syrup poured over him in waves. He tried not to breathe.

The monster said, "I'm sorry about the rest of your bungalow. Your friends. Your friends who made you wear a dress."

"Are you going to eat me?" James said.

"I don't know," the monster said. "Probably not. There were a lot of you. I'm not actually that hungry anymore. Besides, I would feel silly eating a kid in a dress. And you're really filthy."

"Why didn't you eat Bungalow 4?" James said. He felt sick to his stomach. If he looked at the monster he felt sick, and if he looked away, there was Danny Anderson, lying facedown under a pine tree with snow on his back and if he looked somewhere else, there were Bryan Jones's legs poking out of the tent. There was Bryan Jones's head. One of Bryan's shoes had come off and that made James think of the hike, the way Terence lay down in the mud to fish for the Simpson twin's shoe. "Why didn't you eat them? They're mean. They do terrible things and nobody likes them."

"Wow," the monster said. "I didn't know that. I would have eaten them if I'd known, maybe. Although most of the time I can't worry about things like that."

"Maybe you should," James said. "I think you should."

The monster scratched its head. "You think so? I saw you guys eating hot dogs earlier. So do you worry about whether those were good dogs or bad dogs when you're eating them? Do you only eat dogs that were mean? Do you only eat bad dogs?"

"Hot dogs aren't really made from dogs," James said. "People don't eat dogs."

"I never knew that," the monster said. "But see if I worried about that kind of thing, whether the person I was eating was a nice guy or a jerk, I'd never eat anyone. And I get hungry a lot. So to be honest, I don't worry. All I really notice is whether the person I'm chasing is big or small or fast or slow. Or if they have a sense of humor. That's important, you know. A sense of humor. You have to laugh about things. When I was hanging out with Bungalow 4, I was just having some fun. I was just playing around. Bungalow 4 mentioned that you guys were going to show up. I was joking about how I was going to eat them and they said I should eat you guys instead. They said it would be really funny. I have a good sense of humor. I like a good joke."

It reached out and touched James Lorbick's head.

"Don't do that!" James said.

"Sorry," said the monster. "I just wanted to see what the mud spikes felt like. Do you think it would be funny if I wore a dress and put a lot of mud on my head?"

James shook his head. He tried to picture the monster wearing a dress, but all he could picture was somebody climbing up to Honor Lookout. Somebody finding pieces of James scattered everywhere like pink and red confetti. That somebody would wonder what had happened and be glad that it hadn't happened to them. Maybe someday people would tell scary stories about what had happened to Bungalow 6 when they went camping. Nobody would believe the stories. Nobody would understand why one kid had been wearing a dress.

"Are you shivering because you're cold or because you're afraid of me?" the monster said.

"I don't know," James said. "Both. Sorry."

"Maybe we should get up and run around," the monster said. "I could chase you. It might warm you up. Weird weather, isn't it? But it's pretty, too. I love how snow makes everything look nice and clean."

"I want to go home," James said.

"That's Chicago, right?" the monster said. "That's what I wrote down."

"You wrote down where I live?" James said.

"All those guys from the other bungalow," the monster said. "Bungalow 4. I made them write down their addresses. I like to travel. I like to visit people. Besides, if you say that they're jerks, then I should go visit them? Right? It would serve them right."

"Yeah," James said. "It would serve them right. That would be really funny. Ha ha ha."

"Excellent," the monster said. It stood up. "It was great meeting you, James. Are you crying? It looks like you're crying."

"I'm not crying. It's just snow. There's snow on my face. Are you leaving?" James said. "You're going to leave me here? You aren't going to eat me?"

"I don't know," the monster said. It did a little twirl, like it was going to go running off in one direction, and then as if it had changed its mind, as if it was going to come rushing back at James. James whimpered. "I just can't decide. Maybe I should flip a coin. Do you have a coin I can flip?"

James shook his head.

"Okay," the monster said. "How about this. I'm thinking of a number between one and ten. You say a number and if it's the same number, I won't eat you."

"No," James said.

"Then how about if I only eat you if you say the number that I'm thinking of? I promise I won't cheat. I probably won't cheat."

"No," James said, although he couldn't help thinking of a number. He thought of the number four. It floated there in his head like a big neon sign, blinking on and off and back on. Four, four, four. Bungalow 4. Or six. Bungalow 6. Or was that too obvious? Don't think of a number. He would have bet anything that the monster could read minds. Maybe the monster had put the number four in James's head. Six. James changed the number to six hundred so it wouldn't be a number between one and ten. Don't read my mind, he thought. Don't eat me.

"I'll count to six hundred," the monster said. "And then I'll chase you. That would be funny. If you get back to camp before I catch you, you're safe. Okay? If you get back to camp first, I'll go eat Bungalow 4. Okay? I tell you what. I'll go eat them even if you don't make it back. Okay?"

"But it's dark," James said. "It's snowing. I'm wearing a dress."

The monster looked down at its fingernails. It smiled like James had just told an excellent joke. "One," it said. "Two, three, four. Run, James! Pretend I'm chasing you. Pretend that I'm going to eat you if I catch you. Five, six. Come on, James, run!"

James ran.

ACKNOWLEDGMENTS

The book you now hold in your hands is not quite the one you might otherwise have been holding, had events transpired only slightly differently. In the summer of 2005, I set out, as I had in previous years, with Karen Haber in search of the best short science fiction of the year. We had an agreement to edit the book for Byron Preiss and his company iBooks, and if all had gone to plan, that book would have been published in February 2006. Tragically, Byron Preiss was killed in a car accident in July 2005, and his company ceased business in February 2006. It looked as though the book that Karen and I were working on would never appear, and that is pretty much what has happened. The book we had compiled for iBooks was abandoned, and Karen decided to pursue other interests. At around the same time, I received a generous offer from Charles N. Brown at Locus Press to assemble the book you now hold. Using the experience I'd gained reading for 2005, I would assemble a new book, one with different contents and expressing a slightly different editorial vision. This is that book. It would not exist without the early support of Robert Silverberg, the late Byron Preiss, Charles N. Brown, the staff of Locus Publications, the very kind and generous contributors to this book, and Karen, who was a joy to work with for four years and who I hope to work with again. As always, I'd also like to thank Marianne Jablon for support above and beyond the call of duty, and also thank Justin Ackroyd, John Joseph Adams, Brian Bienkowski, Jack Dann, Ellen Datlow, Jeffrey Ford, Nick Gevers, Gavin J. Grant, John Helfers, Rich Horton, Jay Lake, Deborah Layne, Kelly Link, Sharyn November, Robin Pen, Tim Pratt, Gordon Van Gelder, Jeff VanderMeer, Mike Walsh, and Sean Williams for their invaluable assistance with this book.